ANOTHER PLATE AT THE TABLE

Surviving With Love and Humor

Dimitrios T. Karamitsos

ANOTHER PLATE AT THE TABLE

Surviving with Love and Humor

By

Dimitrios T. Karamitsos

Professor Emeritus of Aristotle University

Thessaloniki, Greece

Blog: dtkaram.webpages.auth.gr

Translated into English by

Eleni Phufas-Jousma

Professor Emerita SUNY ERIE

Proofreading and Illustrations by

Despina Karamitsou

Teacher of English and Artist

AMAZON EDITIONS

by University Studio Press, Thessaloniki, Greece

under the title: *Oikogenia Barlabas* [*Barlabas Family*]

Edition in English language by AMAZON 2023

DIMITRIOS T. KARAMITSOS

ANOTHER PLATE AT THE TABLE

Surviving with Love and Humor

A novel

Translated into English by

ELENI PHUFAS-JOUSMA

AMAZON EDITION 2023

The story is in part fiction and in part the author's experience.

This novel can be characterized as an ethnography

and a historical novel.

The names of persons mentioned in the text are fictitious.

Table of Contents

ii

1

The Characters

Georgia and Dimitris: The year was 1902 and young Georgia was living in Agathoupolis, a beautiful coastal village of Northeastern Thrace.[1] She was married to a handsome young man, Dimitris Mavrothalassites, who had been working hard as a steerer on ships that traded between Pontos in Asia Minor and throughout the Mediterranean. Their wedding ceremony had taken place according to the traditional Greek Orthodox customs, which included the marital garb, the songs and the reception to which all the villagers were invited.

A few days after their wedding, Dimitris started traveling again. Whenever he returned from a long journey, he would bring his wife a gift, usually gold jewelry, which at that time - along with currency in gold coins - was the best way to save. With each new piece of jewelry, her husband tried to compensate her for his long absence. Georgia soon had two daughters who were her husband's great pride and joy.

---

[1] The wider region was then called Eastern Rumelia and was, after the Treaty of Berlin in 1878, an autonomous region under the suzerainty of the Sultan. In 1885, in a coup d'état, the Bulgarians annexed this area to the Bulgarian state, and despite various international reactions, eastern Rumelia has since become part of Bulgaria. A great proportion of inhabitants were Greek.

He was greatly pleased when he returned from his travels and found them waiting for him.

Thus, good and happy years passed by until Dimitris' ship was shipwrecked in a great sea storm. Though soaked, freezing, and frightened, the sailors and the captain found themselves unharmed and, after many hours of struggling with the waves of the wild sea, they were finally rescued by a larger ship. Dimitris returned home exhausted but also determined to stop working on boats. By the time he was 40 years old, his financial affairs were in good order. It was, therefore, time for him to do a safer job, although less lucrative, and enjoy his family's warmth. He began working as a tailor, a craft he had learned at a young age when he helped in his father's tailor shop.

From these two work experiences, Dimitris earned a great deal of money. He was a very virtuous homeowner, father, and husband. However, the pleasant days for the Mavrothalassites family ended in 1912. Against his will, Dimitris found himself a soldier on the Bulgarian side fighting against the Turks. A year later, the Second Balkan War broke out. The former allies—Greeks and Bulgarians—were now fighting against each other. Dimitris could not bear to fight against his Greek compatriots and tried to desert, but a lieutenant took notice, shot and fatally wounded him. He was taken to a makeshift military hospital but died of internal bleeding in a matter of hours. Shortly before he died, Dimitiris spoke to Miltiades, an old colleague of his from the ships, who was serving as a nurse.

"I beg you, Miltiades. I don't feel well. Please try to inform Georgia of what's happened. Tell her to get aboard a ship with the girls and to go to Greece. Her brother, Democritus, has been living in Thessaloniki for a year now…he is a shipbuilder and is quite well off. He'll support her."

"Be strong, Dimitris. You will live." Miltiades tried to encourage him.

"I feel everything spinning…lightheaded. Everything is dimming. I'm lost "…the pale and weak Dimitris managed to mutter, and in a moment, he faded away.

In a few months, Miltiades returned from the army and informed the wife of the prematurely dead Dimitris and about the sad events. Georgia, who until then had been driven crazy with anxiety about the fate of her husband, found herself in a challenging position. She had two young daughters, Eftychia and Antigone, seven and five years old, and a full-term baby in her womb. She had given birth to three girls by then, but one daughter died as an infant. As soon as the unfortunate woman learned of Dimitri's death, she cried for several hours and having grown tired of crying, wiped her tears, dressed in black mourning clothes, tied a scarf on her head, and made her decisions. She would leave for Greece. She could no longer live in this oppressive regime.

The very next day, Georgia held a forty-day memorial service for her husband. She wanted to stay ahead of events and an uncertain future. She sold the furniture to the neighbors, along with her silverware and glassware, for as much as she could get. She sold her late husband's sewing machine to a Bulgarian, who was a good, hardworking young man and would open a tailor shop. Finally, she dressed her girls warmly, doubling up in shirts to withstand the cold of the sea, and gathered as many things as she could in a trunk and two suitcases. In addition to dresses, underwear, towels, sheets, and blankets, she took with her a Greek flag, the *Bible*, the *Synopsis* (of the Holy Scriptures), a history of Greece, and two novels: *Les Miserables* by Victor Hugo and *Without Family* by Hector Malot. She hid her jewelry in two large inner pockets deliberately sewn inside her skirt. There were gold rings with diamonds and gemstones, two gold necklaces, three gold crosses, gold earrings, and two bracelets adorned with precious stones wrapped in paper so that they would not bump into each other and be heard. Inside a special wide belt that Georgia wore pressed tight against her body, she had placed several gold coins and a few gold five lira notes which had been collected by the late Dimitris with his honest labor. She agreed to the fare with the captain of a floating coffin of a boat called the *Pipina* and with her two daughters squeezed into the hold along with a small number of her fellow locals who were also rushing to leave for Greece.

The next day after several hours of travel, and while the ship was approaching the exit channel of the Bosporus Straits, Georgia began to feel painful jabs in her belly. At first, she thought she was in pain because her legs felt cold.

One day later, the ship was passing through the straits, and then it entered the Aegean, where the waves started to roll. The old boat was beaten mercilessly and creaked so much that all the passengers started to pray, frightened as they were. Luckily, the captain knew his job well as he sailed this route regularly. Georgia continued to feel small aches every now and then and began to think that she would probably give birth. In any case, with her two daughters by her side, she took a nap for a few hours until suddenly all the passengers woke up from the noisy din made by the anchor that the sailors were throwing into the seabed to stabilize the ship which then anchored for a while in the port city of Alexandroupolis. When the boat set out again, Georgia, feeling nauseous from the shaking, vomited and began having more frequent labor pains. She realized that she was about to give birth.

An old woman approached her. She was a lay midwife who knew about these things, and she supported her. The captain was notified, and he instructed the cook to heat water for the needs of childbirth, provided alcohol and iodine to the midwife, and ordered the woman to be transferred to his bunk bed.

Just as the ship was passing by the Cape of Athos, being mercilessly pounded by the turbulent seas and creaking like an old door with unoiled hinges, Georgia very easily gave birth—this being her fourth birth—to another daughter. As soon as the child emerged, the midwife lit a cotton swab with alcohol and heated a pair of scissors in the flame, using them to quickly cut the umbilical cord, which she had tied with a ribbon, then pouring some iodine on its cut edge. Immediately after washing the child with warm water, she wrapped her several times in a clean sheet provided by the captain. Soon Georgia was lying down with a baby in her arms, covered with her coat and a blanket of the captain's. Sitting beside her, the two little girls looked on with interest and curiosity at their newborn sister. They all fell asleep in a little while, exhausted by the ordeal they had gone through. However, after being in a deep sleep for an hour, Georgia would wake up every so often and gaze at her newborn. It seemed like a very beautiful baby, and it wasn't just her opinion. In the early morning, she dreamt that her newborn daughter was 20 years old, a beautiful young woman. When she woke up, she watched her baby sleeping deeply, checked her belt with the gold coins and the insides of her pockets with the jewelry, and ensured that nothing precious was missing. Then she relaxed.

After many hours of sailing, the ship entered the Port of Thessaloniki, again victorious in the battle with the sea. With her two daughters at her side and the baby in her arms, the nursing mother paid a porter to carry her trunk and suitcases. He loaded them into a cart into which they all climbed, and they sat with their legs hanging over the side as they set off for Vardari Square, where they had been informed that a cheap inn on Monastiriou Street was available. It was an old two-story house with several rooms. Georgia settled in one room with two beds, a wardrobe, and a bureau with a mirror on the wall. On the bureau, there was a metal jug with water to wash. On each floor were two Turkish-style communal toilets, i.e., squat toilets without a raised commode. Georgia bought milk from a passing milkman every day for herself and her girls except the newborn, of course, and sometimes ate a bougatsa (breakfast pastry, sweet or savory) from a nearby pastry shop, as well as tripe, which helped her breasts produce plenty of milk for her infant.

Later she was able to meet her brother at the shipyard, to whom she explained her predicament. Without any delay, Democritos reacted appropriately, and with the help of a special service set up for refugees, the family of four settled in a house in the Upper Town which had been left empty as its previous resident was a Turkish officer who had fled to Turkey. The widow with the three girls spent the first difficult years in that house of the Upper Town.

Her youngest daughter was baptized by a cousin of Georgia's, who had an enthusiastic interest in ancient Greece and gave her the name Electra.

In the early difficult years in Thessaloniki, the jewelry and gold coins that Georgia had carried with her proved to be valuable assets for their survival. When the stack of gold coins diminished, both girls had somewhat grown up, so they could help supervise their younger sister. Then Georgia began to work as a sexton in the Church of Saint Catherine. During her free time, she stitched beautiful embroidery and sold her work to the wealthy ladies she met from the church. Overall, she was earning very little money, but by whatever means and with frugal budgeting, she made ends meet. So, she and her three daughters managed to survive.

In the widespread fire of 1917, the house in which they lived at the time was not in danger since its location was at a distance from the source of the fire, but she was very fearful because many sections of the house were made of wood. When the fire broke out, she prayed and made a vow to the Virgin Mary. If She saved her house from the fire, and if her daughters were married, Georgia would become a nun in a convent, so she would not be obliged to her sons-in-law. The house was spared from the fire, and the vow was later to be fulfilled.

In their first years in Thessaloniki the two older girls went to school, but they did not graduate since attendance was not mandatory at the time. Eftychia attended until the middle of the fifth grade.

Antigone finished the fifth grade. However, starting at the age of ten, the girls would do embroidery and, in this way, helped with the finances of the house, while at the same time they took care of little Electra.

Kotsos Barlabas: He was born in a village located on the coast of the Black Sea in eastern Thrace where Hellenism was then flourishing across from the reigning city (Constantinople). The surname 'Barlabas' seems to have been a nickname, because Kotsos' father was quite a talkative man, not to say quite a chatterbox. From the excessive verbosity that characterized him he was nicknamed Parlapas or Barlabas, from the Italian word for talk, "parla", which in time took its place as his surname.

Kotsos' parents had died relatively young, and he decided to come to Greece, so that the Bulgarians would not draft him into the army. He came to Thessaloniki in 1913 at the age of 20. He was a relatively handsome brown eyed man with a straight nose, a bushy mustache, curly black hair, thick eyebrows, and an adequately tall stature.

For two years he lived alone in shacks in a refugee settlement above the Roman castle of Navarino Square, where he became accustomed to the relative lack of water and filthy conditions. The water was taken from a communal fountain that was about 100 meters away and was next to an ancient sycamore tree. But it was quite an annoying process to wait in line in the evening to fill his pitcher when he felt very tired from working all day. Since that time, he had learned to use water sparingly. As a youth, he washed himself once a week by using some water, running it through a tin can which he had hung high on the wall in a room he called the laundry room. He would use the broom to sweep away the soapy water dripping on the concrete floor and spread it around the courtyard where the earth absorbed a part of it with some flowing into the gutter of the descending road.

While he was still physically fit, he worked at various physically hard odd jobs. One was as a porter in the harbor wearing a specialized straw harness to carry goods on his back from the various ships to the carts waiting with the horses to transport goods to the shops of the city.

In 1921 he found himself as an infantryman in the Greek army in Asia Minor and fought at Eski-Sehir. In this battle the Greeks were victorious, but they were unable to encircle the Turkish army that managed to escape and regroup. Finally, the difficulty in refueling the Greek army, in combination with the change in the attitude of the great powers towards Greece (mainly France, Italy, and the Soviet Union), and the reinforcement of the Turkish leader Mustafa Kemal with weapons and Soviet money greatly influenced the developments. The retreat that followed led to the Asia Minor Catastrophe.[2]

When Kotsos was discharged, he found himself a refugee in Thessaloniki for the second time since he had no one waiting for him. He had no close relatives on whom he could rely for help. The

---

[2] Asia Minor Catastrophe: This term refers to the defeat of Greece's military expedition and the loss of Hellenism in Asia Minor. Up to a million Greeks lost their lives in the barbarities by Turks including the infamous "work battalions" and up to 300,000 of the population in the city of Smyrna lost their lives in just 1922 alone.

difficulties of life – becoming an orphan at an early age and the uprooting from his homeland – turned him into a pathologically stingy man. He always carried all his money with him since he did not trust leaving it unattended in his house.

At one point, he worked in the vegetable market, but upon his dismissal from the army, he was appointed a conductor on the trams with the help of a major. He was his commander in the war and was "connected" with the revolutionary government of Gonatas and Plastiras.

Working on the trams, Barlabas left his mark for the speed at which he cut tickets and returned the change. At that time, the tram consisted of two wagons and had on its staff two people, a driver—the so-called tram driver—and a conductor. Kotsos would start out hurriedly in the first wagon and, within the time it took the tram to pass through two stops, he had cut all the tickets of the new passengers on board and then would start all over again.

After his discharge from the army, Kotsos moved to another neighborhood. His house was on the same street as the house where Georgia's daughter Eftychia lived, whom he had noticed from the first moment he came to this district. Whenever he saw fifteen-year-old Eftychia on the street, he would wink at her and whisper a few words like "Hello, sweety" or "I really like your eyes." It was obvious that he was in love with Eftychia, but she did not initially succumb to his advances.

***Eftychia*:** Even at a youthful age, Eftychia was very lively. Her mother could not figure out how to restrain her. After her fifth birthday she was constantly playing in the street. One time—she must have been nine years old—she bit a priest on his posterior. The reason for this cannibalistic attack was not widely known. She later recounted that she reacted this way because she would not assent to kissing the priest's hand as her mother urged her to do, and which everybody else piously did. A similar accomplishment of hers was when she nailed the tip of her technical compass into the hand of a teacher who tried to caress her while she was at school in fourth grade. In any case, our young Eftychia became famous both for these incidents and for other feats.

In her childhood she enjoyed playing a particular game frequently. She would climb on a makeshift sled with four wooden spools acting as wheels and roll down from the highest point of her neighborhood to the square of **Governor's** Office. Carrying the sled back up again to the starting point was undertaken by her admirers (who have been many ever since), and then they would follow her on her descent, running alongside and screeching at the top of their voices.

Eftychia, who also eagerly played with the boys, was very capable of playing marbles which back then were called shooters. When she won a lot of marbles, she would put them up for sale, showing her commercial acumen even in her childhood which continued to develop in her with the embroidery trade. The youngsters willingly offered her their money to buy the marbles they had lost, but more so, they did so to gain her favor! But the last of our childish Eftychia's exploits was that she fell in love very young at just sixteen with a handsome and wealthy young neighbor, Stratos.

It did not take long for the young man's parents to find out about the romance, and they were not pleased to hear that their only son was likely to marry this impoverished lass who was far too young and was such an unruly creature. Their son had to marry a wealthy bride more suited to their social class. That is why they forbade him to see her if he wanted to inherit their property. Meanwhile, Stratos was conscripted into the military. Therefore, the distancing of Eftychia from her beloved became de facto inevitable. On the other hand, Eftychia's mother was aware of her daughter's erotic activities but could not restrain her because she was a headstrong girl.

Georgia feared the possibility of an untimely pregnancy, which meant things would get badly complicated. The solution was found in a hurriedly made match with Kotsos Barlabas to which an aunt of Stratos contributed, having been properly informed about the danger to the tranquility of her cousin's family. Seeing him from a distance, she somewhat liked Kotsos even though he was 16 years older than her. In fact, during a short excursion they took while still engaged, he managed to isolate her from the rest…with all the consequences! The result was that young Eftychia was already pregnant before she got married. Thus, after a short engagement, the vivacious Eftychia married Kotsos, who was thoroughly infatuated with her. Fortunately, the wedding was set to take place soon. The best man was Stratos whose parents thus wanted to contribute to Eftychia's settling down. This marriage ensured the alienation of their son from her.

The marriage of Georgia's oldest daughter was all the talk in the neighborhood for a long time. It had all the elements and folklore of that era. Eftychia, who was at the beginning of the third month of her pregnancy, had worn a tight corset so that there would be no hint of pregnancy from her belly's appearance. Even without the corset, her belly was not particularly visible, but our young Eftychia had this concern, so according to the proverb "if the shoe fits, wear it", so she wore it.

Everyone remembered the giggles the moment the priest was reciting "*...the woman should fear the man...*" Young Eftychia (according to an old Greek custom) stepped resolutely upon the groom's foot with force. Barlabas, who was wearing pointy dress shoes, felt the pain in his middle toe, which he always had a problem with because it was hammertoed and its top was callused. The pain from the pressure made him exclaim a loud "Ouch!" so even the priest could not hold back his laughter.

The groom reciprocated this pain to his wife the same evening. When they found themselves in their marital bed, Kotsos, being somewhat intoxicated by the wedding feast which had taken place in a very close circle in Eftychia's home, but also to show her that he was the boss, asked her for "other things" besides the classic positions. At the time, the relatively unsophisticated Eftychia probably did not know or did not want to know about these matters, or in any case, pretended not to know about them or want them. Not meaning to, she accidentally elbowed Kotsos in his stomach. Then Barlabas gave her the first wallop and reciprocated the pain he had felt in his callused toe. The wedding ceremony had been performed, and the battle had begun!

Antigone: Antigone grew up in the shadow of her older firstborn sister, who loved and protected her. When she was 17 years old in 1925, she emigrated to Chicago to marry Johnny, a Greek American, who was asking for *"a shoe from his homeland even if it was mended,"* a proverb demonstrating the homesickness of many emigres and their preferences to marry Greek women. She traveled alone on an ocean liner in the awful, overloaded, and overcrowded third class. Filled with expectations, she had the company of Greeks who were going to America to make their fortune and other prospective brides who were going there to marry Greeks who were already living there. She was under the protection of Mrs. Alcmene, a kindhearted woman from her homeland, an acquaintance of Georgia's who had been married for years in America and had been involved in matchmaking. Alcmene had come to Thessaloniki for a month to see her elderly parents, who had refused to emigrate, and she made sure to travel back with the bride-to-be.

Upon her arrival in New York Harbor, and after successfully passing a health examination on Ellis Island and stating that her mother-in-law was waiting for her with her son, who had been in Chicago for a long time, Antigone was permitted to step foot in New York.

Waiting for her at the exit were her mother-in-law and Johnny, who recognized her immediately because he had seen her photo before he decided to become her husband. The prospective groom was in his thirties, quite fair-skinned with straight hair and a receding hairline. He was wearing thick-lensed glasses over his blue eyes. His origin was from Krousovo, which was inhabited for centuries by Greek-Vlachs, and he had emigrated to Chicago in 1913 at the age of 18. After the initial exchange of welcome, they got on the train and finally arrived in Chicago. Antigone was accommodated in the house of her mother-in-law, a good woman who treated her well in many ways. The wedding took place a month later. The maid of honor was Alcmene, who, as the architect of the wedding, looked on smugly, but also because she had been paid quite a few dollars by Johnny for her services!

Johnny and Antigone went on their honeymoon trip to Florida for a week, and on their return they both started working. Antigone worked hard in a fur shop sewing furs while her husband owned a greengrocer's shop and distributed fruit to the neighborhood's households on order. When Antigone was in an advanced stage of pregnancy, she stopped working at the factory and stayed home for a fortnight to knit some garments for her baby. Soon she gave birth to her first child, a daughter.

She followed a similar schedule with the rest of the pregnancies. She stopped working not only when her belly prevented her from working but also for six months after giving birth while breastfeeding. Then she would go back to work since she had her mother-in-law's help. There, in Chicago, Antigone had four children—two girls and two boys. They were Georgios, Dimitris, Eleni, and Dimitra. She made sure to speak Greek to them. She had brought a book with her from the time she went to school in Greece entitled *Complete Curriculum*. Despite her exhaustion, she taught her children to read Greek from this book in the evenings so as not to lose their Greek identity in the great melting pot of America.

Every month she would write a letter to her mother with separate pages for Electra and Eftychia. After her mother entered the convent, she wrote less often, but she sent letters regularly to Eftychia and Electra. She usually wrote to her sisters in the same letter to save on stamps. She started with the phrase *"My beloved sisters, Eftychia and Electra. I'm fine, and I desire the same for you."* She would follow up with information about the weather in Chicago, especially in the winter when it was bitterly cold. Then she explained her finances; how she bought a stove with gas and other banalities. Their financial situation was good. In other words, they managed to get by. After her mother-in-law died, they also had a daily maid, a negro woman who came to her house in the morning and left at 6:00 P.M. From time-to-time Antigone would send parcels of clothes and a few dollars to Eftychia, who usually wept over her lack of money and her stingy husband.

Electra: The youngest child, Electra, grew up in the arms of Georgia and Eftychia. She went to school and finished sixth grade. She was an exceptionally good student. After primary school, she took French lessons for a year and a half under the tutelage of an Armenian multilingual man who had come from Constantinople and subsisted by giving lessons. Georgia also bought the small *Larousse Dictionary* for Electra, which her daughter consulted not only when she was taking lessons with the Armenian but also later on. As she grew older, Electra blossomed into a very attractive young woman. She had blonde hair, beautiful green eyes, glorious fleshy lips, and an almost ancient-looking Greek nose. She was quite tall with broad shoulders and had an athletic appearance.

On Sundays in the summers when she was younger, she would go to Kalamaria at the seaside and hang out with her cousins (the children of her mother's brother Democritus) who had boats. There, together with her cousins, she had learned to swim quite well. They all went aboard the boat in their swimsuits—three or four of them—rowed out in quite deep water to bathe in the clear waters. She once took part in a beauty contest that had been organized on the beach and won first prize. She also won first place in the backstroke in some amateur swimming competitions. Out of her great love for the sea, she would start swimming in April and finish at the end of October. She read everything that fell into her hands from magazines about clothes and hats, as well as novels by Greek and foreign writers. It is obvious the first novels she read were the ones that her mother had brought from her homeland. Although she had only finished primary school, she had gained social education and self-confidence by reading.

At the age of 14, Electra became an apprentice in the sewing studio of Madame Harikleia, the best dressmaker in high society. Two years later, she became a clerk in a hat shop. In her spare time, she either read or sewed hats at home, at first to learn the job and later because she had plans for the future. Women always wore hats in those years, especially with their best outfits. Her vocation had good prospects, and as the saying goes, *"When the going gets tough, the tough get going"*.

At first, Electra sold a few hats to her friends from the neighborhood. Barely in her twenties and having mastered her trade, she decided to open her own hat shop. She had saved a small amount of money to start her business so all she had to do was buy some fabrics, a few hat boxes, and doll heads to place in the shop window with her hats. Molho's bookstore[3] supplied her with French magazines with figurines and patterns for hats.

She also went to Harikleia, the seamstress who had taken her as an apprentice, and asked for her help. Harikleia, who liked Electra because she reminded her of her own youth, responded positively. Thus, Electra started making hats in a more formal setting. Pretty soon, thanks to her work, the hardworking young milliner managed to gain financial independence. She now had affiliations with several seamstresses who sent her clientele to have their hats sewn that matched the dresses they were preparing. But her clients as well—at least those who were satisfied— almost all of them, made positive recommendations for Electra to their girlfriends. Electra's business was thriving to the point of having a staff of three girls - two employees, and an apprentice. She managed to sew for herself not only hats but also dresses, which is why she was always very well-dressed, a beautiful young woman who everyone, both men and women, observed and admired when they encountered her. She was

---

[3] An old classic bookstore in Thessaloniki selling international magazines and books.

very sociable and had gained many acquaintances thanks to her profession.

She found time to play cards once a week with a select group of women—wives of doctors, lawyers, merchants— and from them, she learned to smoke, despite her mother's nagging.

As we will see, Electra fell in love with a handsome young man and married him at the age of 23, an unfortunate event.

2

The Birth of Eftychia's Children

Eftychia had barely been married for seven months when her belly started to show despite the tight corsets and the deceptive clothing. In order not to become the subject of gossip, she often avoided going out in the neighborhood. Of course, she did some outside chores out of necessity, such as going to the bakery incredibly early in the morning for bread and to the well for water. You see, back then, in the refugee shack district, there was no water available inside the shacks. It had to be carried into the houses from the communal wells of the neighborhood. Despite the fatigue, she often thought *May the wells be blessed; what would we do without them?* So, Eftychia did all the chores very early, and when her husband came home from work at night, she would be lying in her bed with an expression of disappointment. Supposedly she had seen blood, and the midwife had ordered her to lie down and not be approached by her husband for the familiar marital activities. With that excuse, she kept Kotsos at bay, although she could not keep him away from her double bed.

Despite all that, she spared herself a part of the stench of Barlabas, who had not changed any of his habits of grubbiness even after he got married. For him, being clean was an uncommon state of being, like those rare and hard-to-find stamps. Nevertheless, his lack of hygiene did not prevent him from having sexual demands. Regardless, Eftychia expressed her objections with her "hemorrhages". Barlabas could no longer bear this situation and began to look around the neighborhood for a chance to unwind. But it wasn't easy. Now familiar to all, his unbearable stink did not allow any advances to the opposite sex.

This situation incensed him quite a bit. One night when he tried to…rape his wife, she unintentionally cuffed him in the eye in her attempt to avoid him. After giving her a retaliatory punch, he rushed to find the tin can with water to wash his eye that had clouded over. When he washed it, she saw that the white of his eye had turned red; he became irrational. Returning to the bedroom, he gave his wife a vigorous beating. She endured it with dignity. It was not, after all, the first time he had beaten her. Then, Eftychia suffered a blow to her belly, making her cry loudly, and the beating stopped. She began to feel some pain, like a strong squeezing in her swollen uterus. *That's it,* she thought. *After this beating, something happened, and I will give birth.*

In the meantime, Barlabas had gone out to the café for an ouzo just to forget his woes. His wife got dressed, went out into the street, and walked to her mother's house which was located two streets below hers. When her mother saw her pale and disheveled, she figured everything out. She helped her daughter lie down and called out for the midwife. The midwife Lydia came quickly and examined Eftychia with her hands, palpating her belly. Her gaze fell on a large area of redness that was visible next to her belly button.

"How long have you had this?" she asked.

"As of today," Eftychia gasped, not in the mood for more words.

"Did Barlabas beat you?" Lydia insisted, who was quite curious and gossipy.

"Hey, and so what?" Eftychia replied. What's happened has been done, and now what's happening is I'm giving birth, isn't that right?"

"Yes. But were you due now or later? You were married in March; now we're in October."

She counted with her fingers, and she added up seven months.

"We may have a problem. The baby will be premature."

Something didn't seem right to Lydia. The uterus was too large to be only seven months pregnant. Moreover, the child seemed to be quite large for the dates. In any case, this was not the first time that Lydia had faced a similar problem. In the previous month, she had delivered Elpida, the wife of the charcoal maker. The charcoal kiln was located in a large vacant lot that belonged to three brothers who could not agree to its partition. So, it remained idle for years and was used by Lambros, "the charcoal maker". Elpida had been in a relationship with Lambros for almost seven years. Her mother was a war widow and had only managed to give birth to her while her husband, the sergeant, was still alive just before he was killed in the deadly battle in July 1913 in the Kresna Gorge.

Elpida had been left an only child without male siblings, so no one pressured Lambros, who waited for his finances to improve and then to marry. Moreover, this situation suited him. He ate and drank at his mother's and spent time with Elpida in his shack at the charcoal kiln. In the meantime, she would slip out in the evening and meet

Lambros—always wearing black shoes and clothes— making the charcoal dust invisible. In this way, she was spared her mother's nagging. So, when she almost lost all hope that Lambros would marry her, she managed to get pregnant, and the wedding—despite the relative delay—finally took place with Elpida in an advanced stage of pregnancy but properly wrapped with corsets and belts. The midwife then pulled a six-month-old child out of her belly, weighing close to nine pounds. Therefore, considering the last incident with Elpida and similar events like this one in the past, nothing surprised Lydia any longer. But she was curious and wanted to know. However, Kotsos, who had prematurely impregnated Eftychia was not foolish enough to consult the neighborhood midwife, so he had taken his fiancée to a doctor for his opinion. This is how the secret remained known to only a few people.

In the meantime, the hours passed, and Georgia's daughter was in intermittent pain. Lydia had been half asleep when a loud voice woke her up. Now the young woman was experiencing a lot of pain and had yelled out the attendant screech.

The screams of the prospective mother continued for hours. Eftychia almost enjoyed these cries. They were the choking sounds that had not come out of her mouth when Barlabas beat her. But soon, the situation grew worse. The child was big and had a big head. However, Lydia was trained as a midwife with a diploma. On her signboard was written *Lydia Papadopoulou, Scientific Midwife*. At just the right time, she sliced open at the point where she was supposed to, and the baby's head finally appeared, flushed crimson from the intensity of pulling. The experienced midwife turned his body appropriately, pulling out the first shoulder and then the other, and the rest was easy. It was only in Lydia's mind that the months after the wedding—from March to October—did not explain the size of the baby.

The baby weighed about 8.8 pounds and was too well-formed to be premature. But now was not the time for chit-chat. She had to tie the child's belly button, then apply iodine to prevent infection and watch the mother for any bleeding. She also saw that bruise on the belly, which may have caused something serious. But fortunately, everything went well without complications. Except that the young mother was in pain for days from the scissor cut and from her son's head, who tormented her until he finally came out.

So, the first newborn of Eftychia grew fast and would have been breastfed indefinitely if the last bite he took on his mother's breast hadn't forced her to cut him off from breastfeeding. She then started giving him what the family was eating. The little one gobbled up everything, but he was especially obsessive about eggs which he ate in a variety of ways of preparation: Sucking them raw, boiled, fried, whole, but also scrambled. This preference remained with him as a habit in his adult life as well. He was literally an ovophage (as we shall see).

Late one icy cold night, Eftychia's infant began to shiver, and he developed a high fever. His fingertips and nails had turned blue. It was a frigid night outside, not much warmer inside, so Eftychia was worried about death and was afraid that her baby would die. Her mother called out to a priest to come to baptize her grandchild lest he die unbaptized. The priest baptized it hurriedly, throwing some water on his head from a beaker, and gave him the name Athanasios. The child eventually survived and did not get seriously ill again for many years.

In the meantime, significant progress had occurred in the refugee neighborhood of Eftychia and Barlabas. The Greek State brought water into their houses. Thus, Eftychia's morning ordeal of hauling water with pitchers and buckets ceased. The end to using tin cans had arrived. Now plenty of running water was available in the kitchen! It was a pleasure to see water flowing out of the new tap whose gilded stain seemed more valuable than genuine gold.

Eftychia decided to celebrate the reality of water in the house with a wide-ranging cleansing bath. She started a fire under the cauldron and warmed the water. In the middle of the kitchen, she balanced the large basin for washing clothes on two wicker chairs, divided the water equally, and began to wash her son first. The little toddler seemed to enjoy the water and did not say a word, even when she poured water over his head to rinse him. Then she lowered the basin to the floor, stepped in, and bathed herself with a feeling of grandeur about the great event—having water inside the house. Scrimping on the water had come to an end. She dipped the sponge in the water and massaged it with soap while she silently blessed the sponge diver who had taken it out of the sea. Bathing herself made her feel very contented.

When she finished scrubbing herself with the sponge, she rinsed off, wiped herself dry with a large towel, and after drying up completely, she put on her underwear and nightgown. Now it was Barlabas' turn, who was slightly annoyed because he had almost fallen asleep on the couch as he waited for his turn. She had persuaded him to wash himself after a long time of not bathing. As expected, he shuddered as he stepped into the basin. At 10:00 PM, it was cold in the kitchen. The kitchen doorway facing an inner courtyard was wide, and at the door's bottom edge, a fairly cold stream of air crept in from underneath. Curiously, Barlabas then began to enjoy bathing, especially because of Eftychia's scrubbings that were necessary to remove the accumulated dirt.

But in the end, something went wrong. During the head rinsing, some soap got into his eye and began to sting him badly. It was the same eye that Eftychia had struck the previous year. An outbreak of anger stirred within him. He hated the water, and now came the tingling in his eye, and this strengthened his old aversion to washing.

"Fuck me!" he started cursing his wife.

"It seems the soap bothers you because you're so unused to it," Eftychia responded flippantly.

With his body covered in soap, Barlabas stood up and tried to hit her. She drew back avoiding her husband's punch, but with the momentum he exerted, his body twisted halfway, wobbled, and he lost his balance. He fell, hitting his head on the edge of the bucket which Eftychia had used to haul water, gashing his eyebrow open just like boxers often do. Horrified, Barlabas realized that blood was flowing from his eyebrow clouding his eye. Unused to the sight of blood, he passed out saving Eftychia from a certain beating.

Meanwhile, her baby was hungry and began bawling. At first, Eftychia was at a loss for what to do. The wretched young woman got dressed as well as she could, put on her coat and a headscarf on her still-damp hair, wrapped her son in a blanket, and took him in her arms. She walked silently away from the house and went down the street towards her mother's house. For her safety, she intended to spend the night there.

When Barlabas came to and opened his eyes, the first thing he saw was an overturned bucket. His eyebrow was stinging, and he was shivering from the cold. He was trembling, literally, as he had remained on the floor for a few minutes soaking wet. He wiped himself dry with a towel and looked at his eye in the mirror. He could not even see it because as soon as he saw the blood, he began to get dizzy again.

I knew I was right not to stomach these things, he thought. *This time it happened. There won't be a next time, and I won't take a bath again. It is not ever happening again. And that woman Eftychia (Joy), I will turn her into 'Distychia (Joyless) from the beatings she will get. So, she never forgets it!*

He searched the house to find her. But his wife and her baby were nowhere to be found. In a distressed state, Barlabas began to curse and to let off steam, he abruptly smashed his hand hard on the wooden table. He then felt severe pain in his arm. He tried to open and shut his fingers, but the pain was almost unbearable at that point. The outer side of his palm had become swollen. He thought he would go to the doctor to get a day off the next day.

Indeed, the following day the doctor diagnosed a fracture of the 5th metacarpal and decided *"Off work for fifteen days"*, and his hand was wrapped in an elastic bandage. Barlabas thought for a moment. *Now I'll be at home for many hours, and I'll be able to beat Eftychia every day, with the other hand of course!*

Five days later Georgia, along with her brother Democritus, went to see her son-in-law. They had a serious discussion about the couple's problems. They told Barlabas that the present situation could not continue by his using various excuses to beat Eftychia every now and then. Having been alone at home for five days and suffering without Eftychia, he quieted down and promised not to beat her again. So, Eftychia returned home, and life went on relatively smoothly with rare exceptions. Barlabas never bathed again, and a sink wash was enough for him on a case-by-case basis. Once he was even heard saying in his prickly voice:

"Whether or not a bath I need it, once a year I take it!"

Well, what he meant by this—a bath, a shower bath, or a sea bath—was never clarified. What is certain is that he took a couple of sea baths in the summer, which happened until a jellyfish badly bit him in the neck, and he stopped taking those too.

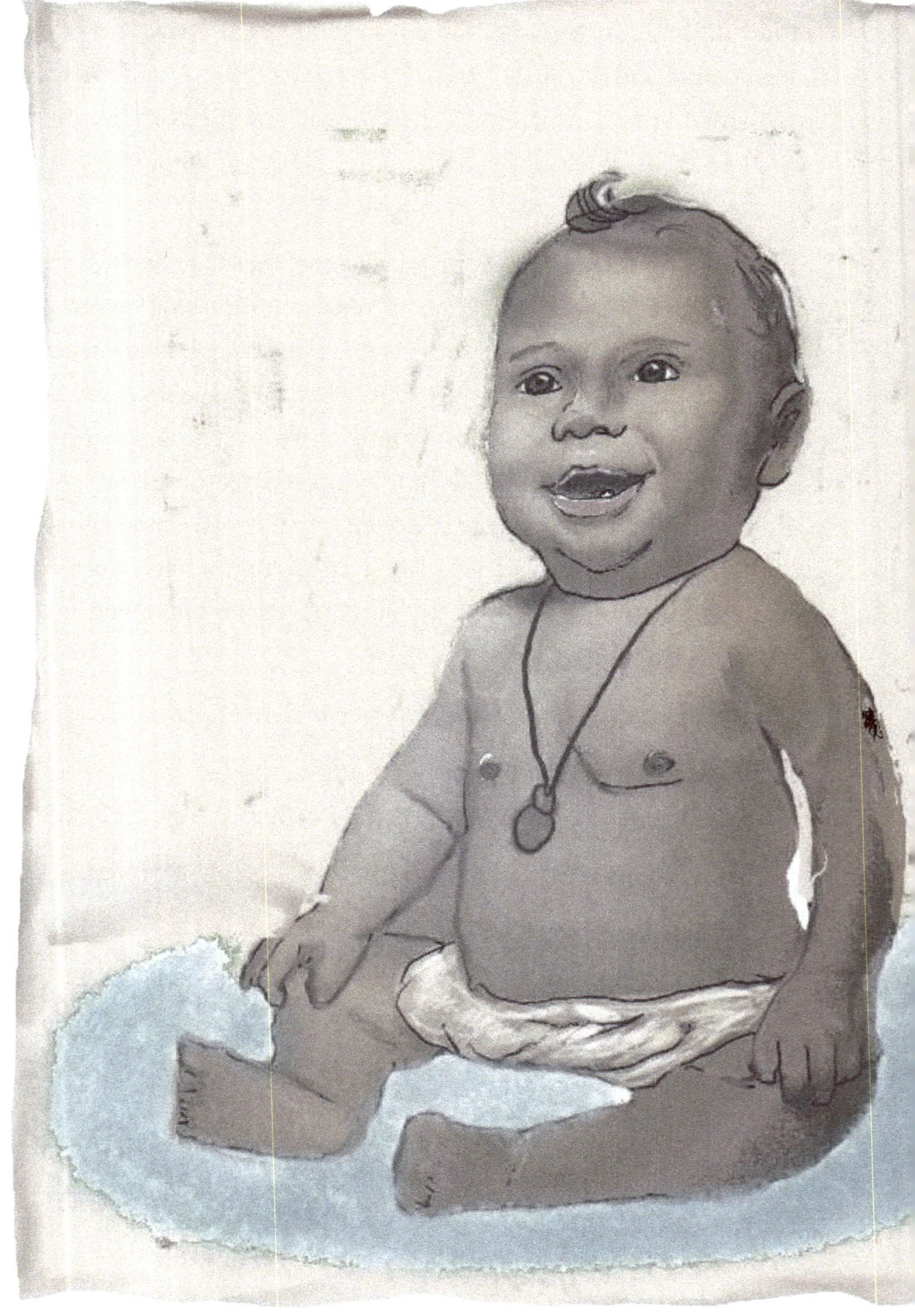

3

The Erotic Revolution

Eftychia may have been unfortunate with her marriage, but she was blessed with a happy disposition. Any other woman would have become deeply depressed with the man she had been almost forced to marry at such a young age. Possessing a cheerful personality and an optimistic mindset, Eftychia was always the center of attention at the party, a woman whose conversations were pervaded with humor. These personality traits made her popular in social groups where she could enjoy chitchatting and telling jokes, drinking ouzo, and pulling shenanigans. After patiently enduring physical abuse by her husband in the first years of their marriage, the young woman began to rebel, and gradually the idea of separating from him matured in her. She discussed it with her mother. But Georgia—committed to the customs and traditions of the time and profoundly religious—could not bear to hear any talk about divorce and other such modern things.

"Mind your place, my daughter. You must raise your child."

"Mother, I can't stand him. He only cares about my body, and that only if he isn't angry."

"My child, what are you saying? This man is the one you married in church. You shouldn't divorce him. After all, he neither drinks nor gambles like other men."

"Yes, dear Mother, but he never takes a bath, and on top of that, he's very stingy. When I tell him that I want money for the house, instead of answering me, he hits me on the head. I'm afraid to talk to him anymore."

"You must be patient and make sure you pray."

Those last words in the conversation were her mother's quite unambiguous advice. At that time, Georgia was preparing to become a nun. She was only waiting to see Electra get married first.

Truth be told Barlabas did not drink much, nor was he prone to drink. But it was his habit to be away from home for long hours. He worked as a laborer in the early years, and back then, there was no eight-hour day. The system required people to work "as long as they could endure it."

He had some friends—refugees like himself—and after the exhaustion from work, he would pass by a taverna on Kassandros Street where he would hang out with them. They drank almost every night, each of them a couple of small glasses of ouzo. The amount of alcohol wasn't much, but when he came home—either from being tired or from the alcohol—he felt a sweet sleepiness that forced him to lie down in his bed often without taking his clothes off. Eftychia was more than happy with this situation. At best, she would take off his shoes and socks, give his feet a quick wash with a wet towel, and let him sleep. Then, unable to put up with his stench, she would fall asleep on a sleeping couch in her small sitting room.

However, being relatively young, Eftychia also had her sexual concerns. Her first love Stratos, who had also become her best man, still had his eye on her. At the first chance, he secretly visited her house and tried to get her to have a go at it. At first, she felt inhibited. She considered her mother's wise advice and kept him at arm's length. Besides, she still held a slight grudge against him for not marrying her. But after the first two and a half years of her marriage passed by, with Barlabas kept at a distance and Eftychia in voluntary sexual deprivation, the timing was right and Stratos managed to bring her back into his arms.

One day, he stripped her completely naked and threw her on the bed, which was just next to her son's cot, just after Eftychia had put the baby to bed for a nap after lunch. While Eftychia had the best man on top of her and partly inside her, little Thanasis woke up from the squeaking of the bed springs, stood upright in his cot, and, holding on to the bars, opened his eyes wide. Eftychia saw him staring at her with his lively eyes wide open, but it was too late to stop her impending stormy orgasm. After all, it had been so long since she had made love that she didn't care about anything anymore. She was determined to live her life to the fullest. She had made up her mind to live freely. No one knows if, at that tender age, little Thanasis could be influenced by the spectacle he saw. However, he did evolve into a very sensual person in his adult life.

Although she enjoyed her sexual trysts with Stratos, Eftychia did not see a happy ending to this affair. She felt that for him she was simply a vessel of pleasure. So, she looked for the opportunity to cast him aside.

Sometime later, Stratos got engaged. His fiancée, a young woman of his class and the daughter of an essential grocer in the Modiano Market was raised with strict guidelines. She would not agree to premarital sexual relations with her future husband. So, her young suitor had no choice but to enjoy amorous impromptu sessions with Eftychia. When Eftychia realized what was going on, she made her second big decision and forbade him to come to her house again. Nevertheless, he kept coming back. But Eftychia was stubborn and resisted him. Finally, although essentially in a forgiving way, she unwittingly took revenge on him. A friend of Barlabas, who was also casting his net around her and who she had rejected, dripped some hints into Barlabas' ear and inflamed the situation.

"Your best man is having an affair with Eftychia!"

Barlabas exploded like gunpowder. He might not have often shared intimate moments with his wife, but the best man humping her was too great an insult to endure. He had a furious fight with Stratos. Out of this quarrel, the best man ended up with a broken nose and decided to put an end to his visits to Eftychia's home. He did not know how to justify his injury to his fiancée. Ultimately, he made up an excuse that he slipped and fell because he carelessly stepped on a rotten lettuce leaf. In any case, he was constantly reminded of this event because it left him with his one nostril being constricted, which closed off completely at the slightest irritation, causing him difficulty breathing. Several years later, he had his nose fixed when his wife—exasperated at his constant snoring—threatened that she would sleep in a separate room if he did not have an operation!

Meanwhile, Eftychia was tenderly raising her son. Her love for him had grown despite her initial coldness. Despite that, she felt her child was an obstacle and a cause of her lack of personal freedom. That is why she never stopped seeing him with some lurking discomfort. Her feelings for her son ranged like a pendulum from day to day. It seemed she was too young to be a mother with all the responsibilities that motherhood entails.

When young Thanasis turned two and a half years old, a childless couple settled in the apartment next door. Lambros and his wife Loukia were both teachers. They had met on an island where they taught in the same school. Loukia was four years older than Lambros, but back when she was younger, the difference was not noticeable. After all, she combed herself in a youthful style—she typically wore her hair in a ponytail—and she was shapely. You couldn't call her particularly beautiful, but she was attractive, except for her barely visible female mustache. (In those years, she would use hydrogen peroxide to make the hairs lighter making it barely visible). She spoke charmingly, exhibited pleasant manners, and so she captivated Lambros, the vulnerable teacher. After the first six months of coexistence on the island, they formed a close relationship, and in time, they married. But despite the years that passed by, they did not have children. When they grew bored with the island—its loneliness and endless winter nights, with the sea moaning incessantly and the air whistling menacingly—they applied for a transfer which was accepted. So, they found themselves in Thessaloniki. There, Loukia soon burst into the religious school environment. In a few months, she converted her ponytail into a bun, lengthened her skirt, and she was "eating, sleeping and breathing" in a "Christian movement," as she used to say. There, the lectures, spirituality, priests, bishops, psalms, prayers, confessions, and "Holy God Holy Mighty..." were ever-present.

Lambros started to feel lonely and gradually felt the need to find a lover. The opportunity for such a thing came up after they were forced to move to another house. (The owner of the rented house sold his property in exchange for it becoming a condominium building and got a very good deal: He became a genuine wealthy man owning six condos.) Lambros and Loukia had to move in a hurry into another apartment which could be seen from the window of Eftychia's bedroom. Lambros began watching and gesturing at her, and at one point, he spoke to her on the street. Eftychia replied with a flirtatious glance, which made it very much apparent that she liked what was going on. It didn't take long.

When two people are attracted to each other, all obstacles can be overcome. So, Eftychia quickly fell into the arms of Lambros, who, being sexually deprived since they came to Thessaloniki due to Loukia's entanglement with the church, had developed into a tireless lover. Their only problem was how to prevent the neighbors from getting wind of their affair. Moreover, Eftychia did not feel comfortable when they met each other in Lambros' home. Apart from the fact that he was afraid that his wife would suddenly come home and catch them in the act, she too could not feel comfortable lying in bed surrounded by walls filled with paintings of saints and holy figures. You see, after icons had completely covered her iconostasis, Loukia began to fill the walls with pictures of various saints. At every visit and celebration, her new friends brought her icons as gifts. So, Lambros' bedroom looked pretty much like a church. Having been raised by her God-fearing mother and nurtured by so many religious imperatives, Eftychia felt a dilemma within herself. On the one hand, she wanted to live her own life, but at the same time, she felt guilty for her infidelities. Moreover, being stared at by so many saintly sunken eyes of saints while she and Lambros were banging each other made her feel even worse. So, she told Lambros that they had to find somewhere else to house their love affair.

"Lambros, I can't stand this situation anymore. I'm afraid we'll suddenly get into trouble in your house. These saints are also all around; I feel like...how do I say this, when I'm at the point I need to relax—you know what I mean— suddenly, if I open my eyes, I'm falling off a cliff and...I strike out!"

"What do you want us to do?" Lambros asked her.

"Let's find another place so that we can meet safely."

"You know, it's not that easy. My finances are tight—two small salaries and that's it."

"I don't know what to say. I don't think we can go on like this. You'll find the solution. You could find a second job for two or three hours. You told me that you worked as an accountant before you were appointed. Why don't you look for something similar?"

"Well, I'll try."

"Don't just say it, Lambros. Are you listening? Look at me when I speak to you. Put an ad in the *Macedonia* newspaper that you are doing accounting work, tax consulting, etc. Something will be found, and we don't need much; just a studio rent is all we want."

A few days later, Lambros took over the accounting of a small commercial business to which he would go two hours each day, but he soon began to do the tax returns of some doctors. The first client he found was a classmate from high school, and the others followed by word of mouth. One doctor would recommend him to another as he was helpful and efficient in this job. With the extra money Lambros earned, it soon became possible to find a studio that he rented at a particularly low price, as it was in the semi-basement of an old four-story apartment building above Egnatia Street. The studio also had a balcony facing an inner courtyard where Eftychia placed two large pots of jasmine and rosemary. Lying on the bed placed next to the window, or if they opened the balcony door, they could see a little bit of the sky. It was very romantic in the evenings, especially in the summer, with the gigantic August moon and the scent released by the jasmine flowers.

Eftychia spent many beautiful moments in this love nest, but a few months later, she became pregnant for the second time. She did not expect this and found herself in great fear and panic. In other words, she began to have a problem with her conscience. How would Lambros' child grow up with Kotsos Barlabas as his father? Up until the child was born, she was filled with anxiety and doubts.

Eftychia gave birth relatively easily with the help of a very experienced midwife. The newborn weighed much less than her first son, who had looked like a three-month-old infant when he was born.

She was used to a much more robust child and began to fear that the newborn might get sick and die. Due to this fear, her second son became the apple of her eye, and this feeling pervaded her even when her children grew up. After giving birth, she was also afraid of the consequences of her sin. She was worrying: *Will God punish me for cheating on my husband?* She was also concerned with the question of whose child it was. *Was it Lambros' or Kotso's?* Her husband had forcibly cornered her once. It was the same night that she was with Lambros a while ago. So, she wasn't certain whose child it was. To avoid any problems, Eftychia did not dig deeper into the matter. The child was definitely...hers! She baptized him when he was nine months old with the name Aristides and called him Dakis affectionately. In any case, this boy resembled Barlabas more in the face, especially when he grew up. Fortunately, though, not in his character!

4

The Move

After the birth of her second son, Eftychia locked herself up in the house indefinitely. The increasing clientele of Lambros, Eftychia's last lover, had limited their opportunities for encounters. Perhaps after this two-year liaison and with the child's birth, their love affair had also suffered the inevitable wear and tear of time.

A few quiet years passed by while Eftychia devoted herself to raising her children. The children grew up unremarkably without much illness. Thanasis, already ten, and Aristides seven, both went to the elementary school in their neighborhood. Thanasis was the protector of little Aristides, who had a weaker physique in contrast to his brother, who was obviously sturdier.

"If anyone hurts you, tell me, and I'll take care of him," Thanasis, who was never afraid, told him. He even dealt with older children.

"But Thanasis, why should they tease me?" replied Aristides, who did not easily get into trouble, as he was aware of the natural weakness that characterized him.

Their mother was fearful of illnesses and even trembled at the idea of polio or tuberculosis afflicting her children. A neighbor had her daughter literally paralyzed by polio. Eftychia visited her quite often, and her heart broke at the sight of a beautiful girl, then seventeen years old, who she was sitting or lying in a bed for the last ten years of her life. Eftychia's younger son was somewhat prone to illness, or that is what she thought, so she took better care of him. Upon hearing that a child had become ill at school from something serious, she would tremble for her little Aristides. She would preemptively have him wear an extra woolen jersey, and the poor lad would burn up in the heat, but that's how his mother felt more secure. At that time, the house where they lived was in the Upper Town and was an old small, detached house of Turkish construction with a sahnisi[4] and a small courtyard, with a fig tree whose delicious figs they honored in the summers and into some tin cans were basil leaves diffused their fragrance. You could feel the fresh air of the area immediately, but at the same time, you sensed that you were living in a community of refugees and poverty. As a result of the many hardships they had experienced, the residents there became ill more often than the more well-off. Even tuberculosis raged there extensively.

Opposite her house lived a family with whom Eftychia had friendly relations. In the evenings, the women would take their chairs outside to the entrance of their houses and chat. Front and center among them were youthful Eftychia with her good neighbor, Zoitsa. Jokes, gossip, recipes, matchmaking, and something about psychics and magic were their usual topics for chitchat.

But suddenly, tuberculosis arrived and separated them. Zoitsa's husband, Savvas, who, while still healthy, worked on the trains as the

---

[4] A floor protruding about a meter from the rest of the wall and resting on special supports with an enclosed balcony and windows all around so that those sitting inside can easily see the people passing by on the street.

fireman (handling the steam injector), became seriously ill. Eftychia then had the opportunity to watch Zoitsa's journey into suffering. Just before Savvas was admitted into the sanatorium, he would cough, and sometimes he would also spit up blood on the cobblestones that formed the cobblestoned pathway on his walk uphill to his house. Eftychia would see the blood, and she would cross over to the other side of the street, holding her breath.

Savvas finally entered the sanatorium, which he never left except in his coffin. His wife, fortunately, was not infected and continued to hang out with Eftychia, but less often than before. Zoitsa, in order to make ends meet, got a job in a tobacco shop. After returning home in the evenings, she was obliged to do her housework as well, even though she was exhausted. There was no more time for chitchat outside the front doors. Zoitsa's quite elderly mother-in-law could offer her truly little help. In addition, she had heart problems, so her legs were permanently swollen. As for the mother of the young widow, she had died of dropsy while her father had perished in 1922 in the genocide of Greeks in Asia Minor.

With all that Eftychia experienced up close, the fear of tuberculosis had become an obsession within her. She no longer trusted her neighbors. In her mind, every neighbor of hers who she heard coughing immediately seemed seriously tubercular. They all looked weak to her, and their daily uphill trudge made her feel afraid.

Eftychia, after being tormented by these thoughts for some time, decided to take the big step and move out of her house and district. Besides, her mother, Georgia, who lived a little farther down the street with Eftychia's younger sister (until Electra opened her own shop and became independent), had decided to become a nun and enter the convent so as not to be dependent on any of her sons-in-law. The house in the Upper Town was no longer convenient for Eftychia.

After weighing all her options, she discussed with her husband the idea of moving and relocating below Egnatia Street. It would be easier for everyone to do so. Eftychia analyzed the positive points of the new neighborhood for him:

"You'll be able to sleep 20 minutes more in the morning since you'll be closer to work. The market below Egnatia Avenue is nearby, and we won't have an uphill shopping climb, and mainly I'll save myself the trouble with the ice in the summers. You know, the iceman pushes his ice cart with the ice chunks with his hands, and as it's overloaded, he doesn't go very high up the street but stops at a crossroads below here and waits there for the clientele from the highest points of our region." (Carrying the ice uphill was a morning ritual every summer, and Eftychia disliked it; one would say that she loathed it; nevertheless, she was embracing the ice wrapped in a sack, and as she was carrying it up to her home, she was cursing her fate that had her wronged and had no help from her husband, not even for these chores.)

"Yes, but how much will the rent be?" Barlabas asked, worried.

"C'mon, how much will it be? A rent like all rents are. It won't be so much that you have to sell your soul."

"I don't mind going to another house, but the rents are more expensive in the lower district, and we don't have enough money."

A long discussion followed that was repeated on other occasions. From these discussions, Barlabas seemed not to have any objection to them moving, but he feared that the rent would increase. Eftychia then promised him that she would look for a house with the same rent, and her husband agreed.

So, the search began, provided they would pay the same rent. That was the hard part. Wherever there were houses for rent with two rooms and a sitting room plus the "other necessities," as they used to say, the rent was more expensive by at least 25%.

Eftychia had walked quite a few kilometers to find a decent and affordable apartment; she had begun to get frustrated. Fortunately, after several days of searching, she found one apartment where the rent requested by the proprietor was only a little more than what she paid in the house of the Upper Town. The apartment's owner, Mr. Prokopis Ladas (Ladas in Greek means oil merchant), was a successful oil merchant (true to his name). During the German occupation later on, he had made a fortune on the black (illegal) market and acquired four flats in the same block where he was already collecting four rents. Eftychia asked him to accept as the official rent showing on the receipts at the limit she agreed to with her husband, and she promised to pay the extra amount herself from her own savings.

At first, the olive oil merchant thought the agreement was in his benefit for taxation reasons. Moreover, he took pity on Eftychia, whom he also…well, after all, she was at the height of her beauty at the time…thought a little slyly about the fact that something could happen in time, perhaps some hanky panky…so he rented her the apartment. The move was decided. The new house was on the street close to the Church of Agia Sophia (in English: Holy Wisdom of God), which being a great archaic church had a large courtyard where many children played. Eftychia thought that her children would have a pleasant time playing after school there, and in addition, they would be safe from careless drivers who drove military vehicles. The only drawback of the new house was that it had a very narrow and small sitting room, which looked more like a wide hallway. Perhaps that was the reason for the lower rent. However, it had a spacious kitchen and a bathroom separate from the lavatory. It also had two balconies: A very narrow one in front facing the street and one in the kitchen roomy enough to stack winter wood. Fortunately, the Barlabas family did not have much furniture. So, when they moved, all their possessions would fit. The front sitting room she would also use as her bedroom; her children would sleep in the back room. In the house where they lived, they used two wood stoves for heating and a cast iron stove, which, of course, was the dominant appliance of the kitchen. They would put a wood stove in the bedroom and one in the sitting room. That way, the heat would circulate in the back room as well.

Eftychia dreamed about the moving day. It would occur on the first of the month so that the already paid days of rent from the previous house would not go to waste. However, the first of the month fell on a Sunday, and Barlabas had asked to enter the Sunday schedule on the trams where he worked as a conductor to earn more wages. When Eftychia learned of it, she became furious. Inside she was fuming with the uncaring man she had. But what could she do?

Having heard the saying from those more educated than her, she thought "*the die was cast.*" So, she found a carter with a Hungarian horse (large muscular horse) that had ''TRANSPORTS – REMOVALS'' written on a sign glued to one side of the cart, and she organized the move. But the cart would need to make two trips because not all their possessions could be carried in one trip.

After putting her life's possessions—clothes, sheets, blankets, quilts, tablecloths, towels, underwear, woolen jerseys. slippers, nightgowns, pajamas, socks, and shoes—in a trunk and three suitcases, Eftychia begged her friend, Katina, to go and wait for her in her new home on Sunday morning after mass, to guard the possessions that would be transported on the first trip. At the same time, Eftychia would wait with her children in her old house until the cart was loaded for the second trip. Unfortunately, Electra could not help because she was away in Athens. She had gone to the convent to visit their mother, who was seriously ill. The aged woman had fallen sick with an unknown fever that would not subside, as the Abbess had telegraphed. The Abbess was even afraid that the nun Eusebia—this was her new Christian name used in the convent—would emigrate to the Lord! So, there was no help from her sister. Fortunately, however, friendships do exist, and Katina was a good friend and classmate from elementary school.

The first trip began at 10:00 AM Sunday. The beds, mattresses, covers, armchairs, kitchen table, divan, clothes chest, and stoves were loaded. In transferring possessions from the house to the cart, Eftychia was also helped by her young son but strong Thanasis, in addition to the cart's owner. On the second trip, the trunk, a wardrobe, three suitcases, a few chairs, a jacket, some boxes of dishes and glassware, the gas stove, some bottles of oil, vinegar, wine, and tsipouro (strong distilled spirit) were packed in a box stuffed among newspapers (so as not to break), a larder sealed with a cover that screwed on and filled with cheese, butter, olives, sausages and a portion of bean soup, small cans and bottles with a variety of contents—creams, colognes, pepper, salt, allspice, mustard, crushed red pepper—all these were loaded. Fortunately, there was also a sack of firewood that had been left over from the previous winter. But there was no room in the cart for the children and her, so the three of them walked all the way down to the center of town.

Thanasis was then ten years old and could walk fast, but Aristides, who was younger, was trudging along slowly, and just before reaching the house, his mother almost had to drag him to get him to walk.

"C'mon, Daki, walk a little faster."

"But Mama, I'm almost running. My stomach's in knots."

After much inconvenience, Eftychia finally arrived at her destination on time and even helped the mover carry her things up to the first floor. The children helped with a few lighter things, but mainly Thanasis, who had supernatural strength for his age. Katina was sitting in the sitting room in an old armchair whose one armrest was about ready to topple over and just watched. But Eftychia did not expect much help from her friend, as she was well-known as a lazy female who pretending to have heart murmur and palpitations to avoid tedious work. (However, as I think about it now, this murmur did not prevent Katina from living in relatively good health until she was 75.)

When all the household goods were transferred, the carter was paid for doing his job, and the family set to work inside the new house.

Katina quickly got tired of sitting alone because Eftychia did not have time to chat, and after wishing her girlfriend good luck with her house, she left. Following their mother's orders, the two children offered her some small help by carrying and arranging minor things. After several hours of arduous work, it had gotten dark early because it was November; Eftychia lit her gas stove and made a trahanas[5] soup for her children to eat while she ate the cooked beans from the day before.

When they finished their simple supper, Eftychia remembered her useless husband. The time was already 8:30 PM, and Barlabas was still absent. Then it crossed her mind. She realized her husband couldn't find the house. *Yes, that's the case,* she thought. Her indifferent husband hadn't even bothered to view the house they were going to rent. He trusted his wife's choice.

When Kotsos finished his shift in the trams, he went to the taverna for a couple of glasses of tsipouro, as was his habit. And when he got bored with the conversations and his eyes would get irritated by the

---

[5] Trahanas, also called tarhanas, is a kind of small-grained pasta usually homemade made semolina, wheat flour, bulgur or cracked wheat. Milk, buttermilk, or yogurt is added and cooked to prepare a quick soup for dinner on winter days.

cigarette smoke—he never smoked for reasons of frugality—he started his usual daily trek to ... the Upper Town!

Halfway there, something enlightened him, and he remembered that it was the day of the move. Cursing gods and demons—*why didn't I remember earlier and got tired unnecessarily going uphill*—Kotsos started walking downhill to the city center. First, he passed by Agia Sophia Church, and he crossed himself begging the Virgin Mary to help him find the house, but when he reached the street, he hesitated because it was impossible to remember the number. At the same time, however, Eftychia had sent Thanasis to walk back and forth on the street, hoping to find his father. Finally, Barlabas saw a familiar shadow approaching him in the middle of the night.

"Daddy, Daddy, we were looking for you," Thanasis exclaimed with relief. "Where have you been all day?"

"Leave me alone, you little bastard! Who do you think you are checking up on me?..." his father replied, in an angry mood but relieved that he would finally arrive at his house.

Immediately after that, he asked.

"Where's the house?"

"Here it is, father. Right here," Thanasis said. "It's a four-story building. We are on the first floor on the left," and he ran off ahead to climb up the stairs so as not to get slapped.

"Eftychia!" Barlabas roared when he entered the sitting room. "I see you arranged the house. Now get me something to eat!"

"Get it yourself. The food is over there. Take some cheese, olives, bread, and tomato and eat," Eftychia replied, irritated by her husband's all-day absence, especially on the moving day.

"What did you say? Did I hear you right?"

"As if it wasn't enough that you left me all alone to move in with two children. I worked enough today. My feet won't hold me up anymore," Eftychia complained with resentment.

"What are you saying, you lazy woman? I worked on the tram all day Sunday. What did you think? That I was sitting with my feet on pillows?" Kotsos replied.

"You knew that we would be moving, and that's why you chose to work the Sunday schedule, so you'd find everything ready!"

"You idiot. Me? The one who works on a Sunday for the double wage? Is this the thanks I get?"

"Of what use are double wages when you barely give me any money? I try to make ends meet and manage the household by squeezing blood from stones," Eftychia complained.

"Hey! You're intolerable," Barlabas mumbled, and he turned to the small balcony where a larder was hanging with a piece of cheese inside. "Lucky for you that I'm hungry because otherwise, I would have given you some smacks to teach you how to behave."

Thus began the first quarrel in the new house where their family would reside for many years.

"We crossed the threshold arguing just so the coming year would turn out well," Eftychia told Electra a few days later. "Whether I was talking, or he was, in the end he was about to hit me, but Thanasis got in the middle and protected me…my precious boy. And my Aristides was also crying and pleading, *No daddy. Don't hit mommy.* So, I was spared a beating. Now that my Thanasis has grown up, I have a protector, and I will show the ne'er do well, the egotist, what's what! But he's really nothing more than a big donkey, sister. Can you believe it?! Moving all by myself with two children and him wanting cooked food!"

Electra agreed. "I wouldn't marry such a man; frankly speaking, if he fooled me into thinking he was fine and I accepted him, I would immediately divorce him afterward."

"My dear Electra, I wouldn't have accepted him either, but let the facts speak for themselves. I found myself in need. I was pregnant. What could I do? Now I've got him, and I'm washed up. But really, now that I've used the word washed, do you know that the house also has a bathtub with a water heater? Do you imagine that my Kotsos will do any washing up, or will he be afraid of his fragrance disappearing? "

A floor plan of Eftychia's home is depicted below.

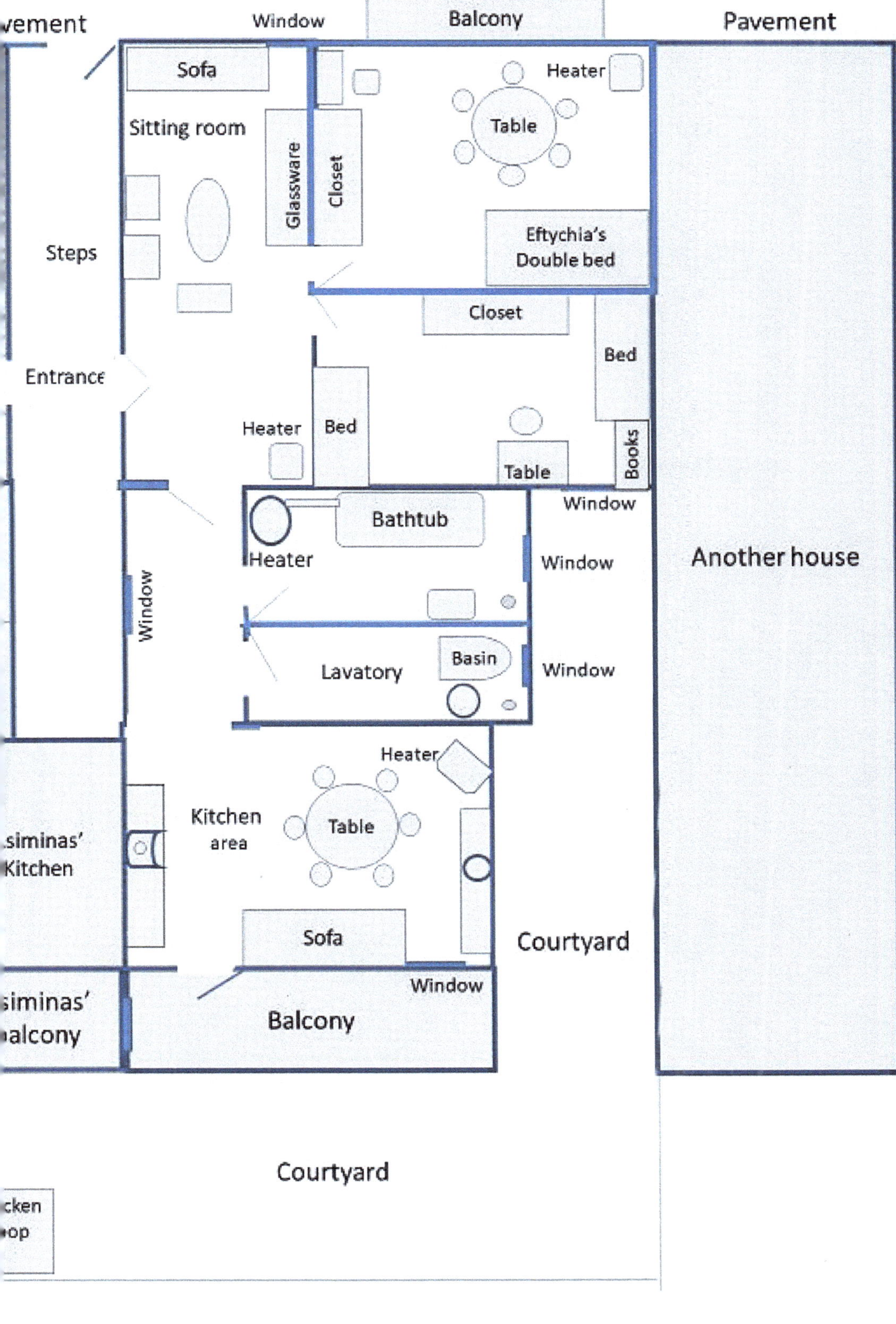
Pavement
Window
Balcony
Pavement
Sofa
Heater
Sitting room
Table
Glassware
Closet
Eftychia's
Double bed
Steps
Closet
Bed
Entrance
Heater
Bed
Books
Table
Window
Bathtub
Heater
Window
Another house
Window
Basin
Window
Lavatory
Heater
Kitchen
area
Table
...siminas'
Kitchen
Sofa
Courtyard
Window
...siminas'
...alcony
Balcony
Courtyard
...cken
...op

ΜΕΤΑΦΟΡΑΙ
ΜΕΤΑΚΟΜΙΣΕΙΣ

5

Zozo

When Eftychia lived in the Upper Town, she knew a couple with two daughters—Sofia and Zozo. The older girl, Sofia, became afflicted with meningitis at an early age. She became considerably mentally disabled either because of this illness or for other reasons. Eftychia had baptized her younger sister Georgia, who everyone called Zozo, a nickname that she had chosen when she was very young and could not say "Gogo" (nickname for Georgia) but instead called herself "Zozo". Eftychia often had conversations with Eugenia, her goddaughter's mother. She felt pity for Sophia's misfortune, a girl who was anything but smart. In fact, she could not understand a single thing and was mocked and teased by the neighborhood's children.

The girls' father, Andreas Krassas, was a subcontractor and supervised a small workshop that employed three to four workers. He would travel to various cities when he was assigned to oversee the construction of a house or a small bridge. He would come home every week. When the girls were nine and seven years old respectively, their mother fell ill with a fever that would not drop despite the efforts of the doctors at the municipal hospital where she was being treated. The medical director ruled that she had liver cancer with metastases, a condition that could not be treated. Eugenia faded day by day; her belly swelled, she had jaundice, and three months after she fell ill, she surrendered her spirit! Andreas was in despair. He could not leave the girls alone at home. The nature of his work often required him to be absent in other places, far from Thessaloniki. He decided to go to his late wife's sister, who lived in a refugee house with her unmarried brother Kostas, who worked as a worker in the Flokas Chocolate Factory.

"Virginia, my job is difficult. I must be away from Thessaloniki often. What should I do with the girls?"

"What do you think needs to be done?" Virginia asked.

"Well, I thought about it, and there are two solutions. One is to put them in a boarding school. But much money is required for this, and I don't have that much left after the funeral expenses. The other solution is for you and Kostas to take care of them, and I'll give you a monthly fee for their expenses."

"This is a great responsibility," Kostas replied, frowning.

"Silence, Kostas. This is a woman's job," Virginia retorted.

"I've thought about it myself. If Andreas gives us something for their expenses—I mean money for their clothes and food—I'll be able to make ends meet!"

Kostas bowed his head, somewhat embarrassed by his sister's remark. He was three years younger than Virginia, and she had taken the upper hand since they were little, so she always had the last word.

Andreas took a wad of money out of his pocket and, without counting it, handed it to his sister-in-law.

"Here, take this for starters. Tomorrow I'll bring the girls and their things. I'll come to see them whenever I can, maybe every 15 days."

On the one hand, Virginia felt sorry for the girls, and on the other hand, she felt her maternal instincts had been left unrealized since she was over forty and still single. For this reason, she accepted her brother-in-law's proposal. Andreas more than wanted to, and he handed over the girls to Virginia, allowing him to be involved in his work without any distractions. Initially, he came to see his daughters quite often, when he would also leave money for Virginia. However, Andreas' visits to his children gradually thinned out, and the money he left began getting scarce until the payments finally stopped completely one day. This happened when a cunning widow wrapped him in her nets tightly and then married him.

Meanwhile, Virginia began to get upset because her two nieces were a great responsibility and financial burden. She decided to look for a good woman to take over at least one girl. She thought it would be an ideal solution for Zozo's godmother to take her, who was no other than Eftychia Barlabas.

One Sunday after church, the doorbell of the Barlabas household rang. It was Virginia holding a box of chocolates.

"Oh my! What a surprise this is!" Eftychia exclaimed and exchanged kisses with Virginia. "I'm alone. Everyone's off somewhere. Please sit down in the sitting room, my dear koumbara (best woman but koumbara is often used for a family relationship in this case being a godmother). I'll bring two cups of coffee in a couple of minutes."

"Thank you, Eftychia; I drink my coffee without sugar." Virginia was trying not to consume too many calories.

Soon after, the coffees were ready.

"Here's your coffee, thickly foamed. Take a cookie for dunking. I made them just today."

"Thank you. To your health," Virginia replied, drinking some water before sipping the coffee.

"To your health and the health of the girls. You did a good deed to take them in," the hostess remarked to Virginia.

After drinking their coffee, Eftychia suggested that she look inside Virginia's cup because she knew Virginia wanted her to do so as she was still single.

"Wow, wow! What I see is quite distressing. A lot of blackness at the base that reaches up to the top. It opens up a little higher, you go through a period of sadness, but you will overcome it," Eftychia concluded.

At this point, Virginia broke down and burst into sobs from all her pain caused by the behavior of the father of the two girls.

"Oh, Eftychia! You have no idea what's happened to us. Andreas, my late sister's husband, left us his two girls with the agreement to give us a sum for their expenses every month, but after eight months, he got involved with a wench in Serres, and now he's an artful dodger—I have no money for his children nor any news from him. He works in Drama and returns to his home in Serres occasionally. My brother Kostas searched for him in Serres but couldn't find him. I'm in a difficult position. I'm exhausted financially but also physically. I see the girls saddened, and my soul despairs. They lost their mother and now don't even have a father. Cursed be the moment he married my sister! I'm thinking maybe I should put the girls in some orphanage."

While Virginia was talking, Eftychia thought about helping in the situation by fostering her goddaughter Zozo herself. She thought: *Being a girl she'll be able to help me with household chores; I put four dishes on the table, another one will easily be added. Zozo is such a cute ten-year-old girl. She'll keep me company.*

So, it didn't take long for her to make up her mind.

"Listen, Koumbara. Stop worrying. I can assume responsibility for my goddaughter as long as Kotsos has no objection. But what am I saying? Whether he objects or not, I will take Zozo! The time when he used to do what he wanted is over."

"Oh, my dear Eftychia, you make me emotional," Virginia exclaimed while tears filled her eyes and, like little diamonds, trickled down her cheeks. She took a handkerchief out of her bag, wiped away tears, blew her nose, which was stuffed up, and said: "Eftychia, this good deed will be reciprocated by God. I will leave now as I left the girls alone and they'll be upset."

She hugged her koumbara, kissed her, took her bag, and added, "I'll be waiting for your answer."

"God bless you, Virginia, and don't worry. I'll let you know soon."

That same evening, Eftychia told Barlabas she would bring Zozo home. He immediately bristled.

"Another plate at the table?! Have you gone insane?"

"Her father will give us money every now and then," Eftychia said, lying. "Perhaps it's more than what we'll spend on Zozo."

"Hey, then that changes everything," Kotsos replied. "Let her come."

The next day Eftychia set off for the Upper Town where Virginia was staying. The uphill trudge reminded her of the hardships she had suffered while she was staying up there, carrying the groceries uphill all year round and the treacherous ice in the summer. *Luckily, I moved downtown and got away from it*, she thought.

Panting and sweaty, she arrived at Virginia's house. The damn house was stuck up there next to the castles. It was impossible to build it any higher. The two girls were sitting at the front door doorstep and playing with a small kitten.

"Hi godmother. What brings you here?" Zozo greeted her while Sophia stared at Eftychia with sleepy eyes. "Look at the cute kitten. We gave it milk to drink. So sweet, isn't it?"

"Did you bring me candies like before?" Sophia asked.

"Yes, my dear Sophia. Here you are. Take a roll of candies and one for Zozo too."

Eftychia entered the front door and found herself in a small courtyard full of pots with basil, rosemary, and geraniums. She climbed ten steps to the top but before knocking on the door, she stood there admiring the view. Thessaloniki looked incredibly beautiful with its church bell towers, the White Tower, and the coast. Several ships were anchored at the piers, and three large ships in the harbor. *Nice view, but you lose your breath getting up here*, she thought.

After a while, she was sitting in Virginia's narrow sitting room.

"Your house is like the monasteries," Eftychia said admiring the panorama. "It's built extremely high, with a beautiful view. By the time you get here, your sins are purified, with so much shortness of breath and fatigue."

"It's very small, though," Virginia replied. "Just look at this sitting room. It's even smaller and narrower than yours."

"The view and the fresh air compensate for that," Eftychia added thoughtfully. "But tell me, how is the neighborhood dealing with tuberculosis?"

"You know, after the first cases, we had no more," Virginia replied with relief. "The Virgin Mary protected us."

"I've come for Zozo," Eftychia said. "I convinced Kotsos, and he has no objection. Did you tell her anything?"

"No, I didn't say anything since nothing was certain, and I was expecting a definite answer from you. Besides, I didn't know if Kotsos would accept it."

"Let's call her. Let's see how she reacts to it, too."

Zozo heard the news and hugged her godmother, whispering calmly.

"Godmother, I love you very much," she said, "but I want us to come and see Sophia sometimes."

"Of course, we'll come. And you'll come on your own when you grow up a little more."

So, after preparing an old suitcase with the little girl's clothes (she had so few) and saying goodbye to Virginia, Eftychia and Zozo began walking down the hill. Zozo was holding a cloth doll in her hand. She had thought about taking the kitten with her for a moment but decided to leave it behind so that Sophia could play with it.

At noon, when they sat at the table (Kotsos was away at work), Eftychia prayed, and then they started eating the leftover bean soup from the night before. In addition to black wheat bread, there was pickled cabbage, savory anchovies, and olives on the table. Eftychia had cut the bread into similar slices and distributed a large portion of a pie made with greens to everyone.

Thanasis saw his portion of the pie and the bread slice and started grumbling:

"I can't fill up with just a slice."

"When you were younger, you filled up and didn't even eat bread."

"But I was eating everything else, but more than just this."

"Shut up and eat," Eftychia replied sternly. "Come on, take one more slice, you Gargantua you!"

After they had eaten their bean soup, Eftychia started speaking.

"Starting today, Zozo will be staying in our house. You will consider her as your sister. You'll take care of her and protect her because she's small and orphaned. She will sleep in the sitting room sofa."

"Will she be going to school?" Aristides asked.

"No. She didn't go to school at all this year," his mother replied. "She's already missed half the year, so why go now?"

"On Monday, they're giving us our semester grades," Thanasis stated.

"Let's see what you're going to bring us," his mother replied skeptically.

When they finished eating their meal, and because she had not bought any fruit, Eftychia took out a jar of sweet orange preserves and gave each a portion with a teaspoon. She didn't have any herself because she had been trying to slim down. When they all finished their dessert, Eftychia crossed herself and proclaimed, "Glory be to God, we've eaten, we've had enough, and we have glorified God."

Immediately after that, she gave orders.

"All of you. Take your dishes to the sink." She wiped the crumbs from the table, turned to Zozo, saying: "Come on, Zozo. Let me show you how we wash the dishes. What do I see? You barely reach the height of the sink. That's not a problem. You're just going to step up on that stool."

She placed a small stool in front of the sink cabinet.

"There you go. Well done. Now take this soapy cloth and scrub the dish. You must use hot water to clean the dishes better if the food has butter or meat. You'll put the hot water in a bowl and put the cutlery in there. We heat the water on the kerosene stove. I'll turn it on for you until you know how to do it yourself. Oh, and something else: I'll show you the mopping tomorrow."

After supper, Eftychia went to her bedroom, sat on the stool of her three-mirrored dresser, and started pulling out her eyebrows with tweezers. When she finished, she took a small tool that looked like weird scissors and curled her eyelashes with it. Then she applied lipstick, tidied up her hair, dabbed on perfume, and got dressed in her good red satin dress. Today she would have an interesting meeting. The deletion of Barlabas from her life had long since begun. She couldn't stand him anymore!

6

Eftychia the Feminist

With two young children to care for and financial hardship to endure, Eftychia became a thrifty homemaker out of necessity; in all matters, she tried to implement the greatest possible savings. So, she was careful not to throw out stale bread, not to forget the milk outside the ice box and have it go sour, to save the olive oil that was left over from frying, to peel the potatoes carefully, leaving as much potato on as she could, not to burn a lot of wood in her stove if the weather changed and it was blowing from the south, and finally not to throw away various papers because one day they might be needed.

Barlabas would always bring home a couple of newspapers. Not that he bought them. He would take them when passengers left them on the tram where he worked as a conductor. So, these newspapers were different each time, and the information that Eftychia reaped was global and multifaceted. She had the opportunity to be informed and educated socially and, thanks to these newspapers, to cultivate her mind more than she had done by attending school through the fifth grade. Obviously, not all days were the same, so she did not have time to read some newspapers. She would collect all the newspapers and use them in various ways. She used some of the newspaper for fuel, that is, to light the coals in the brazier and the wood in the stove. If the newspapers that Barlabas carried home took up too much space,

Eftychia would gather them into large bundles, tie them with twine, and sell them to a merchant in the Kapani Market. She also cut newsprint paper to a specific size and poked each sheet through a nail on the wall next to the lavatory basin. At that time, there was no toilet paper; if there was, it was too expensive, and her budget could not allow such expenses. Eftychia would read these cut-up papers when she sat on the lavatory basin for her needs. She did the same with various wrapping papers that she kept beautifully arranged and used when she wanted to wrap something she made as a gift. It was usually for some cake she had baked herself.

She once heard a debate about women's suffrage. She was an admirer of Dimitrios Gounaris (Greek political leader), about whom she had read that he had been executed along with five others in "The Trial of the Six" — a parody of a trial. Since then, she had become a passionate royalist in contrast to her husband, Kotsos Barlabas, who, despite his namesake, King Constantine I—the same as the leader of the two Balkan wars—was a Venizelist (a follower of Eleftherios Venizelos a political leader of the early 20th century). One day, on one sheet of toilet paper from an old newspaper, she read something that enraged her.

"Some Greek women demand that the vote be given to women. On the same subject, from the floor of Parliament, a very eminent scientist once developed the scientifically known and accurate fact that every woman is in an unbalanced and frenzied spiritual state on certain days of each month. However, because these days do not coincide for all women, it is impossible to find a day of spiritual balance and peace of mind for all women to determine the election on that happy day.

Women's suffrage is a dangerous thing. Therefore, it is repulsive."

Listen to him! Eftychia thought. *The smart aleck journalist accuses us women of not being able to vote because we're on the rag every month. If I saw him in front of me, I would take out the filthy creep's eyes! The only thing we don't do is military service. Oh, of course, the men have organized the issue well, haven't they? If we served as soldiers, we would be killed in the war so they wouldn't find women to keep their house, cook for them, have children, fulfill their whims...*

Eftychia kept the newspaper clipping, and at the first opportunity showed it to her neighbor, Asimina.

"Read it and see what the bugger writes."

"Which is the one I should read?" Asimina asked.

"Here it is, dear, here where he writes about the vote. He insults us; he makes fun of us; he mocks us."

Asimina read the publication carefully. Then she raised her head and looked Eftychia in the eyes.

"So, you think the journalist is unfair?"

"Unfair, what do you mean unfair? Just unfair? Very much unfair, I'd say. Of course, I'm not saying that some days we don't get into our moods, but not to the extent that we can't decide what to vote for. He has exaggerated it."

"It's not worth getting worked up about it," Asimina declared. "Sooner or later, they'll give us the right to vote. But first, women must go to school. In the villages, they don't send the girls to school! How will they read the names to choose for whom to vote?"

Nevertheless, Eftychia had become unhinged with the anonymous author of the comment and was constantly mulling over the issue in her head.

The next night on October 26, 1935, it was Saint Dimitrios Day, and Asimina's husband was celebrating his name day. Eftychia and her husband visited to wish him a happy name day. The first sweet treats were presented with chocolates and banana liqueur, and the second was a homemade cake. Then, a conversation began about the political parties and the King. On November 3, the referendum with the question—"Parliamentary constitutional monarchy or Presidential democracy?"—was to be held. So, in response, Dimitris, the name-day celebrant, revealed his opinion. He would vote against the monarchy. For years, he supported Papanastasiou, a socialist and an anti-royalist. He considered him the most consistent. He added that Papanastasiou had also established the Aristotelian University as a further argument to justify his unconditional sympathy with Papanastasiou and his views.

Barlabas was stuck like glue to Venizelos.

"Venizelos is the father of the nation, and no one can touch him," he declared, with his mind on the relevant poem ("Venizelos, our father of the homeland"). "Unfortunately, he finds himself in self-exile in

France. I wish he could run in the next election. As for the King, who cares. Whether a King or a president, it's all the same for me."

Eftychia was with the People's Party of Panages Tsaldaris, who took over as head of the party following the execution of Gounaris after "The Trial of The Six" and after initial vacillation supported the return of the King. She didn't talk, though, because she was afraid of a fight with her husband. Asimina, who was generally not very talkative, also did not speak out of respect to her husband, although she did not always agree with everything he said. She followed this tactic for years to ensure her peace of mind.

Mr. Pelopidas from the second floor was a Metaxas fan.

"I'm in favor of the monarchy. The king is a symbol of unity as long as he doesn't take sides in politics. As for the government we need, only Metaxas can rule this country with an iron hand," Pelopidas stated firmly. "He is the most intelligent Greek politician today. He was also a professor of Prince Georgios teaching the Prince military tactics when he was a youth."

"Yes, I agree about his intelligence, but he has no popular appeal," Dimitris responded. "Only seven deputies were elected from his party—the Freethinkers—in the last elections. Besides, he caused a lot of friction with Venizelos in 1915, back then during the national schism."

Finally, Mr. Tasos and his wife Frosso, Asimina's cousin, were followers of Kondylis, as Tasos had him as commander when he was in the army, (and in addition, they were both originally from nearby hometowns). However, he did not express himself much because

Kondylis had often changed his ideology and opinions on important issues. Being a Venizelist originally, Kondylis now found himself organizing and preparing for the return of the King. After all, in a few days, the referendum would be held on the initiative of Kondylis who was now acting as regent!

Following this somewhat stimulating banter, a laid-back discussion about the forthcoming referendum followed. Dimitris complained that there was a lot of propaganda in favor of the King, and the old Venizelists were acting as if they were stunned. The Venizelist officers who took part in the coup were expelled. Their party was going through difficult times. *After the failed coup d'état of March and the flight of their leader Venizelos, the Venizelists are fearful*, Dimitris thought. Moreover, being a man who was never absolute but generally had democratic and socialist ideas, he had formed the impression that the Venizelists were not now as fanatical against the King as they used to be. *We are probably disappointed in the democracy not led by a king but with the many political parties and movements,* Dimitris surmised but preferred not to say so out loud.

While the men were talking and the conversation had again gotten animated, at some point, Eftychia also took the floor. On the occasion of the referendum, she started to speak about the great issue of women's suffrage.

"Why don't they ask women what they want? Do they want a monarchical or monarch-free democracy?"

She continued talking about the sarcastic newspaper article she had discovered by chance the day before. Obviously, she did not mention where she found the newspaper! But she did bring up the oppression of women by the male-dominated establishment of society. While saying all this, it was only natural that she was thinking about the clouts she had endured from Barlabas. Her cheeks had reddened in her excitement, and as she spoke, her eyes seemed to grow more prominent, and they glistened, framed by her long-curled eyelashes. Finally, she spoke about the mistakes of male politicians.

"If women were also involved in government, there wouldn't be so many mistakes that we all pay for. If there were women in government, we wouldn't have walked barefoot on the thorns of Asia Minor (referring to the Greek genocide). Venizelos' mistake was the Greek troops landing in Smyrna, an action without a realistic goal. Gounaris was forced to continue the policy of Venizelos as he couldn't bear the psychological burden of Greece withdrawing from Smyrna and then being considered a traitor. Surely then they would have considered him a traitor," Eftychia concluded and paused to take a few breaths.

Pelopidas interrupted to say something about the politician he admired.

"Metaxas had objections to the Asia Minor campaign. He predicts everything."

But no one bothered to listen to him because Eftychia continued unabated, and everyone watched her with different emotions.

"The execution of the six was a criminal error. They executed Gounaris while he was burning up with typhoid fever, which he was infected with in prison. They neutralized Venizelos' political opponents with a rigged trial. Plastiras, yet again—a brave man during the war—but what did he want to get mixed up with the military coups?"

Stunned, the men listened to her narration hanging on her words. For them, it was a revelation. Where did Eftychia know all this? She spoke like a man experienced in years of politics.

"Let's change the subject," Asimina suggested, who realized that emotions might surface. "By the way, what do you think of the new house built on the corner? It has an elevator too! Press the button, and it takes you to the sixth floor lickety-split. I went in to see what it's like. But to tell the truth, I was scared. It stops somewhat abruptly, and you get startled."

"Here in this house where we all live by paying rent, there's no space for an elevator to be installed," Dimitris said. "In any case, there are just four floors."

"And even if we wanted an elevator and space was found to fit it in, do you have the impression that the cheapskate Prokopis would agree to install it for us?" Eftychia said sarcastically. "He only knows how to collect our good money and ask for a rent increase occasionally!"

More trivialities followed, and soon the departures began. Again, wishes, handshakes, and the women kissing each other on the cheeks. Asimina's sitting room finally emptied.

"Bravo to Eftychia. She speaks with her heart!" Asimina exclaimed. "What do you have to say, Dimitri?"

"What can I say, Asimina? Not even a politician could compete with her. I wonder how she knows all the facts in detail and has an opinion on all political issues."

"Eftychia is experienced in life, and she reads whatever she happens to find." She continued. "If she'd finished school, she could have become a lawyer."

Just then, voices could be heard from the adjacent apartment. Kotsos was arguing with Eftychia because he was annoyed that his wife had talked too much about politics in a stranger's home.

"Women should bow their heads down and not talk." He was echoing the traditional male point of view. But Eftychia was a tough nut and proved it every day.

Don't mess with me too much; she had once warned him *because it won't take much for me to ask for a divorce.* At the time, Kotsos had hardly paid attention to his wife's statement. But Eftychia had begun to nurture the idea of divorce in her mind. She waited impatiently for her children to grow up and then she would show him how much spunk she had. After all, her mother lived quite far away in the convent and had ceased dominating her with her old-fashioned ideas.

7

The War

On April 13, 1936, Ioannis Metaxas became Prime Minister of Greece after the death of the acting Prime Minister, Konstantinos Demertzis. Almost the entire Parliament had given Metaxas a vote of confidence to govern the country temporarily until the major parties—the Liberal Party led by Themistoklis Sofoulis, and the People's Party led by Panagis Tsaldaris—agreed to a coalition government. On August 4, 1936, Metaxas, with the agreement of King George II, declared the dictatorship on the pretext of effectively countering an impending nationwide strike and, as he called it, the looming "communist danger!" The Parliament would not function, after the suspension of a few articles of the Constitution, and there would be censorship. Soon, many politicians and civilians were arrested for reasons of "national security", but what that really meant was for the security of the government. Everyone was concerned by these developments. Europe was experiencing great turmoil. Quite a few dictatorships had been established in Europe, and military preparations were going ahead in all nations.

Beginning in 1925, Italy had become a dictatorship with Mussolini at its head. In 1933 Germany chose an extreme nationalist, Adolf Hitler, as a Chancellor. There were dictatorships in Spain and Portugal and a dictatorship in the Soviet Union (of the proletariat, supposedly). Hitler would not accept implementing the humiliating terms of Germany's capitulation in the "Great War". It was evident that a new great war would break out sooner or later.

As was her routine, Eftychia read the various newspapers that Barlabas brought home, and she would become incensed. She often confided her fears to Electra. One Sunday afternoon in August 1938, the two sisters were in Eftychia's sitting room.

"Oh, my dear Electra, I'm very worried. Don't you see where things are going? We are not doing well at all. Remember my words. I'm sure that there will be a war!"

"War! With whom? " Elektra asked, frowning.

"I don't know who the opponent will be, but I've always been afraid of the Bulgarians and the Turks, but now also of the Italians. You see, Mussolini considers Italy to be the same as the old Roman Empire and wants to dominate the entire Mediterranean. He's already attacked Ethiopia. Don't forget that in 1923 Italy bombed Kerkyra (Corfu). That showoff (Mussolini) thinks he is a Roman emperor, and that Greece belongs to him. You'll see. Sooner or later, our turn will come. I'm afraid of the Bulgarians because they desire an exit to the sea. As for the Turks, no explanations are needed."

"Don't be afraid of the Bulgarians. We've defeated them so many times. In addition, we have strongholds on the border—the 'Metaxas Line' as they call it. As for the Turks, we have a friendship pact," Electra said.

"Friendship with wolves is not possible. If they're given a chance, they'll devour us. But the Italians have targeted us. What about them?

They're also in possession of the Dodecanese Islands. I'm more afraid of them," Eftychia muttered.

"Well, and what do you want us to do? We don't have a say; we don't even vote," Electra said to tease her sister since she knew her sensitivity on this issue.

"I think we need to take some measures to survive in case of war," Eftychia replied, "I'll start by collecting food."

"Food? Like what kind of food?"

"Well, let's say olive oil, cheese in a sealed can, flour, beans, lentils, pasta, rice, evaporated milk in cans, canned meat, and stewed sardines, but also salted ones that are cheaper and anything that is preserved and wouldn't spoil quickly."

"Yes, but where will you find the money to buy these things?" Electra asked as she knew about Eftychia's difficult financial straits.

"Well, there's a little something left over with my hard-earned savings," Eftychia whispered. "To tell you the truth, a little at a time, I'm pinching some small change from Kotsos' pockets for the good of us all," she added justifying her actions to herself while a slight blush appeared on her cheeks.

"I don't blame you. I would do the same," Electra replied bluntly. "If, of course, I had such an uncaring man in my family," she added hastily.

"Anyhow. You had a good man until lately, that is, until he started getting drunk every night," Eftychia replied. This nastiness has gone too far, don't you think?"

"Alekos began drinking that time he was left with the rotted, unsold onions. He waited for their price to go up, so he kept them. They asked for them, and he didn't sell them expecting better prices. In the end, almost everything rotted! He sat down, sorted out the ones still in good shape, and sold them for as much as he could get. So, he suffered a great deal of damage. To ease his pain, he eventually took to drinking wine. He was always a social drinker but had significantly increased his drinking lately. He began to drink even in the morning hours. Meanwhile, my work with the hats was going very well, and he started getting jealous. Yes, he's jealous of me…that I do better than him. He starts drinking at ten in the morning. He buys retsina by the barrel. I'm afraid I won't be able to put up with him much longer. As long as he's sober, he's fine, but when he starts getting drunk, and he's in a fun mood singing, he then becomes irritable and doesn't know what he's doing. Of course, since he's drunk for hours at a time, he can't work. He let go of the warehouse he was renting in the vegetable market. It's a good thing I'm working. Otherwise, we'd go hungry. The day before yesterday, I was holding a hot water flask getting ready to drink a cup of tea, and he pushed me angrily; I almost got burned. Fortunately, a little hot water splashed on just my boot. I'm seriously considering asking for a divorce."

"Oh, my dearest Electra, we both married the wrong guys," Eftychia said softly, and suddenly she remembered the issue that mainly concerned her.

"You need to get your supplies too, sister. Your work in the millinery shop is going well. All the rich ladies follow fashion and wear hats, and since you have a bigger house, I'll bring food to you to hide food on my behalf so that Barlabas doesn't see it."

"Well, fine. But don't overdo it with Barlabas' pockets. He could figure it out, and then he'll beat you good," her sister advised her.

After their conversation, they began collecting food. Electra's house slowly became the perfect warehouse! But Eftychia also kept various foods that she stored in her closet, where she had her assortment of clothes; some foods like rice, pasta, and canned goods she stored in suitcases under the beds.

After a year of storing food, Eftychia found that the flour which she had stored in her closet between her skirts had been infested with bugs. She then began sifting it to clean it up, but she was overwhelmed because these demons were endless. She learned her lesson and decided to avoid stockpiling too much flour in the future. However, she told Electra about her blunder so that she, too, could check the flour she had stored.

"Be careful, Electra. The flour I had hidden in my closet caught lice. Check yours to see what's going on."

"What can I do, Eftychia? If my flour caught lice and I needed to use it, I'd make a pie; what I mean to say is a meat pie with the lice. Instead of minced meat, it will have lice," Electra joked as she had calculated these possibilities and did not store flour for a long time.

In March 1939, war broke out with Hitler's invasion of Czechoslovakia. The Anglo-French pretended that nothing was wrong. Electra discussed it with Eftychia.

"Hey, sister! Are these English and French completely stupid? Don't they see that in the end, Hitler will attack them too? They let Germany swallow up poor Czechoslovakia like a spoon sweet," Eftychia said, dismayed.

"England is probably not ready for war," Electra replied, who had read something in the newspaper *Macedonia* the previous day. She continued: "However, ultimately, we won't be spared. I saw Hitler making a speech in the newsreel at the Pallas Cinema, and what can I say…His eyes were glowing like a maniac locked up in a psychiatric hospital. He was screaming and foaming at the mouth like a wild horse."

The sisters were right to worry. The invasion of Poland followed in September 1939. After considerable delay, the British and French finally declared war against Hitler's Germany, with which Mussolini was allied. Things began to get serious, especially after the Spring of 1939 when Italian troops landed in Albania without any local resistance. Eftychia was in turmoil. It was as if she were watching the future.

"You'll see. Mussolini will attack Greece as well," she said on every occasion where there was a discussion.

Electra finally divorced her husband Alekos in October 1940 because the wretched man was now an incurable alcoholic and living with him had become impossible. In the same year, at Christmas, Electra asked Eftychia to let her son Thanasis—who was then 16 years old—live with her to keep her company.

"The glutton will eat with me, and you'll also save money that way. I live nearby, just two hundred meters from your house, and if you need anything, I'll run over. Whenever you miss him, just come and see him. After all, he plays soccer daily in the courtyard of Saint Sophia, next to my house. Do me a favor and do give me your Thanasakis. I'll treat him like my child since I have no children of my own!"

Having thought about it and considered the matter from all sides, Eftychia agreed to let Thanasis stay with Electra. This would also relieve her a little in her financial problem, as her lad ate as much as two men. As for Barlabas, she wouldn't discuss it with him right away. She would reveal it to him slowly. Yes, she wouldn't even mention it. If he asked her, she would say, *Well today the child stayed at Electra's, so she could help him study.* Thanasis of course did not object to staying with Electra as long as...he ate enough! After all, his Aunt Electra was a wonderful cook. Her *pites* (sweet or savory pies) were finger licking good. So, starting on New Year's Day of 1938, Eftychia's older son carried a suitcase with his clothes to Electra's home where he willingly settled in and even had a large room of his own!

Electra quickly found that Thanasis was adrift. He did not study his lessons, and his clothes were not organized. She decided to set him straight. So, every night she checked to make sure he had studied for his classes and had him recite the history lesson, geography, and theories of physics and chemistry. She did not intervene in mathematics because, on the one hand, she was inept in math, and on the other her nephew was quite a math whiz.

With this cornering of Thanasis, under the enforcement of the dynamic Electra, his grades at the Konstantinidis Commercial School, where he had enrolled for the last year, also improved. As for his clothes, Electra showed Thanasis how to iron them and carefully hang them on chairs. No matter how well he ironed his clothes, he got them torn and dirty more successfully. One moment he would be climbing trees, and the next, he would be a goalkeeper in a soccer match, crawling in the dirt.

Thanasis' stay at his aunt's house lasted more than two years until Electra remarried, this time to a much older man. He was a dentist with whom she had become pregnant. Her acquaintance with the dentist, Apostolos Eliades, occurred in his dental office where she went when she broke one of her teeth. She had tried to open a bottle of orange soda with her teeth because she could not find the opener. Thanasis had taken it with him on an excursion. She then lost half a tooth but eventually gained a husband. It wasn't such a bad thing at all. Besides, her new husband did a wonderful job, and the restoration of the missing tooth was quite satisfactory.

If I'd known it would happen this way I would have deliberately broken my tooth much earlier! she thought cheerfully at one point.

She wasn't concerned about the age difference as she thought it was enough for her husband to love her and make her feel safe. With her first husband, they had fallen in love when they were barely adolescents. He was two years older than she was, and they had an enjoyable time at first, but later, it turned out badly. But she remembered the last tragic period of their marriage when every night, she would collect her drunken husband from the tavernas of the neighborhood. Sometimes he became aggressive and hit her. One final beating episode was the straw that broke the camel's back. She started divorce proceedings and managed to get a divorce relatively quickly with the help of some high-class acquaintances she had thanks to her work.

No sooner had the divorce been finalized than Electra got pregnant. Before her second marriage—which took place in a close-knit circle—Electra also acquired a gold tooth, a gold sheath covering her broken one.

In addition to the gold tooth, Apostolos also gifted her a fantastic gold bracelet adorned with beautiful sapphires and rubies. Although she was worried about the age difference between the couple, deep down, Eftychia was happy because Electra was given security and lived near her. She also thought that something would be gained as well. At the least, she would get free dental work at her brother-in-law's dental office!

After Electra's wedding, Thanasis returned to his mother's house, but after finishing the fifth grade of high school, he almost stopped attending. As soon as he escaped Electra's close surveillance, he began playing hooky—going to morning cinemas and taking walks—which resulted in many absences. When Eftychia went to the school to get the semester grades, the headmaster told her there was no reason to continue paying tuition fees, as her son had already missed the year from his absences. So, Thanasis did not finish the six-year high school, as he missed the last year.

Fortunately, Electra, who, as a milliner, had many acquaintances, managed to place Thanasis into an apprentice program as an employee in a delicatessen shop owned by Mr. Stamatis, who was the husband of a client of hers. In this shop, which was located below Tsimiski Street near the port, they sold salted and cured foods. For the first couple of months, Thanasis would have no salary. Then they would pay him provided he had learned the ropes and was hardworking, so in that case, Mr. Stamatis would have been satisfied with the young man's performance.

Eftychia's son turned out to be a workaholic, smart, and mathematically gifted. To everyone's surprise, he could figure out math problems in his head without a pencil. Some had him do math problems in his head to entertain themselves, and Thanasis was always right. Once, a neighbor who owned a souvlaki shop wagered with him about who could figure out a math problem faster and correctly. It was the multiplication of a three-digit number by a five-digit one. They were given the numbers, and the contest started, one solving in his head and the other with the pencil. Thanasis won the bet, of course, and he pocketed five drachmas, which at the time was not a negligible sum if we consider that Eftychia paid 20 drachmas every month in rent.

Thanasis was constantly lifting boxes in the shop, making his arm muscles even more robust. Soon, he began to get a salary as well. Half of the money he kept and half he gave to his mother. He worked six days a week, eight hours every day, as the dictator Ioannis Metaxas had established the strict eight-hour day. After work and on

Sundays, he spent his free time on soccer, fishing, backgammon, and erotic pursuits.

On August 15, 1940, the cowardly torpedoing of the *Elli*, the naval cruiser that had been moored in Tinos for the feast of the Virgin Mary, was carried out by an Italian submarine, as evidenced by the subsequent investigations. The submarine fired three torpedoes, one of which hit the *Elli*, which quickly sank, while the other two hit the pier. No war had been declared yet, and the Greek government was trying not to encourage war, so there was no announcement of the submarine's identity, despite discovering the fragments of Italian torpedoes. Unsubstantiated news from unofficial or unreliable sources raged, even saying that the submarine was British, but had used Italian torpedoes to provoke Greece's entry into the war!

However, Eftychia was sure. She could almost see the future. "You'll see how the Italians are about to invade us, and they'll do it in a sneaky way, as was the case with Elli," she said to whoever was listening.

Eftychia's certainty of impending war grew when they summoned Kotsos Barlabas to the army with a personal invitation for ten days of training in new automatic weapons. It was September 30, 1939. A military mobilization began secretly after August 15, 1940, and the cowardly torpedoing of the Elli. Eftychia was afraid that not having Barlabas at home would worsen her always troubled finances.

She thought of herself as head of the household, including two boys and a girl. The pleasant thing was that lately, Thanasis worked in the market and gave a little money at home, offering his mother financial relief. Electra also helped her a little. As such, a little money was left over every month, so she decided to get a dog to guard her from thieves. In a short time, the bitch which belonged to Persephone, a good neighbor of hers, would give birth. Persephone had eagerly promised to provide her with a puppy.

On October 28, Eftychia woke up early in the morning from the abhorrent whining of the sirens. After a while, the church bells could also be heard pealing. She turned her radio on and listened to the music of military marches. In the brief news segment, the announcer stated: "Our army defends the homeland." She understood. Greece was at war. In the meantime, Zozo was scared and was whimpering.

Soon, the clamor of automobiles and deep male voices singing reached Eftychia's ears. She decided to go out to see what was going on. Since Aristides had not gone to school that day, she took him by the hand, and they walked uphill to Egnatia Street. There, she saw a column of trucks and buses filled with men going off to war with smiles on their faces. It was the first time she had seen so many vehicles on the road. Also passing by were some military vehicles that spewed copious amounts of exhaust fumes from their mufflers. At some point, the exhaust made a loud bang as if a bomb was exploding. Thirteen-year-old Aristides was frightened.

"Let's go home, mama," he pleaded. "Let's go home." Eftychia, who had no reason to stay outside anymore, took the road back. In the meantime, Thanasis went to work but found the store shuttered because with the announcement of a general mobilization, Mr. Stamatis had himself been enlisted in the army. Posted on the metal shutters of the shop was a piece of paper announcing the shop would remain closed for a few days. Thanasis returned home sad as he did not know if he'd get his wages for the second half of the month.

A few hours later, the sirens and buzzing of the Italian planes could be heard again. The two boys climbed up to the rooftop and watched the planes. A bomb fell very close to Electra's house and destroyed the bell tower of Agia Sophia's church.

Eftychia was trembling. She went up to the rooftop and started shouting at the boys.

"Seriously! Are you completely crazy sitting and staring at the planes? What are you thinking? That they're flying in an air show? What do you think this is? Are planes throwing down sugar plums? They're dropping bombs, damned them! God should burn the spaghetti eaters. Get down to the basement quickly. That's what the instructions of the air defense say—to go into basements and to shelters. Do you hear me, you fiends!?" she shouted in her irritated and worried state because the two brothers seemed absorbed in watching the planes and were not paying attention to her.

"Well, Mama, it's the first time we've seen bombings," Aristides replied while Thanasis sorrowfully abandoned his aerial observations. Just at that moment, an Italian plane was hit by a Greek anti-craft fire set up somewhere outside the city center at Neapolis district, and it began to plunge to Earth, trailing black smoke behind it.

"Hurrah, we shot it down!" Eftychia cried out. "Look at it… it's falling."

"Hurrah! We beat them!" Aristides cried out.

"Well done. Our guy has a good aim," Thanasis shouted.

"Look! A parachute is falling too," Aristides added.

"C'mon, let's go downstairs. You don't know what could happen when you least expect it," Eftychia warned them as soon as her excitement subsided, pushing Thanasis along who was lingering.

At that moment, the sirens sounded again. This time it signaled the end of the alarm. As they descended from the rooftop terrace, they met Asimina's brother, Giorgos, on the staircase carrying a sack of sand.

"We need to fill the rooftop with sacks of sand," he told Eftychia. "It's an order from air defense. There are a few sacks downstairs to bring up. Tell your children to help. Carrying up these unbearably heavy sacks has sapped my energy!"

"Thanasis can help, yes, but my Dakis (nickname for Aristides) is weak and cannot," Eftychia said, who always considered Aristides weak and sensitive.

On that day, all those men, who had not been recruited because of their age, had to carry a bunch of sacks of sand doing grunt work as they cursed Mussolini. Those over sixty years old had reached the limits of their endurance. Barlabas also took part in the lifting and hauling of the sacks, but only after a long delay. He had come home late from work. But Thanasis had done credit to himself by carrying up eight loads in the time it took others to carry four or five. The rooftop, however, still had a large area of uncovered space. They would continue the next day.

After a hasty meal of bean soup and pickled cabbage, along with olives and black bread, the members of the Barlabas family found themselves in bed rather early. With the morning awakening from the sirens and the fatigue of the day, sleep came relatively quickly, along with the first dreams. Thanasis dreamed that he was eating bean soup again. Aristides dreamed he was watching the planes in the sky. Zozo dreamed that the food was burned. Barlabas dreamed that he was being recruited into the army and Eftychia that she was being flirted with by an Italian.

Not even a few minutes of sleep had passed, and their dream scenes were not yet over when the sirens screeched again.

"Uh, what's going on?" Barlabas shouted, terrified.

"Quickly, to the basement!" Eftychia began to shout.

"Dakis, Thanasis, Zozo, Carla (Eftychia's pet dog), all of you wake up! Don't waste time getting dressed. Go down in your nightgowns!"

In her anxiety, she also yelled at Carla to get dressed as if she were a human person.

Although not among those called by Eftychia, Barlabas found himself front and center in the basement. The other residents of the apartment building followed. Older adults also went down to the basement, except for the mother of the ground floor tenant who did not come out of her room because she was bedridden by a stroke.

Down in the moldy basement, among mice and rats, the small assembly of the apartment building held a first general council and decided that each family should take down a few chairs or some old army bed or even some old mattress so that they wouldn't get tired standing in the dark for so long. It was also decided that the basement be cleaned by a homemaker every week, but for starters, many of them would participate in the cleaning because the basement was thick with dirt and moldy dust.

"We can also bring a coffee table and a backgammon set," Thanasis suggested, who at the age of seventeen had evolved into a champion backgammon player.

"We can also run contests," Asimina's brother Mr. Georgios suggested to break the chill of fear that prevailed after the destruction of the bell tower.

"What will the prize be?" Thanasis asked.

"All of us will put in one drachma each, and the winner will get all the money that's been collected," Mr. Georgios replied.

"We're going to need light down here. It's pitch black," Kotsos said.

"It's easy to draw a line from the shared power current," Thanasis suggested, and he hurried to add. "Give me a cable, a lamp, and a socket, and I'll hook it up for you."

Within a few days, everything was set up and the backgammon championship could begin. After a few alarms and bombings, Thanasis won his first money playing backgammon, and Eftychia was gloating. Even though he knew how to play backgammon, Aristides was not allowed to play as he had been considered too young. They even had some objections to Thanasis, but in the end, they agreed to let him participate, so the lucky guy screwed them over and collected all their drachmas.

"How did you beat them all?" Aristides asked at some point Thanasis when they got together at home.

"Look, Aristides. Backgammon requires technique, but it's also about luck. But even with luck, you still must think and calculate the odds," Thanasis replied vaguely. "I'll explain it to you some other time."

The next day, Kotsos Barlabas was also called for duty and presented himself in a camp in Drama. He would guard the Greek-Bulgarian border in a stronghold of the Metaxas line. He was assigned to the nursing corps. Eftychia thought scornfully that she was "losing her guardian". However, the truth is that with three children at home, she did not feel very safe. So, the time had finally come for Eftychia to get a guard dog. Persephone's bitch gave birth to five puppies, and Eftychia took one of them two months after their birth. It was a female (of modest size when fully grown), snowy white with plenty of fur, beautiful black expressive eyes, and a tufted tail that turned upward. Her ears were half erect, and she would lower them backwards when someone confronted her. Her breed was the old Greek one called "kokoni." She named her Clara which was the name of the girlfriend of Benito Mussolini, the former leader of a socialist party, who was now Italy's dictator. (Incomprehensible by what psychological mechanism Eftychia chose this name for her dog). Clara would be a security guard in their house since the front door was not secure. It was a cheap double-leaf door that, when pushed, would move back and forth and open even if it was locked.

But unlike Eftychia's front door, the "Gates of Greece" (Greece's borders) were not so fragile, and Clara Petacci's lover, Benito Mussolini, was sweating blood with the Greeks in the mountains of Albania. On that day, the newspapers reported that he had replaced his commander-in-chief in Albania, Visconti Prasca—apparently a failure—with Ubaldo Soddu.

"He'll also be thrown out the door. We forced the spaghetti eaters to escape in disarray," Eftychia commented, chatting with Asimina.

On November 14, the Greek counterattack began. The Italians were in retreat, suffering heavy casualties. The Greek mortars were doing an effective job, and the cries "IN THE AIR!" frightened the Italian soldiers, who could not figure out what they were trying to do in the mountains of Albania, far away from their homes in Italy.

8

The Radio

By the Spring of 1941, the Greek army had repelled the much-publicized spring offensive of the Italians in the snowy mountains of Albania, having already liberated Himarë and Gjirokastër—cities with a predominantly Greek population in Northern Epirus (in the south of Albania). Seeing his ally in a difficult position, Hitler decided to support the Italian effort and attacked Greece. Moreover, most of the Greek army was fighting in the mountains of Albania. The offensive began on April 6, 1941, with the air force and motorized units, so the warfare favored the Germans.

In the strongholds on the Greek-Bulgarian border, the Germans suffered heavy losses in their attempt to break through the front line of the forts. But the German army broke through the Yugoslavian front easily and, unhindered by bypassing the Metaxas line, finally reached Thessaloniki. Continuing the struggle was meaningless for the Greeks. On April 18, Prime Minister Alexandros Koryzis, who had succeeded Metaxas after his death, committed suicide.[6]

---

[6] Many rumors circulated about the unexpected death of Metaxas, including his being murdered by the British. But the truth is that he died because of a peritonsillar abscess at a time when antibiotics did not yet exist. Besides, he had stated to the English that Greece would defend itself to the end and against the Germans if it were attacked. A cardiotonic drug injected by an English doctor into

As commander of the army in Epirus, General Tsolakoglou defied the orders of Commander-in-Chief Alexandros Papagos and decided to capitulate on April 20, after an agreement with the German leadership. The Italians demanded that they also sign the armistice and surrender agreement. On April 27, German troops entered Athens. The British had very few troops in Greece, and they moved quickly towards Crete, hoping to keep this island free because, like Cyprus, it was of great importance for military control in the eastern Mediterranean.

After a month's epic defensive battles, the airborne division of German paratroopers was almost decimated by the heroic Cretan Greeks along with British troops (including Australians and New-Zealanders), but eventually, Crete also fell under the German occupation. The conquest of Greece had been completed, and the grueling era of German oppression had started.[7]

One of the Germans' first actions was enforcing strict censorship of newspapers and national radio broadcasts. Unfortunately, they couldn't do the same for foreign radio stations, especially the BBC, which broadcast from London over short-wave radios worldwide.

John Metaxas shortly before his death—while he was in a state of infectious shock—is ridiculous to consider as a cause of death.

[7] The Germans assigned the Italians to occupy as a military force the Heptanese Islands (Ionian Islands), Epirus, Thessaly and other regions of Greece, while to their allies the Bulgarians they handed over Eastern Macedonia and Thrace, except for the Prefecture of Evros, at which they kept controlling the borders with Turkey.

Despite the static, much of which was of German origin, the BBC transmissions had a fanatic audience.

To tackle this problem, the Germans took two measures. The first and most important was to issue a decree for all radios to be handed over to the German administration to be sealed so that only the national station, which the Germans controlled, could be heard. This way, Greeks, who had no choice but to obey, would be unable to listen to the BBC. If anyone got caught having an unsealed radio, imprisonment or even death were consequences. There was no way to prove you were not a spy who was trying to decipher coded messages transmitted by the BBC. The second measure was to put speakers in several places and transmit their propaganda, starting with the German national anthem in the morning. *"Germany Above All (Deutschland Uber Alles)"*, which made the Greeks furious.

Eftychia wasn't at all happy about the sealing of radios. In 1938 she had been overjoyed when she managed to buy her very own radio from her meager savings. It was a beautiful radio. On its façade were the names of all major cities of Europe and other continents. It was as if it was intended to be used in geography lessons. It had two large rotating buttons—one for the volume and the other for moving the needle to go from station to station, i.e., the tuning. There was also a third smaller button. This was to switch the so-called band from medium to short wave and vice versa. Needless to say, before the Occupation, everyone listened to the middle waves because the Greek radio stations could be heard more clearly, and before the war, they were not interested in foreign stations. When the war began, the short wave became fashionable because they were the waves coming from afar.

Of course, Eftychia wanted the radio for the music and songs, especially folk music. She was fond of "Rebetika" (urban underground music) and "Laika" (popular urban folk music), songs which she sang with a pretty good voice and even danced to on various occasions. Sometimes, she also sang the Greek operettas of Hadjiapostolos as many of her neighbors used to do. So, handing over this impressive radio—the pride and joy of her home—to be confiscated by the Germans was out of the question. In her joy of possessing her own radio, she almost venerated it, just like she did with Saint Georgios and the Virgin Mary in her iconostasis.

When Barlabas heard about the German decree for the radios, he told his wife to hand it over. Eftychia did not say a word. In any case, she was afraid to listen to music. But she had decided. She would not turn the radio over. There was so much she did behind Barlabas' back. She wouldn't stop now for just a radio. So, she took her miraculous and adored radio and hid it in a place that seemed to her to be a perfect hiding place. In her sitting room there was a fairly dated 20-year-old sofa, which her mother had given her when she got married. At one end of the sofa a spring had pierced through the cushion, so to deal with the problem of the torn cover and the spring that vaulted up and tore through skirts and trousers, Eftychia had placed a pillow on the spring after she bent a section of it over to the side. Above the regular fabric of the sofa, she put a damask throw-type cloth to cover the hole in the cover. In this way, she covered the hole which the pillow filled, and it significantly corrected the depression in the sofa. In this cavity under the pillow, she had stuffed many newspapers and old towels so that if someone were sitting on the corner of the sofa it would not sink too much. But it would be far safer if no one was seated there. This problem with the sofa had been known for years, and all the relatives and friends of the family knew about it. So, they would mostly sit at the sofa's other end or in the two armchairs.

Eftychia thought that it would serve as a hiding place quite well. She removed most of the newspapers, cut the fabric with a razor blade, enlarged the opening, and by using a thinner pillow, she created space for the radio to fit. Thus, her radio was hidden in this spot for a long time. She had stopped listening to it every day because she considered it dangerous. Only her older son would take it out occasionally to listen to the BBC news with his brother Aristides. The fact that they had kept the radio was only known by her neighbor and trusted friend Mrs. Asimina, who was always the first to come and listen to the news.

When Barlabas was away, they would shut the doors and windows tightly and invite Mrs. Asimina's family, and they all gathered and attentively listened to the news. The radio antenna wasn't just placed on the wall supported by a nail. They had found that when its antenna was held by a human hand, there would be less static. When they listened to the radio, they connected a wire like an antenna, and it was held high by the window by one of Eftychia's sons, usually Aristides. The others called him the "Statue of Liberty," probably with a bit of irony, but perhaps they literally meant it because it was for this impending freedom they were all crammed around the radio.

Asimina's brother was a lieutenant commander sailing with the submarines, so she was directly interested in developments in combat operations. Asimina was a person of integrity and would never reveal the radio's existence. And why should she, after all? There was no dissension between them. Their children spent time together except for Thanasis, who was much older and had his own friends.

Residing in the apartment building across the street was Loukia, another neighbor acquaintance of Eftychia's. Eftychia did not trust her very much. She lived next to the apartment building at the corner that the Germans had seized. One night some people saw her sneaking into that building after taking precautions. It looked very suspicious. Even so, Eftychia had not cut off morning greetings. But she remained wary of her. Since Eftychia knew how to read the grounds in the coffee cup, every once in a while, Loukia would come over to drink coffee to learn her fate. Thus, she knew Eftychia had owned a radio before the Germans occupied Greece.

Loukia's husband, Alcibiades, had not returned from the battlefront. However, idle neighbors gossiped, saying he never enlisted as a soldier because he was previously tubercular with pneumothorax (collapsed lung). While the tubercular cavities had healed, perhaps, he remained unsuitable for the army. So, these vicious tongues had information that Loukia's husband was in Alexandroupolis with a woman he had met at the sanatorium where he had been hospitalized for some time.

Whether because their relationship hadn't been going well for a long time or for fear of catching tuberculosis, Loukia didn't visit him often. At the same time, he was hospitalized up north outside of Thessaloniki at Asvestochori, where the sanatorium was. She made up the story that she got dizzy traveling in a car. So, just before the declaration of war, Alcibiades was released from the sanatorium showing significant improvement (fifteen kilos heavier) and soon disappeared. Then, Loukia spread the word that her husband was drafted into the army, but nobody believed her.

The main concern of Loukia was whether Alcibiades would return. The last time she visited Eftychia to get a coffee reading, she went over to the end of the sofa to sit on the spot where the radio was buried. Eftychia urged her to sit farther over, but Loukia was curious. So, when the hostess went to the kitchen to make her coffee, Loukia, suspecting that something was hidden in the sofa, lifted the cover, saw a thin pillow and the newspapers, and lifted them up a little too, and the hidden radio revealed itself! Loukia hastily re-arranged the camouflage of the radio and waited for the coffee to arrive, calmly indifferent.

"Come, Loukia. Your coffee is ready; it is special, half chickpea and half genuine coffee too!"

"Awww, thank you very much, Eftychia," Loukia said after the first sip. "You made it perfect and so foamy!"

"To your health."

As soon as Loukia finished drinking the coffee and turned the cup over, she gave it to Eftychia, who, after waiting for a little for the shapes from the coffee dregs to stabilize, took it in her hands and began to articulate the customary and established introductory words.

"Loukia, the cup is not good."

In fact, it was full of thick black specks of coffee, with a lot of dregs, full of pessimism and sadness.

"You're going to walk through a big door," Eftychia continued her analysis. But above the big door, the cup reader could see a sign like a swastika, the emblem of Nazism, which upset her greatly. So, while she told Loukia that the cup was very pessimistic and indifferently mentioned the "big door", she hid the detail about the swastika.

"Oh, my dear Eftychia! And I was waiting for you to tell me that he'll be found alive, and Alcibiades will return."

At that point, Eftychia could no longer put up with pretense, and she blurted out:

"C'mon, dear Loukia. Are you that dumb to be still waiting for Alcibiades?"

The neighbor was greatly annoyed. She could not face reality. Eftychia had spoken out clearly. Alcibiades wouldn't be coming back! Some woman had taken him in. Everybody knew and talked about it. Loukia left visibly furious and reddened. Her blood pressure had risen, and she felt her temples throbbing. Eftychia was now her enemy. Had she spread anything in the neighborhood about her husband, she wondered.

Early in the morning the next day, Loukia woke up still upset. She remembered Eftychia's radio. She was, in fact, a widow; she had no children, and she no longer had a husband, while the other woman had children, a husband, even if he was a good for nothing—but she also had a lover, yes, she was sure of it—and she even had a hidden radio! Jealousy flared up in her chest. She felt a headache coming on. She had trouble sleeping the previous night, and her sleep was full of similar thoughts and dreams. She got up, got dressed, left her house, and headed straight to the German headquarters. She paused just before the entrance, but then she changed her mind. She feared that the neighbors would see her. So, she crossed over to the opposite sidewalk. After going to the baker to get her bread (80 drams a day with the ration coupon equivalent to 256 grams, which is about five current slices), she soon returned home.

By coincidence, Eftychia had been walking her dog and saw Loukia's movements from afar. She started thinking intensely. She saw little but understood a lot.

Oh, that tramp, she thought. *She's going to turn me in because of the radio...she found it!*

She quickly returned home and stared through a mesh curtain behind the window. Tired of staring through the window, she called out to her goddaughter Zozo to sit down, taking turns and watching the door across the way and Loukia's movements. At last, just as it started to get dark, Loukia showed up! She was wearing a scarf, as if she was trying to hide her face.

Eftychia immediately realized her intentions.

That whore! The divorcée! The bitter woman! May fire fall and burn her! Who does she think she is to try and burn me? she thought.

Like a bolt of lightning, she ran to the sofa, took the radio out of its hiding place, and quickly carried it down to the yard.

It was pretty dark. Wrapped in sackcloth, the radio was placed deep inside a chicken coop where a few hens and a rooster were kept. The latter was quite particularly upset by the night visit because he feared that his turn might have come for slaughter…but he could not do anything about that anyway.

Meanwhile, Eftychia put a stool over the radio so that one could hardly suspect that it was hidden there. In a short while, with the droppings that would soon cover the spot, it was doubtful that the hideout would be revealed. Taking quick steps, Eftychia hurried home in less than five minutes.

She filled the hole in the sofa with newspapers and covered the disputed spot with the coverlet. At the last moment, she thought even more cunningly. In her closet, she had hidden a classic pornographic book entitled *The Virgin of Pleasure*. She took it and placed it in the hole of the sofa along with the newspapers. Then she sighed in relief, saying: "Oh, my God! What struggles I go through!" and sat in an armchair to unwind.

Not even ten minutes had gone by when there was knocking at her door.

"Stay calm, Clara," she said as she first gathered up barking Clara. When she opened the door, she found herself face to face with a German in his Gestapo uniform and another guy wearing civilian clothes, dark glasses, a long trench coat, and a fedora. The latter spoke to her in Greek and told her they would search the house.

Eftychia stepped aside and said ironically, "Here you go…at your leisure. Should I make you a coffee with roasted garbanzo beans?" and after finding that there was no response, she stood in front of the couch in front of the spot with the hideout.

As Eftychia later recounted safely, after the Germans had left, these two awful guys at once headed towards the couch, pushed her aside rudely and arrogantly, lifted the cover, and searched underneath.

They quickly found the hiding place and smiled with satisfaction, but only briefly. Old newspapers, a pillow…and a book; that was the treasure. The Greek collaborator of the Germans took the book in his hands and looked at its title. And he looked at Eftychia. She stared back at him, almost mockingly, and even winked at him the moment he lifted his gaze from the "virgin" of the book and looked at the "more experienced" Eftychia.

"I hide it there so the children don't find it," Eftychia commented meaningfully.

The German Gestapo officer did not search anywhere else. His information concerned the sofa. For the sake of appearances, the Greek guy opened her closet and went up to the attic. Nothing was found there either. They opened two suitcases, causing clothes and underwear to tumble out. Of course, they did not think to search the yard to find the radio. And even if they had seen it, the chicken coop was communal. The residents kept it to collect the eggs; eight families shared them on prearranged days. They had agreed not to slaughter the hens except in dire need.

Eftychia had just barely escaped the danger. Having bungled the deed, Loukia did not visit Eftychia again, but in two months, unable to bear the hunger, she left for her village. Emboldened, Eftychia would take the radio out occasionally, and the two families would listen to the BBC news together, as in the past.

Ultimately, the German Nazis encountered problems with the Soviet Russians on the eastern front. General von Paulus was taken prisoner with his huge army, and General Rommel, the "desert fox" in North Africa, had no fuel to move his tanks as he wanted. There, the British had the upper hand. Churchill made his famous speeches, excerpts of which were broadcast by BBC. Hitler made fewer appearances, and rumors circulated he was sick and on the verge of mental collapse. Eftychia also got the news from the BBC that the Gorgopotamos Bridge had been destroyed.

A glimmer of hope arose. Soon the Germans would be forced to withdraw from the Balkan Peninsula. The BBC occasionally reported this news, and Eftychia listened with joy. She was pretty fed up with the Occupation and couldn't stand the oppression, famine, blackouts, early evening curfews, shuttered windows, and the banned radios.

9

The Demijohn

During the German occupation, the Barlabas family suffered greatly from starvation. These three years of hunger indelibly sealed Eftychia's soul. Facing the possibility of future needs became her main concern, so saving money and food became an end and a means for her family to survive.

In 1941 her son Thanasis was eighteen, and Aristides was fifteen. Zozo, Eftychia's orphaned thirteen-year-old goddaughter lived with them. So, the unfortunate woman had many mouths to feed. Her husband, for acquired reasons, but perhaps also genetic, had evolved into a terrible miser and selfish opportunist, so he left little money to support the household. Barlabas hid the little surplus money from his salary in various places, but his main hideout was the lining of a coat he wore almost his entire life. He probably spent money on his visits to a prostitute on some side street who must have suffered from a loss of smell because she was perhaps the only woman who could consent to share physical closeness with him. He took badly his need to visit a prostitute and held his wife responsible for that who in turn avoided him. He was not concerned about where she would find money to buy the bare essentials. Perhaps deep down, he was also taking his revenge because she never slept in their bed as his legitimate wife. She always reacted negatively to his sexual needs and avoided him completely. For Barlabas, living with Eftychia and fantasizing about her was torture as she was so beautiful. Despite her two pregnancies, his wife still looked lovely and alluring. She was relatively thin, with rather large breasts, and her face had attractive features with full lips, transparent green eyes, and a smile or laughter that attracted men. She typically used a coquettish voice, but it could become normal or harsh on a case-by-case basis.

The era of the German occupation was perhaps the only one when all the family members ate at the same time at a set table. As the head of the family, Barlabas had stated that whoever works is entitled to more bread. So, the food was shared by six, and Barlabas enjoyed a double portion. Nobody in the family agreed with this arrangement, especially Thanasis, who was always a compulsive eater.

The hunger and injustice Thanasis felt soon motivated him to find a job. He stopped attending the six-year gymnasium (high school) and never graduated. Then in 1942, he managed to get hired as a worker for the Germans. At 18, his mind was like a sponge, and he grasped foreign languages just by listening. He had studied a little German and English at school. Very quickly, he managed to communicate with the Germans who appointed him to be the head of a group of workers, that is, a foreman. He conveyed instructions of the Germans to the other Greeks who did not know German. In a short time, he managed to make friends with a sergeant called Fritz, and he introduced him to Kiki who was the sister of Dina—a girl who at that time was Thanasis' girlfriend.

Sergeant Fritz was married, but he couldn't stand the ... abstinence. However, he had a fear. He did not dare to approach any female on his own because his wife's brother, Hans, was serving in the same camp as a captain. If he discovered anything, Fritz would find himself in a lot of trouble.

Despite the obstacles, Thanasis succeeded in his plans and drove Fritz to a sinful life. He and Fritz went out with the two sisters and would visit tavernas, but also places Thanasis used himself on his rendezvous. One of these places was at the Jewish tombs, which 1943, the Germans had desecrated due to their anti-Semitism. There, in the deep darkness of the evening, it was a fairly hospitable place for couples. But attention was required as well due to the curfew after 9:00 PM. But also, when it rained in winter, the area became a bleak place for the "lovebirds" to visit because the clay dirt turned into a muddy slush. Thus, in the winter, Thanasis preferred to use the basement of the apartment building where his family lived.

When the sirens screamed to warn of bombings—first by the Italians and afterward by the British—this basement was used for shelter. Down there, the apartment building residents had also placed some mattresses, which they used to lie down on when they were forced to stay in the basement for an extended time. Thanasis thought these mattresses were very convenient for his love affairs. His only concern was the possibility of an alarm sounding during his…erotic encounters! However, he was lucky, or shall we say even proactive because he chose the time for his romantic assignations and went there at dusk, knowing that bombings usually took place in the dead of night.

This devilish coincidence—a romantic encounter and a bombing—happened to him only once. Unfortunately, at the time, Fritz was also with his girl in the basement. At the whining of the first sirens, Thanasis kept calm. He told the girls to hide behind some pillars and quickly began to climb the steps of the basement, where at the top of the staircase, he met the first group of people descending to protect themselves from the bombs. Then, as Fritz emerged behind him, Thanasis calmly told them that Germans were in the basement, and they were investigating a wanted man who appeared to have hidden there. The apartment building residents, who were at that time about a dozen people, were in no mood to be confused with the wanted man by the Germans. A few returned as fast as they could to their homes, and others went to the basement of the adjacent apartment building. With these adventures and many more, Thanasis developed a bond of friendship with Fritz, who, in turn, placed him under his protection.

Eftychia's son then began to eat nicely for the first time in months ever since he had swallowed the ration bread. Every night when he left the camp, he had jam, chocolate, biscuits, cheese, butter, and even soap in his pockets. The latter, of course, cannot be eaten, but Thanasis, in addition to what he left at home for family use, sold some pieces on the black market (underground illegal market).

Gradually, he got Fritz into the black-market game as well, so a pattern of plundering the camp began. Fritz participated to profit, of course. That is, Thanasis also gave him some gold coins for his share. The main thing, however, was that he had done him a favor with Kiki.

One day, Thanasis complained to Fritz that he had no olive oil in his house. The olive oil was generally nowhere to be found in the shops either. The black marketeers had collected the little olive oil that remained. To sell it at a higher price, they would display it for sale in small amounts and accept only gold coins for payment since the banknotes at that time were less valuable than old newspapers.

Fritz took pity on his friend. One night with Fritz's approval, Thanasis stole a demijohn full of olive oil from the German warehouse. With his German friend, they had agreed to engage the guard's attention at the gate while he would pass by with the demijohn. It was his rotten luck that a senior officer sent Fritz to do a job at the other end of the camp, and Thanasis was left with...the demijohn in hand, uncovered.

He had a coat thrown over his shoulders without his arms in the sleeves. This helped him to hide the demijohn, and the daring rascal managed to get it through under the guard's nose. He even spoke to him in German and joked with him, tilting his body to hide the demijohn. Of course, his heart was pounding, and he was listening to it like a drum beating before a death row inmate execution. But what could he do? The hunger would be worse without the olive oil. He almost died of fear until he managed to get past the camp gate!

That's what life was like with the Germans. After this adventure, Thanasis would only steal small bottles of oil. Demijohns? Never again!

In any event, the celebrated demijohn arrived successfully at Eftychia's home, where the whole family gathered to admire it…except for Barlabas, who was absent. Thanasis asked that nobody touch it because he intended to sell it for several gold sovereigns since a regular bottle of olive oil at that time was used to be sold for one gold coins.

Eftychia then exploded.

"You good for nothing! You despicable being! Aren't you ashamed to be selling the olive oil? What about us? What are we here? Children of God, are we not? We're your blood, are we not? For four years, I breastfed you, and you turned out to be such a big stupid lout. This olive oil won't leave my house again unless you kill me! Do you hear? If you kill your mother! I'm going to curse you, you good for nothing, and my curse is binding…do you hear?"

Eftychia had flown into a rage. Her voice had switched to its harsh version. Her eyes were shooting sparks. Thanasis was petrified.

"Mother. Be silent. They'll catch wind of us," Thanasis replied in muffled tones. "Take the demijohn. Just give me a small bottle of it to take to some poor girls who don't have anything to eat," he told her, thinking of Kiki and Dina. Eftychia poured some oil into a bottle of soda and gave it to her son for the girls. She then filled a small bottle with oil for immediate use in her kitchen and dribbled a little into the candle in front of the iconostasis. The demijohn, with the rest of the olive oil, was placed in the bathroom and, to be precise, at the side of the bathtub. There it stayed for two days until they became aware of the sounds of automobiles and German voices. The Gestapo was conducting raids looking for any Jews hidden in the houses of

Christians. Eftychia was terror-stricken. Her mind zeroed into the demijohn.

"What do we do now?" she muttered, half in tears. "We can't drink it. We can't pour the oil out, so they won't find it. I can't do that."

It was a surreal scene. Thanasis reassured them.

"Here. We can hide it, dear Mother."

He took the demijohn in his arms like a lover and took it up to the roof of the apartment building. There were many sandbags placed there to protect against the bombs.

He hid the demijohn among some sacks, but while he turned to leave, out of the corner of his eye, he saw a German guard on the roof of an apartment building almost opposite theirs that the Germans had confiscated. The guard was not looking toward him, but he may have seen him earlier. Thanasis turned to go down the steps but encountered his mother, who was quietly climbing behind him to check where he was hiding the demijohn.

"For goodness sake! Enough Thanasis! We forgot about the guard. Their floor is one floor higher than our rooftop. He may have seen us. Oh, what I go through, poor miserable me! What are we going to do now? They're going to catch us all as a family!"

"C'mon, Mother, just hold on. No one saw us," Thanasis whispered and pushed her gently to start going down the stairs.

That night Eftychia could not fall asleep. As soon as her husband fell asleep, she got up and went to the far end of Thanasis' room.

"Thanasis," she whispered and touched his shoulder.

"Hey, what's going on?" her son grumbled, awakened from a deep sleep.

"The demijohn, Thanasis, the demijohn."

"Again? What about the demijohn?"

"I'm afraid… maybe the guard saw it."

Whether he liked it or not, Eftychia got her son up, and they went up barefoot so that their footsteps could not be heard on the steps. They reached the rooftop, and Thanasis picked up the demijohn again. This time, however, he took it down to the basement. Somewhere down there, was an iron cover from a manhole, covering his secret hiding place. He lifted the lid and put the demijohn inside after first wedging a basket with half a handle underneath. Above it, he placed one of the mattresses that were in the basement.

"For one night, let it stay here, Mother. Tomorrow we'll divide the olive oil into smaller bottles," Thanasis told her.

"But where are we going to keep them?" Eftychia asked.

"Behind the bathtub," and Thanasis explained that the gap between the wall and the bathtub would be an ideal place to hide bottles. "For the cover, we'll put our clogs and a chamber pot in front."

Thus ended the adventure with the demijohn with Thanasis escaping his mother's curse this time. But the oil in the demijohn eventually ran out. Consequently, for the Barlabas family, hunger became a permanent fixture. Needless to say, he was the only one who was not hungry because he was eating from…the German camp! Whenever he could, and with Fritz's indulgence, something was left over for others or, for the most part, for…the girls. Of course, as always, his mother grumbled, so her son had to bring something home as well. Eftychia even went so far as to give him orders:

"Thanasis, don't forget to bring me flour, baking chocolate, and some butter to make you a cake. I don't need eggs, you know. I have plenty from my hens."

10

The German Feast

The winter of 1943 had begun, and nothing foreshadowed that the terrible famine of 1942 would not be repeated. Eftychia was in turmoil. She regularly went to Cedar Hill to collect greens such as chicory, endives, and thistles which she would then boil. She would trickle a teaspoon of olive oil into each portion she served. There was not enough for more. Next to the plate was the bread for each person, just as they got it with the special ration coupon. Occasionally, there was some cheese and sometimes eggs from the hens she kept.

Despite all her efforts to save and put together a meal, they had visibly weakened and suffered from hunger, causing them stomach pains. The problem became worse if someone lost sleep at dawn, which often happened due to some roosters who started their concerts before sunrise. By waking up somewhat earlier, the torments of hunger became worse. When they all gathered at the table, Eftychia would tell them:

"We have to do something about the food problem; otherwise, we'll get tuberculosis and die." Tuberculosis was her constant fear. But there were no answers.

Fortunately, Electra was helping as much as she could with her reinforcements by sharing the gifts brought to her husband by his patients, some of whom paid only in kind since money was of no value at the time. At the same time, Thanasis was doing wonderfully with the acquaintance he had made with Fritz. As already described, he had created an intertwined network of commercial activity with love affairs and was the only one who ate well by stealing food from the military barracks. However, the security system at the camp gate was recently reinforced, so he could no longer smuggle food out. However, Thanasis ate well just as he used to, and often arrived home stuffed. So, he would give his bread portion to Aristides who was going through adolescence and was very thin.

One day Thanasis came home in a fairly good mood and talked with his mother about their circumstances.

"What do you think, Mother? Are we going to survive the winter?"

"We'll survive, but how only God knows. The Germans, but also our allies, the British—to hell with them—set up a naval blockade and don't allow us to get food supplies, just so they annoy the Germans. But we're the ones mainly suffering."

"Look, Mother, I have an idea. Fritz, a good guy we work with in the barracks, has a group of three or four friends, and they want to unwind. But they're having trouble because they're not allowed to entertain themselves in public late in the evening. I told him I could help."

"What do you mean? Explain yourself, and don't beat around the bush. I'm sure you're up to another one of your shenanigans again."

"No, tricks, Mother. Just let me explain. I thought of telling Fritz that we would let him use the house for one night so that he could amuse himself with his friends. They'll bring food, and I'll do the cooking by myself. You won't tire yourself at all. There will be lots of leftovers, so we'll eat."

"It seems like a good idea, but where will we go?"

"We can think about that. You could take Aristides and Zozo and go to your sister's. Dad will sleep in the cooking galley where he works in the afternoons. He has the keys because he cleans it in the evening and then locks it himself."

"And what will we gain from doing this?"

"Don't you get it? They'll give me a lot of food to cook for them. I'll take care of the details. What I'm saying is that lots will be left over for us."

"Go on. Please do it. Just tell me ahead of time so the house is clean. I don't want myself to be gossiped about by the white fat asses."

The following Sunday, the house was ready. They had all disappeared except for the head of the ceremony, Thanasis. Clara, the dog, was already tied to the back balcony to prevent her from biting the Germans.

"You'll get leftover bones to lick all day long," Thanasis told her, stroking her ears.

At 11:00 AM, a German knocked on the door. He was carrying two huge heavy bags of food supplies. He left them in the hallway, greeted him, and told Thanasis that everything had to be ready by 7:30 PM.

For God's sake. Everything must be ready in eight hours, Thanasis muttered and ran to get the charcoal he had forgotten.

When he returned, he peeled the potatoes, washed the tomatoes, cut the meat into portions, counting them to see what would be left over for the family, cleaned the rice by removing specks of impurities, chopped the onion for a salad and sautéing, minced just a little bit of garlic—because Germans did not want to stink to others around them—but the damned garlic made the food taste good, and our cook knew it.

He put coals in a small grill that stood on the balcony and then lit them to make a layer of burning coals to grill souvlakia (skewered meat) and keftedes (meatballs). He kneaded the minced meat with wet bread, onion, and parsley, added egg to bind the meat mixture better, and he added grated cheese and some tomato to make it fluffy. He tasted it to see if the kefte mixture had enough salt and found it good, so he also added pepper as well. He also boiled small pieces of meat to make soup, to which he added celery, potatoes, and rice. He calculated that they would start feeling full after eating the soup, so by not grabbing the meat dish first, there would be more meat leftovers for the family.

He put the first well-lit coals in the fufu (brazier) to boil the soup. He worked diligently like a professional cook and, from time to time, consulted Eftychia's recipe notebooks. He also paid attention to the details. *Add the oregano at the end because otherwise, it makes the food taste bitter,* Eftychia had written in the notebook, and our cook meant to amaze.

The menu was almost ready and consisted of the following:

- tomato salad with cucumber, chopped spring onion, olives, and olive oil with vinegar.

- tzatziki (yogurt sauce) but with a minimum of garlic.

- mashed eggplant salad again with only traces of garlic.

- mashed and fried zucchini balls.

- meat soup with its relevant ingredients along with egg-lemon sauce.

- fried livers.

- grilled keftedes.

- souvlakia.

He grilled the souvlakia last, and the fragrance of grilled meat filled the neighborhood. *Where the heck did so much meat come from?* the neighbors all wondered.

When the cooking was done, Eftychia's son singled out many pieces of meat for the family, mainly cheese, livers, and keftedes as well. Of course, he did not fail to gobble up his own portion on the spot. After all, he had to try out everything to make sure they were tasty enough.

In order to have enough soup left over, he added water to dilute the original mixture in some fashion and divided it into two tins. Before that, however, he also added some flour to thicken the soup making it appear denser. He also threw a generous-sized bone at the dog and thought that Clara was lucky because she would also eat the marrow. Then he spread a clean tablecloth and started setting the table.

At about seven o'clock, he heard the doorbell, and when he opened the door, he saw that it was the same German soldier, who this time gave him a demijohn filled with red wine and extra loaves of bread.

"They're arriving in half an hour," he yelled at Thanasis in a threatening way as he was leaving.

At 7:30 PM, the doorbell rang again, and Thanasis, who just ten minutes before had finished his preparations and was lying on his bed with his legs resting high against the wall to rest them better, stood up.

Oh, those Germans are passionate about accuracy. They came right on time; he reflected and went to open the door.

Four officers were in their uniforms, and one was Fritz. He showed them the bedroom where the large table was always ready. The Germans sat down and began to eat the soup served to them in deep dishes, making exclamations of approval. This was followed by salads, keftedes, and souvlakia, which Thanasis made sure to reheat before serving. Last, the livers appeared, which the Germans duly honored by adding a lot of mustard, even though they had already eaten to bursting. Every now and then, they drank red wine, so they got into the mood and started singing. Various songs were heard, but the one they repeated ever so often was "Lili Marlene," which had become a hit song and was heard on German radio occasionally, even on the battlefront lines.

They had drunk quite enough and were feeling in high spirits. Thanasis had left them a small bell so they could call him if they needed him, and he would respond. At one point, when they rang to bring them more wine, our master of ceremonies, who being Fritz's friend, had a bit of audacity, told them about a joke in German, and their loud laughter woke everybody up.

At two o'clock in the morning, the guests—stuffed, drunk, and satisfied—decided to leave. They straightened their uniforms, buttoned the shirts around their necks, thanked Thanasis, and carefully descended the staircase. It was strange, but whereas a while ago you saw them drunk in a phase of intoxication, now they were standing straight and marching down the street as if they were in a parade, though at a slightly slower pace. It was as if the big feast had not preceded it.

The resourceful Greek made a quick inspection of the table. He picked up all the meat and livers that had not been eaten, as well as a large piece of cheese, and placed them in the *fanari* (a container looking like a lantern that could store leftover food for a few days, like a "meat-safe") which was located on the shaded part of the balcony. He wrapped the bread in towels, put the leftover cheese in a container with water, and added salt to keep it longer. He was too tired to clear off the table, so he left it with various leftovers scattered here and there and went to bed, where he slept like a log.

At eight in the morning, her curiosity having been piqued, Eftychia showed up to find out what happened. Thanasis was asleep. She entered her room, and her eyes greedily fixed on the leftovers.

She chose the ones that seemed cleanest to her and began to eat meat for breakfast.

"How delicious the food my son cooked is," she murmured. "This child is talented. He should be a cook, but when it comes to that...where would he find meat?" Then she singled out some food for Aristides and Zozo. She did not know that Thanasis had already made the appropriate arrangements and placed them inside the fanari. When she untied the dog on the balcony, she saw the tin can with the soup and the meat with the cheese in the fanari. Luckily, she had just eaten. Otherwise, she might have fainted when she spotted them, as they looked appealing and fragrant.

Wow, that rogue! He had a good haul. We'll have enough to eat for three days, she thought, *and not only that, but we need to hurry because it's summer and the meat will spoil.*

At noon the family—except for Barlabas, who would come in the evening—sat around the table and praised Thanasis.

"See that? I told you we were going to eat well."

"You ate last evening, too, shifty dude," Aristides said.

"What about father? Will we keep anything for him?" Thanasis asked.

"I'll give him some watered-down soup, " Eftychia said.

"He always eats something in the kitchen where he works. We are more famished. Oh! My stomach hurts. I haven't eaten for so long, and it's aching," Eftychia complained and began to chew a Chios

Mastiha, made from the natural resin of the mastic tree to digest better.

"In the evening, we will eat tzatziki and mashed eggplant with bread. Tomorrow at noon, souvlaki, and the day after tomorrow, keftedes." (Two leftover livers she had hidden in her closet to give to the emaciated Aristides). But when the time came to give the livers to the younger son (in secret from the others), he asked to share them with Zozo.

They ate the food together in the kitchen, holding chunks of food in their hands as if they were *"kariokes"* (chocolate walnut candies), and licked their fingers. But more than anyone, Clara, who had sniffed the food, was salivating, and even though she was already fed, she would have liked them very much. She was insatiable. It seemed she sensed something and was waiting for a piece of liver that was too tough to eat. Sure enough, Zozo threw it to her, and after grabbing it in the air, she swallowed it in one gulp. Clara had been trained to grab food in the air, but lately, she was eating less and had become quite scrawny. That's why if she was outside and some German passed by, she would start chasing him, barking loudly. Dogs understood these things with their sixth sense!

11

Thanasis in a Convent

In February 1943, the mobilization of the civilian adult urban population was ordered by the German Nazi authorities. Thanasis, who was working in a German warehouse, was afraid of being taken to the weapons factories in Germany. Then a mass demonstration against the mobilization took place in Athens, and the mobilization was ultimately aborted. But nothing was certain in those days. It was very likely that conscription would be decided in the future. The Germans had lost 800,000 men in the Soviet campaign. General von Paulus himself had been taken captive in February of 1943. After his many initial successes in Africa, Marshal Rommel, a veritable desert fox as he was called, was left without an air force, supplies, and fuel. By March of 1943, Rommel's Afrika Korps had been disbanded, so he was moved to Normandy to organize the area's defense in anticipation of a possible Allied landing operation.

Workers were urgently needed for Germany's war industry. The German beast was massing its forces for the last attempt at conquest. Thanasis feared that eventually there would be political conscription, and he would be selected immediately since he worked in the camp and knowledge of the German language was a significant advantage. So, he decided to escape and hide in the convent in Attica where his grandmother lived. He told Fritz, his German friend, that he had to be away on a serious family matter and left for Athens in suspenseful fashion. He decided to enlist the help of his cousin, Kyriakos, who owned a large almost 18 foot boat, and was a "hotshot" in salt smuggling. *What are relatives for,* Thanasis thought. *At the least, he'll help me with the expectation of profit.*

So, one afternoon he went to Kalamaria and met up with Kyriakos.

"Hey, there, Kyriakos, my man. What are you doing? You look very pale. No sun at all?"

"Don't even ask. I'm dying from exhaustion during the night shift and sleeping during the day. Those cursed Germans don't let even a boat pop out. We don't sail in the daytime because Germans inspect everything to stop soldiers from leaving for the Middle East via Turkey."

"Well, tell me this. Can you take me with you on a boat run to Skiathos?"

"If the waves don't bother you."

"Hey Kyriakos, what are you saying? You can't be serious that waves bother me in the slightest. I've had the sea as my best fishing buddy since I was a 10-year-old kid."

"Of course, if the Germans catch us, we've bit the dust. Two young dudes sailing together is a more suspicious matter for them. Keep that in mind."

"Never fear, big guy. I was born under a lucky star. Take these. Two gold coins," Thanasis said, and he took them out of his pocket.

"Gosh, guy. I'd take you even without the gold coins. What are cousins for?" Kyriakos said to keep up with the pretense, but he happily pocketed the gold coins after clinking them, turning them around first to check their authenticity. "Tomorrow night, come over and eat with my mother and brother—we've got some snappers that I fished out this morning—and we'll leave afterward. Oh, and don't forget to bring an overcoat with you because at night, there's frost, and when the boat's sailing along in a strong wind, you'll be chilled to the bone."

The next night, after eating the snappers that his aunt prepared on the grill, they took their essentials and set off for the boat that was waiting for them on the shore three meters from the water. They pushed the boat into the sea and paddled for a while until they were in open water, and the wind carried them out. Kyriakos lifted the sail and set off in the direction of the town of Katerini. Now the breeze was helping, and they inflated the sail, resulting in the boat moving at a fast clip. Outside the Bay of Thessaloniki, as the waves grew higher, Thanasis vomited and threw up the snappers he had eaten. Kyriakos laughed at his passenger's suffering.

"Next time, don't brag that you don't get seasick in high waves."

"Dammit, Kyriakos. I'm serious. I don't get seasick, but it's my fault that I overate and drank wine."

"Lie face down in the boat, and you'll feel less dizzy," his cousin advised him, and Thanasis obeyed finding relief in doing so.

When dawn came, they hid in a secluded cove near the salt ponds. They ate some bread and cheese, drank wine, and then decided to sleep. The rocking boat in the water transported them into sweet relaxation; they slept for hours in the boat covered with canvas. The next night they set off again and reached the island of Skiathos where Thanasis left to go ashore.

From there, Kyriakos returned to Kalamaria after first passing through the salt ponds of Katerini, where he loaded salt illegally, which he transported for sale to Thessaloniki. He had made these itineraries countless times, always traveling at night. The North Star oriented him because lights were forbidden. Without moonlight, you could not even see your nose. This time Kyriakos also stopped at Makrygialos, where he sold salt to a group of insurgents who had ordered it from him.

Meanwhile, back in Skiathos, Thanasis embarked on a boat to take him from Skiathos to Euboea. He arrived at his destination in Euboea uneventfully. From there, he did a lot of trekking and even hitchhiking before getting picked up by some ramshackle trucks—defying description—that strained to go uphill but ran well going downhill. Finally, he arrived in Attica. After strenuous effort and hiking, he managed to reach the convent. As he passed through its gate, his fatigue made him feel that he was purified from his sins. He told the doorkeeper of the convent who he was and was taken to the guest quarters.

After being summoned, his grandmother, the nun Eusebia, arrived shortly after. She was elated because she hadn't seen him for a few years. He begged her to let him stay in the monastery for a while until the Germans left Greece. As he explained to her, the issue was for a few months as the Axis powers were losing the war on all fronts.

His grandmother could not decide on her own. The matter was a serious one. She had to get the blessing of the Abbess. The Abbess agreed to admit the grandson of her nun to the monastery only under the following conditions: He would grow a beard like a priest, follow the ritual of the monastery's liturgy, wear a robe, and help in the monastery's garden. He would also work to repair the wall that had recently been half-destroyed by a stray bomb.

What choice did Thanasis have? After all, he was not lazy. So, he accepted the terms of the elderly nun. This is how he became a jack of all trades. When dusk fell, he slept in a small hut near the convent's front gate. The Abbess made sure to acquire a new identity for him, so instead of Barlabas, she would write Parlapas. The issuing of the identity card was assisted by the director of the Athens police, Mr. Aggelos Evert, with whom the Abbess had collaborated on other identities of the persecuted Greeks and Jews.

Inside the monastery, Eftychia's son did various jobs. He built the damaged wall; he took care of the vegetable garden lovingly and expertly; he looked after the olive trees; he oversaw the few sheep of the monastery—first in line to take advantage of their milk, of course. In general, he was never idle, and his grandmother watched him with satisfaction.

Three relatively carefree months had gone by, when shortly before dawn—after the end of the service and the morning meal—while Thanasis was high up in the bell tower putting the sealer on some joints that were useful for holding up the bells, he heard the whine of an airplane and the sounds of anti-aircraft fire. Soon a plane appeared in flames and smoke, and immediately after that he noticed—with difficulty as darkness still prevailed—two parachutes falling. As he calculated, they would land relatively close to the convent. Immediately he left his job in the bell tower, went down to the courtyard, and ran towards the exit. However, the huge gate door was closed even though he had alerted a nun to bring the keys because he was impatient to get out quickly. So, he grabbed a ladder—one of those used in pruning the olive trees—and jumped over the wall. He ran about 800 meters in the direction he had seen the parachutes falling. As he approached the spot where he guessed the parachutists had landed, he slowed down to walk as noiselessly as possible so as not to scare them causing them to distance themselves.

As he was approaching a bridge, he noticed something under it. He soon found himself in front of two British aviators. One of them had severely injured his ankle and could not walk. The other one, terrified, aimed at him with his revolver.

"Easy boy, I'm a Greek friend," Thanasis said. With the little English he had learned at school, he told them that there was a convent nearby where they could be accommodated. Holding the wounded aviator by the armpits, Thanasis and the other Englishman reached the convent. It was finally dawn, and the doorkeeper was at her post, and even as frightened as she was, she opened up for them to enter. The downed plane had fallen into the sea a few meters from the shore. It was all too certain that the Germans would search for the aviators if they discovered the plane without them inside the cockpit. After all, they would have seen the two parachutes fall. Thanasis took the liberty of disturbing the Abbess to explain what had happened and to beg her to hide the English men. The Abbess was very anxious.

"My child, what you have done is Christian but also very dangerous. We need to move quickly. You're going to give my brother a coded note quickly," she said firmly.

"Where does your brother live?"

"In the village five kilometers from the monastery. He's a priest and, in some cases, helps the resistance."

She wrote a few words on a small piece of paper:

"Papa-Giorgi (Father Giorgi), come to the convent for vespers and eat with us. I have two books to give you. One is a little torn, but I have taken care of it, and it can be read."

Thanasis arrived at the priest's house by running almost all the way and gave him the note. This notification to her brother was written in code and meant that a partisan had to be notified, and a message had to be sent by radio to Cairo so that a submarine could come to pick up the aviators; one of them was slightly injured. They had done it many times, but not with aviators.

Meanwhile, expecting a German investigation sooner or later, he led the English to a stable on the floor of which there was a very well camouflaged hatch with a pile of straw over its detachable opening. The nuns used to stay in this stable, formerly a farmhouse, until the newer building was built with the correct specifications. The Brits holed up in the hideout there after Thanasis had supplied them with water, milk, cheese, and bread. A short while passed, and five Germans came and started their investigation in the convent. They could not find anything blameworthy. Thanasis' identity was perfectly genuine, and they took him for a priest. But he was quite fearful. What if they discovered the Brits and interrogated them? He was involved in this situation way over his head.

Fortunately, a week later, the Abbess was notified that the submarine was finally arriving to pick up the aviators and that they had to be on a particular beach at 3:00 A.M. The Abbess' resistance network had organized things very well. The British were consistent in their assignment. They threw an inflatable boat from the submarine into the sea with a sailor, who then paddled about 150 meters to the shore where the aviators were waiting. He gave oars to one of them, and they were quickly lost in the darkness as they paddled away. In the depths, the massive outline of a submarine stood out, which would set off shortly with the newcomers for the journey to the Middle East.

Thanasis was also involved in this operation phase, but the next day he decided to leave the convent—for his own safety. Having first shaved, he got the blessing of the Abbess, wore a cap that was given to him as a gift, kissed his grandmother, and set off on the return journey home. Once again, he finally arrived in Thessaloniki in two and a half days by walking and hitchhiking. In the meantime, the Germans were belatedly informed about the submarine's approach and went back to the monastery to interrogate the Abbess, which they did for two days rather cruelly. Throughout the interrogation, she inwardly prayed the prayer of the heart: *Our Lord Jesus Christ, have mercy on me,* and did not buckle. The Germans, who had lost their old determination, and in view of their probable imminent departure from our country, were tired of dealing with the case and released her.

When Thanasis arrived in his neighborhood and began his favorite kind of whistling, Clara leapt up and began her barking in a cheerful, almost weeping way. As soon as the door opened and Eftychia caught sight of Thanasis, she stayed as motionless as a figure in a snapshot for a moment.

Her son was emaciated and sunburned. After a few seconds of stillness and surprise, she fell into his arms and hugged him tightly. "How did you get like this, my boy? You look dreadful. Your cheeks are sunken, my child," she kept repeating.

She loved her son even though she scolded him often. The squabbles between them were something of a morning exercise routine. Clara bounced between them, barking. The whole family gathered around the newly arrived, except for Kotsos Barlabas, who was absent as usual.

Eftychia's son had a lot to tell them. He also laid it on thick, as he often did when discussing his adventures. He was quite the braggart and did not hide it at all. Everyone listened with their mouths open and bulging eyes, especially his mother, who seemed anxious about the story with the aviators. Fortunately, however, there were no unpleasant consequences.

After the liberation, the Abbess and Thanasis both became recipients of a certificate from the government of Great Britain, thanking each of them for their contribution in preventing the enemy's capture of the two aviators and their participation in their escape to Egypt.

The Abbess put this diploma in a frame and hung it on the wall behind her armchair, next to and just below the image of the crucifix. Thanasis stuffed his certificate folded in four into his back pocket and took it out every now and then to show it with pride to relatives, friends, and acquaintances. In three months, his diploma had disintegrated into a torn-up scrap of paper. One day Zozo took his pants to iron them and found the certificate that was about to crumble. She took it and put it between the leaves of an old book to preserve it somewhat without more wear and tear. This book by Hector Malo titled *Without a Family* had been carried to Greece by Georgia and was Zozo's favorite book, who, although not orphaned by a father, lived as an orphan in someone else's house.

In June 1943, after Thanasis had returned to Thessaloniki, he found his friend Fritz again through Dina, his old girlfriend, whose sister, Kiki, the German, had fallen in love with. With his acquaintances and his little German, he managed to begin working for the Germans once again as the head of a group of Greek workers who did not know German. He started stealing again and eating butter and chocolates that he had been deprived of for so long in the monastery with the fasting there.

He gradually regained his normal weight. The camaraderie with Fritz was going very well. The two sisters had lodged them. But one day in July, Fritz left urgently with his unit for the front in Sicily, where the allies had landed. The camp with the warehouses where

Thanasis worked carried on with a minimum number of Germans, so stealing became more trouble-free, but the Germans' food supplies were now scarce…along with "their other goods" in Greece!

Three years later, Kiki discovered that Fritz had been killed in Palermo. They alerted her because in his pockets had been found two photographs of Kiki and an envelope with her address that the unfortunate Fritz had not had time to mail. In one of the photos, Dina was pictured with Thanasis. A photo had been taken by an outdoor photographer in the city's central park opposite the White Tower, and Fritz was wearing civilian clothes. But he didn't have much time to enjoy being a civilian or Kiki. He also died too young, like millions of people in these awful wars of human beings who turn into animals to carry them through to completion.

12

Eftychia can also be a little...silly

The Germans decided to depart from Greece, but Thessaloniki's inhabitants continued to suffer great anguish, especially those such as Electra with her second husband, the dentist who lived on the coastal road. This trouble was caused by the German plan to blow up all the coastal buildings so that it would be impossible for the Allies to use the port for a long time. With the explosions, the whole first row of houses would be demolished, and perhaps the second row as well. Large quantities of dynamite were placed in holes in the pier, one meter from the sea. Finally, after many requests to the Germans from the Greek authorities and the Orthodox Metropolitan Bishop Gennadius, this plan was changed, and the Germans simply sank all the ships that were in the port, making it dangerous for other ships to enter it.

A month before the Germans left, there had been an incident with Eftychia too. She almost got arrested by the special pro-German Greek battalion of Colonel Poulos because she had annoyed them. Here's what happened. The men of the notorious battalion had blocked the sidewalk with ropes in front of the house they used as their headquarters on Pavlos Melas Street for their own safety so that in order to get through the passers-by were forced to walk in the street below or on the sidewalk across from their headquarters.

One day Eftychia was passing by, and she became annoyed that they had blocked the sidewalk. She bent over to go under the rope causing the guard to shout at her. She almost got arrested. Eftychia was not intimidated, and she started talking back. Fortunately, Zissis, who was her best friend Katina's husband, and who had joined Colonel Poulos' special battalion, was inside the building watching the street behind a window and got wind of what was happening. He then intervened with the guard to release the woman, telling him that he knew her and that she was also a little...silly! However, before leaving her, they searched her bag and kept a record of her name and address just in case. Not only did they not discover anything that incriminated her as a leftist, but instead, they found a photograph of King George II, which proved it was completely unlikely that a communist would carry the King's photo with her.

In any case, for better or worse, Eftychia stopped passing by Pavlos Melas Street until the battalion was disbanded, many of whose men were killed in clashes with the leftists, while a few who escaped were preparing to follow the Germans back to Germany.

Finally, the time had come. The conquerors departed without even being harassed by the left-wing resistance fighters because such were the orders of the leftist guerrilla leadership. So, on the one hand, the withdrawal of German troops was not hindered, and on the other hand, the rebel groups remained unscathed for the next phase of the struggle, which was the seizure of power using their guns.

But while the inhabitants should have been relieved by the departure of the Germans, conditions turned from bad to worse as the times were wicked, and significant political turbulence followed. Most of the city was now ruled by the left-wing guerrillas under the name ELAS (Greek Popular Liberation Army), whose leadership and many members (but not all) were communists. In the evenings, everyone locked themselves in their homes early and sporadic gunshots and rallying cries were heard, uttered by an assortment of fanatics with improvised loudspeakers. Various rallying slogans were written on the walls, and various proclamations were circulated every now and then. A few British officers tried to maintain law and order, but this was difficult to achieve.

Despite her worries about this state of affairs, Eftychia did not let anxiety overwhelm her. One evening she was sitting on a stool in her bathroom, painting her nails, when the doorbell rang. She was not expecting anyone at such an hour, and she wondered who it could possibly be. But her dog barked and wagged her tail as usual behind the entrance door, a sign that the visitor was a friend. When Eftychia opened the door, her friend Katina fell into her arms sobbing, her eyes swollen in tears.

"What's wrong?" the hostess asked anxiously.

"Oh, a great evil has befallen me! Oh! What's happened to me? The Elasites (men of ELAS) have arrested my husband!"

"How on earth! My dear, how did this happen?"

"As I've told you, my husband was constantly the target of the leftists because he used to be a rural police officer. So, to be safe, he joined the team of the special battalion led by Poulos." [8]

I know all this because he helped me in one situation, Eftychia thought, silently recalling the episode with the rope.

"In the last few days after the Poulos team was disbanded, my husband was caught by the Elasites, and I lost track of him. Of course, he was away from home for ten days because he was hiding, but now I've discovered he was captured, and I don't know what's happening. I'm afraid they'll kill him!"

Eftychia was trying to find a way to help her friend but could not find a solution. She tried to comfort her by saying:

"God is great, Katina. I believe He will intervene."

"If God intervened, my husband wouldn't have been caught by the ELAS men," Katina countered. "I'm now left alone and helpless without money, and luckily I have a few English gold sovereigns just to get food, but how long will those last? I'll run out of them too."

Eftychia made some tea for them to relieve her embarrassment, and after comforting her, when it was time for her friend to leave, she prepared two bags in which she put "coffee" and sugar. She didn't

---

[8] Colonel George Poulos participated in the military coup in 1935 as an Eleftherios Venizelos supporter. During the German occupation, he became National Socialist and received military uniforms and weapons from the Germans to fight against leftist groups. He was arrested after the war and was sentenced to death in 1919.

have real coffee. What she had was made from roasted chickpeas, but she had as much sugar as she needed.

"Take some sugar to have for your coffee and don'i't be upset. If things get worse come here to eat with us. We're five. What's one more? I'll put another plate on the table."

Katina could not thank Eftychia enough. Her eyes were brimming, and her tears were now flowing down her cheeks. Her mind was on her husband. *A retired police officer who is a rightist ... a bad combination in the days we're going through,* she thought.

Finally, after a short trial, Zissis was executed in the Heptapyrgion Fortress in Thessaloniki. For weeks Katina never stopped weeping at his loss. Since that time, she always wore black clothes despite her friend's advice to stop mourning and get remarried. In these matters, she was completely different from Eftychia who reigned supreme in matters of love. Katina preferred to live alone in shoddy conditions, with a small pension, accompanied only by her misery. She had the misfortune of not having children. She often went to Eftychia's house but rarely did the opposite happen. However, both friends were rightists and fans of the king.

Young Zozo, perhaps influenced by Eftychia also became a royalist, so she always had a frame with the picture of the King over her so-called bed, next to it but a little lower than the icon of the Virgin Mary with Christ in her arms. She even kept a notebook (album) in which she pasted photographs of the kings from publications in magazines and newspapers. One could never understand where this devotion of the orphaned and wretched Zozo to the royal institution originated. Perhaps it was because she too waited for a lifetime for a prince to come and ask for her hand in marriage just like it happens in children's fairy tales. But for the time being, she was growing up washing dishes, washing underwear, pajamas, nightgowns, socks, blouses and shirts, wiping and mopping the house in which she ate a plate of food and had a corner to sleep in.

Once a month, a "major laundry day" was held to wash the bedsheets with the help of a special washerwoman, Mrs. Varvara. On such days the kitchen became inundated with water so they lit a fire under the vat in the kitchen so that they would have plenty of hot water. Then the women—Eftychia, Zozo, and Varvara—circulated in the kitchen wearing sturdy wooden clogs, while the men could not go to the back of the house because there were no more clogs. After all, washing was a woman's job!

Eftychia was quite affectionate with Zozo while she was young, but as she grew older, Zozo was increasingly assigned household chores so that Eftychia herself could deal with her love affairs undistracted. But everyone loved Zozo, whose disposition came from having integrity—everyone except Kotsos Barlabas who was generally indifferent.

Zozo was also loved very much by the two daughters of their neighbor, Mrs. Asimina. They went to church together and chatted during their free hours. They had common beliefs about almost all matters, even those regarding the royal institution, despite the fact that the father of the sisters was a socialist. Indeed, they also tried to put together a collection of royal photographs. However, they were unable to compete in number with the photographs in Zozo's album, since she had started this hobby some time before.

Eftychia's family shared an increased interest in politics. Barlabas was an old Venizelist, but since Venizelos had died years before, he now supported General Plastiras. Thanasis admired Georgios Papandreou for his eloquence but was more concerned with his own jobs and love affairs. He often found himself entangled with two women, one, quite young, out of feelings and another older one, out of passion. As for 18-year-old Aristides, he was still searching for his life's goal. Mostly he was interested in finishing the six-year high school. Because of his many outings on Tsimiski Street on safe quiet days, he had again not taken exams in Ancient Greek and French. Lately, he had been involved in a low-key love affair with the sister of a classmate. But he was more concerned about what work he would do in the future. He wanted to gain independence. Seeing the commercial exploits of his brother he thought about becoming a merchant but first, things had to calm down.

As for Eftychia, she was always worried about her finances. She was also involved in small commercial activities. In particular, she knew a recipe for a moisturizing night cream that made the skin soft as silk. She sent Aristides to different pharmacies each time she needed supplies so that nobody would learn the recipe. From one pharmacy he would buy lanolin, from another almond oil, and from a third a tincture of benzoin and rose water. Eftychia would mix them in a utensil she had specifically for this project by combining the right proportions and then distributing the cream in small boxes supplied by a pharmaceutical warehouse. These boxes were made of a thinly cut sheet of wood. She also made glue with flour and water and glued a handwritten label that read "Pure Night Cream" on the boxes. She used the cream on herself first. Being forty years old her skin needed maintenance. When she was seen by acquaintances on the street and they'd start chatting, they were often impressed by her smooth unwrinkled skin and would complement her. Of course, Eftychia did not miss the opportunity to talk to them about her miraculous cream. She soon acquired a significant number of clients who asked to buy her cream every month.

Eftychia had estimated profits of 90% from her sales. Despite the great profit, her cream was much cheaper than the commercial creams of the time especially the famous Swiss night cream "Tokalon". Perhaps Eftychia's cream was better because it was quite oily and softened the skin so much.

One day, Mrs. Magda, who ran a tailoring business came to get a box of cream.

"Hello. How are you doing with work now that the situation is a mess?" Eftychia asked.

"What can I tell you," Mrs. Magda replied. "It seems that women want to wear nice clothes in all seasons, perhaps more so now in these difficult days such as the ones we're going through. I can't find enough time to sew. A girl I had with me for years quit because she got married. So, now I do the work of two. The other five girls I have are only assistants. By the way, I found out that you make moisturizing cream. A client of mine told me."

"Yes, I have an excellent night's cream."

"Don't tell me you put mercury in it because it has an impressive temporary effect but destroys the skin shortly after. That's what happened with my friend Vaso, and now it's hard to look at her. Her skin looks pleated!"

"What on earth are you saying? It's impossible that I'd put mercury in my cream. I only use pure ingredients; the results are obvious. Just look at my skin. There are no wrinkles on my forehead or around the eyes."

They stood in front of the large mirror. Magda, who was also five years older, clearly showed that she was starting to wrinkle.

"So, tell me. How old are you?" she asked Eftychia.

"I'm what I look," our dear 'aesthetician' replied playfully and continued. "All right. I'll tell you. I'm 44 years old." (She added four years to prove the miraculous properties of her cream, which was very effective, but she made this small personal sacrifice to advertise it). Convinced of the miraculous ointment, Magda bought two boxes, became a regular customer, and bought the creams two and three at a time.

Katina, the broken-hearted widow, did not buy creams because now and then Eftychia gave her a box as a gift, each time the last of a batch had been left unsold before it went rancid. The unfortunate lady was already 48 years old. Despite not intending to remarry, she did not want her skin to be wrinkled and gladly accepted the gift of creams.

It seems that the various cosmetics, which our ancient Greek ancestors called *"psymythia"* or decorative body creams, have been in use for so long that they became a part of the DNA of women, which is why they begin to use them as soon as they reach the age of 14 or even younger. Eftychia had come to realize this fact. That is why her commercial pursuits always had something to do with what women wear and use.

13

Sugar for sale

As soon as the Germans left Thessaloniki, various groups of armed men turned the city into a mayhem cf riots, demonstrations, and clashes. Going out into the streets in the evening was dangerous as those who went out at night either out of recklessness or out of necessity would be shot at. In the working-class districts of the Upper Town, the communists were the majority. The middle class was in the majority of those living in the city's center and towards the coastline. Of these, some were Liberal Venizelists, and others were supporters of the Popular party, i.e., the rightists. But the old divisions of the political parties had subsided. At the time, everyone feared the communists who held weapons and controlled almost the whole city. In the evenings, they patrolled the streets in small groups and shouted rallying cries against the king and the rightists.

The rightists, less organized but always hardliners, either hid or stayed silent for their own security or would make sudden attacks on the offices of the KKE (Communist Party of Greece). The British were trying to keep order.

Thanasis Barlabas stayed away from all this. He was mainly interested in being safe and finding enough food to eat. He had no confidence in the political factions, and besides, he had no party affiliation. In other words, he was free and thus felt free, which is precisely what he wanted. When he cast his vote, he would choose based on the "lesser of two evils."

Day by day, things quieted down in the city. The British now managed the food supplies. With the ease that Thanasis learned the basics of foreign languages when he needed them, he had already made an acquaintance with Peter, an Irishman who held a good position in the logistics of his unit. The tactics used by the resourceful Greek had been tried and tested. The bait? What else? Women! Fritz may have gone, but his girl was left all alone. Thanasis spoke to her.

"Listen here, sweety. It makes no difference whether it's Fritz or Peter. One was blond, and so is the other. Besides, the times are full of uncertainty. We must seize every opportunity. You don't know what's going to happen one day to the next. Trust me. You've lost your virginity anyway. Of course, this can be corrected if necessary, but we're not interested in this matter now. With the Irishman, we'll have everything. He's in logistics, I'm telling you. He regulates all the food supplies in the warehouse."

The next day Thanasis and Peter met the two sisters. They went to a small taverna in the Kalamaria district. There Thanasis was well known; they knew him by name as he went there often. Mr. Pantelis was happy to see him because he always left a good tip; apart from that, he would consume an abundance of delicacies with his friends.

So, on that day they ordered salads, potatoes, zucchini, eggplant, all fried, of course, and keftedes in a spicy sauce. And, of course, retsina. Peter began to drink, and his face flushed. After all, he was already ruddy faced by nature. He started singing in English as there were no other guests in the taverna. On a Monday in an age like the one they were experiencing, no one was in the mood for feasting. However, the shop also offered two unique rooms—apart from the others—for illicit couples to rendezvous. In a short while, Thanasis and Peter sequestered the ladies. Thanasis would pay something extra for all that, but he would profit from this after his expenses. About that, he was sure of.

It was 11:00 PM in winter, and the clouds hid the moon resulting in profound darkness. A cart, creaking characteristically, was dragged by an old horse gasping and snorting down a street covered with roughhewn stones, as most of the streets of Thessaloniki were built like that. The cart then stopped in front of the Barlabas house. A young athletic-looking man wearing a cap jumped quickly off the cart and shouted at the middle-aged driver: "Yianni, come here fast to get this unloaded. And you know…just as we agreed!"

The driver got down and went to the back of the cart. There were two sacks full of something that could have been anything. They started work right away. The young man mainly loaded the sacks and took them up to the first floor from a straight staircase, which had about fifteen steps. The Germans had just left two months previously, and now the British had come with strange-looking soldiers, a few of whom were blonde but most of whom were swarthy soldiers wearing turbans.[9] The young man carrying the sacks was Thanasis, who, after

---

[9] India was still a colony of Great Britain and thousands of Indian soldiers distinguished themselves fighting for the allies in WWII.

the German withdrawal, did not waste time and had already made his contacts. Peter, who, in fact, was a clever Irishman, immediately got the message and started work. This was the first delivery of goods. Thanasis had transferred the sacks to the top of the stairway, and in the next five minutes, he had placed them in the bathroom of the house. This bathroom had recently had a problem, and when the firewood was lit to warm up the water, it would smoke quite a bit. It was probably the fault of the chimney, coated with a lot of soot and creosote and was not ventilating correctly. So, little by little, the water heater had fallen into disuse, and the bath had evolved into a storage room, much to the delight of Thanasis, who always needed storage space. For the family, fortunately, five public baths functioned in Thessaloniki.

Now the tub was filled with two sacks that, as it turned out, contained sugar. Thanasis would sell it divided into smaller sacks and give Peter one quarter of the proceeds. He kept Peter constantly in mind, thinking that the Irishman was indeed insatiable; *it wasn't enough that I offered him a girl; he also wanted a share of the profits!* But he had expenses too. He had to pay off the gate guard at the barracks. He figured it out in his head and found that very little was left for him, the guy who had to deal with all the risks and the danger of transporting sugar in the dangerous night hours.

These were his thoughts when he closed the door of the bathroom. As he was absorbed in his thoughts, he did not hear the footsteps of Eftychia, who was approaching to see what was happening as he arranged the full sacks inside the bathtub; his moans and groans awakened her.

"Thanasis, what are you doing here?" Eftychia asked.

"Nothing, Mother. Here…I brought two sacks of sugar I took from the English to sell them."

Her eyes glowed in the middle of the half-dark.

"Thanasis, how much sugar will you leave for us at home?" she asked him, adding as much sweetness to her voice as she could.

"Mother, see here. The merchandise is an order. There's nothing left over. Next time I'll bring some for the house."

Eftychia felt her skin shivering in goosebumps and her head aching. That's how she got when she got angry. Her blood had risen to her head with a vengeance.

"What are you saying, you lout? Aren't you going to leave even a little sugar for the house out of so many sacks? And what's our role in this? Are we suckers? I wash your stuff; I clean your stuff; I provide you with water and food, and out of so much food that passes through your hands, you leave us only crumbs?"

"C'mon, Mother. I told you it's an order," Thanasis said with a decisive tone in his voice.

"Shit on your order," Eftychia said angrily. "Look here. If you continue your behavior, get up and leave the house! I don't believe it! An order!"

"Why are you saying this, Mother?" Thanasis countered. You can't say I leave nothing for the house. Did you forget the olive oil and chocolates from the Germans during the Occupation?"

"Big deal! You annoyed us with the demijohn back then, and so what if once you left a couple of bottles of olive oil, and we survived the Occupation," Eftychia said indignantly. "If I weren't in command of this household to manage our affairs, we'd never have food on our plates. But the foolishness is over. You're a great big hulk of a guy. Anyone else in your position would get married and have a wife and children to feed. And the only thing you know how to do is eat, drink, and go around with sluts, you stupid lout... yeah, you self-obsessed greedy hulk. The sluts are gobbling up your money, stupid fool...wake up and smell the coffee. Wise up."

Thanasis listened with an angry look in his eyes. The argument had flared up. He took a deep breath and said resolutely:

"Listen here, Eftychia. I've already sold this sugar and dare not open the sacks. Do you understand what I'm saying?" Eftychia proceeded to take a few steps farther off from the bathroom door where the quarrel was taking place. She approached a shelf that had her jars of salt, sugar, coffee, linden leaves, and tea. The sugar jar had only traces of sugar on the bottom.

"Do you see the jar with the sugar? Not enough for even one coffee. And the other guy—the great good for nothing, your father, may he rot in hell—neither cares what we eat nor how we survive. We were living better during the Occupation than we are now."

Thanasis turned and began to move away while muttering.

"Mother, I told you the sugar is already reserved. Period. End of story."

Eftychia was holding the empty jar of sugar in her hand. She was staring at it with tear-filled eyes. Her chest started to swell. With difficulty, she held back the first sob. If she were to let go, she would collapse from crying. That's how she was. Only to a certain point could pretend she was tough. Once more she spoke.

"If you don't let me have sugar for the house, I'll curse you, you bastard."

Thanasis shrugged his shoulders indifferently.

"Do whatever you want to do. The sugar is reserved, and if I'm a bastard, what are you? A whore?"

At that point, Eftychia roared and, with all solemnity, cried out:

"I curse you, you ungrateful lout, yeah you, I curse you. May you return with your tongue cut out…calling your mother a whore. D'you hear? With your tongue cut out!"

Thanasis left the house distressed and dazed. His mother's voice, but what a voice—curses and howls—still resounded in his ears. On the one hand, he felt some guilt. When his mother showed him the empty sugar jar, he felt sorry for her. However, he thought that she had behaved selfishly.

He then went to the Kapani market where he found the merchants who would take the sugar. He made the relevant agreements and returned home with a few small sacks with which he would distribute the sugar for sale. It was also more convenient for transportation. As he walked up the stairs and just before he reached the front door of his home, he heard a familiar voice from the inside.

"What are you saying, dear Eftychia? All this sugar will be sold, leaving you with nothing but your appetite! It's not as if somebody got killed. And what are you saying, you quarreled with your son? I had him in my house for many years when he couldn't get enough food in yours. You didn't speak to him about this properly. Do you think I don't know what your mouth is like you have when you're angry?"

Eftychia could be heard saying something, with a voice altered by the crying and the snot-filled nose blocking her airwaves. You couldn't distinguish her words well.

When Thanasis entered the house, he found himself facing Electra.

"Thanasis, hello, my boy. It's been a while since I've seen you. Come here so I can give you a kiss. Kissy." She gave him two kisses on his cheeks. "But really, what have I found out? Are you doing business with the Brits? Be careful, my child, not to get yourself into any trouble. It's also these communists who pretend not to care and pretend to respect everything. They forget about the gold sovereigns the Brits would drop for them with the parachutes, and they would spend them on their own personal needs. Do be careful."

For his aunt to start the conversation with so much diplomacy Thanasis figured his aunt was up to her schemes. He prepared for the sequel. And as he expected, Electra continued:

"My Thanasis, I found your mother in tears. I don't believe it. Is it possible? You brought so much sugar and won't share any for the household?"

Thanasis then understood. That's what it was about. Electra was getting into the game about the sugar.

"Look here, Aunt Electra. You must know what I have to supply. It's been ordered for days. Out of what they give me, half of it and more the Irishman takes, add the guard at the gate so he can look the other way, add up the transportation costs, and there is nothing left. If I start handing out stuff—here, there, here's some sugar—I'll go under. Got it?"

Electra concluded that Thanasis was unwavering. Her gaze hardened. She stopped smiling, and her lips pursed. She took two steps into the kitchen, grabbed a large, pointed knife on the counter, and, holding it firmly in her hand, turned towards Thanasis. Her nephew saw her and became alarmed. *What's this bullhead going to do now?* he wondered.

In the meantime, sitting on a sofa in the kitchen and wiping her nose, Eftychia watched the scene unfolding and got scared too. Her maternal instinct outweighed her anger, and she cried out:

"Electra. No! Not the knife! Thanasis, my child, watch out!"

Thanasis retreated a few steps, passed through the open door at the end of the hallway which connected the kitchen with the sitting room, hurriedly closed the door behind him for safety, and placed his foot at the bottom of it in such a way that one could not easily open it. But Electra did not intend to open the door, nor was the knife destined for Thanasis as he and Eftychia feared. She took three steps to the front of the bathtub, grabbed a basin, and with a skillful movement, nailed the knife into one of the sacks of sugar. White crystalline sugar began to pour into the basin. The stab in the sack had been done high up near where it was tied so that more sugar would pour out. Electra tilted the sack a little. Eftychia watched dumbfounded. Perhaps she thought that Electra did what she herself wanted to do but did not dare to. Although Electra was younger, Eftychia always admired her because she was more intrepid than she was.

Meanwhile, after waiting a little behind the closed door, Thanasis bent down and looked through the keyhole. On the other side, there was silence. Electra was carrying sugar in three jars on a coffee tray at the back of the kitchen. Thanasis then realized that he had lost the game. He loved his mother, but he had weakened her cockiness. He also loved his aunt, but he couldn't cope with her. Besides, he admired her because she was smart and aggressive. She had shown her strong character one other time. He owed her his gratitude as well. She had taken him in for so long, and he ate like a king in her house. For just a second, he thought about going back to the kitchen. But what would he do there? He did not dare to oppose Electra. He chose to leave. He would go to the soccer club's meeting house to play a little backgammon game and calm down. In that endeavor, he was unbeatable. He'd play for money, he thought. So, he would even out the loss he had with the sugar. He would distribute the sugar the following day.

14

The Horsehair and the Curse

Thanasis was not profiting much from the sugar trade, so, having a resourceful mindset, he thought about doing something more financially rewarding. In the British encampment where he worked, he took care of some fine-looking sturdy horses with long tails and manes which young Barlabas had noticed. He started up a conversation with an Englishman, John the stable master, a kind man who had become his friend since he spoke to him often.

John engrossed himself in soccer. He had played on a team before the war and, as he said, he was quite good. Thanasis told him that he was playing as a goalkeeper. His team was in the second division and hoped to climb to the first. Some decent matches were being held. He invited John to attend a match. The afternoon of the match, Thanasis played impressively. He was an absolute master goalkeeper, a real guard dog of the goalposts. He blocked a shot at three meters, immediately jumped up and repelled another one, and deflected the ball to the corner. Against the corner kick, he jumped higher than everyone else and caught the ball with both hands raised up high in the air. But in doing so, he shoved an opposing player to get into a better position to jump for the ball. So, the referee whistled a penalty. But Thanasis had his way with penalties too. Whether because he was able to read the opponent's mind or because he was watching his opponent's feet, he could figure out if the opponent would shoot with the inside or the outside of his foot. The rest was easy. He would take a couple of small steps forward and then fall to the right side. That is what he did in that penalty shot by blocking the ball, which, however, escaped him, and it took a second leap to capture it before the opponent did.

John was thrilled with Thanasis. He had a ball in the camp, and in his spare time, he had him play goalkeeper, and he'd kick from a distance. He even had him learn a special training trick. He had his back turned so that he could look towards the net and suddenly shouted at him: **NOW**! while kicking at him simultaneously. So, the goalkeeper's reflexes became even better.

Thanasis didn't attend his team's training sessions regularly. Because of his work he had little time. However, he was unshakeable in the position of the main goalkeeper. He was way better than his two other teammates who were substitutes.

Naturally, Thanasis took advantage of his relationship with John. With his approval, he began to cut the tails of the horses. Bristles were a valuable material for making brushes. He had already consulted with a craftsman to whom he would sell the horsehair. He had barbered all the horses except one called Buck, who was unruly and who, when grabbed by the tail, would immediately change his position as if he were being tickled, distancing his buttocks from any annoying person bothering him.

Thanasis Barlabas decided to get Buck's horsehairs. However, for this unruly horse not to escape, he tied his hind legs with a rope close together. When he thought that everything was ready, he approached from behind and caught the tail, ready to cut the first hairs.

When he did a job that needed careful attention, Thanasis had the habit of sticking out his tongue, which many people do. I have noticed that some people tighten their lips, and others stick out their tongues. Thanasis belonged to the second group. He stuck his tongue out as he was cutting the horsehairs. Buck, however, annoyed by the clipping of his tail and, as he was unable to move with his legs tied, made a defensive move, and suddenly jerked by lifting his hind legs and kicking backward, a kick that landed on Thanasis' jaw. His tongue, which was between his lips, was crushed by his teeth, which with the blow slammed shut hard, his mouth filling with blood. He fell backward, stunned by the blow.

Nobody's dared punch me in the jaw and now look at what the old horse did to me, Thanasis thought. His tongue started to throb in pain but more so his jaw. Salty blood filled his mouth; his tongue swelled up. He spat out blood, but once was not enough. He realized that he was bleeding profusely.

Just as all this happened, John was sitting outside the stable smoking some cigarettes from a pack with the image of a sailor on it. Thanasis came out and tried to tell him what happened. But he immediately realized that he could not speak. His tongue was sliced and swollen, and his mouth soon filled with blood again. He was severely injured, wobbling, and about to faint. As soon as he saw him pale and bloodied, John understood. He had Thanasis lie down on some sacks and called the unit doctor, who quickly came in a jeep. He glanced at the mouth and the slit jaw of the young man who had turned pale and realized that the job was too hard for him to tackle. He placed the young man in the jeep and sped to the camp surgery quarters, which the organizational skills of the British had developed.

There the surgeon placed a gauze bandage drenched with ether over Thanasis' nose, who began to get even dizzier and calmly began to stitch his tongue back together. As he explained to them afterward, the tongue had been deeply cut by a third and was supported by just one end. However, there was some doubt about the outcome of the restoration. Thanasis, who understood simple English, was petrified!

After some time, no longer faint but still quite distressed, he arrived at his house, accompanied by his good friend John, and met his mother in the kitchen making coffee (not real coffee, but chickpeas baked and crushed, which they called "coffee"). Only the sugar was authentic, the sugar that her sister Elektra had "confiscated" with her intimidation tactics, stabbing the sack of Thanasis' sugar a few days earlier.

Eftychia saw him swollen and bruised and got scared.

"My child, what happened to you?" she cried, running towards him.

Thanasis tried to talk to her, but he couldn't. His swollen tongue filled his whole mouth, so he took a piece of paper and a pencil and wrote:

What kind of mother are you, Eftychia dearie? You cursed me in the sugar incident and your curse came to fruition. My tongue was cut. Your curses come true. You should only curse your enemy! No more curses against me. I will not upset you ever again, I promise you. I did wrong. No more curses!

The English surgeon did a good job, and Thanasis' tongue was slowly restored. Despite all that he suffered, he still stuck his tongue out when doing some delicate work. But he never cut horsehairs again. A lesson learned, and as he used to say, *I have made many mistakes in my life, but I do not repeat them.* He had read this somewhere! The bad thing, however, was that his life was to be filled with a plethora and variety of mistakes.

From then on, Eftychia possessed a formidable weapon in her claims and quarrels with Thanasis. She would threaten to curse him, and he feared her, so he was forced to comply with her demands. Not always, of course, because another event regarding curses came to pass.

15

Correspondence and Matchmaking

The following letters were exchanged between Eftychia and her sister Antigone, who lived in Chicago, married there, had four children, and worked hard. Eftychia would lament her fate as always.

In Thessaloniki on March 3, 1946

My beloved sister Antigone,

We are all well, and I hope you are well, too. Anyway, we experienced difficult days here with the Germans; our stomachs were starving, our insides played music day and night, we could be heard in the next apartment growling like cats, our breaths stank of hunger, we shut ourselves inside starting early in the evening because it was forbidden to be out and about after 9 pm. Don't even mention the bombing. At first the Italians...well, they were the enemies, but then also the British, they were supposedly bombing the Germans, yes, they did well to do that, but Antigone, we were in danger crowded in the basements— supposedly shelters—God only knows what they were. Still, I mentioned God, and I remembered God protected us. No bomb fell on our house, we would all have been killed, and well Barlabas, he is useless, he is a burden on the earth, no one would take notice of his absence, but my children and little Zozo, how would they be to blame if they had such a fate. Fortunately, God protected us. We didn't have olive oil, but I always saved a little bit for the vigil oil lamp...I lit it up for a while every day to save on oil, for the protection by our All-Merciful, not to mention Saint Georgios, who I have on the iconostasis as he is killing Satan, who transformed into a dragon. I've become quite thrifty with this German Occupation. The damned Germans have put us through hell; we've realized the value of peace... dammed them. My Thanasis was in danger with some arrogant Brits who he was helping ... what! ... am I saying helping? He SAVED them from the fangs of the German death, the whole Gestapo was looking for him nationwide, but he had changed his name and identity in Athens, thanks to the Abbess...may she be well at the monastery... who supplied him with an identity card you know the Abbess has a lot of influence... the head of the police serves her in whatever legal help she asks of him... you'll say that the second ID was not legal it was made under another name, but he had his own picture. And the youngster was performing national resistance, that's what they call it here, each person does national resistance whether from the right or the left, but my kid did...he helped the Brits so they wouldn't get caught by the Germans...my little angel was in such danger!

He didn't think about me that if he had been caught, they would have executed him. He thought only of those two young men, the British airmen who...well I mean, these two were also born of mothers waiting for them to return; I am unsure if they were married, and it would be even more complicated—then two women each would be waiting for their return, but those unfortunate ones would be tortured by the German thugs. So as for the rest, little sister, we are going through a tough time even now... my ungrateful husband, Kotsos, is the lowest of the low, a stingy man. He leaves me nickels and dimes and wants me to find luxury food...I have been beaten before, beaten you'd never believe how much, and kicked in my belly when I was pregnant...the barbarian kicked me, but now I have put him in his place, and the divorce is going forward...he signed his signature and for the time being...I'm thinking about it...I told the lawyer to wait, not for anything else, but because if Barlabas dies, I will lose his pension...he's not about to die for years. Still, he is older than me by almost twenty years, so I told him if he wants to stay at home, he should know he will sleep on the sofa in the kitchen, and he will give me rent for his house, his food, and so on that are burdens on us. Aristides complained to me that I had exiled his dad to the kitchen, but in the end, he agreed. It's also his filthiness, you see... he doesn't wash because he's afraid of water and soap, but also because he doesn't want to take off his clothes whose linings are filled with money. In any case, I want to tell you, my sister, that we've had a difficult time all these years, and now again, we're going through hard times.

Fortunately, Electra, who had an excellent job with hats, helps me a little bit.... crazy women aren't they? Their men paid whatever amount for a good hat; what was I saying? Oh yes. Now that our sister married the dentist...he is a little bit older, of course, but very nice, what they call a gentleman. With a husband and two elderly sisters-in-law, Electra could not do it all, so she closed the shop and had her child, little Spyro; in fact, our Spyrakis was born before she got married because her first husband—the drunkard—delayed the divorce...she has probably written to you about it I imagine... really, ...what was I saying? Oh, yes, yes, yes, the truth is that Electra helps me a little, but here we are again, having a hard time with so many mouths to feed, and Thanasis eats enough for two Gargantuas. So little sister, what I mean to ask is don't forget us and send a parcel as you did before the war—that has coffee, cocoa, powdered milk, some cookies, chocolates, pepper, maybe a pair of nylons, some clothes you know...thankfully Thanasis brought me a parachute, and I sewed a dress for myself and Zozo...that girl is now 19 and she's relatively short, but she's started to primp herself to look classy. So far, no nice young man has been found to ask for her hand... perhaps that's better because she helps me at home; after all, that's what every adopted daughter does, so many chores show up daily, just the briefs, long johns, undershirts, and panties are one wash, and that's apart from the towels and the tablecloths...if you can send something nice for Zozo, maybe a cardigan, a blouse, you know. I still remember your last parcel before the Occupation, with so many goodies you packed and those shoes I still have. They really served me well, but now they're about to split apart... if you can send a pair of black pumps so I have them as a good pair, the 'sayiz' as you call it over there is my 'sayiz' number seven, we have the same 'sayiz' feet, so better try them on your feet.

Oh, I forgot to tell you we will have an election in a few days; let's see what government will dawn on us; the Communist Party of Greece, they say, will abstain; I don't understand why since they want to govern us why don't they stand for the elections, or do they want to govern only by force, as they do in Russia?

That's the news I had for you, my Antigone, and have compassion for me if I tire you.

Convey my greetings to your husband and kiss the children for me. With love

Eftychia

P.S. If travel starts up again—if they find and defuse the landmines—why don't you take a trip with the ocean liner so we can see you? Now that there is a space in my double bed, we can sleep together like we used to when we were little kids. ∞

In Chicago, April 10, 1946

My beloved sister Eftychia

I received your letter and was happy that you are all well and we are too, but we get exhausted with work. We all work from morning to night, and we have transportation expenses ...Chicago is a huge city with more people than all of Greece, that's for sure. Our jobs aren't close by...the city is big... Johnny has a black worker Jeff who helps him...he does the fruit delivery to homes. Still, I get tired more than everyone because I leave very early...my job is at the fur factory, and it's pretty far away; in the winter, it's so freezing...the roads are slippery, and the lake freezes over so that the hardships with the cold cannot be described. My Georgios will now go to high school to learn more than me, who is not the sharpest knife in the drawer, and I have to struggle. Dimitris, Eleni, and Dimitra are still in primary school. I am preparing a parcel for you and will have all you want and even more...I will include enough nylon stockings...I know you like luxuries, and I will include powders and lipstick in three colors. You'll see them...give one to poor Zozo, a young girl in her prime...but tell me does she have a boyfriend or not yet? Here there's a nice young man who wants to marry a Greek girl; he is one of our own, a Greek from Eastern Rumelia; his father had left when we left as refugees…his name is Thomas, and they call him Tommy. He is 45 years old…he is probably too old for Zozo, but you know many people, you'll think of something…find him a nice girl to send him to marry him off. If you know someone, first of all, send me a recent photo. My dear sister, that's it for now. Perhaps in two years, I'll be able to come to Greece for a month…I miss everyone, but I miss our sun so much. I got so emotional just now that a tear fell on the paper. That's why the ink is smeared. I wrote a few letters on top when it dried because they got blurry my tear spattered the ink. I'm so emotional now; I remember our mother and how that poor thing was doing in the monastery with the fasting. Well, I'm finishing now because I'm tired and sleepy.

I send you my kisses,

Antigone

P.S. If you're impressed that my letter doesn't have many mistakes, it's because Father Efthymios corrected it…he's very educated because he graduated from the Athonite Academy at Karyes.

In Thessaloniki, August 15th, 1946

My dear sister Antigone

We are all right and hope that you are as well. In your previous letter, you wrote to me how tired you are, and I understand that because I am exhausted too, but we are all tired; everyone has a job to do; my Thanasis, of course, now is a sailor serving the country and he is probably in Piraeus, the good for nothing does not send a single letter, we do not have a phone, sister, who can find the money for the phone, and let's say that if you apply for one, it takes up to several years to get approval. Our neighbor Asimina has been waiting for months, and not a word, her husband went to ask the offices of the telephone company, but they paid no attention to him. Your application is waiting in line they told him.

And I am waiting for my turn to get your letter, and I am waiting for that parcel as well, it has not yet come, perhaps it got lost; I will go to the post office to make a fuss, can you believe it...losing the little people's parcels and I say little people because that is what they call us poor folk—little people—others are the gentlemen and the ladies, they are the ones who lived like kings during the Occupation, the black marketeers, oh what we went through you cannot imagine.

Just before the Germans left, their collaborators almost arrested me outside their offices because I went under the rope they had stretched from the wall to the tree at the sidewalk's edge. It prevented people from walking down the sidewalk, and we were forced to go into the street so that any military car or taxis would accidentally hit us; you know, taxi drivers go fast, and they are dangerous; if you see a taxi, step aside.

The situation has calmed down somewhat now, the gunfire has stopped, there have been some trials, and they have caught up with some traitors, but they may also be innocent, as can be seen from what I read, but there will be elections, and we will see who knows what other wonders and signs... A lot of fanaticism. My dear sister, right-wingers and left wingers fight each other like cats and dogs; even during the Occupation, they started fighting... Again, that Papandreou, or his nickname, the "scammer." A flip-flopper, "we believe in Democracy" at one moment, "we believe in Laocracy" the next. I do not understand the difference, but the communists want Laocracy. Whether they mean with or without an election, that's where the issue lies.

I also have pleasant news. I found a bride for the Greek who prefers to marry the devil you know than a foreigner... what did you call him? Tommy, I remembered it.

She is a very nice, hardworking girl; she works as a self-employed tailor. She has no helpers or apprentices; she does it all alone, I tell you. I gave her the address, and she said to me that she would send a photo of herself...if she likes your guy, invite her to go there to get married. She is getting up there of course, at around 40, but she told me that she is 35... but I know she's older than I am...when I was 15 years old she was definitely 20. She was working at the Yfanet textile factory as a worker. Still, she had a talent for sewing; as soon as she collected money, she bought a sewing machine, she bolted from the factory, and now she is well established; I helped her too, of course, and so did Electra, do you know how many clients we have recommended to her?

I had a skirt made for special occasions from the parachute that my Thanasis brought me...she sewed it for me. The leftover fabric I gave her at a discount. Do you understand? I gave her nickels and dimes; where could I find more? But also your guy; he is not young, forty-five-year-old you said that he is...Thomas or Tommy...and if he is hiding a few years like Mary— because she is surely hiding a few—they will get together and match up, and if the matchmaking succeeds, Mary will give me three sovereigns, yes she promised me, so do what you can complete the matchmaking so I can get something out of it too.

Write to me when you send the parcel because that concerns me, and I can't understand why it is taking so long.

Oh, and more news. My Aristides will take exams again in Mathematics, my treasure studies a lot, together with a friend of his, they study in his house, Kostas, they call him, but they smoke a lot, his clothes stink when he comes at night, I'm about ready to explode. I don't smoke, nor did their ungrateful father ever smoke them; he stank for another reason; we've talked about that at another time, so there is no need to return to that ...how they both turned out to be smokers, I don't understand it. And my Thanasis is supposedly an athlete, sure...an athlete. Is that how the athletes are? That's why he plays a goalkeeper and not a forward. Is that why he doesn't have the stamina with so many cigarettes? But he's good, you know, I'll tell you another time but just think...at 18 years old, he was a key player in the PAOM soccer team. Just now, I remembered something else. The parcels must include enough nylon stockings so that I can sell some. They're costly on the market, so I will sell them at a high price to earn something more; you understand me...right? They go crazy for American stuff.

Well, I'm getting to the finale; I have no more paper, don't forget to write me news about the matchmaking and what's going to happen. That's it, and many greetings and kisses to all of you.

With love

Eftychia

PS: For the stamp, I used the same one that you sent me back. It was in good condition, and I erased the stamp mark that was there with the rubber eraser...it was barely visible...it got dirty, as you would remember, a little on the side. What can we do, Antigone? As the teacher Mister Petros used to say—you know the one who tried to put a hand on me and I bit it. "Necessity is the mother of invention," which means people experiencing poverty learn ways to survive. Don't take too long to send the parcel if you didn't send it.

Mary had sent a photo of herself taken in 1935 at a good photography studio, the respected Photo-Lykides Studio. Tommy liked her, but for greater certainty, he decided to come to Thessaloniki to meet the prospective bride. The meeting was set to happen at Eftychia's home. The groom came first. He was well-built without any extra weight, had straight black hair combed with a part and slicked with Brylcreem hair oil, was darker skinned, but not too dark, with perfect skin, and his only drawback was that he wore glasses for his myopia that he wasn't wearing in the photo he had sent.

When Mary came in, she was dressed in a very nice green dress (green is the color of hope). She had thought about the color and chosen it on purpose, hoping to get married. Tommy got up and approached her up close to see her better. He saw then her many wrinkles on the forehead—despite the bangs Mary had deliberately maneuvered for a kind of camouflage—but he also saw the wrinkles in the tired eyes and around the mouth. His only words were - "Ooooh, sorry," and he left without saying goodbye. Mary stood there immobile like a statue, and Eftychia didn't know what to say.

"But what just happened? Why did he leave like that, as if he'd gotten a case of indigestion?" Mary asked.

"Do you need to ask?" Eftychia said, who figured out what had happened. "What photo did you send him, you tease, the one taken a decade ago with the retouchings of Photo Lykides that you even made into a frame? But is it possible? What did you think? That Tommy wouldn't see you up close?"

Mary stood up deeply offended, and after responding in a sharp tone to Eftychia accusing Tommy of being a crude American with no manners, she took her bag and left, totally bewildered and disappointed.

Eftychia was again inconsolable because she had lost the sovereigns she would have earned if the marriage had occurred.

A few days later, Eftychia was talking with Katina, her devoted friend.

"Well, my dear Katina, this Mary is too crazy for words. She sent a picture from when she was a fresh young girl, and she forgot that she is now like a wrinkled raisin. She acted like the parliamentary candidates who, when they get older, take old photos out of their drawers and turn them into posters. What a situation to be in! To let my sister down like this!"

Katina, who could also cunningly throw a few punches, replied to Eftychia:

"All well and good dear Eftychia, but couldn't you find any younger girl? You went and found Mary, who has become like a wrinkled sun-dried raisin. The man would definitely like to have a child to leave his property to since he works so hard there in America. How can she have a child now that she has forgotten what it's like to have a period? It was probably right that Tommy took off like a bat out of hell."

Since that day, Eftychia never came across Mary, who suffered a severe stroke two years later and died. Some evil tongues said that she "died of her sorrow". The funeral notice mentioned the age of 57, so she was much older than even Eftychia thought!

Some collateral damage was that Antigone was also angry because Tommy furiously complained to her about her sister's selection of the bridal candidate. So, she delayed writing to Eftychia and sending her a parcel for quite a while. The first post-Occupation parcel, however, that our Eftychia was waiting for finally came after much delay, simply because, at that time, the ship needed at least 15 days to cross the Atlantic, and customs controls added more delay!

It was a cardboard parcel box with all one could wish for and a letter with instructions:

Eftychia, the green dress is for you, the red is for the girl, don't take it yourself...I tell you because you can be a little insatiable...the heels are for you. I tried them on they are your 'sayiz,' the green shirt give it to Kotsos, it is a large 'sayiz,' the blue shirt give it to Aristides. The nylon stockings are hidden inside the jacket sleeves so customs officers do not see them and make you pay a duty tax. The jacket is for Thanasis. Give two pairs of socks to Electra and two to Zozo. The swimsuit is for you...it also has an apron that is in fashion here. However, you don't care for modest clothes like that, that's what I had, I got it for myself in September on sale, but when I wore it the following summer when we went for a week's vacation, it did not fit me because I had gotten heavier, I always gain weight in the winter. I eat well so I don't get sick in the cold weather here. Enjoy it, so you remember me. The food is all for you. I also put in some boxes of pudding and others for zelo. The zelo boxes are apricot and cherry flavors. You dissolve the powder in warm water and let it get cold in the fritz (I meant to say in you call your icebox). The cocoa has sugar, and it is not bitter, you know. The 'blek pepa' is very good, and 'ooayt pepa' is for soups, so it doesn't look blek on the soup. The baker's chocolate bars are very good at melting when making cakes and pouring them over the cakes. The coffee box contains milk powder, you put a couple of teaspoons in hot water, and it is ready. Here we got used to it in the morning. The chewing gums are lovely and make giant bubbles. Give a few gums to little Spiros, Electra's son. Give him as well some chocolates from the ones in different shapes. I also included two pairs of galoshes for the kids to wear over their shoes when it rains. The rest you can share as you wish."

16

Fishing and Soula

Having ended the German Occupation left behind experiences, memories, pain, misery, exhilaration, and deterioration. Eftychia and her children, Kotsos Barlabas, and Zozo, had survived the ravages of war and the famine of the Nazi German occupation. Eftychia's and her sister's food stockpile significantly helped them overcome that brutal winter of 1942. Meanwhile, her sons grew up, and Eftychia came out of the ordeal of the occupation stronger.

However, the country's tough times were not over as civil war broke out. It was difficult for this conflict to reach inside the city of Thessaloniki, but everyone was experiencing its consequences. There were no Communists in Eftychia's family, so they had nothing to fear. The first unsettled months after liberation had passed. The so-called "people's courts," murders, hostage-takings, executions, and retaliations continued but were declining. However, Eftychia did not omit the relevant warnings: *Don't talk to strangers about politics. You don't know what might happen. Let things calm down first.*

Thanasis selected to serve in the Royal Navy, thinking that by this choice, he would probably be given opportunities for...fishing. After basic training, he was assigned to the Naval Station of Piraeus. While there, on his first leave and wearing his navy uniform, he went to the monastery to visit his grandmother and get her blessing as he had not seen her since the episode with the aviators. He had a strong religious sense, even though he did not always abide by the ten commandments—especially that seventh commandment, *"Thou shalt not commit adultery,"* which he quickly and repeatedly violated.

It was a sunny morning when he arrived at the monastery. He sat on a garden bench outside the monastery's guest house and enjoyed the magnificent view of the rural landscape, just like an artist who enjoys a natural scene he has painted. At one point, he began to think and reminisce about his sins with Soula.

Soula was married to Stavros, a black marketeer and a German collaborator, who was now in prison waiting to be tried. As she was financially comfortable from the profits of the black market, Soula enjoyed many luxuries—she bought new dresses, shoes, furs, jewelry, and colognes, and the only thing she lacked was her husband. The timeline of Thanasis' sin, the adultery he committed with Soula, had a connection to fishing.

Before enlisting in the Royal Navy, Thanasis did various manual labor jobs, and in addition, following his old habit, he would go fishing for sea breams in the Gulf of Thermaikos in his free time. Many housewives in the neighborhood had heard about his remarkable catches and even placed orders with him.

Thanasis, if you go fishing, keep two large seabreams for me from the ones you catch, OK?"

Thanasis, if you don't catch sea bream, put aside a kilo of various fish for me," another told him, who was too stingy to pay for premium class fish.

Soula first met Thanasis one day dressed in a tight dress with a revealing neckline made of a shiny green satin fabric which would shimmer with a reddish tinge, depending on which direction the light fell from. She wore high stiletto heels and wore her hair in a well-coiffed femme fatale look. She knew Thanasis by sight, and one day she bumped into him outside the door of her house while he was returning with his basket full of fish. It would have been around six kilos (over 13 pounds). As fishermen do, Thanasis had also placed the larger fish on top to draw attention to buyers.

"Hey. You caught all these fish?" Soula said, admiring them.

"Yes," Thanasis said, whose invisible antennas were a kind of erotic radar. "Would you like me to give you a sea bream, here…this big one?"

"Oh, let me pay you," Soula said at the time, "but oh…I don't have any money with me. Come up to the house. I live right next door," she told him, looking him boldly straight in the eyes, but then she added hastily. "Wait…no, I don't want the neighbors to misunderstand me, being single at the moment. You'd better come over later when it's dark. I'll be waiting for you. Right here. I live at number 38, on the second floor."

Thanasis immediately caught on. In his mind, her words echoed for a long time: *So that the neighbors don't misunderstand me. I'm alone now. You'd better come later when it's dark. I'll be waiting for you*, and he conjured up dreams in his mind.

Even though he was carrying the heavy basket of fish, he skipped the steps two at a time to the kitchen of his house as he whistled, emptied the basket into the sink, selected two large seabreams for Soula, and put them in a double paper bag so that they would be ready for later. He left the smaller fish in the kitchen sink and took two more sizable sea breams on a tray which he quickly carried up to the fourth floor to sell to Mr. Tasos, who had ordered them.

When he returned, he turned on the water heater and bathed as he predicted possible developments with Soula. When Eftychia saw the little fish in the sink—bogues, mackerel, well-fed sea bream, giltheads, and some small sargos—she started grumbling.

"You scoundrel! So you're selling the big ones and leaving us the catfish?"

"Oh, Mother, stop your nagging. The big ones are an order. I'll be humiliated if I don't deliver them. And by the way, you're insulting me by calling them catfish. I throw the little ones I catch back into the sea to grow and catch them later. I'd never stoop to bringing home catfish. Look here. Four beautiful bream, three giltheads which would almost be sea bream, and the six mackerels are of top size, two per portion. The bogues are for Dad's retsina appetizers. We'll stuff ourselves to bursting."

"And if you hadn't caught the fish, how would you have delivered their order?"

"But you know that your son has his tricks. With my secret weapons, I always achieve good catches there in the breakwater," Thanasis replied, his thoughts on the unique baits he used with the small crabs and thin lines with the minimum bob so as not to scare the suspicious sea bream, which were carefree, preferring to swim in rocky places. Fresh worms were the key so that the cunning bream would be mesmerized.

"Besides, out of the money I make, I'll give you your share," Thanasis added, providing the last irresistible argument. Eftychia calmed down.

After scrutinizing the fish in the washbasin, Zozo set out to clean them, muttering about her fate of being orphaned with a father who was still living. At the same time, Eftychia lay down to read a newspaper, one or two of the abandoned ones on the tram that Barlabas would bring home.

After being freed from his mother's nagging, Thanasis stretched out and started to solve a crossword puzzle in a magazine called *Thesaurus* to distract himself and relax.

It was finally getting dark with the sun playing its last game of chase with the few clouds over Mount Olympus. Thanasis got up, put on his best clothes, combed his wavy, somewhat blondish hair, brushed his teeth well with Kolynos toothpaste, and applied some cologne to his hair, chest, and neck. So, ready and confident, he held the fish in his left hand.

In a while, his heart was pounding somewhat more strongly, especially when he pressed the bell on the door where a sign read **"Stavros Georgiadis. Food Merchant"**. Soula opened the door with a seductive look and a smile full of promises. She looked at him straight in the eyes at first, and after several seconds, her eyes shifted down his broad chest without even for a moment lowering her gaze as more modest females would have done. Thanasis felt the heat flooding him, but he had not forgotten the pretext for his visit. He offered the fish to her, saying, "Here are two well-fed sea breams," but Soula said straight on, "Come in, Thanasis," and whispered very slowly, "Now let's see what fish we'll catch," and grabbed him by the hand, dragging him into the house. Thanasis left the package of fish on a little table next to the front door and managed to say:

"I think you'll like them. I brought you very nice breams."

"But Thanasis, now that I'm all alone, I don't have much appetite for eating. Well, you know, my husband's in jail. His competitors accused him of trading illegally, and they told various lies. I'm just a poor woman, alone and unprotected with my son, who's 14 years old, a susceptible child. He couldn't stand the rumors and went to stay with his grandmother in Veria for a while."

"Nice dress you're wearing," the young man offered, and then suddenly, as he remembered the smell of fish he had just left, he added, "Do you want me to clean your fish so that you don't get yourself dirty?"

"I'm indebted to you, dear Thanasis," Soula then said. "But before you start cleaning them and I roasting them, why don't you sit down for a drink? Come on, sit on the couch, and I'll come over with the drinks."

Thanasis sat on the couch, somewhat restless but certain he would be starting a new affair. With the drinks, they both relaxed and soon let their bodies talk. Soula, who made the first move, kissed wonderfully and, despite being a mother and 34 years old, had the body of a young woman. For his part, Thanasis had no inhibitions, not to mention that he was an erotically inclined man. *If this mistress is also a good... cook,* he thought this in a flash, *at least for a while, we'll have an exceptional time.*

As we've said, Soula was one of a kind in kissing. As for the rest, and even if she did not perform as well, Thanasis had the drive and the patience...to teach her! But she was a master in making love, and Thanasis gained something... from her coaching!

Our sailor was reminiscing about these and similar experiences when his pleasant daydreaming was interrupted by the arrival of his grandmother wearing her habit. She greeted him joyfully.

"How are you doing, my dear child Thanasis? The Abbess told me you'd come, but I couldn't leave my ministry immediately. Well, how you've changed! You also left a mustache to grow. You look older in your navy uniform. It's been quite a while since you lived in the monastery and hid the English aviators two years ago—why am I saying two—almost three years have passed since then!"

She continued:

"My gosh, you have no idea how you almost got us in trouble. They took the Abbess for interrogation and were about to torture her, but the Metropolitan bishop, who had studied in Germany, intervened. He managed to convince the head of the Germans that the monastery wasn't involved in the case and that the rebels had helped the English to escape. However, you scared the daylights out of us at the time. Our holy Mother protected us...Her grace is great. But tell me, how are Eftychia and Electra doing? Is it true that Electra remarried? Does she get along well with her husband? He's a dentist, as she wrote to me, and you should go and take care of your teeth now that we have a dentist in the family. Tell me about your mother. How does she cope with your cranky father? Does he still beat her? Do tell her to obey[10] her husband, to be patient even if he's wrong, and put aside any ideas of divorce. Even Electra's divorce is a burden on my conscience!"

At first, Thanasis did not know how to respond. After giving hasty answers, he also gave her the money that Electra sent her for the convent. His grandmother took it and gave it to the monastery guest mistress to give it to the Abbess, and then she turned to her grandson, saying:

"Would you like to confess, my boy? Papa-Yannis, who is an excellent spiritual man, is here today. He has a line of people waiting, but he will make time to take your confession because I'll ask him to."

"To confess? But I don't feel that need now. I don't intend to take communion. I will sit for a while longer, you know, to ..." Thanasis did not know how to excuse himself. He felt somewhat trapped. The truth is that his religious sensitivities compelled him to confess, but he was ashamed of the adultery he had committed for three months with Soula until her husband was finally released from prison.

---

[10] "Obedience" is a term common in monasteries and is an obligation of the monks or nuns to the orders of the administration of each monastery (the abbot or abbess). In Orthodox Christianity a wife's first obedience is always to God, but in all other things she must submit.

However, he found himself in a difficult position, did not dare to refuse, and finally agreed to confess.

"Well, all right Grandma. I'll go to confession," he said, surrendering to her pressure.

"Come with me now. Let's go see the spiritual father," his grandmother said, grabbing him by the hand to guide him inside.

They waited for a while for his turn, which was approaching, so his grandmother left him alone with his thoughts and went off because she had some ministry to fulfill.

Shortly, Thanasis found himself alone with the confessor in a small room just beyond the entrance of the church on the right. There were various icons of male and female saints all around who all seemed to be looking at him sternly, especially the male saints who stared at him somberly. *Not even a single one is smiling*, Thanasis thought, and with relief, turned his gaze to a cross that was hung on the wall behind a small armchair on which the spiritual father was sitting. He sat in a chair a short distance from Papa-Yiannis, the priest.

Thanasis could remember no other sin. Some bullies he beat up after a soccer match a while back had attacked him first, so he was not to blame. *Only Christ would turn the other cheek for a second punch,* Thanasis thought. *I simply repelled a blow attempted by one of them and gave him a direct blow at the base of his nose, after which he fell completely unconscious, while the other guy, when the sniveling rascal was sneaking toward me from the side, I threw him a volley kick into his abdomen, and he folded, collapsing.*

But the affair with Soula was a terrible sin.

"I got involved with a married woman Father," he confessed, feeling devastated.

"This sin is serious, my child," Papa-Yiannis said in a paternal tone. "It is the seventh commandment you have broken."

This was followed by his short pep talk with admonitions, and right after that came the punishment of purification. "Thou shalt fast thirty days and make thirty penances every morning for three months. And look, keep away from the women who are betrothed to their husbands who, in some cases, are the devils themselves transformed."

"But Father, I serve in the royal navy. I eat at the naval base. How can I fast?" Thanasis asked, overwhelmed at the idea that he would fast for a month.

"Fine, then don't fast, but thou shalt repent daily for a year," Papa Yiannis said scornfully. "And thou shalt observe the fasts of Pascha (Easter), the fifteen days of August—the Dormition fast and the Christmas fast when you'll be discharged. And see to it to get married to calm your passions."

Starting on that day, Thanasis began to systematically do thirty repentances every morning, making a pleading wish. Finally, after a year—as if from momentum—he continued his repentance. Who knows, he thought, what else will happen to me with women? Let me do the repentances in advance.

As for his getting married, despite the urging of Papa Yiannis, that took a long time, and it is a rather long story about how, where, and when it happened!

17

Koko the pet

Animals always played an essential role in the life of Eftychia and the Barlabas family. Usually, one or two dogs lived with the family. Over the years, various other animals appeared, such as rabbits, hedgehogs, canaries, and a cat (strangely sharing space in harmony with the dog).

In her courtyard, Eftychia used to keep hens in a chicken coop that held a dozen of them, but at the end of the German occupation, not a single feather was left. Her last hen had been stolen by strangers just before the Germans left. No one ever learned who the thief was, nor was the hen ever found. Apparently, it must have been eaten in the blink of an eye due to the hunger still prevailing in Thessaloniki.

Aristides promised to give his mother a hen as a gift when he got his first wages from the shop where he'd been hired a few days earlier as a commercial employee in the market. The young man got the job thanks to his Aunt Electra, who interceded and begged Zizi, the wife of the owner of a large clothing shop. Zizi was her client at the hat shop, and they also played cards and, specifically, pinochle every Wednesday night.

Electra would take her son Akis to these card parties to throw up a smokescreen to prevent her husband Apostolos from discovering that she was playing cards. Akis found it fascinating to crawl under the table and gaze at women's legs.

At one such card party, Zizi mentioned that an employee of her husband's had suddenly died, and they were now looking for a new employee with appropriate qualifications. He had to be good-looking and well-spoken. Electra immediately thought of her nephew and suggested that they hire him. He had just finished the six-year high school and was looking for a job. Aristides was indeed suitable for the job and was immediately hired.

In a month, Holy Week would begin, and Aristides fulfilled his promise to give his mother a hen as a gift. Only it was cheaper to bring home a little chick instead of a hen. This chick was raised in the care of the Barlabas family and, over time, grew into a beautiful brown hen. In the beginning, Eftychia would leave her on the kitchen balcony. Soon they all realized that their hen, growing up inside a home and close to people who loved her, was highly sociable.

Whenever she'd see a human, she would cluck her greetings, or when the kitchen balcony door was open, she would hop in and cluck her good mornings. Even though Zozo would get upset because she was always the "lucky" one to clean the poop that the hen shamelessly left on the tiles, Zozo was the one who finally gave the hen a name. She named her Koko, and this name was accepted not just by the humans but also by Koko herself. When they called her, she would hop over to them, and with a leap, she'd climb up to the kitchen sofa where someone was usually sitting. Aristides, who had a weakness for her, would call her to sit next to him, caress her, and she would cluck contentedly. The dog—the clever Bibo, son of Clara, who Eftychia kept, so she now had two dogs—strangely was not jealous of Koko and wagged his tail with joy whenever he saw her. Clara, however, was probably jealous and did not get too involved with the newcomer. But when Bibo approached the hen too closely, she would move her beak menacingly, so like the smart dog that he was, he kept a safe distance, although he would have loved to play with her.

Once, Koko fell ill with diarrhea. Eftychia had come to realize that the situation had gone on too long with Koko getting in her way. One day her feet got tangled up, and she fell in an attempt not to step on either the hen or Bibo. The hen's diarrhea was the final straw. Zozo had also grumbled for days as she did not appreciate the droppings on the kitchen balcony. So, Koko eventually found herself alone in the old chicken coop of the courtyard.

At that time, Andreas Dermatas, a butcher, was staying on the ground floor. He was a burly forty-five-year-old who had made a lot of money as a black marketeer during the Occupation. This guy tried to befriend every influential man. Various remarks were heard among which was that he had denounced a partisan to the Germans and was now a police informant.

Dermatas had bought the ground floor which he turned into a shop. Behind the back of the kitchen of this ground-floor unit, there was a patio door from which you could exit into a small, paved courtyard, which looked like a sizeable ground-floor balcony. The rest of the courtyard was plain dirt where two trees stood, and a third one which was completely parched.

Koko soon recovered from the diarrhea. On the one hand she was upset by her eviction to the courtyard, but on the other hand she felt much freer, and she'd strut back and forth clucking. In fact, quite shamelessly, she sometimes fouled the tiled area of the courtyard of Dermatas, who since that episode had apparently decided to exterminate her. At first, he quarreled with Eftychia who lived on the first floor right above the ground floor.

"Hey! You up there. Is the hen yours? Come and collect it if you don't want to find it slaughtered."

"My dear Mr. Andreas, what's your problem with Koko? This is a domesticated hen. She is like a human."

"Humans don't drop their shit wherever they are," replied Dermatas, walking back inside because a customer had come.

Koko even soiled the tiles of the courtyard a few times. Eftychia would stalk the scene and, when she noticed, she would send Zozo to clean up the droppings. But sometimes Dermatas witnessed it, and he would clean up before Zozo got there once again complaining about the situation.

One Sunday, Aristides came down to the courtyard to feed Koko. But the butcher got wind of him, and after they exchanged sharp words with each other, Dermatas finally slapped Aristides hard, who at that time was a well-developed youth, but was still quite weak due to his innate physical build and from the hunger of the Occupation. Blushing red, Aristides kept his rage in control and backed off. After all, what could he do to confront that beastly butcher? He ran off and went up to his house, embarrassed.

In the meantime, Dermatas took one of his well-sharpened knives, caught the hen trapped in the chicken coop, and quickly dispatched her. He then placed the dead chicken on one of the butcher's papers, took her to Eftychia's top step at her apartment, and left it outside her door. Then he pressed on her doorbell with force and went downstairs before the housewife could open the door.

Zozo opened the door, and shocked by the sight of the bloody and decapitated hen, she immediately called out to Eftychia, who suffered an emotional breakdown when she saw Koko slaughtered.

"There's going to be a big ruckus with this butcher…his shop will be covered in blood and sand! I'll be damned if I don't do damage to the black marketeer who should have already been in prison. Oh! I'm getting dizzy; my head hurts!" Eftychia shouted, and lay down, almost fainting in her bed. "Oh, my head!" she kept crying. "My head's going to break!"

From the apartment next door, through the lacy curtains of her kitchen window stood Mrs. Asimina who was watching the courtyard events when Dermatas had butchered the hen in the blink of an eye as if he was slicing feta cheese. She ran over to see what was happening with Eftychia.

"Oh, my head's going to break, Asimina; I'm sure my blood pressure has risen," Eftychia moaned.

"I'll bring the blood pressure gauge to measure it for you," Asimina said, who had been hypertensive for years and had come into possession of her own sphygmomanometer since her uncle, her father's brother, who was a doctor, had died. In three minutes, Asimina was wrapping the sphygmomanometer around Eftychia's arm.

"Your pressure is way up," she said, "but I'll count it again for you to be sure. Be quiet," she said to those who had gathered around Eftychia.

"How much is it now?" Eftychia asked.

"Twenty-two, the systolic one, and nine, the diastolic," Asimina replied. "You have to take a pill."

At that moment, Thanasis was heard whistling as he came in from outside.

"What's going on? What's the matter?" Thanasis asked when he saw Zozo putting a wet cloth with cold water on Eftychia's forehead.

"He slaughtered Koko, that black marketeer!" Eftychia whimpered. "And now my head's about to break open. I'm going to have a stroke or something. May he rot in hell, the scoundrel! How was the animal to blame? He slaughtered it out of his wickedness...the sadist...the rat, the...black marketeer... the brute... the BEAST!"

"He slapped me good," Aristides said, blushing in shame who, by revealing what happened to him, was hoping for his brother's reaction.

Thanasis saw little but understood all. Without further ado, he flew down the few steps in three strides and arrived at the butcher shop, angrily demanding answers from the butcher.

"Hey, you! What did you do? My mother is about to die!" he shouted at the butcher at a distance of a few feet.

"I didn't do anything. She asked me to butcher your chicken," the butcher responded mockingly.

"Who do you think you're conning? You—a black marketeer," Thanasis responded, flushed in rage. "My mother is about to die, and you're mocking on top of everything else!" And then he yelled out a curse that he had learned in the Navy.

Instead of answering, the butcher grabbed a hook he used to hang meats with and threw it towards Thanasis, who at the last moment jumped aside, thus avoiding the hook, which instead crashed into the wall shattering it, resulting in a significant amount of cement collapsing on the floor.

Eftychia's son approached the husky, beefy butcher menacingly with his arms ready for battle, but then Dermatas grabbed a second hook in his hand to sling at him. But with his left hand, the muscular Thanasis blocked the blow being attempted by the butcher, while with the edge of his right hand, he managed a whack on the ear of the beast that was threatening him, causing a cut deep enough to flood his head with blood.

Thanasis thought *that was for my mother's satisfaction.* Then he gave him a kick in the shin. *And that was for the memorial service for Koko,* as he used to say every time he narrated the story.

"Ouch! Ouch! You killed me, motherfucker! You've killed me, you asshole!" The butcher moaned in pain. He did not know whether to grab his leg or his ear. But now that Thanasis had calmed down, he turned around quickly, and vaulting the few steps three by three, he went up to see how his mother was doing.

Dermatas' yelling triggered the apartment building residents to come out to see what was happening. Even Eftychia came out, pleased, but also with concern on her face as she witnessed the butcher's sorry state. Completely soaked in blood, Dermatas was gripping his ear. Embarrassed, that giant of a man, who had encountered his superior in strength for the first time, initially went to the neighborhood pharmacy. But the pharmacist told him that his ear was in bad shape, had a deep cut at its base under the hair, and had to be stitched. He placed some gauze on it and tightly tied it around his head so he would not bleed.

Dermatas rode his motorcycle to the Red Cross with his head wrapped, whether he felt like it or not. The First Aid was in a small building next to the harbor entrance. There the doctor stitched the wound, having previously been surprised to learn that the damage to the ear had been done with a single blow from a hand and was not the result of a blow with any board or iron.

"But why did they hit you?" the doctor asked when he finished stitching, tying off the fifth stitch.

"Where do I begin, doctor? It's about someone who's crazy. I butchered his hen, and he cut off my ear. Can you imagine if he'd gotten me on the neck? He would've slaughtered me without even using a knife," the butcher said, who was terrified at just the thought alone. You see, he knew something…about slaughtering!

After the doctor had finished putting on the bandages, Dermatas again rode his motorcycle directly to the Police Precinct #3, where he had several acquaintances. He quickly found one of them and they sat side by side like classmates in the Gymnasium and drew up a complaint against Thanasis.

Very soon, a police officer came by the Barlabas house and left a summons for Thanasis Barlabas:

"Come to the police station about your case."

As soon as he saw the summons, Thanasis immediately understood. *This beefer, the fat butcher, is looking for trouble.*

Thanasis decided to remain indifferent, and he spread the news through friends by sounding off in the café, saying that if Dermatas filed a complaint against him or if he were to be bothered by the police, mayhem would follow.

"I have a clean record. I helped the British during the Occupation. I also have a certificate sent to me by the British Foreign Office. I have served in the Royal Navy more than my allotted time. I am innocent. Dermatas slaughtered our hen and, in addition, threw an entire hook at me as he was bent on killing me, and to defend myself, I hit him once! I can't help it if my hand is like iron. He should've been careful and everyone pay attention, not just Dermatas but also some little guys in the department yesterday who were his friends from his days of ratting. I have no one to fear," he would say to anyone listening, and loud enough for well-wishers to hear and take back to the police station and his injured opponent.

But Dermatas wasn't having any of it. He went to the security commander, the famous police officer Nikos Mouschountis, (who was also his customer), and made the relevant complaints to him. He also had a feisty shrewd lawyer pushing the case.

The commander decided to resolve the matter. Thanasis' refusal to appear at the department was disobedience to state authority. The physical damage to Dermatas' ear was quite severe. He had to act in such a way as to satisfy the butcher and for Thanasis to get away with it easily and quickly. He liked Thanasis because they had lived in neighboring houses in the past, and he had watched Eftychia's struggles in coping with so many misfortunes and with a husband who was more of a burden on her than a mate. Moreover, lately, Mouschountis had been playing backgammon with Thanasis frequently at the premises of the soccer club, which was almost directly across from the police security offices on Prince Nikolaos Street (as Polonia Street had been renamed after the return of King George II).

So, he arranged to go to the club premises at a time when a man informed him that Thanasis was playing backgammon. He got there, sat at the next table over from Thanasis, ordered a coffee, and glanced at the game. When the backgammon game was over, he invited Thanasis to play a game against him for five points, and as soon as the game ended very quickly—5-2 in favor of Thanasis—he leaned into his ear and told him that he wanted to help him with his problem.

"Let's go for a walk to my office, and you'll see that everything will be arranged," he told him with a wink and added. "Don't be afraid. I'm on your side..."

In a short time, they found themselves alone in the office.

"Thanasis, you almost killed the man. What did you hit him with?"

"With my hand!"

"Are you kidding me!? And you did that much damage to his ear?"

"He tried to hit me with a big hook. If I hadn't hit him, I'd be dead," Thanasis retorted, defending himself. "I didn't think I put any particular strength into it. It's just that my hand is, how do I say this…it's heavy!"

"That's fine, but no one else will believe that you did such damage to the man and that it was done with your hand. He almost had his whole ear ripped off, and his eardrum also broke. Besides, there are no witnesses, so the only sure thing is that Dermatas almost lost his ear, and now he's still suffering vertigo and hasn't worked a week."

"He should've been more careful," Thanasis countered. "My mother almost had a stroke when she saw our chicken slaughtered. The fatso had it coming to him."

"I'm not saying you shouldn't have defended yourself, but the point is that he filed a lawsuit and papers are papers. He hired a lawyer, and it'll open up a can of worms."

"What do you propose I should do?" Thanasis replied, who figured that Mouschountis wanted to help him.

"I suggest you give him a little money as compensation because you hit him, which means that he hasn't worked a week."

"Agreed," Thanasis said half-heartedly.

"Wait for me to call him," said the commander, and gave instructions to a police officer. "But let's go to the third police precinct because that's where he filed the complaint."

Soon Dermatas entered the commander's office. Besides the gauze turban on his head, a large bruise that descended from the ear to the neck revealed his plight.

"The situation is very tangled," the commander said. You, Mr. Dermatas, butchered somebody's hen and hurled a crowbar or hook—what it was, I don't know—and you nearly killed Thanasis, and you, young man, gave him what could have been a deadly Japanese body blow to the ear. You can sue each other. But what am I saying here? You've already done what you've done. He looked knowingly at Thanasis as he opened a briefcase and shuffled some papers.

"Here's the lawsuit of Dermatas against Barlabas, and here's the lawsuit against A. Dermatas. You're both going to get badly messed up in this. You'll be eaten alive by the lawyers. These cases with adjournments, interruptions, and appeals take a long time and are not in the interest of either of you. I propose that Thanasis give a sum for compensation and that the lawsuits be dropped."

"I agree," the butcher mumbled.

"How much do you want, Mr. Dermatas?" the commander asked.

"Ten gold coins," Dermatas replied without hesitation, and his eyes glittered.

"I won't give ten. I'll give three," Thanasis said.

"Ten not budging," Dermatas retorted.

"Give seven Thanasis," the commander said. "Let's finish up. I have other work to do."

"Here, take four to end this story," Thanasis said. And he took four sovereigns out of his pocket. All of them were sitting in the right pocket of his pants as payment for old car tires that he had sold for a significant profit.

"Let's do it," Dermatas said, who saw that Thanasis had no more sovereigns. "Let's end this."

Dermatas took the four gold coins and left satisfied.

Thanasis thanked the commander, and he also left. He put his hand in his left pocket and rattled some coins. He took them out while he was still on the staircase of the police precinct and counted them visually. Six. Three of the ten coins he had received were the Englishman's, and three would have stayed with him, but at least he had cleared himself. He had deliberately put the four gold coins in the other pocket, only to make it appear that he had just those during the negotiation with the compensation for the injured man.

He went home and told Eftychia everything. She gave him a jar of candied sweet orange peels to take to the commander with her thanks. Thanasis, who had begun to solve a crossword puzzle delayed taking the jar to the commander by an hour in order to unwind. Eftychia started nagging.

"Come on, Thanasis, it's already dark, the commander will leave. Take the jar to him finally. The man took pains to save you from trouble."

"Alright already mother! I'm going," Thanasis said, and he set out with the jar in hand.

When he arrived outside the commander's office, he almost bumped into Dermatas, who was leaving. Upon entering the office, Thanasis gave him the jar, and in turn, the commander gave Thanasis a large package and told him to give it to his mother. Thanasis did not immediately know what it was, but it seemed to him to be heavy and cold, so he suspected something. He thanked him and took it, quickly running home full of curiosity. When they opened it, they saw that inside the well-wrapped package were ribs, a leg of lamb, some beef steaks, a large chunk of veal, two kilos of ground meat, and many sausages.

The commander, kindhearted as he was, knew that Eftychia had a hard time making ends meet and that she had taken her goddaughter into her home for many years as a stepdaughter, as well as the fact that Thanasis' money had been depleted, and not wanting to accept the gifts of Dermatas personally, gave the meat to Thanasis!

In the Barlabas family home, a feast began.

"Our cholesterol will go up," Aristides said mockingly.

"We will drink to Dermatas' health," their mother said. "We're going to burst from the meat," Zozo said.

But Eftychia's face went dark when all this was said and done. "We have a problem," she said. "How will we preserve so much meat? It doesn't even fit in our small refrigerator."

"Thanasis should take some to Aunt Virginia," Zozo suggested.

"Don't worry, Mother," Thanasis said. "I'll take some to Virginia, but I'm thinking of giving some meat and minced meat to some acquaintances...poor girls! Anyone with two shirts should share with the one who has none—isn't that what they taught us in the monastery?"

The following week Thanasis played backgammon with the commander and lost on purpose. The loser would gift a Tsitsanis album to the winner, and our hero knew that the commander was a collector of rebetika records from when Metaxas banned rebetika music as songs of the underworld. It was a way to give him a gift and the big guy to accept it.

18

The Lavatory Basin

It was past midnight, and Eftychia was getting ready to go to bed. The rest of the family members—humans and animals—had surrendered to sleep for a while. She delayed lying down because she was knitting a sweater for Aristides and wanted to finish it. The next day would be her child's birthday, and it was a good opportunity to give him a gift without her elder son, Thanasis, getting jealous. So, when she finished knitting, she took out a pastry wrapper she had saved for the occasion, wrapped the sweater, tied a colorful ribbon around it, and placed it on the table. She put on her nightgown and proceeded to the lavatory as she usually did for one last visit.

Shortly, in the quiet of the night, a sound was heard as if a tap was running into a full bucket. Eftychia turned on the light to look at the lavatory basin. Indeed, it was what she suspected. The water wasn't draining. For days now, she had been watching it. Yes, it was not drawing well, and the water was not draining as quickly as it should. The dirty mess floated for several minutes, descending towards the drain opening slowly while gurgling noises sounded like the basin was ... a roaring animal. She let out a moan. *Oh, dear. We have a problem; tomorrow is Sunday; where do we find a plumber,* she thought. *In any case, we will do something. We won't drown in shit,* she mumbled and went to lie down.

In the morning, Barlabas, who always woke up first, went to the lavatory, used it as usual, and pulled the chain pull. The basin filled to the edge, and then the water level began to descend but slowly. Realizing the problem, Barlabas shouted out in a loud voice:

"Eftychia, this damned basin is plugged up."

"So what?" Eftychia replied. "Why are you telling me? Am I a plumber?"

"Fix it and fast."

"Hunh? So now I'm going to get mixed up in your shit. Lay off."

"Anyway, I told you," Barlabas replied, and began getting dressed, to go to the café. Eftychia once again felt that she had no man. She was both mother and father alone and always had to take responsibility for everything.

That good for nothing, she thought to herself; *if he thinks I'm going to fix the lavatory basin, he's only fooling himself.*

In a while she felt the need to pee, so she went to the toilet holding a small basin. She peed holding the basin between her legs and emptied it into the small drainage hole located in a corner of the floor. She also poured a basin of water into the hole and all was well. But the problem became more acute as time went by. Over the next two hours they had all gone in to use the toilet—Thanasis, Aristides and Zozo. In fact, the latter avoided sitting on the toilet and went to the adjacent apartment of Mrs. Asimina since the dirty water had reached just a tiny distance from the rim of the toilet basin.

Eftychia gave the finished sweater to Aristides, wished him a Happy Birthday but without a lot of fuss, hugs, and kisses. Then, she asked Thanasis to go up to the attic where she stored relatively useless things, and to look for a chamber pot they had put up there years ago. Thanasis brought the pot down and Eftychia gathered them all around, except Barlabas of course, and with a determined voice announced:

"Look here. I don't have money for plumbers and toilet basins. That stingy man, your father, will have to deal with the toilet basin and dig deep into his pocket to pay. Until this happens, you'll have to go to the public toilets at Aristotle Square for shitting. You will pee in the chamber pot and then you will empty it into the drainage hole on the floor. Let's see what that selfish useless man will do. That loser...who married me, an innocent young girl, just to torture me."

Upon saying this, Eftychia turned her back on them so as not to reveal to them a tear that began to flow down her cheek. The difficult life she had suffered until then had of course strengthened her, but from time to time she would become discouraged.

Barlabas returned at noon to have lunch and went to the toilet where he peed into the congested basin. He held his breath because the stench coming from the toilet bowl was unbearable. He then left panting and sat down at the table to eat, seemingly indifferent. His wife, who had cooked bean soup, placed black bread, some green olives, anchovies and pickled cabbage for salad on the table. "Five olives each and two anchovies," she warned them, "just so that we don't have any misunderstandings."

The food was delicious, and Eftychia and the children gobbled it up, praising its taste. Barlabas ate it without saying a word, with a strange sour expression on his face. This time Eftychia had deliberately added extra salt and pepper to his dish. The children knew about it and looked at each other, winking and furtively giggling. Barlabas either pretended he didn't understand, or, in fact, he really did not understand.

In the afternoon after a nice nap, he needed to use the toilet. Opening the door, he saw a toilet basin whose filthy contents had reached its rim. Others had preceded him. Barlabas cursed loudly.

"Cocksucker! Is this my home or a cesspool?"

He looked around for Eftychia, but she had skedaddled to Asimina's sitting room and told her everything about her toilet problem while they were drinking their demitasses of coffee.

Barlabas continued to grumble and curse to himself. He peed once again marking the sewer hole, but not always successfully, got dressed and went out to the café. He played cards with some old friends of his and lost. He was distracted. He did not remember the cards. His mind was on the backed-up toilet. Before leaving for home, he acted wisely by visiting the café's toilet. In the past it used to seem dirty to him. Now it seemed to him as if it were a luxury hotel toilet.

Half an hour later he arrived home brooding. It was summer and the smell from the toilet immediately hit him in the nostrils. He let out a growl, as he was used to doing, and in his growly voice he shouted: "Eftychia, what's going on here?"

He heard no answer. He went to the bedroom. There was no one there. He went to the other rooms. Nobody was home. *So, what's going on?* he thought.

He went to the kitchen to look for food and found the tin can with a few beans. The food wasn't in the icebox as it should have been. He put bean soup on a plate and sat down to eat, brooding and lacking an appetite. With the first spoonful, he felt like spitting it out. Forgotten in the pot and it being summer, the bean soup had gone sour. He ate some pickled cabbage, olives, and dried bread. He turned on the radio and found that it wasn't working.

"But what's going on in this shithole of a house? Has everything broken down?" he growled. He took off his clothes and lay down to sleep. Irritated as he was, it was difficult for him to fall asleep. But he was also bothered by the stench coming from the lavatory.

He had forgotten the half-open lavatory door, so he got up, closed the door, and returned to bed. Just as he managed to fall asleep, he heard the buzzing sound of a mosquito in his ear. He immediately woke up and turned on the light.

Where is it? I'll kill it, he thought. He searched for it everywhere. Finally, he spotted it sitting high on the ceiling.

He got up, took a hard pillow, and threw it toward the ceiling. The pad hit the mosquito, but in falling, it also hit the bare lightbulb that was hanging from the electric cord. Then what happened scared him. BANG! The bulb burned out, and at the same time, the house was plunged into darkness because the electric fuse had blown out. Barlabas was now cursing all that's sacred, his dead relatives,

Eftychia, and his misfortune. He finally fell asleep after much effort, delay, twisting, and turning. At around five in the morning, he felt he needed to urinate. He got up in the dark and went down the hallway. As he was holding the wall for safety, he unintentionally stepped on Clara's tail. She had chosen to sleep on the corridor tiles because the air current made it the most excellent place to sleep during hot days. Instinctively, the dog turned her head and bit his foot, making a dog-like howl of pain. Barlabas followed with his shouts.

"Ouch! Ouch! The old dog bit me! I'll set poison bait tomorrow. That insolent, ungrateful animal bit me! Me, the one who feeds it my leftovers?! This bitch Clara but Eftychia too—another bitch—will pay for it."

He searched in the dark for iodine, and it seemed to him that he found it in a cupboard where the medicines were and applied some to his leg. But somehow the smell of the drug was strange. It had a totally different smell and wasn't like normal iodine.

"They've spoiled everything nowadays," he thought because it didn't have that characteristic smell of iodine.

Just then, the rooster they had on the balcony to butcher for the next holiday started crowing.

This is not a home. It's a zoo, he thought, and began counting the animals that lived in their homes with people. Two dogs, one turtle, one rooster, one hen, one rabbit, and one canary—a collection of seven animals. In the depths of his brain, it seemed to him as if he heard the voice of Eftychia saying to him: *And one of you, so all the animals together.... make eight.*

Barlabas was in a state of fury. As soon as it dawned, he looked at his leg and found it covered in blood. When he took a better look, he found it wasn't blood but a red stain. That's when he realized that in the dark, instead of iodine, he had applied red nail polish. Regretting that he had blamed iodine earlier that night, he kept on swearing, sometimes silently and sometimes out loud. He got dressed and went to find a plumber.

There was a plumber nearby whose shop was located just below his apartment building. He went there, knocked at the door of the shop, but no one answered. So, he waited outside the closed shop for half an hour until the plumber showed up, who was dressed in his suit like a groom returning from Sunday liturgy with his wife and daughter.

"I need you for a job!"

"What? Today? Sunday?"

"You need to change my toilet bowl. It's urgent."

"Is it broken or clogged?

"Why? Does it matter?"

"Of course, if it's broken it's cheaper. If it's clogged, I put in the bill an allowance for "dirty work".

"It's clogged."

"A lot?"

"Enough."

"What quality toilet bowl do you want?"

"The cheapest."

"Clay, enameled or porcelain?"

"I want the cheapest."

"Well then clay it is."

"The last thing I'd do in a rented house would be to put a luxury basin! How much will all the work cost?"

"As much as the basin, the tank, the cement, and my labor. Don't be afraid. I won't empty your pockets."

"Then let's go."

As soon as they entered the house, Barlabas kicked the dog who was barking. With her tail between the legs Clara hid under a bed. The plumber approached the toilet.

"Wow, wow! What's going on here, dude? How many days has it been clogged?"

"Hmmm...since yesterday."

"What do you mean yesterday...are you kidding me? Hey! There's shit here to the top. I am not taking it on!"

"What do you mean you're not taking it on?"

"Yeah. I don't work on lavatory basins filled to the top."

"But you said clogged and how much you'd charge."

"I said, clogged. Not filled to the top! Empty the basin, and then I'll work on it. I'm leaving now. Call me when you're ready. Anyway, I need to change my clothes too."

Barlabas spit into the basin cursing. He took the chamber pot and carefully began to empty the liquids by pouring them into the hole of the drain but there were also solid impurities that would not easily drain down the hole. So then, he took a wooden stick and stirred the contents of the hole, allowing the revolting liquids to slowly go down. He then added new material with the chamber pot. In an hour he had managed to empty the toilet basin except for its lowest section.

Now it's only clogged Barlabas thought, and he went to fetch the plumber.

The plumber removed the old basin, found that there were accumulated papers that had created the problem (newspapers at that time), poured down plenty of water to wash the pipeline well and replaced it with the new basin, applying the necessary cement.

"Don't sit on the toilet basin for the next 24 hours so that the cement thickens well," he reminded Barlabas while he was taking the money. "And look. Don't toss papers into the basin if you don't want it to get clogged again."

"Yeah yeah…I know," Barlabas replied, who felt guilty because he was the one throwing the papers into the basin despite Eftychia's nagging. As soon as he remembered his wife, he began to worry about her absence. His wife Eftychia, his "wife" so to speak, was nowhere to be found.

Meanwhile, the "runaway wife" was staying in a village outside Thessaloniki where some of her distant relatives and good friends lived. It was still summertime; besides that, she felt comfortable enough to go there and to be accommodated for a few days. Zozo went to her aunt, taking advantage of the opportunity to see her sister as well. The boys had accompanied their mother on Sunday, played with their cousins, went swimming in the sea together, and on Monday, the brothers took the first train home and returned to their jobs.

Late on Monday afternoon after work, Aristides went and found Thanasis, and they ate *souzoukakia* (Greek-style meatballs with tomato sauce) at Rogotis' snack bar in Eleftherias Square and then went for coffee at the corner café called "Poseidon" at the harbor. There, Thanasis played, or rather "gave a backgammon lesson" to a regular patron who bragged that he was a great backgammon player. As always, Aristides was watching Thanasis play. When the game ended, Thanasis took the prize from his opponent, who had agreed to pay five drachmas in winnings. Thanasis gave one drachma to Aristides.

"Take it. You bring me luck, and I win when you sit next to me."

"Next time, if you don't give me two out of five, I won't sit with you," Aristides replied in jest.

In the evening, they returned home, both quite tired. When Thanasis found that there was no electricity in the house, he fixed the burnt-out fuse on the electric panel by fitting a thin wire rod. Then he found that a lightbulb was burnt out and replaced it with a new one.

Finally, he took into his hands the radio—which, at the behest of his mother, he had temporarily neutralized—opened the back with a screwdriver and screwed back tightly a connector he had loosened. So, the radio began to work.

As for the much-coveted lavatory basin? It had been replaced with a brand new, sparkling clean, functional, but ceramic one. The smell was gone. The house was bright and filled with electric current. The next day, Eftychia would also return triumphantly.

Aristides came out of the house and went to the telegraph office. He sent a telegram to his mother in just three words to save money:

"LAVATORY BASIN FIXED STOP"

Barlabas returned in the evening and looked around for Eftychia. His house seemed empty without its head. Yes, it was strange, but Barlabas did feel lonely without his wife at home. He heard a voice whispering to him: *Eftychia is the leader. And what am I?* he wondered. *You're the trash,* his wife's voice came to him from afar.

The next day, Eftychia arrived all cheerful and refreshed, pinkish from the sun, with a bag full of grapes. They were black muscat grapes of the kind her Aristides liked. She hid half of the clusters in her wardrobe.

Let ungrateful people not see everything, she reflected, thinking about Barlabas but also about Thanasis, who was insatiable for food. *If they eat a lot, they might get sick with diarrhea,* she murmured softly. *But in this matter as well, we don't have a problem any longer. After a lot of effort...the lavatory basin has finally been corrected!*

222

19

The Soccer Coach

Eftychia looked at her face in the mirror as she was curling her hair with a heated curling iron. After that was done, she curled her eyelashes with a special tool and applied lipstick and some blush on her cheeks. She looked at herself in the mirror for the last time. She literally glowed in beauty. That day was unique because she would be meeting a new paramour, a veteran soccer player of the team called "Glory of Thessaloniki" who had now become a coach on the team her firstborn son had signed up for and was training for.

But let us take things from the start.

Eftychia's son was an exceptionally skillful goalkeeper. After three months of training, he became the team's first substitute at the age of only 18. At that time, each team would draft eleven players. The substitutes simply watched the game from the sidelines. Thanasis did the same, but something inside him was bothering him. The regular goalkeeper was allowing scores for trivial reasons. He was a coward when pulling out saves and, worse and did not position himself correctly between the goalposts. Thanasis had athletic ambitions and felt bitter, but he did not want to discuss his problem with anyone as they were all senior to him and would make fun of him. One afternoon after they had eaten at the table and everyone else had left, he confessed what was troubling him to Eftychia.

"Mother, you should know that the coach doesn't trust me even though I'm better than Nondas, who allows goals like a knife through butter. In the last match, they even scored, passing the ball through his feet. If we continue like this, we'll fall into the third division. "

As the young man told her all this, he was on the verge of tears. His Mother took pity on him.

"Do you believe you are better than Nondas?"

"Yes, Mother, I'm telling you exactly that. But I haven't played yet to prove it. During training, the first team plays against the substitutes. The defensive players usually leave me exposed. We constantly play three against two. So, it's natural that I let goals in. But if I were playing with a good defense, I'd show them. Not even a mosquito would get through to the net."

Eftychia remained thoughtful for a while. Suddenly her eyes glistened.

"When do you have training?" she asked decisively.

"Tomorrow at 4:00 PM."

"Good. I'm thinking of coming to see how you're playing."

Thanasis did not believe her, but the next afternoon there she was. Eftychia was on the field sitting in the front row of the stands. At the first opportunity, she would speak to the coach. Of course, the coach spotted her from the very first moment she arrived. It was uncommon for a woman to come to the field during training time. Eftychia was wearing a tight shimmery red satin dress that accentuated her curves.

At some point, the coach whistled to the players and yelled, "Sit and take a break for five minutes." This is when this woman, who attracted everyone's eyes, moved towards him. And as she approached, she took better notice of him. He was a man in his fifties, with straight black hair combed back without any baldness, nice features, a straight nose and a strong jaw, dark melancholy eyes, and gorgeous lips. Eftychia smiled at him and said:

"Good afternoon Mr. Spyros. I'm Thanasis Barlabas' mother, and I'd like to talk to you for a moment."

The coach looked at her with amazement. He had never had anything like this happen to him before. He felt that with this woman, there would be a sequel. He also felt a sudden attraction and affection. If he hadn't been olive-skinned, he would indeed be blushing.

"What would you like to tell me?"

"Well, I'd like to talk to you about my son, Thanasis. I saw that he was coming home from the training sessions very upset. I asked him what the matter was, and he explained to me that you don't use him in matches. So, I wanted to ask you how you see him. Does he have prospects? Is he likely to take the place of the team's goalkeeper?" Eftychia asked as she looked at the coach boldly in the eyes. The coach thought for a while and replied:

"You know he's still young. He has no experience and has only been training for only three months. He came in January, quite late. The team was already formed with another goalkeeper. But I'll see what I can do. He's currently a substitute. I'll keep an eye on him. Don't worry."

Eftychia threw him a look filled with sweetness and extended her hand to him for a handshake. Spyros grabbed her hand and felt a beautiful sensation, as Eftychia was not content with a simple handshake. No. She covered the back of his hand with her left hand and, almost stroking it, said to him:

"Thank you very much. I'll see you soon." And as she was saying this, she looked at him directly in his eyes with a bold look full of promises.

At the next training session, Eftychia was back on the field. This time she wore a narrow black skirt that barely covered her knees but had a deep opening on the back side where her legs could be seen. She had shaved her calves with a Gillette razor and felt confident that her pale calves looked smooth and lovely since the weather had warmed up, so she wasn't wearing stockings. The first chance she got, she spoke to Spyros again.

"Mr. Spyros, let Thanasis play in training with the first team and see what a performance he'll give!"

Spyros had already thought about some things when he saw Eftychia on the field. He gave orders. The players formed two teams. The defenders of the first team would play against the strikers of the second, and vice versa. Thanasis would be a goalkeeper with the defense of the first team. Looking troubled by all this, Nondas took a position under his goalpost, and Thanasis ran to take his own place.

The match lasted 30 minutes. Thanasis did not allow anyone to score any goals. He blocked the ball twice and made three saves with bounces over the heads of the forwards, a save at the feet of the center forward, and overall, he made a brilliant appearance. Nondas allowed four goals, showed instability in his saves, and the ball went through his hands once. In general, he was a mess. Eftychia saw little but understood a lot. She stayed until the end. When the players retired to the locker room, she approached Spyros and said to him:

"What did you think of Thanasis today, Mr. Spyros?"

"The young man is doing very well. He's a natural born goalkeeper and performs like an experienced player," Spyros replied. "Soon, he'll become a staple."

It seemed as if he was thinking about something, and after a momentary hesitation, he said, "Actually…would you like us to go for some appetizers at the taverna that is a little farther down to chat more comfortably?"

"Why not," Eftychia replied. She had become quite fond of Spyros, both in appearance and personality.

Soon, they arrived at a small taverna, which was very close to the stadium. They ordered fried keftedes, zucchini, fava beans, and tzatziki. And there, after drinking their ouzo and eating their appetizers, Spyros gave her the first kiss. They had both consumed tzatziki, and not only did they not smell the garlic, but rather its fragrance stimulated their mood for love. But this time, things stayed that way. That was just the beginning. In those years, love affairs followed a slow pace to prevent misunderstandings, and the men would make assumptions that the females were easy. Besides, young Barlabas was still playing in training matches. He was not yet playing in a full-scale official match.

In any event, Thanasis soon played in an official game and particularly distinguished himself. He kept his nets untouched and became the match's most valuable player. Spyros now found another advantage with Thanasis. Being sturdy and robust, Thanasis struck fear in his opponents whenever he went out to jump for the ball. At his first exit from the goalpost, he collided in the air with a striker (chest-to-chest) and broke two ribs of his opponent. Eftychia's son was evolving into the lord of the goalposts. No one could budge him from there.

The following year he played in the goalkeeper position with the second-division all-stars, and his team prevailed against the first-division all-stars scoring 1-0.

In the meantime, Eftychia, in love with Spyros, became his mistress for a few years, and it seems that after all is said and done, he was her great love. But love had come relatively late because she had already been married to her deplorable husband, Barlabas, for 19 years. But even worse, Spyros was also married. Eftychia did not know it at first, perhaps even did not expect it because he looked like quite a bohemian guy and wasn't wearing a wedding ring. Even so, their romance lasted a whole year until Spyros found a coaching position with a higher salary in a provincial team and left Thessaloniki for two years. With no intention of ruining his home, Eftychia did not grumble but broke up with him amicably, keeping for herself pleasant memories.

A little later, she met Manthos, who ran a small taverna in the market, which operated every night. Musicians and singers often played various folk songs there. Eftychia had gone there a few times with Spyros and Manthos noticed her, not only because she was indeed remarkable but also because she was one of the few women at that time who got up and danced the "hasapiko" (lively traditional Greek dance), not to mention the "tsifteteli" (traditional Greek dance, of a more sensual type).

The first summer after Spyros left Thessaloniki and after the Occupation ended, Eftychia would go to the sea in Kalamaria for a swim with Sultana, a newly made friend of hers, and they'd hang out together. One morning, she ran into Manthos at the beach, and they started talking.

From the conversation, he realized that Eftychia was unaccompanied, and then Manthos asked: "What's going on with Spyros? I haven't seen him for a while." She answered that the romance was over, and she was free to do as she pleased.

Manthos did not need further encouragement and quickly became the new boyfriend of the always beautiful and lively Eftychia, who was already 38 years old. The visits to "Kalamaki", the most remote taverna on the Kalamaria coast, which in the mornings served bathers while in the evenings functioned as a nightclub with music, continued throughout the summer and more sparsely in the winter.

The following year, when Eftychia went with Manthos to *Kalamaki* for summer's first swim, in the taverna next door, called *Kalamitsa*, there he was—Spyros, who had been watching her discreetly. He had finished his obligations with the provincial team and was once again in Thessaloniki. The two tavernas—*Kalamitsa* and *Kalamaki*—were separated by a fence made of reeds so that if someone approached it, he could see between the reeds to the other side.

As soon as he saw Eftychia sitting with Manthos in *Kalamaki*, Spyros went to the store's gramophone and put on a rebetiko song whose words were filled with meaning:

At dusk, we parted both in tears
with broken hearts beyond repairs
in my mind, you wander, Missus.
As I recall your hugs and kisses.
On those nights, you gave me sweet
promises you could not keep.
To have you back, my desire is deep
and in my heart, a fire
that soon your charms
perhaps will return to my arms.

Then he put on another song with an interesting meaning too:

Without hope, I stay awake
endless nights for your sake.
All alone, I roam the streets.

My heart's pounding 'n missing beats.
Standing at your window's grilles
with a bunch of daffodils.
I stop and stare
in great despair.
The sad hours I suffered through
I so much yearn to meet you.
The old joy to rediscover
And once again, to be your lover.

Eftychia, who knew that these two songs were Spyros' favorites, realized that something was transpiring and, at the first opportunity, looked behind the reeds into the courtyard of *Kalamitsa*. Ah yes! There at a table, almost next to hers, but with the reeds as a partition, Spyros was sitting and drinking ouzo! The truth is that she had not forgotten Spyros at all. So, she went inside the shop and asked the waiter to play a song she wanted on the gramophone. The disk began to turn, and soon the singer's voice poured out:

With a double-edged knife
I will take away my life
And my cries will be heard
Why I love you is absurd
To be or not to be?
You have hurt me bitterly.

Another song was also heard immediately after that from Kalamitsa, which went like this:

So many sacrifices I made, all in vain

I have nothing more to gain
She couldn't care less
The shrill adulteress...

Eftychia realized that Spyros still loved her. After a few days, she let Manthos understand she was still in love with Spyros and wanted to break up with him amicably. He understood. He was an old hand at love relationships and knew that every love comes and goes. After all, he had his eye on a new singer who would soon begin to appear in his club, and he wanted to be undistracted. So, it was no big deal.

The following week Eftychia went swimming in Kalamaria... with Spyros! They even planned to take a water boat to the seaside beach village of "Baxe-Chiflik" (lit. garden farm, now called *Neoi Epivates*, which means New Passengers), whose water was cleaner. Besides, Spyros' finances were better with the new team he was coaching in Thessaloniki.

The taverna owner who saw them talking, cuddling next to each other, and looking into each other's eyes like pigeons, had a few thoughts. *Hey! See what love can do to you. You make concessions and compromises, rejoice, break up, regret, cry, and again set out for a new love.*

He came out of his store and shouted at the couple.

"To your health, Eftychia, you straight-talking woman." As she drank her retsina with cold soda water, she shouted out an *"Aallaa"*! and threw her glass down behind her shattering on the concrete dance floor. With Spyros, she was truly happy, and it was obvious!

20

Electra's Second Marriage

Electra lived quietly with her relatively older second husband, Apostolos Iliades. His gentle personality, along with his steady job, made her feel secure. Moreover, she thought she had fulfilled her role as a woman with the birth of her only child, a son, son in 1942. They rented a beautiful home on the old seafront of Thessaloniki since Apostolos owned no property. He had lost all his money with the involvement of Greece in the Greco-Italian war when the state bonds, in which he had invested all his money out of excessive patriotism, lost all their value. His dental office was in one room of the house, whereas the sitting room served as a waiting room during working hours. After the liberation, his clientele had increased, and he was slowly saving some money that he converted into gold sovereigns because, as he used to say, "Once bitten, twice shy."

Despite the significant problems during the war, Electra's husband was an experienced dentist and managed his finances well. His elegance was immediately apparent. He always walked around well-dressed—a habit he formed from the time he was single—and wore a suit, vest, tie, and fedora every day. He was very affectionate and caring towards his wife, ensuring she lacked nothing. He was able to support her sister Eftychia now and then, who constantly struggled with her finances.

Just one problem troubled Electra, and that was that she lived with her husband's two sisters, Pelagia and Irene, who had both remained single because they had fallen in love with the same man—a military doctor. The sisters had decided that neither would marry him so as not to spoil the close sisterly relationship that existed between them. Apostolos had been waiting for his older sisters to get settled first so that he could also have a family (as was customarily expected at the time), but the years passed by…that is until he turned 57 when he met his future wife.

For him, it was love at first sight. Electra was initially flattered and did not take long to become fond of him to an advanced stage, that is, fond enough to invite him for dinner at her house with candles and French red wine. After dessert, she put a slow waltz dance song on the gramophone, a very slow and passionate piece, and they danced it tightly hugging each other. Apostolos, who by then had relaxed with the wine and had loosened up, bent down and kissed her. The kiss was at first soft, but it evolved into a very erotic one. The rest followed in the bedroom, and their sexual union was ecstatic and careless because of the lust that had gripped both of them. From that very night, Apostolos asked her to become his wife, but Electra reserved the right to think about it and asked for a short time limit until she gave a definitive answer. A month and a half later, she realized she was pregnant and decided to marry him. When his two older sisters were informed about the forthcoming marriage, they reacted strongly. Would their brother marry at such an age, with twenty years separating him and his wife?

As expected, they were infuriated at first, but the moment they first saw their newborn nephew, who was as beautiful as an angel, their hearts warmed up, and they felt their maternal instinct vibrate in their breasts. So, after conquering Apostolos, Electra managed to be accepted by both sisters, Pelagia and Irene.

The wedding took place in the Apostolos' home with a few relatives present, and in fact, after the child had been born. The long delay in the marriage was due to the initially strong objections of his two sisters.

Electra didn't wear a wedding dress at the wedding. Instead, she put on an elegant dress with garlands of flowers in place of the collar and white gloves. Aristides and Zozo held the candles, and Thanasis threw sugarplums with all his might while the couple and the priest danced the Dance of Isaiah around the dining table. The maid of honor was Despina, a close friend of the bride. Some good neighbors of Apostolos also attended the wedding and naturally admired the bride for her beauty.

At first, life in Electra's new home was not at all rosy because the young woman was caught between the two spinster sisters who saw that they were losing a share of their brother's love now received by their daughter-in-law. When Electra's son was two and a half years old—a proper rascal he was—he got twisted up at his Aunt Irene's feet, who lost her balance, fell, and broke her leg high up where elderly people often break it. From that moment on, she was bedridden until she died a year later.

The German occupation went by without great difficulties for the family of Apostolos because patients who came from the villages surrounding Thessaloniki to fix their teeth would bring eggs or chickens, beans, walnuts, almonds and hazelnuts, village sausages, and cheese. Many did not have money, which, after all, was losing its value day to day, and instead paid with food. With this and that, hunger did not make its presence felt in the new home of Electra, who, as usual, helped Eftychia a little.

Electra's son was baptized Spyros with his Aunt Pelagia as his godmother. At first, they called him Spyrakis and, even more affectionately, Akis, which became his established name over time.

After the first year of cohabitation, Electra and Pelagia harmonized with each other and acted in a complementary way at home. When Apostolos and his wife went out to entertain themselves, Pelagia kept Aki company and told him fairy tales, Aesop's myths, and Hercules and Theseus' labors. When he was older, she told him the stories about the Battle of Marathon and the Naval Battle of Salamis, as well as about the political systems of Sparta and Athens.

Liberation from the German occupation found Apostolos' family sailing in calm waters and an aura of happiness spreading everywhere in the house. In the kitchen, which was very spacious, the two women coexisted strangely enough, very congenially. Pelagia cooked meals, and Electra baked pies and sweets. On name days, relatives and friends gathered at home, the first and foremost being Eftychia, who, with her words, spread "kefi"—the spirit of joy—among the guests.

However, as is usually the case, the happy days did not last long, and when her son was five years old, Electra became seriously ill. She had suffered from two months of anorexia and bloating in her abdomen. The doctors who examined her decided that she needed to be operated on with a possible diagnosis of a stomach tumor (that's how they described it back then), and probably to exorcise the evil, they did not mention the term "cancer".

The most renowned surgeon of Thessaloniki operated on her, but when he opened her up, he realized he could not do anything. He could only whisper *God guard humanity against such a thing.* Electra's whole belly was full of metastases. It no longer mattered where the evil had begun because it was already an incurable cancer. The postoperative course of Electra's health was full of problems with continual and rapid deterioration. After a month, no one recognized her—so much had she changed. That beautiful woman had become a shadow of herself. Perhaps that's why one day she didn't permit her son to enter the room—it was a few days before she died—and she shouted with as much force as she had left in her lungs:

"Take the child from here! Take him away!"

In despair, Eftychia was spending the nights at the bedside of Electra, who was fading away. She had carried and placed on the bedside table and the headrest of Electra a whole array of icons, amulets, holy wood, and an old Book of Holy Scriptures bound in gold, and she constantly prayed. But no changes occurred, and Electra was counting the last painful days of her life.

In the worst days of his mother's illness, Akis was taken to an aunt by marriage who lived in a refugee residence—half a shack, half a house—in the Kalamaria district. The little one stayed there for two weeks and learned to walk barefoot on the dirt road like all other children. At first, it was a bit difficult with his delicate feet, but he got used to it. So, playing carefree with the poor children of Kalamaria, he did not experience the last nightmarish days of his mother.

Electra's funeral was held with great solemnity. The dark mahogany coffin was placed on a hearse by two black horses adorned with violet colored fabric wings. The procession began from the house accompanied by a multitude of people who followed to the church, and then at the end of the funeral service, they all went to the municipal cemetery.

Apostolos had become a hollow shell of a man. Pelagia was as pale as the dead with dark circles around her eyes, and Eftychia, her children, and Zozo were crying continuously. Electra's mother in the monastery was not notified of the event because Eftychia felt it would be too heavy a burden to learn about her daughter's death, who was not yet forty years old. A year later, the nun Eusebia also died and was buried in the monastery.

After things had calmed down and the funeral troubles and visits had ended, they brought Akis back home, who immediately sought out his mother. They gave him a cheap excuse: Electra had gone to America to visit Aunt Antigone. This lie lasted a few years. When the little one was playing out on the street, he was asked by the other children where his mom was, and he would reply: *She is in America,* until one day an older child threw into his face this blunt unrestrained cruelty:

"Hey! What America are you telling us? Your mother's dead!"

Six months after the death of his wife, Apostolos' health deteriorated, and he began to suffer bouts of angina pectoris. He would have attacks when he walked uphill, so that he would walk slowly and, if necessary, take a sublingual trinitrin pill. His great consolation was his child, with whom he became more attached than usual. He helped him in his school classes, taught him French, and had long conversations with him before bedtime. The maternal absence was covered by Aunt Pelagia as much as she could. The fairy tales and sweet words were on the daily agenda, or to be literal, in the nocturnal arrangements.

Apostolos lived with angina pectoris for another six years. One day, while dawn was approaching and he was lying in his bed, he felt a stronger than usual pain and shortness of breath in his chest. The pain was not relieved with the sublingual tablets he took. He realized he had suffered a major heart attack, possibly a myocardial infarction. According to the perceptions of the time, the patient was not to be moved, so he would not be admitted to a hospital. In the morning, while they were waiting for the cardiologist, Apostolos, who was standing up to breathe better, hugged Akis and said to him, "My child, who will I leave you to?"

He realized that he would soon die. Then, when the cardiologist came, he injected the patient with morphine and asked for his permission to be given oxygen. A central pharmacy on Tsimiski

Street had an iron container with oxygen from which it was possible to fill a rubber bag with this life-giving gas. Eleven-year-old Akis ran to the pharmacy and dashed home with a bag filled with oxygen.

The back-and-forth runs with the oxygen bag happened four times, but on one evening, the fifth run was unnecessary because the patient became comatose. Akis was picked up by a neighbor and put to bed in her house. Around midnight the little one woke up from a voice that said to him, *Goodbye Akis. Be careful, my boy.* Was it a dream, or was it the soul of his father who, at that moment, was leaving the body to go to where people's souls dwell when they leave life? Then Akis, already orphaned by his mother, realized that his father had also passed away.

His father's death was confirmed the next morning when from the window he watched the hearse with the horses waiting down in the street until the coffin was placed on the carriage. He did not want to see his father or go to the funeral. He preferred to remember him as he knew him— alive and smiling—and not with the severity and rigidity of death.

The following year and throughout the sixth grade of primary school, Akis stayed in the big house with the aging Aunt Pelagia. Eftychia often paid them a visit and cooked for them and swept the home a little because Pelagia was too old and helpless. During this time, a concierge of the apartment building made sure to steal from Pelagia's room various jewels and one hundred and twenty gold coins that Apostolos had collected during seven years of work after the liberation. The thief was revealed when he tried to sell the jewels and was sentenced to prison for a year. But only eighteen gold coins had been found, as the rest he had spent or did not confess to hiding them. Pelagia, who was almost confined to an armchair, died the following winter of pneumonia. Then Eftychia took Akis to her house, and Zozo gave him the sofa where she was sleeping in the small sitting room, and she lay on the floor between the two beds where Thanasis and Aristides slept.

Barlabas was annoyed by the presence of the two orphans—intruders—according to him, and now and then, he'd say: *Crowds, crowds, so somebody needs to go.* He was bothered by the overcrowding, especially since Eftychia evicted him from her bed, and he found himself sleeping on the narrow sofa in the kitchen. In the meantime, a guardianship committee had been appointed for the orphan child, and the committee sold the attractive furniture of the large house that had been left empty to the junk dealers for next to nothing. They sold the dental tools of Apostolos very cheaply to a young dentist as well.

From a house with a sitting room and four rooms full of furniture and silverware, Akis was left with some jewels, the few gold coins which were spent relatively quickly for his needs, and a collection of stamps. The head of the guardianship committee had taken the old bonds for safekeeping. Still, ten years later, when the Greek government gave some small reparations, the bonds had already vanished into thin air. No one remembered where they were except for Akis, who knew who had taken them, but the culprit denied having them. Then Akis, who was already a university student and was paying tuition fees and for expensive books, gritted his teeth and thought: *It doesn't matter. There is little difference between a little and nothing. I will start from scratch.*

At some point, he had to sell his father's gold watch. The following Christmas, he opened a stall in the market, which helped him cope with the expenses and matured him. He figured that no one gets lost in life when he has guts and that no job is too shameful to do.

21

The Wristwatch

Aunt Antigone is coming on Saturday," Eftychia announced to the family as they were all eating at the kitchen table. Everyone had heard about Aunt Antigone's trip and were awaiting her arrival. The transoceanic liner *Queen Frederika* would arrive in Piraeus after sailing for fifteen days, and from there, she would travel by train to Thessaloniki.

Aunt Antigone had been living in Chicago for many years and was especially beloved by the Barlabas family. Besides being a close relative, she was surrounded by an air of glamor because she lived in a great country. They loved her also because of the parcels she often sent, which had benefited all her relatives in Greece.

In the last shipment three months earlier, Eftychia was lucky to receive ten pairs of excellent quality nylon stockings and a cardigan with a fur collar. Thanasis was blessed with a jacket stuffed with cotton like a quilt, Akis with a jacket and golf pants, Aristides with a coat and two shirts, and Zozo with two pairs of nylon socks and a dress. There was nothing to benefit from these packages for Kotsos Barlabas except two bottles of deodorant! The distribution of items was arranged in Chicago with an enclosed letter which Antigone made sure to put inside the box with the description of the goods.

During the difficult years of the German occupation, 1941-1944, the two sisters had not communicated. Now that it was safe for ordinary people to travel, it was an excellent opportunity for them to meet and talk in person. After all, four years had already passed since the liberation, and Eftychia was pressuring Antigone to make this trip. When Eftychia announced that Antigone was arriving on Saturday, Barlabas asked: "And where will this 'Americana' stay?" Eftychia grimaced with discomfort at Barlabas' question and answered: "Do you need to ask? She will stay with me and sleep in my bed." At that time, Barlabas had been exiled to the kitchen sofa for some time. His glory years, when he beat Eftychia at the slightest provocation and was the fear and terror of his children, were now irretrievably gone. Now his sons were adults, and he couldn't influence them; besides, he was well past sixty. Eftychia was now completely independent, mostly living with Spyros, and had removed her husband from the marital bed.

Barlabas muttered with that characteristic guttural tone in his voice, "The wild has come to drive out the tame," and rose from the table. The others, however, were all very happy and impatient. They could not wait to see Aunt Antigone up close—who they imagined in their mind as an angel—but also to receive the gifts they considered certain their aunt would be bringing.

In the following 48 hours, a complete state of frenzy was apparent in the house. Eftychia changed sheets, couch covers, tablecloths, and curtains. In a fury of haste, she whitewashed the kitchen walls herself. Then, she made Akis help with the cleaning work in addition to Zozo who was always in the "front line of fire". Keeping a home clean was hard enough, so even though he was still a young boy, Akis had to help. So that's how he learned to mop. She would prepare the mopping rags for him and throw them at him from a distance so he could start mopping. The first mopping was watery so that it would leave plenty of water on the floor, and the next two moppings would be done with a tightly squeezed cloth to collect the water so that the floor was ready to dry quickly.

On Saturday, the house was ready. Zozo had become exhausted with the housework and, to a lesser extent, Eftychia, who, like a general, mainly gave orders to the rest. Thanasis did not noticeably participate in the preparations. Only once did he undertake to cook, and he made a great complex omelet with eggs, peppers, cheese, and potatoes, for which he had to use the pan three times because one pan was just for himself!

Nevertheless, on Saturday afternoon, everyone was ready for the welcome reception. Eftychia and Aristides went to the train station. The hugs and kisses of the two sisters mixed with tears seemed endless. Eftychia, who always had tears ready to unleash on the right occasion, came home with swollen eyes and dark stains dripping down from her eyes. Antigone seemed somewhat more restrained. She had adapted to some elements of the rather aloof American character without losing any of her Greekness. She spoke English in a distorted form, in the typical Greek American way. For example, she called hospitals 'hospitalia' and automobiles 'kara'! But she didn't forget her "French" either. When needed, she would spurt out some pretentious words with naivety and innocence that made everyone laugh.

Antigone was carrying three large suitcases with her. The process of doling out the goods, which were mainly clothes, began again. This time she even brought Barlabas a pair of black, slightly pointed, shiny patent leather, nicely soled shoes. They even smelled of genuine leather. Barlabas accepted the gift with a sly smile, saying, "Now, in my old age, I'll become a count." Then he tried to put on his new shoes, and after that, everyone ran out of the room to escape the unbearable stench of his feet.

For Thanasis, Antigone brought a pair of soccer shoes as well as various items of clothing. She brought Aristides a suit and tie, and for Akis gloves, a deflated soccer ball, and a small box, which she said she would give him later. For Zozo, she brought socks, a blouse, a kitchen apron, lipstick, powder, and cologne. For Eftychia, she brought so many things that I consider it unnecessary to list and describe. Imagine whatever you can think of, and you'll be right. It certainly wouldn't have crossed your mind that she brought not simply an ink pen, but a permanent ink one, an electric flashlight with rechargeable batteries, some large boxes of cocoa, coffee, milk powder, cans of black and white pepper, but also bath salts, shampoo and bubble bath, hair dyes, even a salon dome for doing hair perms.

Most important was that she hauled a radio to Greece. After going up and down to the roof and then to the basement and the chicken coop, the radio they had during the Occupation finally suffered irreparable damage. But there was a problem with the new one because of the voltage: 110 volt circuits in Greece and 220 in America. Surely there would be some way to make it work. Eftychia would take care of this by calling Epaminondas, the electrician, who never refused her calls because he was secretly in love with her.

In addition to the large radio, Antigone also brought a small radio with batteries. That's when everyone heard the word "transistor" for the first time. Thanasis noticed this little gadget, and at the first opportunity, he took it with him on a date with a girl—his new conquest—to Seikh Su, the hilltop forest (now called Cedar Hill). Zozo figured this out because when the radio was returned to its base it had resin stuck to it and it smelled of pine from the pine trees.

In any event, the two sisters were sailing in a sea of happiness. After almost thirty years, they had found each other. They sometimes spoke loudly and sometimes in whispers. Eftychia's and Antigone's lives passed by in oral chatter and became their common property. Until this visit, they had corresponded regularly, but there were also some gaps, so there were still some things that had not been said, and now it was time to confide in each other.

Eftychia took Antigone on a tour of the places that she thought were interesting for tourists. She took her to the Castles, to Hagia Sophia Cathedral, to the Church of the "Acheiropoietos" (lit. not made by hands in reference to an icon in this 5th-century church), to Agios Dimitrios and his crypt with so many miracles ascribed to him, to the Red Church, to the catacombs of Agios Ioannis and to the Rotunda. She walked with her to see the "jewel houses" on Vasilissis Olgas Avenue (designed in the neoclassical style) and the tavernas of Ano Polis (Upper Town) and Aretsou.

On this occasion, Antigone met her sister's "other circle of friends"—the taverna owners and waiters who knew her by name and treated her most superbly, as Eftychia had a way of becoming beloved. She had a good word to say about everyone and knew their family matters, but she could also crack a few shocking jokes to help them drown their sorrows and feel better.

This is how Antigone met Spyros, who had long been Eftychia's chosen one and who was now proud to show him off to her sister as her most precious conquest. The three of them ate their snacks together at *Paparounes* (lit. "Poppies"), a small quiet taverna in Kalamaria, where they listened to a few of their favorite rebetika songs on the gramophone with the big horn. And when the two sisters returned home and found themselves alone, the relevant discussion occurred about the Eftychia's relationships.

"How will this relationship of yours end up?" Antigone asked, who possessed rationality in her thinking.

"I don't know. For now, we're having a good time," Eftychia replied.

"Yes, but you're married."

"But I'm essentially divorced, and Spyros and I are in love. What can we do? That's life. Barlabas happened to me, and Spyros happened to have a wife who only takes care of her children."

"What about the divorce with Barlabas?"

"We've reached the signature stage. He has already signed it. But I'm the one who hasn't decided yet. I'll have a pension if Barlabas dies, and I'm still formally his wife. But if I get a divorce, I won't be entitled to anything like a pension. Who'll marry me at 45? Spyros' wife won't give him a divorce. After all, marriage is the tomb of love. I've read this and believe it, although I didn't experience it exactly since I probably never fell in love with my husband."

"Anyway, you know best," Antigone was forced to agree.

The next day Eftychia counted several pairs of nylon stockings that she had stored for a time of need from the various parcels, plus those of the last batch brought by her sister. While counting them, she thought there were more than she needed and decided to sell several pairs of them. Each of her friends was soon informed that Eftychia was selling stockings, and they began to buy them at an advantageous price because at that time, women's stockings were quite expensive. With her own eyes, Antigone became aware of her sister's commercial acumen. She saw this endeavor positively and decided to send more stockings with the parcels since they were very cheap in Chicago but in Greece were inaccessible in price!

In a few days the 26th of October arrived—the day dedicated to the patron saint of Thessaloniki, Saint Agios Dimitrios. While they were all at the table, Aunt Antigone took out a small box from her bag and gave it to Akis. Inside, there was a small wristwatch. In size, it was a little smaller than a typical watch. Apparently, she chose it that way to fit his little hand. Her nephew put it on feeling proud. He wouldn't need to wind it up because it would automatically wind up with the movements of his hand.

Thanasis' eyes sparkled when he saw the watch. His gaze was not one of envy but of admiration. He would have wanted it as his own watch. The same afternoon he had a date with his new girlfriend Dimitra, who was celebrating her name day. Thanasis got dressed, got dolled up, and splashed on his new cologne (made in the USA), but he did not have a watch. It seemed he had lost his own, maybe in the bathrooms or soccer locker rooms. He may have sold, donated, or even lost it in backgammon. (The last version seemed the least likely because he usually won in backgammon.) In any case, Thanasis could not bear being without a watch for long, so he made the relevant request to Akis. He wanted the new watch to wear it for just an evening. Without much hesitation but with a secret worry, his young cousin gave it to him.

Thanasis went to the rendezvous with his current girlfriend, Dimitra. He also got her a bouquet of chrysanthemums. The girl was overjoyed. They had met at the house of a friend of his who was away on a hunting trip and had left him the keys. There, among the kisses and hugs, Dimitra noticed the watch her lover was wearing.

"Ah, how nice your watch is, so small and elegant," Dimitra said.

Thanasis saw her greedy gaze pinned to the watch.

"Would you like it for your own, Dimitra? If you like it, take it," he told her as he took the watch out of his hand, and without delay, he placed it into Dimitra's hand.

From that evening, Akis' watch was lost. The poor kid had only worn it for four hours. Thanasis did not make any serious excuse for the watch.

"I can't figure out how I lost it," Thanasis tried to justify himself. "I'll buy you a watch at the first opportunity. Don't be upset. On Sunday, I'll take you to the stadium."

Indeed, on Sunday, he took Akis to the stadium. He had him hold a wooden suitcase with his sports uniform to enter without a ticket. Almost every soccer player had a protégé, a young man who entered the stadium as a carrier of his sports attire. When they passed through the gate, Thanasis took the suitcase in his hands and told Akis to go and sit in the stands. Akis' eyes were mostly fixed on Thanasis: How he took a position, guided the defenders, caught the ball, and jumped on the corners. He was a real lord in the field. He did miss a goal that he shouted was offside, but his team eventually won 2-1 anyway.

When the match was over, Akis entered the locker room that smelled of men's sweat and was full of steam from the showers and took Thanasis' sports uniform in the suitcase. Dimitra would be waiting for the goalie a little farther down at the bus stop. Akis had figured it out and, after taking a few steps outside the stadium, hid behind a booth waiting for Thanasis to come out. Ten minutes later, the hero of the match came out and met up with Dimitra. Hugging each other, they proceeded towards a road that went up next to the stadium and led to the so-called Jewish tombs.

The Germans had excavated the tombs, and there were several large pits left in which couples found shelter. A few scattered bones and, from time-to-time skulls would emerge in the grasses and the red soil. Despite the macabre conditions, many couples went there for their romantic adventures. Akis, who was guarding, saw it clearly. The young woman was wearing the watch on her left wrist.

Thanasis grabbed her by the waist and smashed her a hasty kiss. After the leaps on the soccer field, other kinds of "leaps" would follow. And after catching the soccer balls, Thanasis would touch other balls now. That's the way he was. Thanasis was an integrated personality. He lacked nothing. But he never had...a watch.

That same night the goalkeeper returned home exhausted. Red clay soil, pine needles, and other stains of unknown but probable origin were glued to his clothes. He took the suit off himself, wrapped it like a rag, and threw it into the bathtub. He fell asleep, and in a minute, he was snoring. He was happy. He was sleeping the sleep of the righteous. He had no guilt. Everything he did was spontaneous and instinctive. Dimitra was a poor girl. She didn't have a watch. He gave her one. He also gave her his love. As for Akis, he was still young. Of what use was the watch on his wrist? To wear it at the risk of losing it?

22

Liza, the guest

Eftychia was a very sociable person. Despite her meager finances (which were always in deficit rather than surplus), she came up with ways to visit her friends and to also welcome visits from others. When she scheduled to see someone, she would make a spoon-sweet or baked dessert or yogurt cake as her mother had taught her. Because she had a somewhat vulgar sense of humor, she often told her friends spicy jokes that many liked to hear but would not dare to say to themselves out of modesty. She would even sing some humorous songs between appetizers and ouzo that were successful at gatherings.

Every two or three years, Eftychia would take a trip to Athens and other nearby places around Thessaloniki. On these trips, her girlfriends provided accommodation, and in return, she was eager to return the hospitality.

Obviously, the conditions of hosting guests in her home were tough. There were few beds and even less free space. However, as Eftychia always used to say, *a thousand good people could fit*, and despite her poverty, she took upon herself the relevant rewards of hospitality. Knowing of her financial hardships, these friends she hosted usually brought more than enough food, as was customary on the part of every guest who did not want to burden the host.

On one of her trips to Athens, Eftychia met Lula's girlfriend, Liza. Liza was a middle-aged woman who had married somewhat late and was childless. Her husband abandoned her for another younger woman - a divorcee and a rather lively one at that - who had even become pregnant, unknown of course whether by himself or by another man, but he believed that he was the father of the child and was willing to restore her honor with a wedding wreath. So, he abandoned the withered-up Lisa in their apartment, which was his property, and left to live with his mistress while also filing for divorce. He even promised Liza that he would give her a good amount of compensation so that she would grant him the divorce, which she, having nothing better to do, was thinking of accepting.

During the phase of negotiations for the divorce, Eftychia was also in Athens. So, one day Lula, Liza, and Eftychia sat together over afternoon coffee. Liza shared her dilemma for joint reflection after having a few meaningless conversations about the general situation and high prices in the marketplace.

"My husband got a slut pregnant and is now seeking a divorce."

"Don't give it to him," both women shouted simultaneously.

"He wants to give me money," Liza said.

"Don't give it to him," Lula said yet again.

"Give it to him," Eftychia replied, changing her mind, and continued arguing.

"If you don't give him the divorce, all you gain is to continue sitting in a house that is his property, but he abandoned it, leaving his wife for another, to his detriment. However, you have no income, and the house has expenses: Light, water, telephone, utilities, heating, the concierge, and food is a separate matter. Not to mention clothes, shoes, and things you will need regardless of how much you follow fashion. How are you going to make ends meet?"

"My brother's been giving me an allowance for the past two months," Liza replied, embarrassed.

"Well, I think it's in your interest to solve the compensation issue," Eftychia insisted. "With the money he gives you, you can rent a small apartment and rent one room to a student from the province, receive the interest on the money you invest, and live modestly."

The discussion continued with more elaborating details and predictions. Liza was caught between a rock and a hard place. The dilemma was a serious one. That night she could not sleep from the thoughts that flooded her mind, but by morning she had decided to grant the divorce.

After staying in Athens for ten days, Eftychia decided to return home. She said her goodbyes to Lula, kissed her on both cheeks, and invited her to reciprocate her hospitality. Then she rang the doorbell of Liza's apartment, across from Lula's, and said goodbye to her. Because she felt pity for Liza and for her own predicament, Eftychia invited her to stay for a week in Thessaloniki whenever she wanted so that she could *drown her sorrows*, as she told her.

Upon her return to Thessaloniki, Eftychia's life returned to its normal routine. Her dog gave birth to five puppies, and the standard process of choosing the lucky ones who would live began. Eftychia chose the three most beautiful and sturdiest and called Akis to do the dirty work. When Akis asked her why she didn't keep them all, she replied that, firstly, she had no intention to let her bitch die by letting five puppies feed on her, and secondly, that she did not intend to make her home a dog farm. With the three puppies, something good could happen, and because they were the most beautiful, someone would indeed be found to adopt them. Moreover, this was not the first time. *This is always what happens*, Eftychia said resolutely.

What could Akis do? With a heavy heart, he took the road to the beach with the two puppies in a paper bag. Fortunately, the newborns had their eyelids glued shut because if Akis had seen the wide-open eyes of the two little ones he had to throw into the sea, he would not have been able to do it.

It was afternoon, and the wind was gusting landward. He threw the unlucky puppies overboard with the bag twisted shut as tightly as he could, but it quickly opened, and the poor ones began to float and would have suffered for a long time if the sea was not disturbed. They soon surrendered to their fate, which was death by drowning. Over the next few weeks, all members of the Barlabas family and Akis watched the development of the remaining puppies. In about a fortnight, they opened their eyes.

One day while Aristides, Zozo, and Eftychia were eating lunch, there was a knock on the door, and the dog began to bark. Thanasis hadn't shown up for several days because some woman had housed him, and Barlabas, after finishing his main job, was working in a taverna where he ate in the early afternoon.

"It must be some stranger for the dog to be barking like that," Eftychia said and got up to open it.

"Oh wow! Who do I see? Liza, it's you," Eftychia's voice was heard.

"Since you invited me to stay, I came for a change, just for two or three days," Liza said.

"My dear, just for three days? By the time you came, you'd be leaving right away. I insist that you stay at least a week."

"I've brought you something to remember me by," Liza said, who had sat down in the sitting area and removed a package from a bag like the ones they carry as hand luggage on planes.

"Yes, it's a handmade embroidery. I've been working on it for six months," she added with pride.

"Thank you very much. I'll put it on the table here. It fits perfectly," Eftychia told her, and she replaced an old handiwork of her own, putting Liza's gift in its place. It looks so pretty. Thank you so much Liza...but now let's eat. We had just sat down at the table. I'll put another plate on the table."

"Oh, I shouldn't," Liza said. "I've had something on the road, but well anyway, I'll sit down to keep you company," and she dashed into the kitchen where the relevant introductions were made before she sat down.

"Clara, sit quietly, calmly, don't bark," Eftychia ordered her bitch, who had been whimpering anxiously for a while, especially now that the visitor had come close enough to her basket, where her puppies were.

"She has recently given birth," she explained. "Don't get too close to her little ones because she gets angry and could bite you. Otherwise, she only barks, so don't be afraid of her."

Everyone noticed at the time that Liza, although half-full as she had told them, ate with a ravenous appetite, and Eftychia had to prepare some more salad. It also turned out that Lisa ate quickly and rather a lot. Only Akis and Thanasis could compete with her.

Akis felt the first adverse effects of Liza's arrival that very same night. Liza displaced him from the sofa he was using as his bed. He would have to sleep on the floor on a mattress that Eftychia used in emergencies. *Never mind*, he thought. *It's only for 5-6 days. I'll pretend I'm camping.*

In the following days, Eftychia showed Liza the sights. She took her to the White Tower, the park, and the forest with the thousand trees. She also took her by bus to the coast of Kalamaria. The steamboat, *Lefki*, took them to the seaside villages of Perea and Neoi Epivates, in any event, to all her familiar hangouts. She also introduced her to her beloved Spyros, and sometimes they shared ouzo and appetizers in Kalamaria. She did not take her to the museums, as these locales did not belong to their…well… lowbrow repertoire!

Despite her sorrow, Liza seemed pleased. The first few days passed by without her realizing it. After the second week, the mood seemed to get a little heavy. Eftychia began to get tired. One day when she dashed next door to her neighbor Asimina to borrow an onion,

Asimina asked her how long her guest would stay. Eftychia openly and officially breathed her first sigh.

"Oh, Asimina! I don't know when she's going to leave. She's just about exhausted me!"

"To tell you the truth, I've counted almost three weeks you've been hosting her," Asimina reported and then continued.

"Hospitality requires work and is an extra expense. You're not exactly flush in cash…what else is there to say? You can't be a bleeding heart."

The old fart, Eftychia thought and returned to her kitchen, determined to confront Liza. However, when she saw Liza teary-eyed, she felt sorry for her.

"Crying again, dear Liza," she said compassionately.

"Oh, just my bad luck, isn't it?" Liza whined. "Thank God I have you standing by me."

"Yes. But for how long?" Eftychia decided to say aloud, and she said it as softly and as sweetly as possible.

Liza burst into sobs. Her eyes reddened even more, and she began blowing her nose into a handkerchief. Eftychia took pity on her.

"I'll host you one more week," she stated, but her voice and gaze had now taken on a harsher countenance!

The week passed by, and Liza wasn't making any move. Akis had gotten sore from sleeping on the floor. The doors had a large opening underneath, and the chilly air currents made him shiver as if he had been accidentally uncovered in his sleep. That's when he figured out why dogs lay near the door in the summer and away from it in the winter. Akis began to get annoyed with Liza. She was constantly in everyone's way. Someone would go to the lavatory only to find out that Liza was using it. He would look for a slice of bread to eat with cheese, but he wouldn't find anything. Either Liza had eaten it, or after a while, the hostess Eftychia deliberately ensured it didn't exist!

A war of nerves began to take place. On some days, Eftychia gave money to Akis to get a gyro sandwich from the corner grill and eat it for lunch outside the house.

"I'm tired of feeding her. I'm not a charity," Eftychia would say and repeat to everyone else when her guest wasn't within hearing distance.

In the meantime, Liza said she would return to Athens as soon as she received some money from her brother, who had agreed to send it to Eftychia's address. But Eftychia was boiling mad. She had lost count of the days Liza had stayed in a stranger's home just because she wanted to. Every once in a while, Eftychia (who was a little superstitious) would place a broom behind the door and mutter some 'spells' for Liza's departure from her home, but all in vain. Each day followed another, the days would turn into weeks, but Liza was still there, immobile and resistant to the "spells." She sat like a Buddha in an armchair, and occasionally she would let out a sigh. She also read the *Treasure* magazine (in Greek *Thisavros*), whose trademark and main caricatures were of the Fat Lady and her tiny little man, Zacharias. Every week Thanasis would faithfully buy the magazine.

Eftychia often asked about the issue he recently brought home but could not find it because Liza had it with her and read it in the lavatory. Of course, Thanasis, who was only at home briefly, was probably the least annoyed.

In the meantime, while at first, everyone counted days and weeks, they had now counted months of hospitality or, rather, the occupation of the family sanctuary. Eftychia was about to explode. She felt deprived of her freedom. Also, the others were generally frustrated. How much longer would this squat take?

At first, Barlabas showed no interest in the case, but when he did not find any food one day due to Eftychia's passive strike on cooking food, he began to shout.

"This is not a home; this is a transit center! We'll catch lice from the crowded conditions. Somebody's gotta go..." and other such...courteous words!

"Don't worry. I'll be going away soon," Liza replied to Barlabas, embarrassed.

Fortunately, and by coincidence, the very next day, the remittance sent by her brother arrived. After proudly proclaiming that her brother may have been late, but did not forget her, she began to gather her things. Eftychia was on top of the world.

When it was time for Liza to leave, after collecting two lucky brooms she had behind the doors, Eftychia said her goodbyes to Liza.

"Dear Liza, c'mon…I wish you all the best. We may have gotten on each other's nerves in the end, but here I am. I also have problems, my knees hurt, and I can't do long-term hospitality."

"It's not our fault, Eftychia, but my ill-fated destiny. I was a queen and became a beggar," Liza said. "In any case, thank you anyway."

"We'll take you to the station with Aristides' car," Eftychia said, who had thought of encumbering Aristides, who was driving the company car where he worked as a commercial agent.

Indeed, at his mother's request, Aristides found the time and took the two women to the train station. Liza had boarded the train and was watching them through the window when Eftychia remembered to hand her an envelope through the window, saying:

"This envelope was given to me for you by a friend who heard about your situation."

Liza grabbed the envelope just as the train started moving. When she opened it, she found quite a bit of money and a short letter.

Liza, a lady liked the embroidery you brought for me and asked to buy it. I sold it to her, and I'm giving you the money because I understand the difficulties you are going through!

Thus, the hospitality for Liza ended, and Eftychia's ordeal did too. That very same night, Akis found himself in his bed again. At last, he would sleep comfortably again. But something bothered him for a few more days. It was a cheap lady's perfume that had permeated the mattress! For the past five months whenever he passed near Liza, he had hated the stench of her cheap cologne combined with powder or talcum powder.

23

The Transfer

In mid-1949, Aristides' class had been called up, and he enlisted in the Army. The Civil War would soon be ending. But the risks remained real in some border regions of the country. Eftychia, like the excellent and loving mother that she was, not only supplied him with various goodies for the first days when he would be at the training center in Corinth but also with lots of advice: How to take care of his health, not to joke around with pistols, to be careful especially where he steps, not to be distracted, and much more. In particular, she warned him about avoiding mines, that deceitful weapon that kills and cripples anyone who steps on one.

After kissing her according to the traditional customs and wiping off his mother's tears from his cheeks, Aristides reassured her that everything would be fine. He also had the assistance of the prayers of his grandmother, who had become a nun after the death of her husband, so he felt protected from all danger. When he noticed Eftychia's intention to accompany him to the station, he angrily dissuaded her. He did not want his mother to come to the train station as if he were a spoiled kid. So, he took the bus to the station himself. He almost missed the train by a few seconds, and his heart was pounding from this anxiety. He had been delayed due to his mother's endless instructions, almost missing the train by a hair since it was already sounding its horn and rolling out.

He breathed a sigh of relief, moved forward in the carriage, and settled into a compartment where other young men his age were on their way to enlist. After many hours of travel and after switching trains in Athens, he finally found himself at the training center in Corinth. There he experienced his first challenging moments, first because he was shorn of his hair with the fine bristles of a hair clipper—that is, his head became as bald as a globe and second, because the instructors—non-commissioned sergeants and corporals—were hollering and mostly swearing at the slightest whim. Even walking was forbidden. They had to run to perform all chores whenever they moved. If they happened to be walking, the sergeant would yell: "We're running now!"

Training also had its funny moments. The trainees had a gripe with a corporal who browbeat them quite a bit. One day a recruit left a backpack deliberately where the corporal would stumble if he weren't watching. As he was furiously striding forth, he tripped over the backpack and fell. Everyone present burst into laughter. Then the corporal angrily barked:

"Who does this damned backpack belong to? Come and get it!"

"Prima Facie's," its owner replied.

"Haul ass and find Primafacie (pun using a law term) so I don't break your bones."

Naturally, the recruits burst into laughter, and one of them took it upon himself to explain to the corporal what prima facie meant.

After a month and a half in the recruitment center with training and marches, weapons shooting, and other related aspects of army training, Aristides took some intelligence tests and apparently did well, so he was chosen to become a lieutenant. He also successfully finished the Officers' Training School and was transferred to the Greek-Albanian border. The conditions were difficult, although the civil war had recently ended. Groups of left-wing rebels had persisted in some places and were cut off from the bulk of their army that had retreated beyond the borders of Greece.

For twelve months, Aristides commanded a platoon of infantrymen and patrolled areas near the border. But there were two dangers: The mines, because of which many had been killed or crippled, and the ambushes set up by small groups of rebels. Eftychia, who had learned about all this, was very anxious and was trying to find a way to bring her son back to Thessaloniki. There were very few positions for second lieutenants, which were grabbed by those with connections, usually descendants of those with "special surnames." At the time, this convenience was evidently for the people of southern Greece. If they could not be transferred to Athens, they were placed in Thessaloniki. For the Thessalonikians, there were no available places in or around their city where the Third Army Corps was based. Eftychia seethed with this situation. Twenty months had passed, and Aristides was still on patrol in danger of stepping on a mine.

Thanasis had enlisted in the Royal Navy and was then serving at the naval station that was located in Piraeus. Eftychia felt trapped. Her two sons were away from her, and she had only her husband Kotsos Barlabas near her, tormenting her with his unscrupulous character and demands! Wherever she found herself, she talked about the problem she had with her two conscripted children. At the time, there was no telephone in the house. The letters were slow in coming. Also, Aristides had his own worries and did not write much.

Thanasis was even worse about writing letters and did not write more than three when he was a sailor in Royal Navy. She learned more about Thanasis from the letters sent to her by her mother, the nun at the convent. Since the time of the German occupation—when he had hidden in the monastery when the Nazis were pursuing him— he had become quite familiar with the area and used to visit it. He liked the tranquility in the monastery and the wisdom exuded by the words of some monks and nuns. In any case, by having a fear of God and visiting there, he had the feeling that he could atone for his petty sins.

The sins of Thanasis were undoubtedly not serious. He committed some petty fraud, such as telling a few lies to save himself from difficult situations and using deceitful words to girls that he supposedly loved very much, that is until he succeeded in his goals, or selling a few cigarettes and watches in the underground market on ships, or trading with other merchant ship sailors. In short, these were the sins of Thanasis. He would confess all these sins to his confessor at the monastery but, shortly after that, would again commit them without much thought. He possessed an innate but also disarming…innocence!

Eftychia was not worried about Thanasis, a true beast of strength and endurance. Her main concern was Aristides, her younger one, the skinny one, the crybaby, the delicate and sensitive one. And for a long time, her child was walking in the minefields, and she was about to lose her mind from the constant worry.

One morning the newspapers wrote about three soldiers who were found mutilated by an exploded mine near the border. Eftychia fell into one of her sporadic bouts of depression. The next night she dreamed of Aristides with a severed leg and a missing eye. The nightmare woke her up at 7:00 AM. By the following day, she had made her decision. She would bring Aristides to her at all costs.

Eftychia began her preparations to play her last remaining cards. A major of the military police, an old neighbor, advised her to speak to the Lieutenant General.

"It's not a matter I can do anything about Eftychia. You must go to the Lieutenant General. I'm sure you'll manage to do it. Tell me when you're going, and I'll call him."

She replied that she would go the day after tomorrow and early in the morning. That is precisely what happened.

Eftychia took a bath the night before and styled her hair with rollers and special hair curlers. Having done all this, her hair formed beautiful curls. She also applied her own formulated night cream based on lanolin, almond oil, and flower water. In the morning, she dabbed on some expensive cologne that her last admirer had given her as a gift. She used her eyelash curler, rubbed some blush on her cheeks, and wore a little discreet lipstick, but not overdone to resemble any loose woman. She wore a soft green satin dress with a wide neckline, and bursting with stubbornness mingled with anxiety and self-confidence, she set out.

She paced forward slowly because her special occasion high heels were killing her feet. On the way, she was harassed by at least three men. The third was quite persistent and took after her. They both reached the headquarters simultaneously, but just before she turned into the entrance, and just a few meters in front of the guard standing with his gun in front of his watchtower, the annoying guy grabbed her hand. Then, Eftychia raised her voice and, with her bag, started hammering the rude flirt. A small commotion next to the watchtower followed. As it turned out, the annoying man had received a strong whack, and because of the bag's metal protrusion, his skin was torn over his eyebrow, and he was bleeding just like a boxer. The guard asked for help, and soon the pestering man was taken to the doctor's office and Eftychia to another office to calm her down. The duty officer tried to find out what had happened. Eftychia briefly explained to him the events of the episode and quickly got into the subject of her visit. The Police Major had called to have her meet with the General, the appointment was made, and as she was arriving at the headquarters, the incident with the annoying guy took place, so she reacted and hit him with her bag. The officer graciously took her by the hand and led her to the General's office.

After taking a deep breath, our Eftychia was about to give quite a performance. The General was impressed by her beauty, but also surprised, so he was forced to listen to her story.

"Good day, my dear General. I have come to talk to you about a hero! My son!"

The General immediately figured out her real mission. Like this woman, dozens of people passed by every day asking for permission to be given to conscripts serving in his area of responsibility.

"Madam, tell me your name and how long your son's been serving."

"My name is Eftychia Barlabas. But regardless of my name—what I mean is my name is Eftychia (Joy)—but I am "Distychia" (Joyless)," she said almost in a whisper. "My husband, though alive, is non-existent. Indifferent to his children, indifferent to me, you understand...," Eftychia said meaningfully. "We are also refugees. We came here with just the clothes on our backs. But let's leave my troubles aside: I am a young woman with so many needs...he plays cards and drinks. He is incapable of anything included in the terms marital duties and obligations. But I don't want to talk about myself but about the children. My two sons both serve. The older one in Piraeus has completed two and a half years as a sailor in Royal Navy, and the younger one for months now is at the border at risk by exploding landmines. If I were a widow, I would have one child with me because he would be a protector. But because my worthless husband is alive, that exception does not apply. I became both a man and a woman to take care of everything. I feel like a reed blowing in the fields. So far, I have managed to get by. But after the dream I saw, I am about to go crazy."

The General bit the bait like a hungry fish.

"What dream?"

"What dream? It was a nightmare! I almost had a heart attack. And I have a sensitive heart, my General."

The General began to look at her with interest. He understood that he had in front of him a mother who was doing her best for her son, but also a beautiful woman in her forties.

"The dream was obvious, General. We are just about out of time to prevent evil. Please do something. I saw my son hit by a land mine, I have premonitions, I read the future, I am almost something like a psychic, I have not investigated that, but I must be something like that," Eftychia stated with unshakable certainty.

The General began to feel entertained. There was a dosage of performance in the invasion of Eftychia into his office. This woman was particularly attractive, immediately arousing a man's interest. He could not just throw her out gently nor in the strict service style he knew how to use. But then her words provoked his interest. For a moment, he wondered why Eftychia had aroused his interest. Could it be because she was beautiful, and she referred to her "nonexistent" husband? Could it be she was throwing herself at him? Though her story did not provoke any sympathy for her (she wasn't the only mother whose children were serving), the General felt favorably disposed toward her.

"Look here, my lady. I will take care of the matter," he said. "Come by again tomorrow so I can let you know."

"What time should I stop by?"

"Around 3:00 PM. My lady...what did we say your name was?"

"BAR - LA - BAS," Eftychia said, emphasizing each syllable, "and my son's name is ARISTIDES. I depend on you, my General."

"Rest assured, Mrs. Barlabas."

"Please call me Eftychia...and I am going to bring you good luck," she replied, her eyes conveying meaning. "But will you not write down the name to remember it...here let me write it for you."

As she approached him, she delivered to him a strong dose of the intoxicating aphrodisiacal fragrance that her body produced in combination with the expensive perfume she had worn. She took a small piece of paper from a notebook in her bag and wrote down her son's name, bending over the desk. She did not fail to write his initials "A. K. B.", his military number, and his unit. As she was bending over in front of the General to write, she revealed her breasts to him.

The General had been a widower for a year after a horrible illness sent his wife to the grave. He missed female companionship. He was victorious in many battles with fierce opponents. But in this battle, he felt his back on the ropes of a boxing ring. Defeat! At the same time, he was attracted to her.

When Eftychia finished writing, the General got up to see her out of his office. Eftychia extended her hand to him, smiling mischievously, "I hope you will help me, my General," he took her hand and brought it to his mouth in a chivalrous kiss after effortlessly uttering an *Of course*. Eftychia took courage from the scene and went on:

"General, thank you very much for your understanding. I honestly don't know how to thank you...you have overwhelmed me."

The General inwardly thought of an obscene rhyme with the "overwhelm" part, thinking...*and you've aroused me*, and he gently pushed Eftychia towards the door, holding her around her waist. Before going out, she turned around and gave him—an apparent but full of promise—innocent kiss on the cheek that slowly slipped to the corner of his mouth.

"Thank you for your understanding and forgive my spontaneity. Tomorrow I will come at 3:00 PM just as you told me."

"Yes, yes, do come," the General whispered, his mind almost completely clouded over. *This woman possesses something enchanting,* he thought.

Eftychia descended the steps of the building, being careful not to fall because her heels were particularly high, and she was not used to them. She soon found herself in the street. She took some deep breaths. The air smelled of pine from the tall pine trees of the open-air area of the headquarters. Her younger son, the sensitive one, the weak one, the pampered one, for whom she had a weakness, would finally be coming home. She passed by the guard who had previously helped her.

"Hey, my young man," she told him. "You have my best wishes that you return quickly to your home, a good citizen. How much longer do you have to serve?"

"Ten months which goes by too slow, lady," the guard replied in a strange city accent.

Where are you from?"

"From Nafplio."

"I've heard it's a nice city. Are you going to be on watch again tomorrow?"

"Yes, I'll be here from 12:00 to 3:00 PM."

"Then at 5 minutes before three o'clock, I will bring you sweets to remember me by," Eftychia told him, and in her mind, she could envision the countenance of Aristides. The road to her house seemed too short. She was almost flying despite her high-heeled shoes bothering her. She arrived at her apartment like a bird returning to its nest after a long flight. She changed her clothes, wore her robe, and was soon in her kitchen. She sent Zozo to get minced meat, parsley, and onion to make keftedes, and she started preparing the dough with flour, butter, and eggs to make the bases for the petit fours (delicate little cakes).

She worked non-stop that day until she saw her work finished. The keftedes were made ready to be fried the next day and were placed in the icebox. She also made a sauce that she treated with all the necessary spices, including pepper and basil. The petit fours were ready with a filling of apricot jam she had made days before. She divided them equally into three boxes. She had saved these boxes for a long time just in case. These boxes were from a confectioner's shop from previous uses. The first one she intended for the guard of the headquarters. The second one was for the General. The third one she would keep untouched until Aristides came back home. Three petit fours remained outside the boxes. One she gave to Zozo, the other she gave to her dog, and the third she ate herself with her coffee on her kitchen balcony.

As she sipped her coffee, she planned the next day. Her brain was working at a furious pace. When she had planned everything in detail, she imagined it coming true and was satisfied. That night she fell asleep early because the day had passed filled with tension and fatigue. She slept deeply without dreams and, fortunately, without nightmares.

The next afternoon, after getting ready according to her familiar routine—bathing, arranging her hair, plucking her eyebrows, applying blush and perfume and lipstick—she set out confidently. She was carrying a large shopping bag. Inside were the keftedes with the sauce in a container closed by screwing it airtight and the petit fours in two cardboard boxes. Today it was afternoon, and the sun was burning hot, so no one was around to bug her. She greeted the guard to whom she gave a box of petit fours. He thanked her, but they did not chat further. Eftychia's attention was focused on other matters. Mainly the TRANSFER. The concept of transfer was ingrained in her mind and had become her ultimate and exclusive goal. It was now an end in itself!

The duty officer announced her to the General who was waiting for her appropriately...cologned!

"Good morning, my General. Have you got any good news?" Eftychia asked, smiling.

"The news is that your son will come tomorrow or, if he catches up with any means of transport, maybe even today, on a five-day leave. Then, I imagine very soon, as soon as his replacement is determined from the recruits who come out of the Reserve School, he will come with a transfer very close to Thessaloniki. I was promised by a friend from the staff that the transfer would occur. After all, he has more than fulfilled his duties at the border."

Filled with emotion, Eftychia felt her heart beating like a drum.

"I feel like crying out of joy," she said. "You are a very good man. Really what can I do for you so that I can reciprocate this good deed that you have done for my sake? My gratitude will be eternal. My mother is a nun. I'll send her your name so they can remember you in their prayers and supplications." She paused for a moment. "Well, anyway. Now if you allow me to give you something I made for you (and she took the box of petit fours out of her bag). I have also brought you some hors d'oeuvres made with my own hands that whoever's eaten always remembers. Keftedes with sauce." Saying all this, Eftychia took the sealed container where the keftedes were placed and opened it under the General's nose.

The only thing the General wasn't expecting was to be confronted with homemade keftedes! As soon as he opened the container, the smell of onion and spices emerged. He hadn't eaten homemade food for 14 months, and at 3:00 PM, he was already hungry. Although it seemed ridiculous, he couldn't bear it any longer. He grabbed a kefte and put it in his mouth. It was mouthwateringly delicious. He licked his fingers like a child to remove the sauce. Eftychia watched his facial expressions. It was evident that he found it delicious.

"Mmm…" the General mumbled. "They're delicious. "Where've you been for so long?" he added, and then he felt like the words had escaped him.

Eftychia was emboldened.

"Seriously, my General, if you don't have any work to do, with all the respect I have for you, I know a taverna at the Kalamaria coast where we can go to eat the keftedes at your leisure and with a little retsina from the barrels. I know the owners. It will be so pleasant in their courtyard, in the shade under the trees, and they'll pamper us like lords."

The General was briefly speechless. That this woman found such courage and how simply and gracefully she said it! It was a mystery. In the meantime, the idea passed through his brain that he could enter into at least a temporary relationship with her. He began to feel his heart beating faster and louder. He thought. *Keftedes in the office or the taverna. What difference does it make?*

"It's not a bad idea. Let's go," he said after a few seconds of thought. He continued pondering how those great generals were distinguished for their determination, and so was he. He was making the decision, and the dye was cast.

The General called his driver and gave him instructions. The sedan came to the front of the entrance of the headquarters building. He came down with Eftychia, and they sat in the car's rear seats.

"We will go to Kalamaria coast. Take Vasilissis Olga (Queen Olga) Avenue," he told the driver.

Following Eftychia's instructions, they arrived at the taverna called "The Tulips" in 15 minutes. Stathis had been a faithful admirer of Eftychia ever since she interceded with the director of security to get his license to operate his taverna again. They had temporarily suspended it "due to the facilitation of debauchery!" Honestly, it was nothing serious, but there it was.

The taverna had two separate rooms for those few couples who, for obvious reasons, wanted isolation and discretion. But also, in its courtyard, it had tables surrounded by tall plants that were relatively isolated and looked like private summertime dining tables. It was to one of these separate tables that Eftychia was directed.

"Stathis, please make us a good salad, like the kind you know, and fry up some zucchini and eggplants. Add two hot peppers to the coals and bring feta cheese with oil and pepper. Please reheat these keftedes. We will drink retsina from your cellar. Put some lamb chops on."

Stathis hustled to take care of her. He thought about *Eftychia - what a woman! What on earth was she? The last time she had come in with the director of security, who was wearing civilian clothes. Now here she was with this General! This woman will drive me crazy with her acquaintances,* Stathis pondered as he entered the kitchen.

The taverna owner soon brought them the salad, retsina, and a bottle of soda water. He remembered that Eftychia never drank retsina straight. *I drink it with soda, so I don't drink too much and do crazy things from my natural instincts. Too much alcohol for me is unnecessary, anyway my disposition is always good*, she had once told him, and he had not forgotten.

That afternoon the General ate with an excellent appetite and, after so much time, regained his sense of joy. The death of his wife, official matters, and the lack of social contacts—apart from the official ones—had made him slightly melancholic. He struggled not to show it. After a few glasses of retsina wine, Eftychia told him some things about her life—truth be told, quite moving—but as they were both in a good mood, she later shared some shocking jokes that she always told very cutely. The obscene words she only uttered with the initial syllables. The General laughed heartily.

The meal with the keftedes and the delicious other preparations of Stathis would remain indelibly engraved in the memory of the General, together with the jokes of this well-preserved beautiful, and cheerful forty-something female. In the outdoor secluded dining spot, he had an excellent opportunity to practice some of his thoughts concerning Eftychia. However, in the end, he restrained himself. He thought about his position, remembered his wife, whom he loved dearly, and ultimately did not succumb to temptation.

When they decided to leave, he asked for the bill. Stathis was adamant.

"Dear General, what are you saying? It is my honor that you came to my business, and after all, I have a great obligation to Eftychia."

The General insisted though, and he left a banknote.

Three and some hours after leaving the headquarters, the sedan stopped in front of Eftychia's house by order of the General. They said a few farewell words, and Eftychia thanked him once again and exited the vehicle. She climbed the stairs of her house, thinking of Aristides. She opened the door and found herself in her sitting room. Her heart was pounding. An officer's hat was hanging from the coat rack. Obviously, Aristides had come home.

"Aristides, my child, where are you?" Eftychia shouted joyously. Aristides immediately appeared at the balcony door. He looked sunburned and a little emaciated; he had also grown a thick mustache. One of his eyes was taped over with gauze, but he was smiling strangely. Eftychia immediately remembered the dream. A *severed leg and a missing eye*, she recalled in horror. *I can see his legs; they're fine. But the eye?*

"My God, why did you do this to me!" she shouted and fainted right in front of Aristides' feet.

Aristides laid her down on the sitting room sofa, put his mother's feet on two inflatable pillows, and rubbed her hands, which were pale and sweaty.

"Oh, Mother. What's wrong with you? Is this the first time you've seen me?"

"Oh! What happened? Where am I? Ah! Here you are, Aristides…what happened to your eye?" Eftychia mumbled.

"I got a stye in my eye, and the doctor covered it with gauze and an ointment," Aristides replied. "What were you afraid of?"

"My boy, I had a bad dream," Eftychia said, a little embarrassed.

"C'mon, Mother. Don't be afraid. I didn't step on mines. I wear my crucifix, and it protects me. After all, the minesweepers move ahead of us. Now warm some water so I can take a bath. I'm going out tonight," Aristides said. As he was chatting with his hand in his pocket, he could feel the… yes, a condom!

Like all military leaves, this one passed by quickly, but in 15 days, Aristides came back with a transfer to the Thessaloniki garrison. Eftychia's fears were finally allayed. To her delight, she made two pites—one cheese and one spinach. He put several pieces of both in a pastry box and set out for headquarters. Her gratitude for the General was immense! Besides, he was also a charming man with diamond stars on his epaulets and greying temples.

24

An Ill-Fated Romance

The love affair between Eftychia and Spyros, whom she had met when he was Thanasis' coach, lasted a few years. They would meet each other about once or twice a week and go to various tavernas for appetizers with ouzo or retsina. Eftychia drank little but had a natural cheerfulness without needing the effects of alcohol. In the summers, they went to the beach, sometimes for half a day in Kalamaria and sometimes for a day trip with the motorboat to Perea, a small seaside village.

There they preferred a beachside taverna that was the farthest from the dock where the motorboat docked because it was quieter, and where they had befriended the owner who took special care of them since they were also regular customers. Eftychia and Spyros enjoyed delightful times together since they did not have to deal with the daily friction as being husband and wife, so their bond of love was always strong.

Spyros had finally divorced and was pressuring Eftychia to get married, but she didn't want to lose old Barlabas' pension. She kept her nominal husband at home so that mainly the emotional Aristides would not grumble, but she had banished Barlabas to the kitchen, where he slept on a couch. Now that he was getting old, Eftychia had the upper hand, evident to all.

However, the lovers' happiness did not last long, and after several years of great love, their bond abruptly dissolved because her lover died suddenly from a cardiac arrest. Eftychia was inconsolable about the loss of Spyros and went to the funeral wearing black, just as if mourning her husband.

The late Spyros had a deposit book in the postal savings bank under three names, one of which was Eftychia's name and the other in his daughter's, Aliki, a teacher appointed on Astypalea island in Aegean. Due to rough seas, the ship could not travel, and Spyros' daughter was unable to attend the funeral that took place under the care of Eftychia, who even made sure to go to the savings bank and withdraw the money that Spyros had deposited in their two names before the news of his death became known.

When Aliki arrived, Eftychia asked to talk to her, and after explaining to her the love she had for Aliki's father, she gave Aliki all the money of the late Spyros to the exact drachma. Though she never sympathized with her father's love affairs, Aliki felt sympathy for Eftychia, who, dressed in black and with her eyes swollen from crying, demonstrated love and integrity in her behavior, and the daughter fell into her arms with a mute lament. From that moment and for many years, the two women kept up a correspondence. Eftychia also went to Aliki's wedding which took place five years later, and even bought her a gift from her surplus funds, a silver dinnerware set.

Eftychia wore black mourning clothes for a year. Those who did not know her story with Spyros asked why she wore black, and Eftychia answered in various ways, such as *because that's how I look slimmer*, or she replied playfully *I wear black so that you can ask me about it.*

A year after Spyros' death, Eftychia again got involved with another man. This man was Michalis, a wine taster in a large distillery. Her new lover was single because he liked the bohemian life; he was a party reveler type and even played a little guitar. They met one carnival night when Eftychia dressed as the carnival "Hooligan of Athens" with a painted mustache—which she had painted using burnt cork—went to the famous bouzouki taverna of Georgios Dalamagas called "Koutsoura" with her friend Sultana, who had dressed as a gypsy. There they gyrated to the zeibekika and tsifteteli dances, and the whole shop was in an uproar with their vivaciousness. Michalis sent a bottle of wine to the girls, and shortly after, they found themselves sitting and singing together.

From the very next day, Eftychia began to date Michalis regularly. After a few weeks, one night, when they had stayed up late at the taverna of musician Tsitsanis called "Ouzeri", at Pavlos Melas street, Eftychia suggested that Michalis sleep in her house because he had missed the last tram. Michalis had no objection. So Eftychia, without hesitation, pushed Michalis into her room, and they slept as husband and wife in the double bed. The dogs barked at the night visitor but soon calmed down after Eftychia's constant shushing them.

At that time, Thanasis was sleeping elsewhere and did not go home often, while Aristides was still in the army as a reserve lieutenant. Eftychia explained loudly to Zozo—who had woken up from barking—that Michalis was something like her husband and she was going to marry him and that actually, she was waiting for a formal decision for the divorce to come out. She asked Zozo to tell Barlabas, who was supposed to be sleeping, but had woken up and heard what Eftychia was saying, and not to make it an issue of it because otherwise Eftychia would drive him out of the house altogether. To her new amore, she had explained beforehand about her broken marital relationship with Barlabas, and that she kept him at home out of compassion, and all was above board.

The only detail that made things somewhat difficult was the use of the lavatory and the washbasin. The two men should never intersect. To this end, Eftychia stretched her antennae and notified Michalis when he needed to leave their room. In addition, she would put a chamber pot under her bed so that the guest could use it and would not have to go to urinate in the lavatory.

Typically, Barlabas would awaken before everyone else and return late because he worked in a galley kitchen in the evenings. As for Michalis, initially he was shy, and as soon as he entered the house, he would lock himself in the bedroom with Eftychia and would not make his presence felt. However, with the passage of time, his existence became provocatively obvious, and even in the evenings, he would return home in the throes of cheerfulness after he had passed by a taverna and drunk his retsina. So, he would grab his guitar to relax and sing.

His favorite Tsitsanis song was one about a young maiden:[11]

"Don't speak to me about love,

my maiden fair.

My heart is full of tears.

Women took away my fears

made me heartless, cruel

and in love a deceiver.

To love you, I cannot

my maiden fair.

So, in the course of life,

in secret on the pathway

those hearts who have loved

shed tears in dismay

my maiden fair."

In addition to the double bed, Eftychia's bedroom had a triple-leafed wardrobe, a makeup vanity with her cosmetics, and a large square dining table with its chairs. Of course, there was also the iconostasis with various icons. Among many was an icon of Saint George on his horse killing the dragon.

---

[11] The song's title is "Apo Gynaikes Dakria", ["Tears Caused By Women"] Vasilis Tsitsanis, composer. 1948)

As a rule, whoever came into the house first had to enter this bedroom which sometimes also functioned as a sitting room. On the big table that dominated the center of the bedroom, Eftychia would set out her appetizers, the room soon displaying a festive atmosphere. Michalis would come from work in the evening, and after eating some of Eftychia's delicacies, he would begin to sing, accompanying himself with his guitar. Every week with Eftychia, they would go out to various tavernas and enjoy themselves singing songs and listening to the tunes of the bouzouki.

Michalis' mother, a virtuous woman from a village outside Thessaloniki, regularly visited Eftychia wearing her long peasant clothes and black scarf—as a widow—and never failed to ask Eftychia to hasten her marriage to her son. She hoped that she would see a grandchild if they did not take too long to get married. But things turned out differently because Eftychia did not intend to lose Barlabas' pension. This grotesque situation continued with Michalis in the bedroom and Kotsos Barlabas on the kitchen sofa for a year and a half.

During this time, Aristides was a second lieutenant at the head of a platoon that patrolled mountainous areas of Western Macedonia, looking for forgotten guerillas and clearing minefields. (He was lucky because his brother was also serving, so he went into the army later and escaped the murderous three-year civil war period between 1947-1949 when brother was killing brother).

In any case, the army enhanced the confidence of Aristides. He had enlisted as a young man, and now after almost two years of service, he felt like a genuine man. He had gained a few pounds and no longer looked as thin as he used to. He admired himself in his uniform and the mustache he had left to grow. After serving in the army for two and a half years—which went by without any serious complication, illness, or injury—he was discharged. He then returned to his family home and resumed his job as a commercial employee in a shop on Hermes Street. As for himself, he asked a change to be made, and that was for his mother to stop calling him affectionately "Dakis" (diminutive of Aristides). After all, he was now older and even a reserve officer.

But there was a severe second problem he wanted to change: The presence of Michalis in the house. He soon bumped into him in the narrow corridor outside the lavatory at an hour when Michalis was, as usual, in the throes of cheerfulness. Aristides felt quite humiliated by the presence of his mother's lover. So, the following day, as soon as his prospective stepfather left for work, he started a serious argument with Eftychia.

"It's impossible to continue to have your lover in the house where I live," Aristides said angrily.

"Your father and I have broken up," Eftychia replied, "but I allow him in my house out of compassion. I have a right to live my life."

"This situation cannot continue," Aristides countered, who had learned to command in the army. "Tell your Michalis to collect his stuff and go to hell so I don't plant any bullets in his head and go to prison!"

"What are you saying? You've become quite the bossy type. In my house, I commandeer."

"If Michalis doesn't leave, Thanasis and I will leave!" her son fired back his ammunition.

At the time, Eftychia expressed to him much about the difficult first years of her marriage, about the beatings that Barlabas would decide to inflict on her spontaneously in the past, about the little money he left at home, and how she tried with great difficulty to raise them. She tried to dissuade him by taking out her spare weapons, that is, her tears. But her son was adamant. Harsh words were exchanged, and the situation had reached a critical juncture when Aristides opened Eftychia's closet and, irritated as he was, began to throw all the man's clothes on the floor, which of course, were Michalis'. His mother was screaming to no avail. At one point, sugar even fell out all over the floor. It was the sugar that she had hidden in her closet according to her old habits.

Just when the quarrel was at its peak, Thanasis showed up in the room. Provoked by Aristides, he immediately took his brother's side, accusing his mother of having gone too far with her lovers. Bibo and Clara were also involved in the commotion, barking between them, apparently seeking to calm them down, and when the loud voices stopped, they licked the spilled sugar.

"Look who's talking," Eftychia said, meaning Thanasis.

"This man who sleeps with a new slut every day."

"Be careful how you talk, Eftychia. I am a man; I can do whatever I want. No one condemns me, but you are a married woman, and in addition, you have us as your children, now adult men."

The two brothers had formed a faction with a solid majority. Sitting on the sidelines, Zozo did not speak and continued knitting a shirt for Akis, but it was evident that she applauded Aristides' view, to which Thanasis had also joined. Eftychia did not give up easily and, as a final argument, added:

"But look at this. The rent control with the old rents frozen was abolished, and Prokopis, the landlord, has raised the rent to double what it was."

"We'll pay you the rent. Never fear," the brothers said in unison.

Deeply distressed, Eftychia realized that she was losing the battle and, after throwing around a few more words without convincing anyone, wiped away her tears, washed her face, dressed in a hurry, combed her hair quickly, placed Michalis' clothes in a suitcase—a suit, four shirts, two woolen shirts, three trousers, some changes of clothes, socks, and pajamas, that is, his whole wardrobe, as well as his shaving tools,—and she went out to find him. In one hand, she held the suitcase and in the other the guitar. She caught up with him in a taverna in Ladadika where he used to go after work. Relieved, she left the suitcase and guitar on the floor next to him, told him everything, and with tears in his eyes, asked them to separate. She turned her back on him and left without even listening to what the stunned Michalis was telling her.

When Eftychia arrived home, Thanasis was playing backgammon with his father in the kitchen. Still angry from the previous arguments, Aristides waited for Zozo to finish sewing a button on his jacket. Without speaking to anyone, Eftychia locked herself in her room, banging the door loudly, and after crying for a while about her lover whom she had just dismissed, sat down and wrote an informative letter to her sister, a redemptive letter for her. Eftychia thought, *Antigone understood me better than anyone else. Only she could understand me in this case!*

However, there was another soul that sympathized with her. While Eftychia was writing to her sister, with a dog's intuition, Clara looked at her with watery eyes. Her mind understood something. That night Clara slept on the double bed with Eftychia and was trying to comfort her!

25

An Important Match

Thanasis continued to be the main goalkeeper of his team even if he did not go to training regularly. His team participated in the second division championship and, at the end of the championship season, was in the middle of the leaderboard. That year, however, the last match of the season was very crucial for the opposing team, which would move up to the first division if they won the game, while for Thanasis' team, there was a "defeat without pain" and they would not lose or gain anything regardless of the result.

The match was to occur at the ARES team stadium on a Sunday afternoon. Thanasis had fallen asleep late the night before because he was playing backgammon in the café, so he was late getting up. Fortunately, Takos, a friend and teammate, came by to accompany him to the Stadium. They arrived at the Stadium's locker room, put on their soccer shoes and other accessories, put on their jerseys and shorts, and went out onto the field.

In the stands, most of the fans were supporting the opposing team. The match began with good omens for the team seeking promotion to the league. The team wanted to win anyway because otherwise, another team would have moved to the first division.

The match began and soon seemed to be uneven. Thanasis' team was limited to its zones. But the desired goal for the opponents had not been achieved. The ball had been driven back five times from the corner as Thanasis managed to catch it up high in the air or repel it. Time passed, and the goal was not achieved, and then the opponents began to get nervous.

Then forty-five minutes was over, and the teams retired to the locker room. There, the teammates congratulated Thanasis on his performance, and he was proud, but at the same time, he was thoughtful because they still had another forty-five minutes to play.

The second half rolled around like the first but with more pressure and tension. At one point in the match, there was a counterattack by Thanasis' team, and Takos found himself in an advantageous position to score a goal, but he received an unsportsmanlike marker and fell to the ground writhing in pain. The referee was even afraid to whistle the penalty because the fans were terribly upset, and an incident might happen.

Shortly afterward, Thanasis was set up under the goalposts to take a penalty that his right defender committed. The opponent's shot, although artfully kicked, was caught by Thanasis because he figured out to which corner of the goal the opponent would send the ball.

In the last fifteen minutes of the match, a forward approached Thanasis and informed him that the president of the opposing team would give him as much as two salaries to miss saving a goal. However, nothing changed until the end of the match, and the final result was a goalless draw, i.e., 0-0. The fans of the team that lost the promotion to the first division with the draw were furious not only with their team because they did not win but also with Thanasis, who kept his goalposts intact.

When the two friends and teammates came out of the locker room, many furious fans (may God turn them into genuine sports fans) yelled and cursed at them, hollering that another team had bribed them to play hard because with this tied result, they were moving up to the first division.

"Don't respond to anything," Takos advised. "They're crazy and don't know what they're doing."

So, they kept moving while watching their surroundings lest they should be suddenly attacked. A little way down the street was the bus stop, and a bit farther over the tram stop. They waited between the two stops to take whichever would come first. But then a small crowd of indignant fans began to form, surrounding them. These fans were upset with the amazing performance of the goalkeeper, who, with his performance, had condemned them to the misery of the second division for another year. The two friends kept moving, retreating a little farther back and resting their backs against a wall. Better that way, they thought simultaneously, so at least our backs were secured.

An enraged fan of the opposing team approached them and raised his arm to punch Thanasis, who dodged it by bending over abruptly so that the extended hand slammed into the wall causing the attacker to howl in pain.

"Barlabas hit me!" he lied and started shouting and calling others for reinforcements. Several approached in a threatening mood, but they did not dare to hit them because not only was the supernatural strength of Thanasis well-known, but also, with his height and long arms and legs, Takos was almost as legendary too. So, the two lads who approached them to beat them up, hoping for the support of the rest, found themselves in trouble. Thanasis punched the first one in the jaw, who then fell unconscious, and the second guy collapsed folded in two with a kick to the ribs by Takos and was gasping for breath. A third one was about to approach but, before even raising his arm, found himself several meters away holding his belly after being kicked by Thanasis.

Just then, two police officers approached, and the furious fans realized that the attacks had to end. After all, their attacks led them nowhere, but only that they themselves were being beaten to a pulp. The police officers who realized what was happening imposed order by distancing the fans from the two soccer players whom they even helped to get on the bus while preventing others who participated in the incidents from boarding.

The two friends arrived in the city center and went to the club's premises to play some backgammon. There they became the focus of cheers from those who had been in the area of the "Kickboxing fight." After the cheering stopped, they started to play backgammon. But an hour later Akis came running to talk to his cousin.

"What's going on, Akis? What brings you here?"

"A policeman is looking for you. He previously came to the house for what he said was an offense committed by you. There's a complaint saying you broke two teeth of a fan out of the blue, and another suffered something serious from a kick from Takos. How did he say it? Yeah…something like a thorax; oh yes, I remembered it; he said pneumothorax! They're looking for both of you."

The savages came to drive away the tame, or better; the thief cries out to frighten the housekeeper, Thanasis thought.

"What do we do now?" he wondered aloud.

"It seems that the policeman is your acquaintance because before he left, he told me that if you're not found within 24 hours, you won't be taken to court immediately, and the case will take time. It seemed to me that he said it so that I could pass this information on to you," Akis said. "But where you're here right now, logically, well…he'll get here in no time. You'd better leave to hide somewhere else."

The two friends glanced at each other and immediately got up and hurriedly left towards Egnatia Street and went to a friend's and teammate's house. The friend had broken his leg at the fibula and could not go out yet.

"Themis should be at home," Takos said. "Let's go there to continue the backgammon."

Akis followed them because he didn't want to miss any phase of…any action.

Indeed, Themis was at home, distressed that he could not attend the match and glad to see them. Takos quickly told him about the case, and Thanasis continued in much more detail, adding extra information for the two who put up with a bunch of enraged punks. Themis was curious.

"How many punches did you give him with his two teeth gone?" he asked.

"I don't even remember, but I think once, but I gave it all I had," Thanasis replied. "My middle finger still hurts. Fortunately, the matches are over for this year. It'll take me at least two weeks to feel my hand healed."

"And the other guy suffered a collapsed lung?" Takos asked. "I've heard that they do this for the treatment of tuberculosis. Was the chest punched or kicked?"

"Kicked!"

"Then they should hire you as a special therapist in the sanatorium," Themis said, laughing with relief that his two friends were not hurt with so many thugs attacking them.

"C'mon. Let's play backgammon like a championship one-on-one with everyone and the winners against each other," Takos said.

Eventually, the runner-up competitions increased in number, and after Thanasis was initially crowned champion, the others all wanted the backgammon matches to be repeated. So, as the playing of games went on, time flew by, and they started to get sleepy.

"What time is it?" Takos asked.

"Four AM," Themis replied.

"I'm hungry," Thanasis said tentatively, as he no longer wanted to burden Themis.

"Why don't we send Akis to bring us something to eat?" Takos suggested.

"I suggest he bring us tripe from Egnatia Street. The *patsatzidiko* (tripe restaurant) is nearby," Themis said, and he got up. He went to the kitchen, relying on his crutches, taking Akis with him. They soon returned with Akis holding a copper kettle in his hand.

"Here, Akis. Take the kettle and money for four servings."

"Five," Thanasis piped up, who wanted a double portion.

"Six," Takos added, who also intended to eat a double portion. Thus, in a short while, sixteen-year-old Akis was carrying back a kettle full of steaming tripe. When the tripe soup was poured into the dishes, Akis realized he could not eat it with its strange smell. In fact, he couldn't even try tasting it, so the others rolled the dice to see who would be the lucky one to eat his portion.

Eftychia's son was indeed born fortunate enough to eat three servings of tripe! In fact, Thanasis had initially wanted to order that many, but he was embarrassed to say so. Now he would be eating the third serving without feeling guilt.

Akis was getting very sleepy and decided to leave to go to bed. It was 7:00 AM and he promised to bring them something to eat at noon. The 24-hour quarantine from the complaint of the offense would be over at 5:00 PM. Until then, they had several more hours of…backgammon.

At the same time, back at the police station where the complaint for unjustified beatings and bodily injury had been made, the commander was receiving information about the incident from two eyewitnesses cooperating as informants for the police. He immediately understood that the soccer players who got involved unwittingly had no intention to fight and therefore held no responsibility. He sent policemen to bring in the two guys who had made the charges. One could not come as he was being treated in the public hospital. The other one came with a huge bruise, swelling on his jaw, and two missing teeth that made him speak like a toothless man with a ridiculous accent.

"Listen here. We know you from other times. You get involved and start the trouble first. Withdraw the complaint if you don't want me to put you in jail for good. And tell the other guy who's hospitalized the same thing. As soon as he gets out of the hospital, tell him to come here. You deserved what you got. You encountered two tanks. So…is that how stupid you are? Are you dense? You tangled with Thanasis Barlabas and Takos Mavridis! These guys are like two tanks. Don't you have even a bit of brain? Piss off, and don't let me see you in front of me again. Get the heck out, you scum!"

26

Holy Friday

Thanasis had completed his service in the navy, and it was Aristides' turn to serve the country, so he joined the infantry. To Eftychia's great joy, he became a reserved sublieutenant. In this way, her son would get some money for his personal expenses because Aristides had always been the apple of her eye. As a young boy, he was pretty thin, and unlike the sturdier Thanasis, he often caught a cold and was frail and delicate. His brother Thanasis had never fallen ill except once as an infant when he was hastily baptized lest he dies unbaptized and to exorcise death hence his name "Athanasios" (i.e., immortal). And this was separate from the fact that he was so independent and resourceful that he had managed to be quite well-fed during the Occupation. He could be accused of being a collaborator of the Germans because he worked as a laborer in German warehouses. On the other hand, he could also be decorated as a partisan patriot because he had robbed the Germans. And let us not forget to consider that he endangered his life with those English aviators he rescued under the nose of the enemy.

In any case, and without having to look for the causes, her second son was Eftychia's weakness. She never quarreled with him, never raised her voice at him, while with her Thanasis, not a week passed without a formidable quarrel between them. One of the frequent causes of quarrels was financial. Since her marriage to Barlabas (who was indifferent to his family), Eftychia struggled through years of hardship between the ages of 17 and 35. Fortunately, in the early years, she was helped by her mother, who occasionally gave her a gold coin, one of the hidden ones she had in the attic under a tile, which, when lifted, revealed a bundle of them. But year after year, the number of gold coins diminished.

When the gold coins could be counted on just the fingers of two hands, Eftychia's mother—who had arranged marriages for all her daughters and had been a widow for years—left and became a nun in a monastery in Attica. She was unwilling to be dependent on her sons-in-law, and after all, she had already made a vow. She chose a distant monastery to dedicate herself to because she did not want to see the disobedient Eftychia any longer serving her own whims, changing her lovers like shirts every so often. She left five gold sovereigns to Eftychia and took the other five sovereigns with her. With this life story, she was accepted into the monastery. Eftychia's children were now older, and they would work, and her daughter no longer needed her mother's charity.

In any event, things were not easy for her first-born daughter. As the saying goes, *The younger the children, the smaller the afflictions, the older the children, the greater the afflictions.* Eftychia's sons had a lot of personal expenses. They wanted clothes, a suit for Sunday, shoes for every day and other clothes for special occasions, shirts, ties, etc. They also spent some money on women. Thanasis, who slept with many women, spent more and additionally fed them in return. Aristides, who spent less money on women for the time being, paid a standard sum for his sexual trysts every Sunday. However, there was very little money left over for the household expenses.

Eftychia began to get annoyed. One day she gathered together her two sons and husband and told them the following:

"Listen here, you three. If you want to find a plate of food and washed and ironed clothes, you must pay me an amount every week. I am the bank. If you disagree, I'm dismantling the household. So many men are asking for my hand. I'm still considered attractive. The divorce is at the end of the process. A signature is all that awaits. *Capisce?*" (Italian for 'do you get it?')

The men of the house agreed to the terms of Eftychia. But every now and then, they wouldn't pay their total share, and she would become as mad as a Turk!

There were days when the cooking oil had run out, and the grocer declared that if the accumulated debt in his accounts was not repaid, he would not give her any more credit. In one such case, Eftychia asked Thanasis to give her what he owed her. He either had no money or pretended not to have any. Following this big argument Eftychia began a phase of passive resistance. For the next five days, there was no food in the house. Thanasis would leave in the morning and return in the evening. Aristides was away for army drills during this time. This was part of his mother's plan, who would not leave Aristides hungry for any reason. Zozo lived through this time eating some forgotten walnuts and water-boiled lentil soup.

Barlabas worked in a kitchen galley in the evenings and usually ate something there. But Pascha Holy Week was approaching.

Aristides had now returned from the army, and Thanasis was ashamed and paid a part of what was owed, and there was a temporary calmness in their house.

Holy Thursday had arrived. Eftychia—like an excellent traditional housewife—dyed the eggs red. On some of them, she even stuck some parsley leaves and wrapped them in old nylon stockings, creating pretty designs on the eggs. She kneaded her sweet *tsoureki* loaves (similar to brioche), and when Akis brought them back from the public oven, the house was fragrant with the smell of freshly baked tsourekia.

As soon as Thanasis took notice of the tsoureki—at first with his nose and visually right after—and as they were freshly baked and steaming, he grabbed one with his hands and began to wolf it down, growling with satisfaction. His mother started shouting:

"You ne'er do well! You pig-headed creature! Is nothing sacred to you? Christ is on the cross, and you're making me say filthy things. Can't you control yourself at all? I want you to know that too much food and women will destroy you!"

To escape her shouting, Thanasis left half of the tsoureki in the pan and said loftily:

"Hey, Mother, what do you want? I'll pay you for the tsoureki," and took a coin out of his pocket. Eftychia saw the cash, which she considered trivial in comparison to the cost of the tsoureki that her son had eaten, and started shouting again:

"My God, look at what the ungodly rascal is doing! He mistook Pascha for New Year's Eve and left a coin for...the Vasilopita (New Year's sweetbread)!"

These troubles frequently occurred in the house of the Barlabas family. Without them their lives would have probably been mundane and meaningless.

The next day was Holy Good Friday. Having collected the arrears of money, and after the starvation that everyone had endured through the previous week with the water-boiled lentils, Eftychia decided to compensate them. She went to the Modiano Market, where she bought mussels and squids, which she cooked with great skill. In the evening, she set the table and waited for them to eat. Just then, their neighbor, Mrs. Asimina, came into her house through the door of the kitchen that shared a common balcony with the kitchen of the next apartment. When she saw the table set, she exclaimed:

"Girlfriend! On Holy Good Friday, we don't set the table. We consider it a sin."

That's when Eftychia answered with the impressive words:

"My dear Asimina, we have Holy Good Friday every day. Not just today. It wasn't planned! Besides, we'll be eating fasting food; I''s late in the day, and as for the strict fasting... it's also ending soon!"

On that Holy Friday, Thanasis was late coming home. After Eftychia had waited for him for quite a while, she decided to call the rest of them for dinner. Eftychia, Aristides, and Zozo had gone together to the Epitaphios service (Pascha funerary lamentations).

Barlabas was bored with the comings and goings of the churches. For him going once a year for the Resurrection service sufficed.

After they had finished eating, Eftychia put a little of everything on a plate for Thanasis and covered it with the lid of a copper kettle to keep any flies away. He was late as usual.

Tired as she was, the housewife decided to lie down. After some time, she heard his whistle and footsteps as he leaped up the stairs three steps at a time. It was her son. His jacket was covered with some strange yellow and white stains. Eftychia got up to tell him about the food and saw the colors—waxy candle drippings.

Here' what had happened. Thanasis was checking out a girl, one of those who decorated the Epitaphios and, during the procession, would sing *The Myrrh Bearers* hymn, etc. Thanasis, being well-known for his carelessness about his clothing and in order to seduce the girl, stayed for hours in the church, and his suit was stained with the dripping wax from the candles. But he was delighted. He had handed her a love note saying he was in love with her and would be waiting to see her at the performance of the Karagiozis puppet[12] show opening on Pascha Sunday. After reading the love note, the young lass looked at him sweetly and nodded in agreement.

Our lover man was overjoyed. He had just broken up with an older girl, who tired him very much with her quirky nature and jealousy,

---

[12] A shadow puppet and fictional character of Greek folklore.

while now, in the spring (it was April and even Pascha), he would be starting a new relationship with a beautiful young girl!

"C'mon, my child. We've been waiting for you to eat together after the Epitaphios."

"I was at church, Eftychia," Thanasis replied, focusing his mind on the girl and the future with her.

He thanked his mother for the dish she had prepared for him and ate it in a hurry, as he was accustomed to doing. Instead of a fruit, he served himself two servings of sweet orange preserves from a jar. Eftychia caught him in the act and shouted.

"Hey, you! Thanasis! What are you doing there? The sweets are for treating guests. They're not for your pleasure. Put it down now…not saying it again!"

His mouth stuffed by the second spoonful, he swallowed hastily and replied:

"If you don't want me to eat your sweets, buy some fruit Mother, so we can eat that for dessert."

"You good for nothing! Where will the money come from to buy fruit with? With the pennies, you leave me? You pay for a 5-star hotel and want to pamper as if you were in Mediterrané Hotel. Listen to that. Fruit, he says…What do you think this is here? The Mediterrané Hotel or Grand Hotel de Paris?"

On the night of the Resurrection, they did not eat genuine *magiritsa* (traditional Easter soup made with the lamb's offal) at home. Simply put, Eftychia had managed to prepare a magiritsa—

though not authentic—but still a substitute for it by using a little ground meat. They all ate it with relish since they were ravenous not only because of fasting but also from their poverty.

But the first-born son was absent. On Holy Saturday, he had not slept at home and had not left her any money for the next fortnight. At around that time, Aristides had bought a suit and left her less money than he should have. As for her husband, as usual, he almost totally abstained from his financial obligations.

On Pascha Sunday, everyone in the neighborhood would be happy to be eating their lamb meal. Folk songs would be heard on the neighborhood radios. Many neighbors were already singing. Unlike all of them, however, Eftychia was in a sour mood. She had decided to slaughter the rooster, who was the lord in the henhouse of her yard. She didn't have the money to buy lamb. On the day of the Resurrection, she wanted her table to be somewhat festive. She could not tolerate continuing Lent. She resolutely went down to the yard carrying a pan and a knife she had sharpened at the Kapani Market the day before to slaughter the poultry.

As soon as she opened the chicken coop access and tried to catch him, as if sensing the danger, the rooster flew out terror-stricken and, flying uncertainly, managed to find himself on the branch of a dead tree that was in the yard. Then with a second leap, he jumped to another branch even higher. Eftychia tried to lure him in a sweet voice but had no luck. The rooster remained high and safe, gazing at his lady from above. She then removed the cover from a tin can and took some corn kernels from inside.

The corn is almost finished, she thought. *In a little while, there will be nothing left for my chickens to eat,* and she threw five kernels right under where the rooster was perched. Full of pride, he was lured by the sight of the kernels and jumped down to eat. Eftychia left three more seeds farther away, closer to the coop. The rooster devoured them rapidly, fearing that the hens might eat them, as one had already protruded from the opening of the chicken coop. Eftychia made the final move and threw a lot of corn into the chicken coop. The rooster and the hen instantly found themselves inside the coop, pecking away greedily, competing to gobble them up as fast as they could.

Just as she was about to grab the rooster more carefully this time, she heard the whistling of her Thanasis. He always whistled loudly the Russian melody "Otchi Tchornye"(Dark Eyes), a song that had stuck with him, and he whistled it very often, especially when he returned home pleased with his escapades.

Eftychia closed the chicken coop door again and ran to her son to ask him to help her in the slaughter. Upon seeing her son carrying half a lamb she became filled with joy and shock.

"Thanasis, is it lamb?"

"But of course, it's a lamb, Mother," Thanasis replied boastfully. Would I leave you without a lamb at Pascha?"

"And why didn't you bring it yesterday, my child?" Eftychia sweetly asked as she reopened the chicken coop so the still-living animals could go to graze and eat some worms. After the appearance of Thanasis, the rooster had, for the time being, escaped being slaughtered.

"Look here Mother. Yesterday I bought a whole lamb, but as I was bringing it home, I met up with Babis, the tubercular guy, and gave him a piece of lamb to get a solid meal inside him. Then by chance, I bumped into a girl I had recently met who lives in poverty. She's a divorcee living with a small three-year-old child. So, I told myself since it was the Pascha season, I should support her, and I went to her house, where I cut off the rest of half the lamb and gave her the intestines and liver to make magiritsa soup. In the evening, we went to the Resurrection service together, ate the magiritsa, and then...well, I want to say, but it's unsuitable for minors...I sinned on these holy days, but we had a good time; that is, we ate well... in all respects!"

"My Thanasis, I missed you, and you hurt me with your absence yesterday, but today you are compensating me," his mother replied, who was pleased even if only half the lamb had reached her hands. "Now, let's prepare the roasting pan so that you can take it to the neighborhood oven. Ah! What do I see here, the lamb's head? I'll give it to you exclusively. I know you like it!"

A few hours later, they all sat at the table and began eating, licking their fingers. Aristides had brought wine from the wine shop that was on the corner just below their house (a Brusco, red dry, with added some sweet wine to make it a sweeter drink). He did not want to straggle behind his brother in his mother's eyes, seeing that Thanasis had brought half a lamb.

While finishing the meal, Eftychia handed them some red eggs she had dyed on Holy Thursday.

"Come all. Let us clink our glasses and say a toast," she urged them. And I hope that the rest of the year our "clinking" will be reduced," she said as she engaged in discreet eye contact with Thanasis!

27

The Blue Suit

When on the rare occasions Thanasis had to wear a suit, he didn't wear a tie. His neck was broad and muscular, so he felt uncomfortable being squeezed by a collar and tie. Moreover…well, how do we say this…he looked like an ordinary common man, and if he wore a tie around his neck, it would look like a misspelled word. In fact, he didn't even own a tie. Since he did not have a suit, what would he need ties for anyway! But sometimes, according to the circumstances, he had to wear a suit and a tie. This was when he wanted to make a good impression on a new girl who seemed to hail from a higher-class family.

Something similar happened in the case of Mary. This young woman was the daughter of a merchant with a respectable shop in the market selling lighting fixtures. She had finished high school and held two foreign language certificates in French and English. She could also play the piano. Mary's house was in the same square as that of the Barlabas family, and the balconies of the respective kitchens were somewhat facing each other with an almost common courtyard divided in two by a low wall.

Young Barlabas had a lot of work in the yard then. Specifically, he had installed a dovecote of his own construction and spent many hours with the doves. Mary watched him from her balcony, and as she liked doves, they exchanged a few words about them. As soon as he realized that the girl liked him, our 'Casanova' found the courage to send her a pair of beautiful doves which he placed inside an elegant cage. He gave a kid a five-drachma banknote to deliver the gift. The gesture touched Mary very much. He then chose a time when her mother was at the market so that he could also give her a love note.

Thanasis, the seducer, then made his move with the note, inviting Mary to go to the cinema with him. The celebrated long-duration film *Gone with the Wind* was being shown. Thanasis had read the novel and started a conversation with her about the film. The date was soon arranged, and they found themselves together at the cinema where the film was being shown in its extended multi-hour version. During the intermissions, they would discuss the plot. The young woman was impressed by her neighbor's knowledge of literature and thought that the young man who spoke so beautifully and seemed well-read would have a similar education to hers. Finally, after the last intermission, they were seated in the dark hall of the theater. Thanasis had psychoanalyzed his victim. He had to make his moves very slowly so as not to provoke her reaction during the film; therefore, the only action he took was to hold her hand.

After the film was over at last, they finally came out of the theater excited not only by the film but also by the smooth progression of their acquaintance.

A few days later, it was the Dormition of the Holy Mother of God which is celebrated on August 15 and Mary, who was observing her name day, would be hosting a small party at her home. In her spacious sitting room, there was a gramophone with a wide variety of records so that they would be dancing the "La Cumbarsita" tango, "The Blue Danube" waltz, and other dances. She told Thanasis the news and invited him. He asked how he should be dressed and got the answer: "Usually, young people at my parties come in a suit." Then Thanasis replied, "Fine," but secretly he suppressed a nervous gulp because he did not have a suit available.

On the day of the party, Eftychia's son was in turmoil. He was looking for a suit and couldn't find one. His brother was wearing his only suit and had gone for a walk with a friend at the harbor.

When Aristides returned and took off his suit late in the evening, Thanasis sneaked it away and put it behind a curtain, and when his brother lay down on the bed, he took it and stealthily put it on. It seemed to him a little tight, of course (but what else could he do?), and he tiptoed out from the house like a thief lest he be noticed.

Thanasis' appearance in Mary's sitting room made a sensation. The blue suit with a white shirt and a white pocket square in his jacket pocket created an impressive outfit. After accepting his best wishes, the celebrant, who had begun to worry about his lateness, complained to him that he was very late. Thanasis justified his arrival time, saying that he was tired from training with his team and had overslept. The excuse was accepted, and after Mary had calmed down, she asked him to dance. He told her that he only danced the waltz, and they did him the favor of playing records of Johann Strauss waltzes on the gramophone.

After they danced two or three waltzes, Thanasis asked if they had any other songs like a Hasapiko (or Hasaposerviko, a traditional lively

Greek dance). The record with the Hasapiko was found, and the dance began, so the young man felt he was in his element. He had drunk two glasses of vermouth and was in a good mood. After the Hasapiko, they also played rebetika songs of Tsitsanis. Mesmerized as he was, Thanasis got up to dance, and while at one moment he was bending down to smack the floor with his hand, he heard the sound of a 'whizz'—of fabric being torn. And what a whizz that was…more like a mega whizz! The pants were the right size for Aristides but were too tight for him. So, it happened. The pants pulled apart at the middle seam. Everyone heard the ripping sound, and Pavlos, who was also after Mary, began to laugh boisterously. Thanasis restrained himself so as not to spoil Mary's party, but from that moment on, he sat in an armchair and did not get up again. When everyone started leaving, he got up, said his goodbyes to the hostess, and went out into the street. A little farther down the road, Pavlos was waiting for him with a friend, Nikos, and they said something to tease him. They were perhaps a little drunk. Thanasis answered them calmly.

"What do you want, guys? Looking for trouble?"

"Why, what kind of trouble are we gonna find, you boor?" Pavlos replied. "At most, we can tear up your jacket too."

Thanasis restrained his rage and took two or three steps away to distance himself. But arm in arm, the two friends proceeded towards him. When they reached his position, Pavlos forced Nikos to rush at Thanasis. The reaction was immediate. With his left elbow, Thanasis whacked Nikos' ribs, who, for a stunned moment, came to a standstill and then he gave a caressing back punch to Pavlos, saying, "Get outta here and leave off with the jerkoffs, you spoiled sissies."

However, Pavlos was not backing down, and he lifted his arms, preparing to throw punches. He tried to hit Thanasis with his right hand, but Thanasis stopped his punch with his hand. Pavlos then attempted to punch him with his left hand. He stopped that one with his hand too. Thanasis was now holding both of Pavlos' hands. Unable to strike with his hands, Pavlos kicked Thanasis' calf, but by now, Eftychia's son had lost patience and, having both of his hands occupied, gave him a head butt in the face. Blood began to spurt from Pavlos' nose, and his friend Nikos, seeing the blood, seemed about to faint. Thanasis held Pavlos in his hands so that he would not fall and helped him proceed to a public water faucet near the roots of an old sycamore tree, where he washed the blood from his face.

Nikos remained behind. Thanasis waited a while, made sure that the blood stopped running from Pavlos' nose and that he was not dizzy, and told him:

"Listen, Pavlos. Mary and I are a couple. Don't get between us, and don't pretend to be a bully because whoever annoys me learns his lesson. Do you know what that is? Then learn this. One of my punches means a concussion, and my whack means unconsciousness. One of my head butts means bleeding. You learned about my head butt, so don't go looking to learn the rest. Ah, I forgot to tell you. My kick in the abdomen means surgery. I see that you're ok so you can go home. After all, you don't live too far away. Go on now and be well. And know this. If you stay away and don't chase after Mary, I might even make you my friend!"

Pavlos said nothing, but what could he say, seeing how all messed up he was. He got himself together and took the road home. Thanasis walked around the block to get rid of the tension and finally headed for the house.

Thinking that everyone was inside and asleep, his mother had locked up and even left the key inside. Besides, even if Thanasis had a key with him, which he did not, he could not go in unnoticed. He had nowhere else to go to sleep at such a late hour, and of course, he didn't intend to sleep on the stairs. But he turned things around. He went down the stairs and out into the street. His house was on the first floor, and on the ground floor, there was the butcher shop with a perforated-mesh enclosure. He didn't think much of doing what he did. He climbed quickly by grasping the lattice and, with one leap as if on a monkey bar, found himself on the first-floor balcony.

From there, he could not get inside because it was his mother's bedroom, so he stepped on a cornice of the building there and quite easily found himself in the adjacent window that was half open. He squeezed into the house quietly, finding himself in the sitting room. He took off Aristides' suit, which was a mess—pants ripped, blood on the lapel from Paul's bleeding nose—and threw it like a sack into the bathtub without thinking twice. Zozo would find it there the next day and take care of it. Of that, he was sure.

The next day it so happened that Zozo didn't go into the lavatory or, if she did, she didn't bother with the suit. The lavatory was a completely separate space. But Aristides had planned a formal outing in the evening and started searching for his suit. He did not find it in the closet, and his mind immediately went to his brother. He had taken it without asking him another time, but this situation had gone on too long. His brother was asleep at the time, and Aristides thought that his brother's suit had been bartered off, as he always lacked cash. So, he started shouting. Thanasis was sleeping soundly and was not waking up. What could he do? Irritated as he was, he took a jug of water and poured it all over Thanasis' head. That's when everything went amuck. The older brother got up furious that he was being woken up so harshly, while at the same time, the younger one felt totally vindicated.

"You sold my suit, you rogue! You're going to pay me for that."

"Which suit did I sell?"

"You know which one. The one and only good one I have—the blue one."

"And who told you I sold it?"

"So then, what happened to the suit? Did it fly away?"

"I don't know. Find it. I didn't sell any of your suits." Right then, Zozo, who knew Thanasis' tricks, began to look for the suit. She searched behind the curtains first, searched behind a permanently hanging door, and finally entered the bathroom. There it was. The suit was bunched up in a tangle. She took it in her arms and inspected the mess. Apart from the ripping on the seam and the blood stains, the suit had crumpled quite a bit as Thanasis had tossed it into the bathtub.

"Here it is. The suit's been found. I had it for ironing," Zozo said to calm Aristides.

"Yeah…ironing. Hogwash!" Aristides shouted. You ironed the suit the other day. Let me see it. Oh, it's torn! Oh, Oh!… smeared with red paint!"

"It's not paint. It's blood," Thanasis said, who accidentally blurted it out.

"I'll kill you and go to jail, by God!" Aristides yelled, moving menacingly toward his brother.

Passing by the sink—probably for show—he grabbed a knife that was there. Thanasis saw the knife, retreated, and held a chair which he lifted in front of him like a shield.

Just then, hearing the commotion, Eftychia stormed into the kitchen. Along with her, Carla came in too, who hearing a fight, positioned herself between the brothers and began to bark. Seeing Aristides holding the knife, Thanasis holding the chair, and Zozo holding the suit, Eftychia figured out what was happening and decided to act. She let out a scream:

"Oh, my children! Don't…!" and promptly fainted. Eftychia rarely fainted. But her fainting spells were done diplomatically and were highly effective. Her sons forgot about the suit and set out to help her. So did Carla and Bibo, who both licked her in the face. That was it. The tension had dissipated.

Zozo took over—washing off the blood, sewing the seam that had torn apart, and ironing. In about half an hour, the suit was ready. The brothers had calmed down. Aristides found a fifty drachma note in the trouser pocket, which Thanasis had forgotten from the previous night, and said to his brother:

"Oh, I'll keep it, you butthead. For the rent and mental anguish. Yeah, you shifty dude. I'm keeping it because you're too much of a stubborn guy or, better yet...a mega-stubborn guy!"

"Fine. Keep it and have a beer on me," the older brother replied, subduing his anger. He realized that he was the cause of the situation that had arisen. Considering where things had gotten to, what else could he do? He accepted.

At the same time, Eftychia, exuding the fragrance of a perfume from the cologne that had been sprayed on her so she could recover, held Clara and Bibo in her arms and exclaimed:

"My darlings! I don't have two children. I have four. These are not dogs. They are my furry children too. My sweethearts! Oh! How they were kissing me when I fainted!"

28

The Rescues

As already noted, Thanasis Barlabas had a very caring heart and was very kindhearted, mainly towards strangers but less so to his family. His lack of interest in his family led to quarrels with his mother, who felt constantly wronged. Generally speaking, he was a defender of those who were weaker.

When he attended school, he had under his protection a weak and nearsighted classmate, Soulis, who the other children made fun of, that is, until Thanasis, who felt sorry for him, stopped them in their tracks.

"Whoever hurts Soulis will have to deal with me," he announced, taking a grim tone in the classroom in front of all his classmates who took this statement seriously. He also made similar statements to make it loud and clear that he did not want them to make trouble for the music teacher, who could not impose order in the classroom. This teacher was a small-framed, frail, middle-aged man with a high-pitched voice, whose wispy mustache was incapable of providing him with the masculine strength he lacked, and the violin bow he held was not as an effective disciplinary tool as the often-used birch rod of the gymnastics teacher!

Young Thanasis did not waste time messing around with being the president or leader of the class. But no one dared cross him on account of his physique. His minor entanglements in disputes had ended with knockouts of opponents of even the oldest kids or adults. Hence, while he was in school, he was generally recognized as both the physically strong child he was and for his sense of justice. This widely accepted respect he continued to retain throughout his life.

The era of his early youth had passed by and through the influence of the soccer club president on whose team he played goalkeeper, the twenty-five-year-old Thanasis Barlabas was appointed an employee of the Electric Company. At that time, four factory ships moored at the port, two in the harbor next to the Red Cross building and the other two at the Electric Company coast, located about seven hundred meters beyond the White Tower. These ships were essentially small power plants.

Thanasis' post was located inside a small substation at the port's entrance, where a panel filled with levers served to distribute the electricity produced by the two ships of the port. By moving the levers up or down, Thanasis was transferring power to some streets or cutting off the power to others so that the other two factory ships could undertake this task. Inside his workplace was a small desk, an armchair, a small wardrobe with shelves, and a telephone from which he took the relevant orders. In this post, one employee was always present, and it was operated around the clock in eight-hour shifts.

One winter night and even though an icy winter wind was blowing, our hero stepped away outside a few meters from his work site to do a few jumping jacks to stretch and unwind. Suddenly he spotted a young woman rushing to the dock and then jumping into the sea just beyond where he was. Without a second thought and in one quick movement, Thanasis took off his coat and suit jacket as well as his shoes and, in a flash, ran to the dock and, with whatever was left of the clothes he was wearing, dove into the sea, which was moderately agitated. But what is certain is that the water temperature did not favor...recreational swimming! With a few quick strokes, he approached the girl who had begun to sink, grabbed her by the hair and dragged her, swimming on his back with one arm towards the nearest steps at the pier where, with difficulty due to the waves, he pulled her out of the water. Then, while his underclothes were still dripping sea water, he carried her to the sidewalk and, holding her with her head downwards, carried her to his substation.

From his service in the navy, he knew what to do in case of drowning, so without delay, he began mouth-to-mouth resuscitation. He shouted at the sailor who was on watch in front of the two ships to notify the Red Cross by phone of the attempted drowning event and to come to take the girl to a hospital immediately. Indeed, shortly a nurse with an ambulance came from the adjacent building of the Red Cross, and soon the girl was taken to the Municipal Hospital where in the emergency outpatient clinics, the diagnosis was reported as "Attempted Drowning" and written in the admission book in large letters.

Meanwhile, Thanasis was shivering as he was wet and cold but had no way to notify anyone from his home to bring him dry clothes. The Red Cross gave him a towel to wipe off, some white pants worn by the nurses, and a white shirt in which he somehow settled in. Luckily his coat and jacket were dry. He loaded the stove with wood and turned his space into an oven, trying to warm up but also to dry his wet clothes (underwear, shirt, pants, socks).

After he finished the remaining four hours of his shift, Thanasis' clothes were still somewhat wet. As soon as his replacement came, Thanasis proudly recounted the night's events and then put on his still-damp clothes over the dry attire of the nurse and began to run towards his house. Once there, his yelling woke up Zozo and all the others who were sleeping. After recounting to them in a booming voice the rescue of the young woman, that is, how he jumped into the icy waters without his heavy clothes on, etc., he then asked his mother to give him a hot drink and for Zozo to provide him with underwear and pajamas. Eftychia decided to give him preventive alcohol rubbing as well because, as her son had described the events to them, pneumonia was likely to visit him. As soon as the rub down was over—which he greatly enjoyed—he drank two cups of hot linden tea, ate two large slices of bread smeared with butter and jam, and fell asleep exhausted as he did after each night's shift.

Two hours later, someone was knocking at the door, and Clara woke the world with her barking. Eftychia opened the door and saw a young man holding a briefcase asking to see Thanasis Barlabas. Her first thought was that he might be a court officer, and he was looking for her son because he owed money. His luck would not allow him to rest.

But before Eftychia could utter an excuse for Thanasis' "absence," the young man identified himself as a journalist and wanted to interview Thanasis about the remarkable deed he had performed that evening! So, whether he wanted to or not, her son, who was now awake as was to be expected from the barking, stood up and, with his still bloodshot eyes from the cold salty sea water and insomnia, began to narrate his accomplishments—let's be honest—filled with pride.

The journalist was taking notes in his notepad. When Thanasis finished his narration, he told him that the owner of the newspaper *Macedonia,* Mr. Giannis Vellidis, wanted to meet him personally. For this reason, that same afternoon, he would be at the "Poseidon Café", located opposite the spot where he worked in the port, right next to where he jumped into the sea and saved the girl.

In the afternoon of the same day, Thanasis went to the Poseidon Café and asked the waiter to tell him who Vellidis was.

"Really? You don't recognize Vellidis?" the waiter said with surprise. "He's over there in front sitting near the window, smoking a hookah."

Thanasis had heard a lot about the owner of the newspaper *Macedonia,* but he did not know him. He approached Vellidis and introduced himself. Vellidis stretched out his hand, congratulating him, and asked him if he wanted to give him a gift as a reward for rescuing the girl. Thanasis replied that he did not need anything, but if he had free time, he would gladly play a backgammon game with Vellidis because he had heard that he was good at backgammon. Vellidis gladly accepted the invitation, and soon the backgammon would begin.

"What are we playing for?" Vellidis asked.

"For a backgammon board," Thanasis replied. "A backgammon board nicely decorated like those made by prisoners."

"Fine," Vellidis replied, and he threw the first roll of the dice.

Several idlers had already gathered and were preparing to watch the match. The backgammon showdown kept the attendees' interest undiminished and lasted a long time because they had agreed to end the match play in the best of seven wins.

The game ended 7-4 in favor of Thanasis, and Vellidis congratulated the young Barlabas again.

The next day the news of the attempted drowning appeared on the inside page of the *Macedonia* newspaper with just a few lines. When he noticed this, Vellidis was furious. He called out a few editors and shouted at them.

"C'mon, you guys! Didn't you realize that rescuing that girl in the icy waters of the Thermaikos sea in winter weather was a journalistic scoop, and you had to emphasize it much more!" He gave them some instructions and even a note to that effect.

The next day, an employee of *Macedonia* brought to Eftychia's house a wonderful backgammon board that was decorated with various decorative patterns that had been created with thousands of small shiny mosaics. Along with the backgammon board, he gave them the *Macedonia* issue, which this time had on its front page and in a prominent position as its lead story, the rescue of a girl from the icy waters of the Thermaikos Gulf along with a photo of Thanasis from the newspaper's archive. The photo had also been published a month before on the sports page of the newspaper when our hero as a goalkeeper contributed a lot to his team's victory and was asked for a transfer by the ARES team in Thessaloniki. Our rescuer was sailing in a sea of happiness. He had become famous overnight.

That same afternoon he went to the hospital to visit the rescued young lady thanks to his self-sacrifice of diving into the icy cold waters without most of his clothes. He found her sitting in her bed and her suitor holding her hand, who she had quarreled with before her suicide attempt. With her youthful mind, she had thought for a moment that she no longer deserved to live. She was feeling fine but had a slight fever, so she was still hospitalized. Thanasis introduced himself to her and wished her well. He turned and said to her suitor, smiling:

"And look here. Try not to upset her because she's a good girl."

He took the chocolate they offered him, and he left satisfied with his chest puffed up with pride.

One night the following winter, Thanasis put on an American jacket that had been sent to him by Aunt Antigone from Chicago and went to his evening shift. Left alone after making some arrangements for the program of electrification of the streets over the phone, he went out for a while to smoke a cigarette, leaving the front door of his workplace ajar so that he could hear if the phone rang.

He went up to the watchtower of the port entrance and chatted with the guard. He asked when the young sailor was being discharged and Thanasis told him that he also served in the navy and even most of the time in the naval base of Piraeus and thus knew about conditions in navy service.

As their conversation was ending, the voice of a woman calling for help was heard. Thanasis took a step back for better visibility and in the darkness saw some male shadows surrounding a woman shouting for help. He ran towards them and started talking to them.

"C'mon, big guys. Leave the girl alone. What are you bothering her for?"

"None of your business, you faggot," one of the three men replied while the girl was struggling to get away.   But she could not as one of them was holding her tightly by the hand.

Thanasis approached the one man who was gripping the girl and gave him a sudden blow with the edge of his hand on the inside of his elbow, and in reflex, the nasty man immediately released the girl, who began to move quickly away. But before the man realized what was happening at hand, he got a hard punch to the face that felt like lightning and fell down. The tallest of the three men then approached Thanasis (who like a guardian angel was protecting the girl) with the apparent purpose of beating him up. But before he could do so, Thanasis kicked him in the stomach, and he folded in two, gasping for breath. Before the third man could react, Thanasis punched him in the jaw as well, and he collapsed half-unconscious on the sidewalk close to another of the group.

The first guy, who had previously been holding on to the girl, got up and tried to attack Thanasis, but Thanasis was not an easy opponent. After repulsing the opponent's punch, Thanasis gave him a hard punch to the stomach which made him crouch over, and, as he was bent over, Thanasis grabbed him in a headlock and threw him on his back to the ground. He even sat on top of him and raised his fist to punch him again when the neutralized opponent began pleading, asking to leave him be, and even calling Thanasis by name.

"Barlabas, have mercy! Let me go!" It seems he knew Thanasis from soccer or some other occasion. Thanasis then stood up and said to them loudly:

"Buzz off, you delinquents, and next time behave like gentlemen with women, not bums. Get out of my sight so I won't damage you even worse."

The sailor guard witnessed this scene but could not get involved because, by regulation, the guard was not allowed to move from his guard post. But he shouted, "Bravo! Well done, man! They deserved what you gave them."

The three hotheads ran off unnerved, their heads hanging down. A little farther off, they began to quarrel with each other. The tall man blamed the others who did not help as a team. The last person who had previously begged Thanasis to let him go said, "But what strength Barlabas' fist has! I felt it as if it was made of iron. I'm still in pain…feeling dizzy…I don't feel well," and, while saying this, he fell unconscious to the ground.

The other two tried to help him but in vain. Then the two of them lifted him by the armpits and carried him to first aid at the Red Cross, making sure—as best as they could—not to pass near Thanasis. After the unconscious man was treated by elevating his legs, the doctor diagnosed a fractured cheekbone and referred the injured man to the on-duty ward.

The following day, as soon as Thanasis' replacement came to the Public Power Corporation substation, our hero excitedly narrated the events that took place the previous night. He then left to go home to sleep. When he got there and after stroking the dogs that provided him with the usual joys and caresses, he heard Zozo say to him in a reproachful tone.

"Thanasis, where did you rip your jacket?"

He took off the jacket to examine the rip and found that he had a small tear in the middle of its back.

"But your shirt has also been torn," Zozo added. "Take it off so I can sew it up."

Thanasis took off his shirt, but then Zozo saw some dried blood at the point where the fabric had been torn. Immediately afterward, sensing something suspicious, our hero also took off his undershirt, which was similarly torn and had blood. In the meantime, Akis also showed up and visually examined his cousin's back, noticing that just below his shoulder blades, there was a wound that apparently had been made by a pocketknife or other small knife. The depth of the damage was minor, probably because the thick cotton jacket prevented the sharp killing tool from sinking deep into his lung. Akis, a dental student at the time, applied iodine and covered the small wound that was at most one centimeter deep with sterile gauze and bandages.

"So…that louse! He kept begging me to let him go and not hit him anymore, even though he had stabbed me while we were fighting! I felt like something was stinging me, but I figured it was from a kick I'd gotten in the match the previous day. Can you believe that bum stabbed me?"

This is what Thanasis was saying, and everyone who listened wondered how he could not have known he was being stabbed.

"When the wounds from a knife are still hot, what I mean by hot is very recent, they're often not felt," Akis explained.

The next day a young woman came by Thanasis' work and left a small package that read:

"For the courageous man who helped me last night at midnight."

Thanasis was away because he had a day off, so he got the gift the following day. It was a bottle of Old Spice cologne and a note saying that she thanked her savior for saving her from three drunken bums who wanted to rape her. She added that she worked as a private nurse and had previously attended to a sick woman to inject her with penicillin which is done every six hours.

The sailor on guard told all his colleagues that Thanasis beat up the three louts. From that moment on, many asked him to tell them about the battle he fought simultaneously against his three opponents. So, after reporting to them the various phases of the struggle with a complete description of the details—after all, the battle had only lasted only a minute and a half— he ended with this conclusion:

"From now on, they'll know that one of my whacks means a concussion, and my punch knocks you out. Besides that, a pocketknife does nothing against me. Next time they need to bring a sword!"

29

The Burn

When Thanasis worked as a clerk in the Electric Company, he was popular among his colleagues because he treated those around him kindheartedly and was known as a soccer player. After all, his feats—saving a drowning girl and beating up three bullies who badly harassed an on-duty nurse—had become widely known, and his name was on everyone's lips.

One day three of his colleagues approached him. They suggested that he run as a presidential candidate of the "HOPE" party in the elections of their trade union, which consisted of "non-partisan supporters of the republic," as they assured him. They explained that many colleagues considered him to be the most suitable person for this position, and as he was widely known and popular, he would be voted for by almost all the voters.

"C'mon, guys. I've never dealt with such matters," Thanasis objected half-heartedly to their proposal.

"Look here. You're a smart young guy, and you'll make it. You'll learn the tricks. Incentives make the world go round."

"Do you think they'll vote for me?"

"That's for sure. Just now, as we were coming here, we met a crew that was going to install cables on the street, and they asked us who was running for president. We told them that you might step up, and they got excited and started shouting rhythmically, 'BAR-LA-BAS PRE-SI-DENT! BAR-LA-BAS PRE-SI-DENT!' as if there was a demonstration going on."

"What would my obligations be?"

"You would preside over the meetings of the Board of Directors, usually one per month unless serious extraordinary issues arise, in which case there will be extraordinary meetings. You will go to Athens for contacts with the Athenian Union and perhaps for protest demonstrations at the Ministry of Industry. You will also preside over general meetings of members."

"Well, guys, how can I be away in Athens if I work in Thessaloniki?"

"Don't worry about that. A law allows the president and board members to be absent for union jobs."

"When are the elections?"

"In a month."

"OK, I accept. But be aware of this. I like clean jobs. If I see fraud and shenanigans, I'll give it up."

"Hey man, c'mon… don't worry. Everything will be fine, and we'll stand by you."

Thanasis ran around vigorously in that pre-election month: He visited the headquarters and talked with the pencil pushers. He went to the "Doxa" (Glory) district where he met the electricians and the linemen, boarded the specialized ships on the coast—which, as we said in a previous chapter, functioned as small power plants—went to construction sites and small workshops, and presented the platform of his candidacy in general terms. But at the same time, he also learned about the various existing problems and requests.

On election day, he asked for a loan from Aristides.

"Aristides, would you give me two hundred drachmas on loan, and I'll return it to you as soon as I'm paid."

"Broke again?"

"The union is having elections, and I'm running for president, so if I win, which I probably will, but why am I saying probably—wrong about probably—I'll definitely win, so I'll have to treat people with something."

"And how do you know I have any money?"

"Come on now...you're like an ant. You only know how to collect!"

"OK, bro. You're lucky that I love you, and I can't refuse your request, but I want it back fast because I have a promissory note to pay in 10 days."

"Yeah, bro! You'll have it on Saturday when I get paid."

"Just be aware on Saturday that you don't get into trouble and don't come home with empty pockets."

The elections took place, and Thanasis was elected first in ballots by a large margin from the runner-up. His overjoyed constituents greeted him with handshakes, some kissed him crosswise on the cheeks, and some more well-known types gave him friendly slaps on his prematurely balding head. The newly minted trade unionist spent his brother's two hundred borrowed drachmas on treats, plus his own money. The first council meeting was held that evening, and the executive committee was voted in. He was the new president.

A month later, there were problems with workers claiming an allowance for dangerous work. Thanasis had to go down to Athens. In the meantime, the other councilors asked to go together.

"Hey, guys, why should we all go to Athens? Three people are more than enough," the president said. "Let just me, the secretary, and the vice president go so we don't spend much money."

"No, we must exert pressure. The more of us there, the better."

"Well, fine then." Thanasis compromised and added, "But be aware our union fund doesn't have a substantial reserve."

The council traveled to Athens by train. They went to the Ministry, but the minister was away on a service trip. They tried to see the general secretary, but he was constantly busy. *Now he's in a meeting; now he's talking to the minister on the phone; now he's been asked to speak on the phone by the secretary of another ministry…*

The hours went by, and Thanasis began to get hungry. At three o'clock in the afternoon, they were all fed up, and as soon as the president said, "Let's call it a day and go and eat something because I'm starving," there was a consensus, and they left to find a restaurant serving good food at reasonable prices. At the restaurant, Thanasis' portion was too small to satisfy him, but he had his mind set on trade union matters and didn't mind.

In the late afternoon, the ministerial building was closed. The next day they went there again early in the morning but found the doors shut and then noticed a sign informing them that the Ministry was open to the public on Mondays, Wednesdays, and Fridays.

"Now, what do we do?" the president asked.

"We have no money to spend on staying extra days," the treasurer said. "I suggest we go back and come again another time."

"I could stay in Athens longer," Thanasis said, thinking of staying a night in his grandmother's monastery. "I'll stay another day and see the minister."

"It's not possible," the others replied in unison. "We must stick together. We'll go back and come back again."

So, they returned to Thessaloniki without having accomplished anything. The trip to Athens incident—with the failure to meet the Minister—was conveyed by the experienced "trade unionists" to the general assembly that was held as a result of the Minister's refusal to see the executive committee, the general secretary's misconduct, the government's mockery of the workers, etc. Thanasis was more restrained, but the old-timers advised him by saying, "This is what they must tell them for the employees to rally and fight together."

An emergency financial contribution from the workers was requested for the council to take another trip to Athens. Some gave a little money, and so the next trip was organized. The outcome was the same. The Minister was away in Parliament, then had a meeting with a committee of technicians, then left for the town of Ptolemaida for some inauguration so they couldn't meet him. After all—as a beautiful red-haired secretary told them—they had to make an appointment.

Here Thanasis messed up.

"Miss, where can we meet to discuss matters quietly?" he asked, winking at her, but she threw a dismissive look at him and turned her back on him. Fortunately, the other council members did not notice his blunder because they were viewing a poster of the new unit of Ptolemaida. The assumption was that they would have to return to Thessaloniki once more. But that evening, to find solace, they took refuge at the bouzouki club where a new singer would perform, who—as a taxi driver assured them—was a rising star.

So, they went to the club at 9:30 PM and were the first customers there. The club was empty, and they waited half an hour smoking and chatting. Finally, a waiter appeared and took orders. The drinks came, and at 11:00 PM, the first dishes came. At 11:30 PM, some strangely smelling meats were served, and at midnight, they were fed but disappointed; two more groups came, and the musicians took their seats. Soon the band, which was made up of six people seated in a row of chairs on a platform half a meter higher than the floor, began to play. Other customers arrived, who apparently knew that the program started after midnight. A singer also appeared with a squeaky voice singing light pop Greek songs. They were near the loudspeakers, so her voice drove them crazy. Then came another female singer of a certain age, who had a voice almost like a man from all the cigarettes she smoked and sang some urban folk songs. They waited for the headliner to appear, but nothing.

In the meantime, they were getting sleepy, so they called the waiter over and asked him when "the big guy" would come out to perform. He replied to them that it would be around exactly 2:00 AM. It was still 1:00 AM. They had all awakened early in the morning to catch up with the minister before he got caught up with other obligations. Regardless of whether they had failed to see him, they had eaten enough and were now in the phase of digestion, so they were sleepy and felt that it was impossible to wait any longer. After a quick conference (what the hell…they were trade unionists), they unanimously decided to leave. They asked for the bill, and when they saw it, they found out that in addition to what they ate, they would also be paying for something they didn't eat, called a "cover charge." Quite embarrassed and with empty pockets, they all left to go to bed. They also paid a night fare in two taxis and arrived at their hotel on a side street off Omonia Square. They would sleep four in one room and another three in another to save some money.

In the morning, they woke up early, having learned their lesson. They did not attempt to go to the Ministry because it was closed to the public. Instead, they took the first train back to Thessaloniki.

A general conference was held in the following days. The experienced trade unionists, cunningly but fanatically opposed to the government, voiced their exaggerated opinions, such as the minister's refusal to talk to them and the bad behavior of the Ministry's bureaucrats. Many people took to the floor and expressed their views. The government trade unionists argued that communication and discussion with the minister should be made by being adequately prepared. Opponents agitated the audience with various speeches.

After six hours of discussions, most of the men with families gave up and went home. At 11:30 PM, with very few union men left, (in relation to the total number of registered union members), it was decided, at the suggestion of some, to hold a five-day strike by the union. Even though he was President, Thanasis disagreed with the idea of a strike because he understood the existing hostility and considered the strike a premature action, so he voted against it. Those trade unionists who had endorsed him as a presidential candidate verbally attacked him and called him a coward and a servant of the bosses when they saw that he was not towing their line. Tired of hearing speeches and his eyes stinging from the smoke of cigarettes, Thanasis realized that political games were being played behind his back, so without giving it much thought, he replied:

"I fundamentally disagree with your tactics and resign as president." He turned his back on them and walked away.

As he walked out of the room, two burly trade unionists followed him at his heels and suddenly rushed at him in the darkness of the street. One thug caught him by his arms, crushing him from behind to immobilize him so the other guy could hit him. But the recently resigned president was experienced in such matters. He raised his arms over and behind his assailant and locked them on the attacker's back. At the same time, he abruptly bent his head down, bending his torso. As a result, his attacker was disgorged with his head on the ground and was even dragged, smashing hard into a pole. The second bully, intending to attack Thanasis, was taken aback by Thanasis' immediate reaction, thanks to which his accomplice was neutralized, so being a wiser collaborator, he decided to cease and desist.

So, ended this disgraceful attack on their former president by the two fanatics. One of them was pretty frightened, and the second one, dazed with a bruised face and full of abrasions and blood, set off to find a pharmacy to get first aid. Since there was no longer any intention of attacking him again, our hero turned around and said to them, "Well dudes, next time when you see me, switch sidewalks. Capisce?"

That same evening after this episode, the newly resigned "president" immediately went home. Coincidentally, no one was there except the dogs who were overjoyed, not having seen him in days. After cuddling and quieting them down, he opened the door for them to go to the yard for their needs. Then he looked around to see what he could eat. There was nothing ready, but he found enough eggs. He took eight of them, broke them into a plate, beat them with a fork, mixed them with plenty of cheese, and thus made a large omelet that he fried in the large pan where the butter had previously melted. He also sliced a large tomato for his salad. The omelet was delicious, so he ate it satisfactorily, along with half a loaf of bread. He searched for fruit, but there was nothing except lemons. He took two of them and squeezed them with a lemon squeezer, added a whole spoonful of sugar and some water, and drank his lemonade. He lay down, grabbed the *Thesaurus* magazine to read a little, and solved the crossword puzzle. In just a few minutes, he was fast asleep.

When all the family members later returned, Thanasis slept through the noise with the sleep of the righteous, and nothing could wake him up, no matter how much commotion there was. The following day was Sunday, and when Eftychia returned from church, she found her son sprawled awake in his bed and stroking Clara, who was making cheerful yaps.

"Thanasis, lately you've been sleeping around in other places. Who's the female whose bed you're sleeping in now?" Eftychia asked.

"Leave me alone, Mother. I went to Athens for jobs for the union where I was president. We had a union's meeting afterward, but now I've resigned and I'll rest easy."

"That's fine, but with all this and that, it's been a week since you were supposed to give me your share," Eftychia retorted anxiously. "I don't have any money to cook anything. What kind of people are you leaving me hanging here, and I've got so many mouths to feed."

"I'll give you the money when I get paid."

"When. What does that word mean...when? The when doesn't exist. I want it now. Otherwise, I don't cook today."

Thanasis dressed in a hurry and left so that his mother's grumbling would not continue, but at noon when he returned, he found Eftychia in a state of fury.

"Thanasis, who took the eggs I had in the kitchen? There were twelve eggs, two for each of us to eat today, and now four are left."

"C'mon, Mother, two eggs aren't enough for me," said her son puzzled.

"And is that why you ate eight eggs?"

"I came home hungry from the assembly—so many hours of blah-blah—I'd only had some nibbles of kebabs, and I was hungry," Thanasis retorted, feeling justified.

"You rascal! Can one man eat eight eggs for lunch? Aren't you afraid of either cholesterol or your mother? Get up now and go and get me ten eggs if you want to eat something. Otherwise, Zozo and I will eat two eggs, and you men can go to the devil!"

Although he knew his pockets were empty, Thanasis searched them anyway. He found only a note he had used in his speech to the union assembly.

Then Eftychia boiled over with anger when her son said:

"Give me some money to go get you some eggs!"

"Are you saying you don't have money for eggs either? You're unbearable. Which slut did you spend it with?"

The quarrel began to intensify, and in an instant, Eftychia, irritated by her son's apathy, opened her mouth and said with a booming voice:

"Just like you infuriate me every so often, and I burn in anger, may fire fall on you and burn you too!"

"You're cursing me again, Mother," Thanasis uttered fearfully. "No curses again. The last time you cursed me, my tongue got cut. Now what do you want for me? To be struck by lightning?"

"Just leave so I don't have to look at you and get upset," his mother replied faintly after uttering the curse, but she immediately regretted it as she thought of the possible consequences of the curse if, of course, her curse could come to pass.

With his head bowed, Thanasis left the house and went to play some backgammon for money. If he won, he would at least have a few coins in his pocket; if he lost, he would owe them. As was the case most of the time, he won, and with the money, he got a cheese pie which could not satisfy his hunger but was better than nothing.

In the afternoon, he started working the second shift of the day. The room he was working in was chilly because the mistral winds blew demonically under the door, which had a large gap. So, he turned on an electric heater to warm up. After the two electric coils of the stove turned red, he decided to light a cigarette. As was his habit, he first spit on it on one side and then tapped the edge of the cigarette on the packet. Finding no matches and holding the cigarette in his mouth, he bent over, approaching one coil of the heater, and tried to suck air to light it. But what he did not notice was that the cigarette's tip rested on the coil, and since his saliva moistened the cigarette paper, a short circuit developed, and a kind of lightning flash burned his face and chest.

"Oh God! What just happened? The curse has come to pass!" He shouted for help in despair.

The addicted smoker, whose mother had cursed, spent the next ten days hospitalized in a private clinic and could not smoke, not only because he was not allowed but also because he had blisters from burns on his lips and face. A whole army of colleagues, friends, and fellow athletes visited him daily. On the very first day, his mother visited him and, showing her concern, said:

"What have you done, my child?" she asked tenderly, her motherly instinct awakening.

"I told you, Eftychia. Your curses are powerful. So, please, no more curses. I'll do whatever you tell me," Thanasis kept repeating every so often.

A few days after he was released from the clinic, the soccer team of the burnt man was scheduled to play a crucial match. The madman played with the burn on his hand, still bandaged. However, he still sustained his reputation by allowing only one goal resulting in adoration by his team's fans who knew he had suffered burns just two weeks before.

After the burn, Eftychia's older son's character took shape and became beyond reproach in his obligations. Each time he collected his salary, he would place his share in his mother's hands. Eftychia would then smile secretly, thinking that it was her luck that her curses could be fulfilled. After all, as the saying goes, *Silence is golden, but the squeaky wheel gets the grease.*

Of course, with the passage of time, in some ways, Thanasis slackened and the problems with his unreliability began again. But his mother never cursed him again. She had come to fear the power her curses hid.

30

The Mini Denture

The two front teeth of Thanasis' upper jaw had been missing for the past three months. Instead of kicking the ball, that tough center-forward, Vasilis, of the THERMAIKOS team had given Thanasis a solid kick in the face when he fell at Vasilis' feet in the act of self-sacrifice to make the save. When Thanasis recovered from the shock, still covered with blood, he wanted to ask the forward what made him do that but could not mumble even one word because the field doctor had stuffed some gauze in his mouth to bite on to stop the bleeding.

That evening they met in the café where many soccer players would frequent, and the following dialogue occurred:

"Thanasis, I apologize. I didn't mean to kick you. I was going for the goal, and you were preventing it."

"Sure, Vasilis, but you almost killed me today. Is that how we play? We're talking about playing ball, not getting killed. Look at me now. My lips are swollen, and my two teeth are gone."

"It's not my fault, Thanasis. I was trying to score goals, and you had your head in front of my leg!"

"Next thing you're gonna tell that your foot was in danger!"

"Well yeah…actually it was. What do you think? It was moving against your head, and going against a player's head is forbidden," Vasilis teased.

"Look here. I'm talking serious. Two of my teeth are gone, my whole mouth is bruised, my lips are double in size, and I don't have the guts to go out with my chick. Figure it out and pay me the costs of the repair. Dentists are expensive as hell. They don't care about whether or not you can afford it."

"C'mon, take five hundred," Vasilis offered, who never had a problem with money because his father had owned a house on Vasilissa Olga Avenue and had exchanged it with a developer for several condominiums.

Thanasis took the money but did not immediately go to the dentist because he was afraid. Besides, in the first few days, he was still very swollen. Of course, when he smiled, the people he spoke to saw a significant gap in the center of his upper jaw. Seeing he was being watched, he would hide his mouth with his hand when he remembered to.

One morning during that time, the following dialogue took place:

"Thanasis, you have to go to the dentist. Your teeth are in bad shape," Aristides told him.

"I can't stand that drill, so I've put it off…but now there's no avoiding the bitter pill," Thanasis replied.

"You should go to mine. His name is Antonis," Eftychia interrupted. "He has a gentle hand and is also affordable. I consider him my trustworthy dentist since Electra's husband died. Ah…it's sad how we've lost them both," Eftychia sighed. "He doesn't take much money from me because I'm his mother's friend. But you guys too. He'll charge you a good price. Look here…I broke these two front teeth a long time ago when I tried to crack open an almond with them, and Antonis made me a prosthetic that goes in and out to make it easier to clean. It's attached to the side teeth with hooks."

"Is that the Antonis I used to punch when he was little? He'd hold it against me," Thanasis replied thoughtfully.

"C'mon, don't talk nonsense. He's an excellent young guy and quite the expert," Aristides interjected. "He's given me two fillings, and I was very pleased. He doesn't remember when you smacked him 20 years ago."

"OK. Anyway, I'll go," Thanasis said half-heartedly and went to look at his teeth in the mirror.

One evening we were sitting on the balcony to cool off since it was almost summer and we heard the whistling of Thanasis. In the last few years, he would whistle the tune of "Otchi Chornya". Elated, Bibo began to bark behind the door because Thanasis often brought him a small piece of chocolate. When he entered the apartment, he announced the news cheerfully.

"I went to the dentist. In a week, I'll be getting a new mouthpiece."

"May you wear it in good health," Eftychia said.

"I'll need a few loans," he added. "They cost two thousand, and I only have 800 drachmas. And we're only at the start of the month," he added.

"Don't look at me. I'm not the Bank of England," Eftychia quickly stated firmly.

Aristides put his hand in his pocket where three thousand drachmas were temporarily resting.

"I got paid the day before yesterday. I can lend you a thousand."

He took the money out of his pocket and left a thousand for Thanasis on the table. Then he gave a thousand to Eftychia.

"Here, Mother. Take it for my share for July. I have a thousand left to spend for the month. Too bad I was thinking about taking a week's vacation. You've left me broke. Let's see how I get by."

"C'mon, Mother. Give me a five hundred at least, and I always come back with even more," Thanasis complained.

"If I give you the five hundred, what's left won't last for ten days," Eftychia said, thinking about the rent and what she owed to the grocer, the greengrocer, and the butcher.

"Well, are we, or are we not a family? I happened to find myself in need. Just a little help is what I'm asking for…temporarily. I'm not asking for a handout like a beggar. I'm asking for it as a loan," Thanasis complained, distressed.

"I'm not giving you the five hundred," Eftychia repeated and, at the same time, grabbed the thousand that Aristides had placed on the table for Thanasis. "I'm taking it and keeping it on your behalf. When you need to pay the dentist, I'll pay him myself. First off, there will be profit. Until then, you won't waste the money with the chicks, and secondly, I'll make the relevant negotiations with Antonis."

"How can I squander the money with this disgusting mug that's prevented me from even daring to approach a woman for so long!"

A few days later, Thanasis showed up with his dental bridge. The dentist had extracted another tooth that was loose and unsuitable for support, and now there were three false teeth fixed in his mouth with some hooks but had impressively restored his appearance when he smiled.

A short time went by, and Thanasis returned home one evening looking exhausted. He had spent the day with Zetta, a new conquest who worked as a bar waitress and took a day off every Monday. At that time, Aristides and Thanasis slept in the same room in two single beds placed parallel to each other. Content with his new teeth, Thanasis lay down to sleep, but his gums were bothering him. He wasn't used to his new teeth yet, or they didn't fit perfectly well, so at some point, he took them off and put them under his pillow.

He slept deeply and, in the morning, got up refreshed and ready to go to work. After washing up, he began his customary daily prayers of forgiveness by taking deep bows to the floor as his grandmother, the nun, had taught him. As he played with his daily morning cigarette, his coughing began waking up the whole world.

At this time, Akis was a little late getting up in the morning as he was studying very late at night, taking advantage of the quiet of the night to prepare for exams at the University. During the day doing research and reading were problematic in a house which was more like a transit center.[13] Asimina would come over from next door; the postman would ring the doorbell; then the iceman in the street was shouting selling the ice; a friend of Eftychia's would come over; a tallyman who sold on credit women's items, panties, bras, robes...anyway those kinds of things. And all this hubbub was apart from the two dogs barking each time somebody knocked on the door

---

[13] From Akis' personal diary. "I'm taking an Anatomy exam at 3pm today. We take this course along with the doctors and we use the same huge book by Savvas. I woke up at 7 am hearing the song "alpha beta to-ro-ro" that a troublemaker kid from the upstairs apartment wouldn't stop singing this early. I studied until 9 am. I ate something in a hurry, drank coffee and tried to continue studying. But as my luck would have poor me, I was only able to study until 10:15 am. From then on, the house became a transit center. The dogs barked every now and then because something was happening. Thanasis was lying on his bed and as soon as he woke up he started coughing, the turtle was crawling somewhere and making a 'crunch crunch' noise, the bird was singing, the doorbell was ringing downstairs like a possessed demon. Not even brainwashed in the cellars of the GPU would be worse. The seamstress came, the iceman came, Thanasis got up, Pitsa came with her snotty baby—the one who married a friend of Aristides although five years older than him and now they're having problems and she was telling my aunt her sorrows—I switched rooms to find peace, but then Thanasis entered the room again. He started blowing his nose like a peasant and as always coughed to clean out his lungs. He did not fail to do his penances, so another stormy coughing episode commenced. The seamstress left. Pitsa and her baby and my aunt went to the kitchen for coffee, very close to where I was studying, so again I changed my spot and went to the front room. The conversations of the women from the kitchen sounded annoying. I went and closed all the intermediate doors. Not 15 minutes passed, and the women came back to the room, where I had just devoted myself to studying. Then I went back to the back room with my nerves broken and to let off steam I sat down and wrote the narrative of this day. The day when, most likely, I will be cut in Anatomy or hopefully pass, despite all the adverse conditions I had trying to do a final review of the lesson!"

or climbed the stairs. At that time, there were two dogs in this house of marvels.

The coughing awakened Aristides just as Thanasis was finishing his customary prayers. As soon as he settled down with the last fit of coughing and cleared out his lungs, he searched to find his dentures on the bedside table. They were not there. He looked under the pillow. Nothing. Now angry, he threw the pillow off the other bed and lifted the sheet. His dentures were nowhere to be found. He leaned under the bed and looked in front of a suitcase. Nor had they fallen there. He pulled out the suitcase in case they had fallen behind it. They weren't there either.

"Hey, you good for nothing! Are you making fun of me and hiding my teeth?"

"No, Thanasis…seems to me you must be joking," Aristides replied, hiding his laughter with difficulty.

Thanasis vaguely remembered taking out his teeth while lying on the bed, but doubts set in that he might have taken them off and left them somewhere else. He went to the bathroom to look there too. Three minutes later, after toppling everything over—drawers, cupboards, containers, etc.—he found a mini denture. It was Eftychia's, not his. This denture consisted of two teeth missing from Eftychia's upper jaw, so it was impossible for the two dentures to match each other! However, in desperation, Thanasis tried testing them in his mouth. In vain. Eftychia's artificial teeth could not be secured because they fastened on only one hook on one side, and both teeth leaned towards their free side. In addition, they left the position of one tooth uncovered.

Aristides and Zozo noticed Thanasis' attempt to use Eftychia's teeth, and they began to laugh; the more they laughed, the funnier it seemed to them, and they held their bellies from so much laughter, the most boisterous fit of laughter erupting after Thanasis lifted the mattress off his bed and searched underneath as if the metallic dental bridge had legs and had walked under the mattress to hide.

Naturally, the denture wasn't there, and Thanasis, tired of searching, exclaimed, "Oh my God, help me!" and, disappointed, lay down on the mattress after putting it back on his bed. But as soon as he lay down, something scratched him on the shoulder blade. He thought it might be a safety pin, and he put his hand on his back to check it, so he touched…what else? The denture! This playful bauble had caught itself on the shoulder strap of his flannel undershirt.

The amazing thing was that in the last few minutes, Aristides had noticed it. Still, his uncontrolled laughter prevented him from saying even a word since, just then, his brother was trying to see if he could fit his mother's denture into his mouth. Neither did Thanasis expect such a quick response from God after that. "Oh, my God, help me!"

Relieved, he inserted the denture in his mouth and hurried out because he was already late. *What an adventure on this day, too* he was thinking as he smiled with self-assurance at the good-looking neighbor from the adjacent apartment building who just at that moment happened to be going out shopping.

31

Aristides the Merchant

After his discharge from the army, Aristides continued to work in a large shoe store in the central shopping district where he was responsible for men's merchandise. But his department was in the shop's basement, so he worked continuously in dark and humid conditions.

Shortly before he started working, the worst had happened. A co-worker in the same shop contracted tuberculosis. When Eftychia found out, her anxiety knew no bounds. She began including meats often in meals such as chicken and forced her son to take vitamins every day to strengthen his stamina.

Aristides endured the work in the basement for six whole years, stubbornly and carefully saving enough money to accumulate a small amount of capital with which he intended to start a business of his own. Unlike his brother, who was a wastrel, Aristides was frugal and systematic in everything he did. Even though Thanasis was then working at DEH (Public Power Company) and was paid every Saturday, by the time Monday came Thanasis would be asking for a loan from Aristides. It became an inexplicable phenomenon!

"Aristides, please give me a hundred. I'm broke."

"Well, gee whiz Thanasis! When did you have time to spend it? You just got paid the day before yesterday, didn't you?"

"Of course, I got paid, but…well…you know…I've got a lot of expenses. I gave my share to our mother, paid for outstanding loans—grocer, greengrocer, butcher—bought a shirt, ate out with Marina, and, without realizing it, the money ran out."

"Marina! Is that your new girl's name? What happened to Georgia? Did you break up?"

"Hey, Aristides. Leave off with the interrogation. Just give me a hundred. I'll return it as soon as I'm paid."

"No, I'm curious. First, you answer me what happened to Georgia."

"The schedule with Georgia is Monday, Wednesday, Friday. The other days are scheduled for the new ones, and Marina is one of the new ones."

"But how do you manage this, Thanasis? Is your pocket like a bucket with holes? Don't you realize that your women consume all the money you make? And you did make a lot of money with the jobs you were doing selling old car tires when the English were here and considered these tires useless!"

"C'mon! Hand over the hundred now because I'm in a hurry!"

"Well, fine then, take it again. What's the use? I love you even with your faults. But you'd better repay me as soon as you get paid because I owe some installments to my tailor."

"Why? Are you getting another suit made?"

"Yes, and I'm warning you—don't you dare hide it from me if you wear it because we'll start a feud!"

Listening to her children, Eftychia injected herself into the conversation.

"My dear Thanasis, I just can't understand how you've become so wasteful. Who did you take after? Why do you spend your money on sluts like that?"

"Oh, Mother, please! Enough is enough! Please don't say such words about the girls I've got relationships with. They're not sluts! They're just in love with me, and not only that, they're also destitute. That's why I feed them with some lamb chops now and then and a head of cheese to fill their bellies. Please don't blame them. Marina is orphaned by a father. Her mother's sick with swollen legs and has only a small pension; she worked for a few years to raise her three children. Her husband was a merchant, but he wasn't paying his retirement taxes, and when he died suddenly from a heart attack, his widow couldn't claim his pension. Let them be. What drama! After turning forty, the woman went out to work and became a janitor in a factory, where she worked as long as she could. And Marina is a student working for nothing with a well-known seamstress. Luckily for her, fancy ladies with tailored clothes give her a gratuity every once in a while. But as I've already said, I'm in a hurry now, and we've been caught up in this conversation for too long. I'm already late, and the guy from the previous shift will start grumbling."

Thanasis left with the hundred drachma note in his pocket.

Aristides hesitated and then entered Eftychia's room:

"Mother, I want to tell you something serious, and don't make fun of me."

"You look very serious. You're frowning, and you're getting wrinkled. What do you want to tell me?" she asked him.

"I want you to know I'm considering opening my own business!"

"My dear Aristides. What money will you use to start your own business? Have you thought it through enough?" his mother asked. When it came to financial budgeting she was very conservative.

"Look, Mother. For five years now, I've sacrificed to save money. With Elpida, we're almost engaged. We manage to take walks on the beach and in the park, snacking on cheap pumpkin seeds. But I have set aside thirty thousand drachmas; if you give me another twenty, the total becomes fifty. My friend Stathis has also collected 50 thousand. We'll become partners, and we can start after we each put our half together. As soon as I put aside some money from the profits, I'll return it to you with interest."

"Hey…the question isn't when you'll return it to me… and I don't want interest. But what I'm afraid of is losing it. Will the business do well? That's what concerns me. What kind of work do you plan to do?"

"Well, we're thinking about wholesale and retailing women's items."

"Good idea. We women are fascinated with clothes. Merchants of women's clothing always do well in business."

"Will you give me the loan we need?"

"Can I refuse your request, my boy? You know how I sacrifice for you. You'll have the money when you ask me for it!"

That's what Aristides wanted to hear. The next day he went with Stathis to a notary who was the father of a classmate from high school and they signed a corporate agreement. They immediately started looking for a shop to rent.

The following week they found a shop that had been closed due to the death of the merchant who had been operating it. It was located in an alleyway on the main street of the central market area, very close to the corner. It was not particularly large, but it had a basement and a loft; that is, it had handy storage spaces. They rented it without a second thought. They bought the merchandise stocked at almost half price from the widow, procured additional inventory, and got started. To some merchants, they sold wholesale women's items, namely nylon stockings and underwear, but they also sold at retail. Aristides was still working in his old job as a clerk, with the thought of resigning only if the enterprise was working out.

Initially, only Stathis worked regularly in the shop, and they employed a youngster for help only in the afternoons since he went to high school in the morning. Aristides would work there after the central market hours and kept the accounting records of the concern. Business seemed to be going well, and in a year, Aristides resigned from the shoemaker shop and began to take trips to the countryside promoting the merchandise.

On one of these trips, he met Ahmed, a Muslim from Komotini who bought from them quite a large quantity of undergarments and even asked for larger sizes because Muslim women (locked up most of the time in their homes) were overweight. Ahmed supplied these undergarments to shops in Thrace and Constantinople. However, as the saying goes, "the early bird gets the worm," and the two partners soon decided to take one step further by establishing a small undergarment sewing workshop. The reason was that they had to have substantial quantities of large sizes. So, they rented a small apartment, installed two professional sewing machines, and hired three workers. The business ran like clockwork for two or three years.

During this time, Elpida would meet with Aristides at most once a week due to his frequent travel in the countryside. At some point, she gave up on him and got married to a doctor in a wedding arranged with a matchmaker. Their separation could be described as having gone smoothly, as Aristides was not in much mood to get married then. But after a year of being uncommitted, a neighbor in the marketplace made Thanasis an offer to marry a niece of his, Koralia, who was quite a young girl, given she had just finished hairdressing school after high school. The young woman also had a dowry—a small apartment—which was a significant factor because the new husband and wife would not be obliged to pay rent.

During the six-month engagement, Aristides and Lia (that's what they called her) argued several times for trivial reasons. Lia, his fiancée, a relatively immature, moody, and temperamental woman, was always responsible for starting these quarrels. These troubles foreshadowed a troubled married life, and Eftychia began to worry about the viability of Aristides' future marriage. But her son was genuinely in love with his fiancée, who was twelve years younger, and encouraged his mother and himself by saying *C'mon, Mother, she's young. She'll settle down with marriage.*

Without considering his mother's reservations, he finally married her. At one point, at the wedding ceremony at the church, Eftychia became emotional and started crying as she remembered how many difficulties she went through raising her children. Her son's mother-in-law commented on these tears in a spiteful way to her daughter. So, Lia found an excellent opportunity to instigate her first duel with her husband. She always wanted to have the last bitter word.

After the marriage of Aristides, Stathis himself soon got married. But instead of helping even a little in the shop since they did not work elsewhere, their wives began to argue with each other and create problems for the company. A frequent cause for trouble was that the wives would go to the store and take a bundle of merchandise—of course without paying—and compete about who would get the most. In turn, each accused the other's husband of damaging the business and that his partner was making more money than he was entitled to.

Besides these problems, after the first five successful years, Ahmed opened his own workshop in Komotini and ceased to be their customer, thus significantly reducing their sales. Then the arguing between the two friends and business partners began too. They objected to some promissory notes that they failed to pay, and so the slump started. As a result of all these circumstances, their business declared bankruptcy.

After seven years, the two partners and friends separated and went their separate ways out of necessity. Aristides found work in a large company manufacturing orthopedic mattresses and Stathis continued commercial work with other items in a shop he opened in his mother's name. He also took over as the sole representative of an Athenian company's satellite in Thessaloniki but was paid a tiny commission; that was a problem because it left him little profit, and his expenses were considerable.

Despite their separation, Aristides' friendship with Stathis was not impaired, and even on one difficult occasion, Stathis borrowed a good deal of money from Aristides to pay a promissory note before it went to collection. Lia found out because she overheard a phone call. A big fuss followed. As the argument escalated and became more intense, his wife, like a rabid cat, threw herself at him and scratched him in the face with her nails, so Aristides was forced to slap her. But soon after, to avoid becoming enraged, he left the house in frustration banging the door loudly.

As it was late in the evening, he slept in his mother's house. Eftychia listened to her son's explanations for a while and did not fail to remind him. "I told you, my son, that this girl does not seem well, and you won't enjoy your life with her, but you didn't listen to me." She had him sleep in his old room.

Meanwhile, Lia stayed awake until very late at night waiting for him but could not endure until morning. So, at 4:00 AM, she left and went to Eftychia's house where everyone woke up with the barking dogs. Then another distressing episode ensued. With the loud shouting paralleled by barking dogs, pandemonium ensued. Lia was unrestrained, but also irrational, to the point that Eftychia at one point told her, "Girl, you need to be seen by a doctor, I mean... a psychiatrist."

After her mother-in-law's comment, the bride became hysterical and collapsed on the floor, where she began to shout, gasping like a fish out of water and pounding herself. That's when Akis took action. Being a former Boy Scout who had been taught first aid, he put a paper bag over her face so she could breathe her own air for a few breaths. In this way, Lia began to calm down.

Throughout the commotion, Zozo had hidden in fear in the dark kitchen because Aristides' young wife suspected that Zozo had long been in love with her husband and even believed—entirely mistakenly—that she was also his mistress.

After his wife's fit of hysteria had ended and things calmed down, Aristides took her into his room and began talking to her slowly and calmly. Thanasis was missing. (As was his habit, he was sleeping somewhere else). Akis, as always, lay down on the couch in the sitting room. Having no other choice and after making sure that the shouting stopped, Zozo tiptoed in front of the closed door of the couple's room and went to sleep in the double bed with Eftychia.

At some point, muffled cries like weeping could be heard from the room where Aristides and Lia had locked themselves up. But instead of tears, the sounds were the erotic sighing of the woman who was thus sealing her reconciliation with her husband whom she nearly lost for good that night with her unbridled anxieties and whimsies.

Nine months later, Lia gave birth to twin boys. However, the marital quarrels continued at a steady pace. There was at least one serious episode every month, apart from the minor squabbles. For his part, Aristides, like a "patient Job," endured everything to avoid divorce. He thought about the twins he wanted to raise with a father and a mother in their home. Towards this end, he sought to make trips to the countryside, so he was away from home for many days and thus escaped the frequent marital quarrels and the tension they caused. Thanks to his patience, he saved his marriage and stayed with his wife and children. When they grew up, these children were also engaged in commercial work, and Aristides always advised them with wisdom and insight. They did very well in business even during economic crises, which in Greece were, and continue to be an endemic phenomenon, apart from the significant and imported concerns.

After her menopause, Lia's nerves also calmed down to the extent that she wondered at herself when she remembered how many marital storms had hitherto intervened in her life. When things had calmed down, she would talk about this issue with seventy-year-old Aristides and attribute the responsibility for her explosions to her hormones.

"It wasn't my fault, Aristides. Those damn hormones were to blame, not me!"

ΝΕΩΤΕΡΙΣΜΟΙ
ΣΤΑΡ
ΕΚΠΤΩΣΕΙΣ

32

The Lottery

Even though Thanasis Barlabas had earned a lot of money through his involvement in various financial opportunities, strangely, he had not managed to set aside a single drachma in savings. His pockets seemed to have holes. Scarcely two days would go by since getting his wages, and he would have no money left due to his generally wasteful habits and doling out a lot of money to charity. But mostly, he spent it on his girlfriends. If a young lady told him that she liked a dress she saw in a shop window, he would rush to buy it for her if, of course, at that moment—and in exceptional circumstances—he had money in his pocket. Or he'd buy it immediately after getting his wages. This situation of an almost permanent lack of funds had led him to buy many lottery tickets in the hope of scoring a bundle of money and thus solving his life's financial problems once and for all.

One day when Thanasis had a day off, he woke up in a cheerful mood. Before getting out of bed, he called out to Akis, who had awakened early to go to classes at the university.

"Akis, would you please take these two drachmas and get me the *Macedonia* newspaper?"

"Hey, Thanasis. Did you dream about it in your sleep?"

"I want to see the results of the National Lottery draw because, well…even in my sleep…I saw that I won!" he replied.

"And so what? Even if you won, you'd spend it soon enough," Akis replied, and, after taking the two drachmas in his hand, opened the door calling to the dogs to take them out:

"Carla, Bibo. Let's go out."

The dogs raced each other to see who would be first to descend the fifteen steps, and they dashed to the yard, where they first began chasing the cats. After clearing the field from their age-old enemies, they devoted themselves to the rest of their morning duties by sniffing the various spots on the ground.

Shortly after, Akis returned home with the newspaper in his hands, sat in the sitting room, and began to read the sports page. Thanasis, who heard him return, jumped out of bed and snatched the newspaper from him. He began to check the winning numbers in the lotteries. Suddenly he started running from room to room, shouting in a loud triumphant voice:

"I WON THE WINNING NUMBERS IN THE LOTTERY! I won! I won! Wow! Wow! What will happen now? Lo and behold! Come and see with your own eyes! I WON!"

"How much did you win?" Akis asked, with his eyes wide open.

"200,000 drachmas, I'm telling you, the jackpot! Oh, what do I see here? I won some small change in the State lottery too, but that's just for treats."

"Well done, Thanasis. OPA! Yaaay! You said you would, and you did!" Akis said cheerfully, and he, too, started jumping up and down joyfully.

Amidst the cheering of Akis and Thanasis, Zozo, who was ironing at the time, calmly said:

"Now that you've won it, you can spend it like a maharaja."

In the meantime, Eftychia, who had come out of her room, ran and hugged her son and cried joyfully.

"You were always lucky, my Thanasis! The fates who came to my bed when I gave birth to you made you lucky. How much did you win?"

"200,000 drachmas."

"Now look. Don't start giving it away to your girlfriends and not have anything left in the end. With so much money, get an apartment to live in if you get married without being drained by paying rent."

"Let it be for now. I'll think about it," he replied as he was getting dressed. Soon Thanasis found himself at the lottery agency where a small celebration had started with Thrasos, the agency owner. Thrasos had sold him the lucky lottery ticket and always boasted that his shop was lucky…and he was looking forward to a bountiful gift (naturally) since he was aware of both the character of the lucky guy and the related mood of the moment.

After completing a few bureaucratic procedures, our lucky guy went to the bank to collect the money. While there, he opened an account with a booklet, into which he deposited 160,000 drachmas while the remaining 40,000 drachmas he took in cash in precisely five hundred drachma bank notes. Immediately afterward, he went to Thrasos' shop and gave him four, five hundred drachma notes as a gift and did not fail to buy some lottery tickets for the next draw using his smaller winnings from the bonus number. Then he went to the café, and after informing everyone loudly of his good fortune, pandemonium broke out. He offered to buy all the patrons a beer with sausage or ouzo with meze (appetizers), depending on the preferences of each one. He also did not fail to pay off his debts to the café barista. Soon an acquaintance approached him and asked him for 1000 drachmas on loan—obviously unreturnable—and he handed him the funds. He passed by his girlfriend's house—a ground-floor apartment on Kassandra Street—and whistled his secret password.

After a while, Marina came out into the street, and he told her the news. Then and there, his girlfriend began jumping up and down from her joy. Thanasis then gave her two five hundred drachma notes to do whatever she wanted, and they agreed to go and have some fun at the nightclub called *Kalamaki* that very evening where the popular musician Tsitsanis was playing his bouzouki and singing. Then he went to his brother's shop and gave his brother two, five hundred drachma notes along with 200 drachmas that he owed him. Finally, he passed by the kitchen where his father worked as a helper and gave him some "emergency aid" as well.

With all this commotion that day, time flew by, and our hero began to get hungry. So, he went to the "The Swiss Place" restaurant in Agia Sofia Square and asked for eight servings of moussaka. The cook wondered about the size of the order, but what could he do? He prepared the order and gave it to him. Thanasis made his way home with his stomach rumbling, and as he was approaching, he started whistling his customary song "Otchi Tchornye". Hearing the whistle, the dogs were already prepared and waiting for him behind the door, but when they got a whiff of the moussaka, they started leaping, overjoyed more than ever. Thanasis told his mother that he brought the moussaka—one portion for each, two for himself as he always ate more than the others because he worked out in the club (that was his excuse)— and one more for the dogs. Since he was hungry, he plunked the two moussaka portions into a deep plate, cut a large slice of cheese, and started eating like a glutton without even sitting down but half bent over the table with one knee on the chair.

Observing him gulping his food, Eftychia complained:

"Why are you eating like that, my child? Sit at the table properly like a human being or wait a while so the rest of us sit down. Aristides will be here in five minutes."

By the time Eftychia finished saying this, her son had finished the first portion of moussaka and was starting the second.

"Leave me be, Mother. I'm hungry now."

"Sure…are you ever anything else? You're always hungry. You're like the shadow puppet Karagiozis, who's always hungry with the only difference is that he's a glutton for punishment and you're a glutton for food—and unlike him, nobody would hurt you because you're a strong child and everyone's afraid of you."

"I'm the way I am from being so hungry because of the Occupation famine. What can I do? It's my weakness."

"I know. So…what about the lottery? What happened?"

"I netted 400, five hundred drachma banknotes."

"What will you give us?" his mother asked coquettishly.

"Sit down, Mother dear. Let me eat, and don't rush me," he replied, finishing his food.

Right after that, he opened a kitchen cupboard, grabbed a jar of syrupy orange preserves which Eftychia had made a while before, found a clean fork, and placed two large pieces of sweet orange on a saucer. His mother, who was watching him, would otherwise have griped about the preserves which she kept serving to her girlfriends, but because of the circumstances, she said nothing about it except that after it had been devoured, she said with as much sweetness as she had:

"My dear boy, Thanasis. You didn't tell us what you were going to give us!"

"I haven't thought about it yet, but for now, I'll give everyone here two, five hundred drachma notes."

As soon as he said this, he took out a wad of banknotes and began to separate them into pairs.

"I gave two to Aristides in the shop. I also gave two to my father as well, two for you, two for Akis, two for Zozo, and that makes ten."

Eftychia was not satisfied with the two five hundred notes, but hoping for a second round, she said nothing.

Thanasis mixed a portion of moussaka with plenty of bread and singled out two batches for Clara and Bibo to eat separately. *It's the only way dogs can eat bread because even when starving, they won't eat plain bread. They're aristocrats*, he said to himself while preparing their rations.

That night, Thanasis and Marina had more fun at the *Kalamaki* nightclub. The generous, lucky man of the lottery bountifully distributed gratuities to the waiters, the musicians, and the cloakroom attendant. He would have certainly spent more, but fortunately, he had not taken all his money with him.

In the late evening, he accompanied Marina to her house and waited for her signal, namely that her mother was asleep so he could enter a place not his own like a thief and share his girlfriend's bed. He had done it before, and no one knew if her mother was asleep or if she accepted the invasion as an unavoidable event, hoping for the future legalization of their relationship.

The following day Thanasis had to get up very early to leave undetected, which he struggled to do because he did not want to give up Marina's warmth and the inhalation of her estrogen that was permeating the room like an intoxicant. As he passed by Iasonidou Street, he noticed a new apartment building that was in the final stages of being built. He approached and asked the laborers if the apartments were for sale, but they referred him to the contractor. He was a slightly balding middle-aged man with a thick mustache and red cheeks, lethargic eyes, sparse eyebrows, and dyed hair that stood out by its intensely black color. He had completed construction in one of the apartment building's shops and was temporarily using it as his office until the sale of the apartments was made. He greeted the prospective buyer with a complacent smile while he occupied himself with his worry beads in his right hand.

"What does the gentleman desire?"

"Are there apartments for sale or are they all sold?" Thanasis asked.

"I have a two-room apartment on the first and a three-room apartment on the third," the contractor replied, looking bored because the prospective buyer's looks did not impress him.

"How much are you selling them for?"

"The two-room is 80,000, and the three-room is 120,000 drachmas."

"Why so much difference for just a room?"

"The two-room apartment has small rooms, and the three-room apartment has a large sitting room, a larger kitchen, a storage room, and a double balcony."

"Let's go see the triple," Thanasis said.

"Do you have that much money?" asked the contractor. He scrutinized the youthful, plainly clothed prospective buyer, as he did not believe he could afford to buy a house.

"For me to be asking, it would seem I have enough. Let's go see it."

They went up to the third floor on foot and the showing took place. Thanasis liked the apartment and decided to buy it. When they returned to the office, they discussed the method of payment, and without much difficulty, they agreed. The contractor asked for a small deposit, a promissory note, as he said, and young Barlabas also gave him the warranty on the spot. The contractor could not believe his eyes, but Thanasis was overjoyed.

Three days later, the contract was signed. The newly purchased apartment was already completed except for the elevator which was not working yet. *But it is not difficult for anyone to climb the stairs to the third floor on foot unless he's sick or very old,* Thanasis thought and put a "For lease" sign at the entrance.

Ten days later, the apartment was rented by a family with three children, and the lucky winner of the National Lottery began to collect as rent a third of the salary he had as a public utility employee. In other words, he was not doing badly at all.

A year went by, and Thanasis—observing the success his brother had in doing business—wanted to deal with commercial business as well. After thinking about it intensely, he made the big decision. He stopped working at the public utility, sold the apartment, and with the money he made, bought a corner shop near Agias Sofias Street and turned it into a convenience store. His friends and teammates would come and find him in this shop. There, he would treat them with orange juice and ice cream but would also give many of them beer and cigarettes to be paid for, supposedly at the beginning of the following month. Strangely enough, the business did not go badly at all despite the waste and benevolence of Thanasis, who often gave small loans to poor people or those who would shed tears, making him feel sorry for them. Marina also helped in the shop volunteering a few hours.

But the time came again for harsh changes. Thanasis had a neighbor and friend, Stamatis, also a former soccer player who stopped playing soccer prematurely after a severe injury. After the lottery events, this friend constantly urged Thanasis to become partners and engage in commercial business.

So, at some point, Thanasis found himself selling the shop, and with the money he got, invested his capital in his new endeavor. They bought a car with a large trunk and the ability to drop the rear seats to carry goods comfortably, and they rented offices with two spaces on Ion Dragoumis Street. They took over the dealership of flexible plastic toys—some dolls that, when pressed, would make a sound— but they also traded in other items such as balls, pens, and pencils. Moreover, they were always looking for other merchandise to have a larger turnover. When he learned which items had been procured, Aristides warned his brother that they would not make ends meet easily.

"You're not wholesaling a single merchandise category, and I don't see satisfactory profits. You have rent, car expenses, lights, telephone, the tax authority…I'm afraid you'll go under trading in these items only."

"Don't worry, Aristides. I've got the bones of a bat, I'm lucky, and everything will be fine." ("bones of a bat" – Greek expression to describe someone who always lands on his feet)

"Look. Don't be giving loans on merchandise now. You're not in a convenience store selling retail and be careful that you're paid money in your hand. I've been in the market for so many years and I know what I'm talking about."

"Rest assured, I'll be careful!"

That same year during the Christmas holidays, Akis and a fellow student, Petros, decided to open a stall in the market as vendors. They applied at the police station and then went to the workers' central headquarters where the drawing of the location spot took place before the interested parties. Based on the draw, they were given permission to sell in a perfect spot on Venizelos Street in front of the Karasos Arcade.

On the opening day of the holiday season, they opened a folding table at the arcade and arranged their merchandise—just plastic flowers—on the table. But these had already been in circulation for several years, and they left little profit, so they also procured balloons that left them a massive profit since they sold them at inflated prices at ten times their cost. Akis also took squeezable plastic dolls—*The Snow White and The Seven Dwarfs* of the fairy tale—from the wholesale representative, Thanasis. They cost precisely 6.5 drachmas each wholesale and were sold at retail for ten drachmas each.

Their business was going very well, but at the end of the day, the two partners couldn't feel the difference between their feet and their shoes after standing on the frozen ground all day. Fortunately, they did not suffer frostbite, and their profits more than paid for their textbooks that year.

Early in the afternoon on New Year's Eve, there was an exciting incident starring Akis. A woman came to their table to shop.

"How much are you charging for the dolls?"

"Ten drachmas each."

"Goodness me! Farther down, they're charging only five drachmas."

"It's impossible!"

Another customer came by, and the same conversation occurred with a similar result. *Down there, they're selling them for five drachmas.*

Acting like an experienced merchant Akis' quick-thinking brain made a decision. He informed Petros that he was leaving for a while and walked down Venizelos Street. Thirty meters away, he saw three young men selling dolls that had been thrown into a pile on the ground on a sheet.

"Guys, how much are you selling the dolls for?"

"Five drachmas each."

"OK. So how can you sell them for five drachmas since I sell them too and I bought them for 6.5 drachmas a piece? Are you selling at a loss?"

"You know, dude, we don't have refund rights on them. We prepaid for them, and if we have any left, we'll have a loss. So, we sell them for five drachmas, and we'll take whatever we make. It's the last day…let's leave for the New Year's Eve celebration!"

"So then. I'll take them all from you for five drachmas each. Here…count it."

In no time, Petros saw Akis returning to his table carrying 352 dolls.

"Petros, that's what it was. They were selling at a loss. I took everything from them since we have the right to return them to my cousin. So, 352 times 1.5 = 528 drachmas of profit in one go."

"Way to go, Akis. You made a checkmate move. You cut out the unfair competition, and we have a profit," Peter said cheerfully.

The business of Thanasis and Stamatis was not going as well as the two partners expected. After a year and a half, they analyzed their financial situation. The balance was positive but could only be considered satisfactory for one partner, which was enough to feed only one family. Though he was wasteful, Thanasis had no family, but Stamatis had gotten married before he started trading when he was still a commercial employee and already had a three-year-old daughter. The bottom line was that only one of the two could keep the business. Thanasis then suggested that he withdraw from the operation with a possible move to Chicago in mind. His mother's sister had long before been flirting with the idea of him going there to work.

Both he and Stamatis sat down, discussed matters, and parted amicably. Thanasis took the car and a little money, and the partner kept the business. After a few months, the lucky winner of the lottery sold the car, but that money was also spent on his favorite passions: love and charity.

So ended Thanasis' short tenure in the official trading sector. But it also wiped out the lottery winnings. The words that Zozo had said came true. *Now that you've won it, you can spend it like a maharaja.* Of course, as a matter of fact, he didn't spend it quite like a maharaja, but in the end, he did lose it all. This confirmed the proverb that says: *Sow the wind, reap the whirlwind,* which apparently also applies to lotteries.

The worst part was that Thanasis had long since stopped working at the utility company and had only a small pension due to an "injury while on duty". Here's what had happened. In the last three years at his job and to get a better salary, he had changed his specialty and was climbing utility poles and laying the electric cables. One day some heavy irons fell on his leg and he was injured in the lower part of the tibia. The wound healed badly because while the injury was still recent, he was kicked right on the injured spot by an aggressive player in the soccer league, and he eventually developed an "indolent ulcer on varicose veins," as a renowned professor of surgery to whom he had consulted wrote in an opinion, with compensation of course. So, now Eftychia's older son had only a small pension as income, and he began struggling to survive since he had learned to live by spending while now he had to start saving. The quarrels with his mother began again—she was dissatisfied with the little money her son left her. During the most intense arguments, aside from the fact the whole neighborhood could hear them, the barking dogs would also get involved in trying to calm them down.

This period, fortunately, did not last long because soon Thanasis was thinking of leaving Greece and becoming an immigrant to

America. In many ways, the idea of his departure to the promised land, which was at that time the USA, was slowly maturing.

33

Thanasis Falls in Love

Thanasis rarely fell profoundly and truly in love. He was mainly attracted to females sexually. However, this time a young woman from a very respectable family—her father was a senior diplomat—who had fallen in love with him for real had become entangled in his nets. But love is contagious. So Thanasis fell in love with her differently from his usual love affairs. His feelings for Maro were similar to those she had for him.

She was even poetically inclined. As she was the best student in the language arts classes of the school, she wrote poems for the school's magazine. She was touched when the love-struck Thanasis, who had been summoned for further training by the public utility (DEH) and was forced to be in Athens, sent her a poem in a letter. It was written on a paper cut out from a small notebook. With this poem, her beloved was not aspiring to reap laurels in the literary world, but it was infused with a very human element, and it touched her soul as she read it.

My Maro,

You came suddenly, without my asking you,

humble and enamored,

and thou hast sent me into a world of dreams.

My sweetheart, dear beloved

I love you; I love you; I love you

I tell you.

And now, far from you,

I mourn and weep for you.

But after two months of Thanasis and Maro knowing each other and a month of closer contact, the girl's father was transferred to Germany and took the whole family with him. Thanasis grew weary and Maro was utterly inconsolable. In Munich where she lived, her father took her to various receptions. At one, she met and began to spend time with an Australian, Albert, who was a commercial attaché there. Albert fell in love with her and started to besiege her. Due to his persistence, once the conditions were right and after a few drinks resulting in a relaxed and less resistant Maro, he made love to her…once. Maro regretted it and had since avoided being with him. In fact, with the excuse of taking piano exams for the diploma of the conservatory, she took the opportunity and came to Thessaloniki for a while. She immediately met with Thanasis in her house, and they made love without obstacles or distractions. Their bonding was something that could not be described. Unquenchable lust and endless passion without limits. They stayed together for a few days, but the girl could not extend her stay any longer. So as soon as she got her hands on the conservatory's diploma, she abruptly left with unbearable pain inside her and without saying goodbye to Thanasis. She wasn't sure of herself. She was afraid of her reactions, so she left Thessaloniki.

A week after she arrived in Munich, she sat down and wrote a letter to her beloved. She even put it in a consulate envelope she found in her father's office because she thought it would be more challenging for a letter with such a reply address to get lost. Then she mailed it to him.

Four days later, the postman gave an envelope with the letterhead of the German Consulate to Eftychia, who, at the time of the mail delivery, was alone at home. As soon as she saw the address of the consulate of Munich on the envelope she was surprised. What business does Thanasis have to correspond with Germany? Is it possible he's planning to emigrate and work there? That idea came to her. She positioned the letter upright on her buffet sideboard in the small sitting room and went to the kitchen to continue cooking. Later she began to tidy up the house. As she was sweeping the sitting room, she noticed the envelope again. Her curiosity was rekindled, but she held off. She continued doing the chores, and when she began dusting the sideboard where the letter seemed to be teasing to breach its privacy, she could not control herself. She decided to open it, but she didn't want Thanasis to know of course. So, she heated some water in a pot and held the envelope over the steam. Slowly she managed to open the letter without tearing the envelope. Her eyeballs nearly fell out when she read what was written:

"My love

As you know, I am in Munich. I feel so blue in Munich, away from you.

I'm writing this to you in the middle of the night now that everyone is asleep. I don't want anyone to bother me when concentrating on you. I shut my eyes, and your beloved form accompanies me on thoughtful journeys. I escape for a while seeking to live the unfulfilled. No matter how much time has passed, the wound remains unhealed. No matter how many years pass, my longing will stay just as excruciating and your absence as painful. As the years go by, I will love you even if I can't tell you in person. I am telling you, and I am sending you my words with a ray of sunshine passing through your window, with the breeze caressing your cheek, with the waves of the sea you love so much, and with the stars of the night we gazed at together and made wishes when they were falling. Please close your eyes, and let's travel together in the fantasy airship. This—the right to the imagination and love—cannot be taken away from us.

Maro

P.S. Do not write back to me. The address is that of the consulate. I don't want my folks to know anything about our relationship."

Eftychia was thunderstruck. But also, as a woman, she was moved. What a romantic letter this was! How did the God of love urge Maro's hand to write such beautiful words to her Thanasis?

She took a piece of paper and copied the letter, thinking of using it herself in a possible affair of her own! She then took care to close the envelope very carefully again without it appearing that the secrecy of the correspondence had been violated.

When Thanasis arrived, not realizing that his correspondence had been tampered with beforehand, he eagerly opened the envelope and read Maro's letter. He felt a sweetness permeating his being. His beloved wrote such tender words to him. At that moment, he decided to go and meet her in Germany. Without much delay, he began to prepare his papers to get a passport. Eftychia took a dim view of this. As long as Thanasis stayed at her house, he participated in the expenses. Now that he was leaving, how would she make ends meet? But Thanasis was determined to go to Germany. There were only a few formalities left.

In any event, Eftychia had a plan. She began to tell Thanasis various things about Maro.

The girl is educated and rich...impossible for her parents to accept you as their son-in-law.

She also involved Aristides in the campaign. She took him aside and brainwashed him.

"If Thanasis leaves, the money you give me, and your father's little bit won't be enough for us. We need to survive. We have expenses such as rent, lights, water, telephone, food, clothing, heating, and more. So, you won't have money left for your individual needs and, of course, nothing to save. We must prevent this fool from going to Munich. Most likely, he'll return unsuccessful and penniless. Come on...you know what he is. A piggy bank filled with holes."

With his clear, practical mind Aristides immediately understood that his mother was right. So, he, in turn, conducted psychological warfare on Thanasis.

"Hey you, Thanasis. Did you think twice about wanting to go to Germany? All the old soccer injuries will ache with the humid climate and snow. Why would you want to emigrate from Greece, our beautiful country? Doing it for a woman? I cannot even recognize you. Women chase after you, and you usually have two or three at a time. It appears to me that you're out of your mind!"

With a mishmash of advice, Thanasis found himself between a rock and a hard place. He couldn't decide what to do. But he decided to delay doing anything for a few months to see if his love affair with Maro would stand the test of time.

In the meantime, however, there were complications in Munich. Maro was late getting her period. A pregnancy test was performed, and it turned out that she was pregnant, apparently by Thanasis, with whom she had occasions for sexual intercourse. Her mother decided to provide a solution. She psychologically prepared Maro for an arranged marriage without saying anything to her husband. *Thanasis belonged to another social class. Maro belonged to the higher class then and was an educated girl with French, English, and piano certificates. Her marriage to Thanasis would not last long.*

Her mother's constant bickering convinced her. The arranged marriage business was quickly set up. The groom would be Albert, who seemed to desire Maro very much. They went together on an excursion to the Alps organized by the consulate. Maro was forced to pretend to be in love. She did not want to interrupt the pregnancy. In any case, what else could she do? The marriage took place quickly, with Maro's pregnancy at a very early stage.

Immediately after setting a date for her wedding, Maro sent Thanasis a letter informing him that she was pregnant and would get married to an Australian officer. Eftychia's son had already almost decided to move on from Maro and did not take the rejection to heart. He even believed that her pregnancy would not continue. He wasn't sure if the child was his or the Australian's. Maro had left this point unclear. Meanwhile, a new neighbor had caught his eye.

But he decided to send a letter to his great love after he convinced her in a phone call when he made her give him her address. Maro then gave him the address for a post office box. Thanasis wanted to put a ton of drama into their breakup and sent her just a single rhyming letter saying:

My Love

I walk on the same street

that we once walked together

and it seems to me like a lie

that our love is not forever.

It was seemingly fatal

what's done is done

but it would be pivotal

if staying by me you had again begun.

But now you've strayed

401

and all I have are memories

your face,

your voice,

your kisses,

and so many reveries.

Thanasis

When Maro read the poem, she broke into tears. But what could be done now? Things had taken a different path. Moreover, she had begun to get used to her husband, almost to love him. She felt some sadness for him, and she felt obliged to love him because she had deceived him with her clandestine pregnancy.

The child was born about nine months later and was a boy. He was swarthy-skinned and in no way resembled the fair skinned blonde Australian, but the baby's mother was also a brunette, which muddied the waters. Only Maro knew the truth about the child's father.

Thanasis could not believe that a child of his own would be born. If it was his child, then why would Maro marry another man? The fact that Maro got married had overshadowed everything. In her last phone call, she had asked him not to interfere in her life anymore. Thanasis was disappointed and decided to stop thinking about her. The circumstances and people, albeit convoluted, began to find an escape into, at least, an artificial familiarity.

Thus, they would each take their path.

The child Maro gave birth to was the spitting image of his father! Same eyes, same forehead, same nose, similar wavy hair, and robust physique. As the child grew, Maro saw Thanasis in him every day. Even if she wanted to forget him, she couldn't.

However, when Thanasis was informed that Maro had left Germany, already married and now living in Australia, he ceased to hold her memory in his mind. He thought that his beloved probably betrayed him and—without having taken it to heart—mildly disagreed with her choice to move away from Greece and marry a foreign man. He never imagined that he had become a father and already had a son!

34

Thanasis in Chicago

In the meantime, Thanasis had not remained erotically inactive. His long-term love affair with the much younger and dazzlingly beautiful Marina had ended after the first calm waters of happiness, and then a time of distance intervened when Maro entered his life. Then his previous relationship with Marina was restored, but she was now more mature. During the hours when Thanasis was away from her, she would go to the university canteen, her goal to wrap a suitable young man around her finger for the purpose of marriage. She had already scoped out a medical school student and artfully managed to entice him into her arms. She was even two-timing both for a period of time, maintaining a parallel relationship with both men. In the end, however, Thanasis discovered it. After having emotionally charged sex for the last time, they separated for good after Marina told him that she was in love with a future doctor. They planned to get married as soon as he got his degree, probably in a few months.

Thanasis suffered a tremendous psychological shock. He fell into a severe depression, even to the point of taking his own life. He hardly spoke and had lost his legendary appetite as he spent hours staring at the ceiling.

During that time, Antigone was about to come to Thessaloniki from Chicago to stay with her sister for two months. She had learned that Thanasis was inconsolable and that Eftychia was grumbling that he was not giving her money despite their agreement to share in the family expenses. So, she decided to take him with her to Chicago on her return. She believed that his departure from Thessaloniki and the new experiences in Chicago would also cure him of the disease caused by his traumatized erotic egoism. However, they would agree to let his pension remain in Greece to be handled by Eftychia. In this way, his mother would be spared from financial stress and quarrels, and Thanasis, who would work in America and "collect the dollars on the street," as many immigrants believed at the time (until they saw how much hard work was required to accumulate a wad of bills), would also be secure.

For weeks, Thanasis was inconsolable with Marina's duplicity in ending their relationship in favor of the future doctor, especially after having had a bond with each other for so long. His mind could not grasp such a misfortune since, until then, he was the first to abandon his girlfriends, apart from the fact that he sometimes maintained relations with two and three ladies at the same time because—as kind-hearted as he was he would say—he did not want to upset any of them.

An example was Gina. After being his paramour for two years, they had a severe clash when she learned of his exploits, particularly having romantic relations with her at the same time as two others, one of whom, Marina, was much younger than her. Then, she pounced on him, scratching his face with her claws like a cat, and Thanasis, who had never hit a woman, slapped her lightly on her face. But no matter how light the slap, it did its damage and bloodied her nose. Immediately after this incident, Gina went to Eftychia's house with whom she'd had an excellent relationship up until then (often going to their home at will) with cotton in one nostril and a bruise on her lips and complained to her about her son's behavior. She even told Eftychia that when he hit her, she saw stars, apart from her nose bleeding. But his mother, without directly making excuses for him, left her to understand that her son was not one for family life and not the marrying type. So, for her best interest, the best step would be to find someone else.

After he let a couple of weeks go by to let matters settle down, Thanasis decided to go to Gina's home, where she lived alone because her parents lived in the countryside. There he found his successor, so he exited, as the saying goes, "running scared." Gina had swiftly applied Eftychia's advice meticulously.

Generally, nothing was going well with his affairs lately, erotic or otherwise. He was now receiving a small public utility pension, and his partnership with Stamatis had been dissolved, so the lack of employment had irritated him, plus the misfortunes he had with his sexual escapades. He played endless hours of backgammon in the café, smoked many cigarettes, and when he was at home, he would lie around doing crossword puzzles or playing solitaire to pass the time.

Eftychia was worried about this development in her older son, apart from the fact that most of his pension was spent on himself, and there was almost nothing left over for the household needs. Moreover, he was always in debt to Aristides, who now had many expenses with his family and was not giving him any more money—as he had told him—unless he paid him the debts he owed.

One afternoon while they were sitting at the kitchen table and eating, Eftychia announced the good news to Thanasis and Zozo.

"Aunt Antigone will arrive in 15 days. She'll stay with us for a month and go for her swims, and we can enjoy her company. Of course, she's bringing many things with her, just like the other time. The most interesting thing is that she's also bringing us a new machine, something like a radio that can play back our voices hours later. It can write and play back songs. I'm very curious to see it."

"Is she gonna bring us any jackets?" Thanasis asked. "Because the one I had was torn by the guy who knifed me in the back the year before last."

"I don't know about that, but it's very likely that she'll also bring a jacket because I wrote her about your escapades. Of course, I also informed her that you're inconsolable, that Marina abandoned you, and that the girl was right to do so. Don't forget that you spent so many years with her, and if that wasn't enough, you went around with other women when she went to her village to help pick the olives. Oh… what was I saying… Yes, I wrote to Antigone to find out if it's possible to take you to Chicago now that you aren't working here so that you can find a job there. As the educated recall the ancients, 'Idle hands do the devil's work."

"Now that we're talking, I thought about it too," Thanasis interrupted. "I've got to find a job. I've had it with sitting around, but it isn't easy to find work here in Greece at my age. But in America, there are many good opportunities."

A couple of weeks later, Thanasis undertook to pick up his aunt Antigone at the airport. At one point, he saw her coming out through the customs gate. She was carrying a small suitcase in her hand in addition to her handbag, and she was pushing a baggage cart with two large suitcases on it.

"Aunt Antigone! Hello!" Thanasis said, and they kissed each other on the cheeks.

"Oh, Thanasis! Grab this damn tape recorder! My hand is cramped from carrying it from Chicago. What an idea it was to bring it. I was also made to pay a tax of $25 by the customs agents."

"Is this what speaks with our voice?"

"Yes, it writes every sound, voice, song… you'll see."

"Who are you bringing it for?"

"Ah, Thanasis, I'm not that dumb. I'm bringing it to Eftychia because if I'd given it as a gift to you, you'd have sold it the next day or given it to one of your girlfriends as a gift. Besides, I hear your news. Your mother writes to me every now and then. But tell me. What about that pretty one you had as a girlfriend? Have you separated for good?"

"It's more than certain. Listen here, dear Aunt. I suffered a big shock when I found out she was messing with a student, and I couldn't come to terms with it. But slowly, I made up my mind and recovered. Now I'm in a relationship with Maro, a neighbor. She is an excellent educated girl with her piano, French, and German. Her father's an important man; he is a diplomat in embassies. Never mind. I don't know how I made her fall in love with me. I pulled many strings as they say," Thanasis finished his answer, thinking of some poems he sent to Maro, which had filled her with emotion.

On the way home, they talked about various trivial matters in the taxi. (Taxi drivers are snitches, Eftychia used to say. Don't talk about serious issues in their presence. Her children and Antigone had taken the advice to heart).

Just as the taxi arrived at its destination, Eftychia was returning from the bakery carrying a baking pan of moussaka. She saw her sister and Thanasis holding two suitcases, and her heart started beating faster than ever.

"Antigone, Antigone! Welcome home!" she shouted, but she could not hug her because she held the pan tightly. "Take the pan, you deadbeat so that I can kiss my sister."

"Hey, Mother…Stop it! My aunt hasn't yet arrived, and you've already started mocking me! What 'deadbeat' was it that you called me? Can't you see I'm carrying two huge suitcases? Which hands should I hold the pan with? Mmmm, how good that moussaka smells!"

Antigone approached and, bending over, kissed her sister on both cheeks, who had turned her face to the side so that the huge pan would not prevent them from getting close to each other.

"C'mon. Let's go to the house to eat, and you can all kiss each other there," Thanasis said, whose appetite was whetted by the irresistible smell that emerged from the freshly baked moussaka.

As soon as she entered the house, Antigone greeted everyone warmly, kissed Zozo and Akis, and plopped down on the sofa in the kitchen, elevating her swollen feet on a chair. Overjoyed, the dogs most likely remembered her from the last time she had come.

But as soon as everyone entered her apartment, Eftychia faced a dilemma. Should they first open the suitcases and see what her sister was bringing her, or should they eat beforehand? She wanted to open the suitcases before eating. After all, she had already snacked on something an hour before. But Thanasis didn't give her time to think about it. He had already taken out the dishes and started serving the food. So, they all sat around the round table. They were Eftychia, Antigone, Zozo, Thanasis, and Akis. Kotsos Barlabas was away at work, so they felt more comfortable speaking freely. The food rivaled in taste the permeating fragrance that everyone had previously enjoyed.

As soon as they ate the first hurried bites, Antigone began to talk about her news, in particular, her grief. Her eldest daughter had broken up with the Greek she had married and was now involved with a German.

"He's a good guy otherwise, but how can I say this? The German doesn't cease to be German. You endured them for three and a half years."

"How do they communicate with each other? Does the German know Greek?" Akis asked jokingly.

"In America, everyone speaks English," Antigone replied and immediately turned to Thanasis.

"Tell me…you know a little English, don't you?"

"Yes. I studied English and German for five years at school but reinforced them with practice in various opportunities. I talked with the two aviators I hid in the monastery for many hours, and then with the British who came as soon as the Germans left. I even did a lot of jobs with them. But I also talked to the young American guys who came with the fleet. I don't know many words, but we understand each other."

"That's what I wanted to know, Thanasis. Because your mother and I are thinking about taking you with me to Chicago."

"Is it easy to do?"

"Not very easy, but I've found the way. You'll come as a tourist, and we'll marry you off—of course in a sham marriage—to a neighbor of mine who's a widow."

"How old is the widow?"

"C'mon! It's a sham marriage, not an ordained one," she replied.

"Your mind is always focused on naughty stuff," Akis added, who now that he had grown up, often teased Thanasis.

Meanwhile, Antigone had opened the small carry-on case she had placed next to her and, without being noticed, pressed a switch, resulting in their conversations being recorded.

"Just pay attention now. Be quiet, please."

From inside the "magic box," which everyone later learned that in Greek is called a *"magnetophono"* (tape recorder), the dialogue that had preceded began to be heard. It ended with Akis' statement about naughty stuff. They all laughed with Thanasis, who was first and foremost to laugh.

They ate some fruit and got up from the table together, eager to see the gifts that Antigone brought them. What followed was the opening of one suitcase and the sharing of gifts. Thanasis got a new jacket, some shirts, and cologne. Akis also got a jacket and a pair of pants that Antigone called jeans. Zozo also got her gifts and was very happy, especially with some underwear and nightgowns, which this time were precisely in her size as Antigone reassured her.

As always, Eftychia took the lion's share. She was very happy with the preeminent gift: A synthetic fur that could not be distinguished from the real thing. Then she also got some synthetic "see-through" blouses, which, as her sister explained, were "vas n ver"—that is, they did not need ironing—nylon stockings, skirts, nightgowns, and slippers. Eftychia was also delighted with the food items that included cocoa, coffee, milk powder, spices, fruit jelly, which Antigone called "zelo", fizzy vitamin C pills, the American painkiller Tylenol, but also creams, lipsticks, nail polish, scissors, an air heater, and an electric curling iron. Eftychia counted the nylon stockings. There were 24 well hidden in sleeves, in pockets, and wrapped inside men's old socks.

Immediately afterward, they plunged headlong into the tape recorder functions taking turns speaking so that everyone could hear their voice. After quite a bit of time had elapsed, they lay down in their beds to rest. That same afternoon Thanasis took the tape recorder with him and carried it around his hangouts, showing it off. When Eftychia discovered that the tape recorder was missing, she became furious.

"I've barely had the gift you brought me, Antigone, and that hardheaded stubborn man took the tape recorder and will damage it. He does stuff like this to me and upsets me. He's gonna be the end of me!"

"That's why I say that as soon as possible, to take him with me so you can calm down. You should both arrange one thing only: His pension stays with you. That way, I'll also find peace from worrying about whether your money isn't enough for you to live on, and I have to send more to you."

"My dear sister, if I just had my own apartment, I'd be fine and feel secure!"

"That too will happen," Antigone replied thoughtfully. "I have a hefty amount in my own account in the bank. You put Thanasis' pension money in the bank for two years with interest, and I'll send you my share. That way, you'll get a small apartment to save you from paying rent!"

"Oh, Antigone! I love you as my sister, but now I love you even more…so much more…because you care about me. I get so emotional with all you've done and continue to do for me."

"But Eftychia, you should know that the Greeks mainly do the same thing and less so the Italians. The English and the Germans could care less about their own. Listen to this. Their children turn 16 and are kicked out of the house. And if they live in the same house, they pay rent to their parents. Can you imagine such bewildering things? There are no other people like us."

"What are we going to do about the worthless Thanasis?"

"He needs to get his paperwork, passport and visa, and to have a few dollars with him. That's absolutely necessary to enter my country, and the rest with his sham marriage is my business."

Eftychia was flying in the clouds with joy.

In the evening, she did not fail to wait up wide awake to see whether Thanasis would return with or without the tape recorder because she considered every possibility likely. *That rascal sold the watch that Antigone brought for Akis the first time she came to Greece after her emigration*, she thought, raging inside. Luckily, her son didn't have enough time to sell the tape recorder, but when he brought it back and opened it, Eftychia found that the tape was crumpled, giving her an extra reason for a nightly fight with him.

"Who said you could take the tape recorder out of the house?"

"So what? Nothing's happened to it. I showed it to my friends in the café and now I brought it to you."

"You ruined the tape."

"Aw c'mon. If it doesn't get untangled we'll cut a section off. The rest is ok."

"Gosh darn already. Just leave and go to America so I can find my peace," Eftychia said, and she kept repeating it.

Antigone, who had remarkable stoicism and wisdom, would shake her head and smile.

"My dear sister, that time will come too and then you may be troubled by loneliness

"I'll never suffer from loneliness," Eftychia replied. "The world gathers around me like bees to honey. By the way, I said honey and remembered something. Tomorrow morning I'll make you *lalagites* with honey good enough to lick your fingers."

"I don't remember what lalagites are."

"Well, here it is. It's fried dough. In the patisseries they're called *loukoumades*. They're eaten with honey and cinnamon."

"Give me the recipe to make them too. When I return to Chicago on "thengeevin" (Thanksgiving) day when all my children gather with their children in my house—it's a whole army—I'll send you a picture."

"But be careful if Thanasis is there because he's voracious and eats lalagites with both hands. Leave some aside for others to eat."

When the time came for Antigone to return to America, Thanasis' papers were already prepared. Three months later, it was time for his own departure as well. The letter came from America with the final OK from Aunt Antigone. She had finished the relevant preparatory work, and everything was ready. The bride of the sham wedding, the merry widow Katie, also called Kay, waited for the groom, secretly hoping her wedding would become a reality. They would stay in the same house for a year, so the immigration authorities would not notice their marriage was a sham. Katie confided to Antigone her hope of turning the sham marriage into a real one despite being older than Thanasis by five years.

"That's not my concern," Antigone had replied. "Let my nephew stay here in Chicago, and you can screw all you want. Besides, he's good at that."

After Antigone's answer, Katie was full of sweet anticipation and hope.

On the day of Thanasis' departure, his mother was at home crying before her son left for the airport. No one understood whether she was crying out of sadness or joy. But Akis understood that her feelings were mixed. He discerned a joyful sorrow in Eftychia, for on the one hand, she would cease being able to see her son probably forever or for years, and on the other hand, she was glad that she would be spared from the hassles of their quarrels. Not only that, Eftychia thought, she would be left to collect his pension—a big deal for her to have at least a small, but stable monthly income—and if she bought the apartment as well, everything would be fine.

They took the Olympic Air bus to the airport where before her son went through passport control, Eftychia hugged and kissed him and then warning him:

"Be careful, my boy. Emigrating is difficult and has risks. Avoid the blacks because I hear that many of them are thieves and thugs, not that the whites are any better. Italians are also a dishonorable breed. You know, mafiosos. They look like us, *Una faccia, una razza*, as we say, but they are thieves too, and even worse, they are mafiosi, especially those from Sicily. Be careful; work honestly. Over there, nobody puts up with stealing like you did with the Germans and the English. Don't get into fights. There, they don't use small pocketknives, they use big knives, and you better know…well…that a stab from those and you're going to the next world."

"Don't worry, Mother, I'll open a restaurant, and I'll prosper."

"Oh. And I'll send you my notebook with my recipes. I don't need it anymore. Had you told me sooner, I could've saved on stamps."

Eftychia waited next to the large viewing window, and every now and then, the glass misted over from her breath and her eyes from tears. Only when the plane took off did she decide to leave, and she got on the airport bus for home.

During the trip, Thanasis had a conversation with the person sitting next to him. As it turned out, he was a Greek American who spoke Greek in a cute "broken" way because he had been in Chicago since he was seven years old. During the conversation, the time came to talk sports, so Thanasis flattered himself for playing soccer.

"I used to play soccer as a *termatofylakas*."

"What's a termatofylakas?"

"Oh, you don't know that word…it's a goalkeeper."

"Oh! A goalkeeper. Very nice."

"I hardly ever let any goals in. I also played in the mixed team of the Second Division. I even played on the navy team."

"That's quite interesting. You know something? I'm on the board of the soccer team "Olympiacos Chicago". Take my card. Come and find me if you manage to get a residence permit because we need a goalkeeper coach."

The prospective immigrant was over the moon with joy. Here he was still inside the plane and already he had almost found a job.

The flight lasted many hours, and they were served food twice, so Thanasis ate it all even "licking the dish" as they say, but the portions were too small for his needs. Eftychia had made provisions and he had taken some sandwiches with him that satisfied his hunger. He also offered a sandwich to the person sitting next to him. They talked like they'd been good friends for years.

When they landed in New York they switched to another aircraft which they boarded finally arriving in Chicago. Once there Thanasis got through the passport control procedures with some inconvenience that lasted over half an hour. A simple interrogation was done, but in the end they let him enter as a tourist. He was first to exit the airport because he only had a large bag with a few clothes in it. Immediately he saw Antigone who was waiting for him with her son Dimitris, that is, *"Tzimi"* as he was called. His aunt hugged him welcoming him saying: "C'mon let's go…now be a good American."

Dimitris urged them to hurry up and take the *"caro"*, as he said, to go home. Thanasis shuddered. *"What caro is he talking about?"* he thought, but after a while he realized that with each other Greek Americans call cars "caros" and they do not mean the old-time carts with horses and donkeys which is what *caro* means in Greek.

Soon they entered a large Chevrolet driven by Dimitris. *So, this is the car,* Thanasis thought. *The kind I'll get after a while, not like that little katsarida (cockroach) Volkswagen I had in Greece.*

Not quite ten minutes had elapsed since their arrival at home when the doorbell rang. It was Katie who was looking forward to seeing the groom. She literally could not hold herself back. Thanasis looked at her from head to toe.

She was a relatively tall mature woman of 48, a brunette and quite presentable. She had recently had surgery to correct her double chin in view of her impending marriage in the hope that this would make her more attractive. She was nearsighted but wore contact lenses to avoid glasses. She spoke Greek quite well—like Antigone—because she came to Chicago when she was 12 years old. Her late husband was also Greek with a large restaurant of his own, but four years earlier died suddenly of a heart attack. Katie was inconsolable with his loss, but she wanted to rebuild her life because she felt she was too young to be accompanied by the loneliness of widowhood. She had two daughters who had married well, and she could not stand being lonely as she told others.

However, the issue was that at her age she was not very likely to find a groom because men prefer younger women. So, the sham marriage with Antigone's nephew came into her life like frosting on the cake. She also had the hope that the sham marriage would turn itself into a genuine one!

They quickly agreed on the formal issues, and in twenty days the wedding took place at the City Hall. Thanasis started living in Katie's quite large house and worked for a while in the restaurant, which was now co-owned by Katie's late husband's brother. There he learned various secrets of cooking, which being a food connoisseur, he had an inclination and natural talent for. Meanwhile Katie treated him as if he were her legal husband and it didn't take long for her to get him to share the same bed.

To be honest, at the start Thanasis probably liked this development since his sham wife was a warm Mediterranean woman and their hugs were pleasant and not at all fake. So, he was cured of his broken love affair, his serious illness—an *erotopathy* we might call it—and it turned out that the best cure for an erotic disappointment is to find a new love.

In the first letter that Thanasis sent to his mother, he wrote about this development and even added at the end that every night Katie told him *Come over here now hani. Tire me out so that I can sleep beautifully.* (He explained to his mother that the word "hani" -honey- meant "my sweetness"). To these entreaties by Katie, the imported, now iconic man, always responded to with eagerness. After all, what did he have to lose?

After some time Thanasis got a job in a radio factory called Zenith. There, one day the head of the accounting department assigned him to count the stored merchandise that was in boxes on the shelves of the huge warehouse. Thanasis pushed aside the boxes a little and moved some of them farther away, so that they would form a few large groups of squares. After counting the boxes at the base and height he multiplied them, so he quickly found the right number for each group and wrote down their number. When he was finished, he immediately took a piece of paper where he had written down the numbers for each stored item to the chief accountant, who was amazed at the speed of the completion of his count of hardware. He could not believe that he had actually counted the boxes. He instructed another employee to repeat the count. The employee in question took six hours to finish the count, for a job that Thanasis had needed an hour and a half and found a similar result. This incident contributed to Thanasis' promotion, and he soon became the general manager of the warehouse and was also given a higher salary.

At the same time, as a previous goalkeeper that he was, he took over and coached the two goalkeepers of Olympiacos Chicago team two nights a week after work. At the training sessions he also sat behind the goalposts and constantly gave instructions on how the goalkeepers should move. In fact, once when one goalkeeper was injured, and his sub had pneumonia Thanasis was forced—with pleasure of course—to play in a match despite being 41 years old. The Greek community that attended their team matches were surprised to see him at first—he was balding on the top of his head and his age could not be hidden—but after he successfully blocked a couple of kicks, he was cheered enthusiastically.

Thanasis sent all this news to his mother congratulating himself. Eftychia was in turn proud and often read his letters to Aristides, Akis, and Zozo.

Once Thanasis also sent a parcel with several items for his father, who replied by writing some verses:

The words, the letters,

and the parcels

what to do with them I cannot realize.

Since you left us, it still seems like lies.

Gradually however, the letters dwindled. The time had come when Eftychia was learning the news of her expatriate son from only the letters of Antigone, who each time she saw him, scolded him for his profligate ways and for not putting any money aside.

When at some point international phone calls became somewhat more affordable, they began to call each other. Thanasis had stopped working at Zenith and had now opened a pizzeria called King's Pizza. His shop was located near a hospital, so business was good with the on-call doctors who ordered by phone. In addition to the new business which kept him busy for quite a few hours every day, he was always involved with various women, as was always his custom. He only called his brother to send his wishes at Pascha and Christmas.

Meanwhile, Kotsos Barlabas, who was now advanced in age, suffered a stroke resulting from a severe embolism. Eftychia was terrified. How would she take care of him now that he was helpless? Kotsos' blood pressure was usually elevated. She bought a sphygmomanometer (manual blood pressure machine) and would call Akis or Aristides to measure his blood pressure.

One day when Akis had taken Barlabas' pressure, she heard him say: "I'm tired of living like this. I want to die." To tease him and lighten the mood, Akis took a fever reducing pain pill, strikingly red in color, and told Barlabas that it was hydrogen cyanide poison like the one with which Hitler's generals committed suicide.

"Uncle, if you want to die, come take the poison and drink it," Akis said with faking seriousness.

"Get outta here!" Barlabas said, frightened, "and throw the pill in the trash!"

So, it seemed that he did not wish or intend to die by killing himself despite the misery he was in.

In any case, six months later, old man Barlabas suffered another stroke. At the hospital where he was taken, they said the cause was uncontrolled hypertension—despite the medications he was taking—which had caused a heavy cerebral hemorrhage. He was after all quite old at 82 years of age as Eftychia guesstimated his age. He died in the hospital eight days later. His funeral was attended by seven people. That's it. Thanasis found out too late about it in America because Antigone could not find him. He had gone somewhere on vacation, but no one knew where he was. Finally, as his aunt learned afterwards, he had rented an RV camper and had been in Florida for ten days with a girlfriend. Of course, Eftychia would now be receiving an additional pension although she had been authorized to receive this pension after Kotsos had his first stroke.

Gradually, the years passed by and Thanasis did not seem to feel homesick for Greece and his relatives. After being in Chicago for twenty years, he called and informed his mother that he would be coming to Greece on a vacation. He had the impression that his two Greek employees were stealing from him regularly, especially when he was away fishing. He was tired of the pizzeria whose work he considered to be no better than servitude. As he told his mother, he would sell the business to his two employees—to also be spared from their thefts—and then, free from obligations, he would come to Greece on holiday.

35

Zozo Falls in Love

Zozo grew up in the Barlabas family and lived like a squatter, as if hidden in the shadows. She felt a bit like an intruder, especially when she would hear Barlabas say in his grumpy voice, "Jam-packed crowd… somebody shouldn't be allowed…"

Zozo did chores every day, at first simple ones, but as she got older, she dealt with more housework and eventually did everything: Washing the clothes, then hanging the laundry to dry, ironing, cooking, washing dishes, wiping, dusting, and mopping.

While Eftychia was still somewhat young, she constantly ran around hither and thither enjoying herself and only rarely cooked. Of course, it must be admitted that the food she prepared was delicious every time she did engage in food preparation. However, the home was maintained chiefly by her orphaned goddaughter. In general, Zozo spoke little but worked a lot. When she had free time, she hung out with the children of their good neighbor, Asimina, but since her youthful teenage years were filled with obligations, she had hardly any time for fun. At 23 years of age, Aristides returned from the army and would take her out with him on recreational outings and excursions with his friends occasionally. His feelings towards her were brotherly, and he sympathized with her because, on the one hand, his mother had done a good deed by taking her into her home like a daughter. Yet, on the other hand, she had taken advantage of Zozo from an early age and treated her as a maid.

As soon as Aristides married Koralia (or Lia as everyone called her), Zozo became the reason for their first quarrel. Lia believed that Aristides had a romantic relationship with Zozo and could not believe that Aristides, like Thanasis and Akis, viewed Zozo as their sister. Her obsessive suspicions never ceased to torment her. Still, she was temporarily satisfied when she learned that she—"that woman"—as she called her, had fallen in love with a neighbor, and thus Lia calmed down a bit. This happened when Zozo was 26 and started dating Zachos, who was four years older than her and had just returned from abroad, where he had been studying mechanical engineering for the past six years. He then gave physics lessons in a tutoring school for prospective university students. During his spare time, he devised various electrical apparatuses related to his academic specialty. In general, his hands could fix anything that was broken.

Zachos bought an almost-beyond-repair movie projector in a junk shop, but it turned out to be significant after he repaired it. This projector was Zachos' occasion to engage in the cinema industry. He also bought a second-hand car weighing one ton, loaded it with the projector and necessary tools, and began to travel to villages near Thessaloniki, screening third-rate movies that he would find for sale at low prices in the relevant marketplace.

The car—the means of transport for hauling the necessary items for his screenings—was also used for his erotic adventures with Zozo, who, however, according to the morals of the time, was very conservative in her relations with Zachos. They would meet in a dark alley, and as soon as the filmmaker's car braked, Zozo, wearing a headscarf and black glasses so that, in her opinion, she would not be recognized, hurriedly climbed into the passenger seat.

The screenings took place inside cafes with several chairs and a whitewashed wall. If no white wall were available, then Zachos would hang on the wall a white tablecloth that had small buttonholes at its edges, through which he inserted nails to support the "screen."

Well before the film screening, the car would roll through the village streets, and the loudspeaker trumpeted and advertised the upcoming movie. Because Zozo had a pleasant voice, she was the one who spoke into the microphone, reading the necessary words of the advertisement for the film. In the related announcements, superlatives and adjectives abounded:

"A sensational film! An unforgettable work! Starring an incomparable actor! A masterful plot! Mesmerizing direction! The premier of the one and only young leading man! An inconceivable adventure! The film with many golden awards! An enjoyable evening!" etc.

When the time of the screening approached, Zozo would sit behind a folding table at the entrance of the "theater" - so to speak - and cut the tickets. If there was a good turnout and their daily wage was earned, Zachos and Zozo would go to a taverna after the screening, usually in another village, and eat their souzoukakia there and drink some retsina. Zozo, who was not used to drinking, made great efforts to accompany Zachos in his drinking.

Meanwhile, her godmother soon realized that something was going on with Zozo's frequent outings and her delayed returns late in the evenings and tried to get her to confess to her, but in vain. Zozo kept her secret well hidden. But one day, the sneaky Eftychia decided to watch her, which she did by taking many precautions to avoid being noticed. She saw her goddaughter suddenly get into a car but could not make out who the driver was. She repeated the surveillance once more, but this time when she figured out that Zozo was getting ready to go out, she ran and hid in advance on the correct side, very close to where the mysterious car would be stopping and managed to see who was driving it. *Ah, the goody-goody! She's going out with Zachos. And she pretends to be holier than thou!* Eftychia muttered.

The next day she started a conversation with Zozo, telling her that an acquaintance had come and told her she saw her with Zachos.

"Make sure to be careful not to get pregnant as you're a virgin," she told her, showing maternal interest since she had a bitter experience.

"It's impossible to get pregnant," the blushing Zozo assured her. "I don't let him get that far."

"Will he marry you? What do you think?"

"We haven't discussed it, but I find it a little difficult," Zozo said thoughtfully. "His mother is greedy, and his brother is a notary, and I'm just an uneducated and orphaned woman. Without a dowry, what can they want me for?"

"I can promise you that I'll give you your dowry for all the comforts," Eftychia said, having recently accumulated a substantial nest egg with her savings. "Your sheets, blankets, pillowcases, tablecloths, and kitchenware will be from me. Besides, I'm waiting for Antigone to send me dollars to buy an apartment. I'll give it to you as your dowry. Anyway, make sure to talk to him sweetly and so on…you know how. Just don't get pregnant, although, for that matter, if you do get pregnant, it's also a way to get married!"

Eftychia probably sensed, almost knew it, that Zachos would not marry her goddaughter. She consciously or subconsciously preferred this outcome so that she would always have Zozo at home doing all the chores for her. So, she said these things to her goddaughter while deep down she wished for the opposite!

As for Zozo, despite her godmother's words about her dowry, she was constantly thoughtful and constantly frowning, so a vertical wrinkle was close to becoming permanently etched between her eyebrows. Several scenarios were playing out in her mind, and she wanted to make the right decisions. But these worries made her more serious and sadder than before.

The critical day was not long in coming. The two of them were lying on a foam mattress in the car, and in between their hugs, Zachos, who appreciated her character and honesty but had also been captivated by her adorable face—in fact, many at the time found that she looked like a Greek starlet of the time—made the serious decision to propose. He told her that he wanted them to get married. After all, he thought, he was the first and only man in her life. At that time, the issue of virginity had a great deal of value, which was a particular advantage that his girlfriend possessed in addition to the others. But she was preoccupied with a serious issue that had crept into her mind like a thorn. So, without hesitation, she answered Zachos, saying:

"If we get married, sooner or later, we must take with us—what I mean to say to the house where we would stay—my sister. I can't leave my sister in the street with the problem she has. My aunt and uncle, who care for her now, are aged, and they'll die one day. Do you accept that eventuality? If you accept, I'll marry you!"

"I can't answer you now. I'll think about it," Zachos replied, deep in thought.

The answer to this question on Zachos' part was slow in coming; in fact, it never came. After a few weeks, Zozo's dates with him grew further apart until Eftychia, who kept a secret diary of these appointments, discovered that her goddaughter's beloved also had another girlfriend. She was a wealthy girl with a lawyer father and a mother who played cards with Zacho's mother. Eftychia saw them hugging in a dark alley and immediately rushed to tell Zozo. Zozo, for her part, had already decided that their relationship would not lead to marriage, and having become disenchanted with the information that Eftychia conveyed, her feelings for him came to a complete end.

On a subsequent call from Zachos to drive for a screening of a film—*An Affair to Remember* with Cary Grant and Deborah Kerr—Zozo replied that he would do well to take his new girlfriend with him and that the great "love affair" between them had come to an end. Thus ended, this love story, and Zozo remained forever unmarried.

She rebuffed various matchmaking attempts without even seeing the prospective grooms. Her mind was preoccupied with her younger, mentally disadvantaged sister. She lived in Eftychia's house continuously until two years later, when they both moved to their privately owned apartment that was bought with money sent by Antigone from Chicago and very magnanimously given as a dowry to Zozo. Zozo was then already 40 years old.

In the meantime, Barlabas had died, and his widow was receiving his corresponding pension, while she was also receiving a reduced pension from Thanasis, who had fled to America and previously authorized her to do so as his mother. This was the best time for Eftychia from an economic perspective, but the worst for her health because she suffered joint pains, especially in the knees. As the years passed and she got older, she gradually became more immobile from joint pains while her goddaughter, younger by twenty years, also began to have problems with arthritis.

At one point, Zozo's aunt, who was caring for Zozo's sister, Sophia, suffered a stroke, so Zozo moved in with her, at first temporarily, and slowly began to stay almost permanently with her sister to take care of her sick aunt. Every so often, nearly every week, she would come down to help Eftychia a little too.

Two years later, her aunt died after suffering a second and more severe stroke, but very soon after, her uncle died suddenly as well. So Zozo was forced to stay permanently with her mentally disabled sister because she had a heightened sense of obligation and felt the need for selfless giving. Her finances were relatively meager since she was only receiving her sister's small disability pension and for herself a small pension from the Organization of Welfare Benefits and Social Solidarity after Aristides had taken action to do the paperwork. She had not been educated, had not learned to work outside the home, and had been obligated for years to her godmother, aunt, and helpless sister, so her financial situation could not improve.

For the most part, Aristides and Akis, and somewhat less Thanasis, supported her at times, but nearly all of the money they gave her she returned to them as gifts on their feast days, New Year's Day, or other occasions. In the end, Zozo's sister died of cancer, so after her death, Eftychia expected that her goddaughter would return to her and would thus care for her. But Zozo, who had now reached sixty years of age, not only did not return but thought about giving back the apartment to her godmother and putting it into her godmother's name. It was this same apartment that her godmother had supposedly given her as a dowry, but Eftychia still lived in. Still angry that her goddaughter had left her, Eftychia constantly talked about Zozo's lack of gratitude, reminding her conversation partners that she even bought her an apartment and this ungrateful one did what? Abandoned her!

As soon as Zozo was informed of all this, she rushed to give her answer through the notary without a second thought. She switched ownership of the house to Eftychia placing it in Eftychia's name. Obviously, the proud and quite distressed woman thus wanted to dispense with all obligations to Eftychia.

There was another reason Zozo didn't want to continue staying with her aging godmother. The latter, despite her elderly years, continued her youthful ways and always had some paramour about. She dyed her hair blonde, plucked her eyebrows, curled her eyelashes with her eyelash curler, and at the time, had also had "discount" plastic surgery on her chin. In general, she was what we would call "vivacious" and even disproportionately so, considering her age. The surgery in question was performed in Athens in secret from her children, with Eftychia pretending that she had been hit by a car there to justify the scars that the operation had left behind her ears.

This libertine conduct was not forgiven by Zozo, who, the older she got, the more religious and steadfast to moral values she became. Just before Zozo left Eftychia's house for good, they both lost their temper and lashed out at each other. Zozo criticized her godmother for her lifestyle and having lovers even at her age. She was over seventy then and did not mind people's snide comments. This episode happened when Zozo found out that a seventy-five-year-old fan of Eftychia's was secretly visiting her.

"I saw an elderly man hiding behind the electric utility pole. He was waiting, hidden in the darkness, for me to leave the house with the dog so that he could enter. I can't understand how at your age—constantly lying in bedridden with arthritis—how you can still have a boyfriend!" Zozo exclaimed at one moment, indignant at Eftychia's behavior. She then continued. "I really wonder how you expect I could possibly live in this house and go about my business in the neighborhood?"

"You seem very jealous because you're a spinster," the irritated Eftychia answered her harshly. "Yes, you're jealous. It cannot be explained any other way. Why do you blame this man?"

After this sparring with words, Zozo settled permanently in the house in the Upper Town and completely ceased even her rare visits to Eftychia. The glass had shattered for good.

Eftychia was very angry with her for abandoning her so heartlessly, especially when she needed her most since arthritis she suffered made her quite helpless. She had hoped that since Zozo had not married, she would take care of her and have her assistance in her old age. But such an outcome was not to be, and this misunderstanding remained impossible to resolve. Apparently, they were both quite stubborn and decided to grow old separately from each other—Eftychia with her grievances and Zozo with her pride.

36

Thanasis Returns to Greece

After selling his pizza business to the Greek couple, his long-time employees, even though they were cheating him, Thanasis paid the bank some promissory notes he owed and arranged to travel to Greece by plane. He arrived in Thessaloniki quite exhausted because he had a connecting flight through Munich, and he had to do a lot of waiting for a connecting flight. Besides that, he was well over sixty and did not have the old stamina, apart from the fact that too much smoking had damaged his lungs significantly.

When he arrived in a taxi at his mother's house, he rang the apartment bell continuously and triumphantly, as sports fans do with their car horns when they celebrate their team's victory. He was carrying a small travel bag, much smaller than the one he had when he left for America, more than 20 years earlier. He heard Eftychia's voice shouting in the distance:

"Who is it?"

"It's me, Thanasis."

"Thanasis? Who?"

"Who? Is there any other Thanasis in the world?" he replied wryly and began to whistle in his familiar way.

"Oh! I don't believe my ears. It's my son!" his mother whispered in amazement and opened the door. Immediately, they fell into each other's arms.

"Thanasis, I don't believe you came. What happened? Are you okay?"

"I'm fine, Mother. Only the good die young, as the saying goes."

At 79 years of age, Eftychia was emotionally moved to see him after all those years since she believed that she would die without seeing him again. She lived alone at home after Zozo's final departure, but she had visitors now and then, and this fact was remarkable because she no longer left the house at all. Aristides would check in, see her at least every other day, and bring her groceries. A woman also came by twice a week to clean the house since Eftychia's arthritis had made her completely helpless. Most of the time, she spent lying down in her bed.

After some time went by and their emotions subsided, his mother noticed that her son had come without any luggage except for that little bag and was wearing neither a jacket nor a suit, even though it was the month of November. He was wearing a pair of blue jeans and an orange shirt over a short-sleeved t-shirt. When she opened the bag to arrange his clothes in a closet, she saw that all he had was a thin woolen shirt, a light blue shirt, two pairs of underwear, a couple of socks, and pajamas with short bottoms. However, the prodigal son had not forgotten about his mother's coquettishness, and he took two bottles out of a duty-free bag and gave them to her. One was cologne, and the other a particular cosmetic—a body lotion he told her—to be applied after her bath.

"So Thanasis, where are your suitcases? Did you lose them on the plane?"

"No, I didn't bring a suitcase with me."

"After so many years in America, you returned without suitcases?"

"Oh Eftychia! How can you possibly know what kind of life I had in America? I made a lot of money, but I also spent a lot. When I'd go on a simple fishing excursion for a few days, the employees who kept the shop robbed me blind. Not to mention that the banks which I borrowed from charged me high interest because I didn't have any property as collateral. So now I'm going to stay and rest for a month and then I'll go back to open new business…I have some money left in the bank."

"Oh my! You've always been the same. You made a lot of money but had holes in your pockets! I'll notify Aristides, Akis, and my grandchildren to come and see you."

Without waiting for an answer, Eftychia called Aristides first and then Akis. She invited them for dinner the next day, which was Sunday, so everyone could come. She sent Thanasis to buy ground meat and eggplants to make moussaka which was always successful, and everyone was incredibly delighted. Thanasis also bought flour, cheese, and ham to show them what an excellent pizza he knew how to make. Again and again, he said that this was the kind of pizza he made that excited the hospital doctors in Chicago.

The next day Akis came to the house first.

"Well, well, well! My Thanasis! What a surprise this was. You've been away for so many years. It's like you muted us. No letter, not a word! But say…what a bright nice color your shirt is."

"Do you like it? Shall I give it to you?" Thanasis asked, ready to take it off for Akis, forgetting that he had brought only one other shirt with him.

"No, Thanasis. I didn't compliment you so you'd give it to me, but to...well, the color seemed to me too flashy for your age," Akis replied with a smile.

Just then, the doorbell rang, and, as it turned out, it was Aristides with his eldest son, Kostas. The other son was absent as he was doing his service in the army. Of course, Zozo, who had wiped the slate clean, had not been invited either. Koralia had not been invited since she had an emotionally distant relationship with Eftychia for years because of the Zozo matter, and neither of the two would feel pleasure or even any comfort from their coexistence at a table. Eftychia had long explained to her son: *My dear Aristides with your wife, it's better to keep our distance and stay beloved, in words only, but anyway, that's how it's better. I'm only interested in you enjoying a good relationship.*

Since then, they hadn't had frequent get togethers and thus, squabbles.

The two brothers hugged and kissed each other on both cheeks. Eftychia's grandson, who was seeing him up close for the first time in his life, also formally kissed Thanasis. After a few scattered conversations, Eftychia sent her grandson to take the pan out of the oven and bring it to the table where she had placed two thick towels on which the pan would rest so as not to damage the tabletop glaze. Around the pan, she had placed plates, one for each guest, and forks. There was also a large platter of tomato salad sprinkled with small pieces of cheese, oregano, finely chopped onion, and parsley. Around the salad plate, there were large black olives from the Chalkidiki Peninsula. Thanasis had cut slices of bread that he had kneaded and baked himself that morning. He didn't make pizza because his mother insisted on making pizza another time when there was nothing else on the menu.

"Everyone. First, serve yourselves the salad on your plates to finish with this dish, and then you'll serve yourselves from the baking pan, as is the custom from our homeland. According to the custom, we eat from the pan, but here we'll modify it a little. And we shall also make the sign of our cross because we thank God that we overcame so many difficulties, and now we have Abraham's and Isaac's blessings," Eftychia reminded everyone.

They all made the sign of the cross.

"Wow!" exclaimed Aristides, who hadn't eaten food made by his mother's hands for ages.

"The eggplant is not very tasty," Akis observed, who had already had a fork of food.

"Maybe because the eggplants are from greenhouses. It's November," Eftychia replied.

But no one was in the mood for conversation, and without any further delay in chatting, they all threw themselves into the food and honored the eggplants of the moussaka, even if they were grown in greenhouses.

After dinner, Eftychia made some coffee, and they all started chit-chatting. The conversation constantly revolved around Thanasis' life in Chicago.

"Thanasis tell us. What happened to that woman you had a pretend marriage with," Akis asked, who was always curious but also a little bold in his questions.

"We broke up after seven years. The marriage began as a bogus one but evolved into a real one. Katie was in love with me, but in the end, we broke up because she was very jealous of me. I had an enjoyable time with her. I had a black waitress in the pizzeria, and my wife had her in her sights."

"So, was it Katie or you that had your sights on the waitress?" Akis remarked sarcastically.

"Hey, I'm telling you. Katie was jealous. Of course, I wasn't an innocent dove. The waitress was mulatto and very beautiful. She was slightly in love with me even though I was twenty years older."

"Always with young chicks," Akis observed. "I remember Marina, as she was young, and because you didn't dance much, you sent me twice to accompany her to dances so the girl could enjoy herself a bit."

"How did you do with your business?" Aristides asked.

"How would it go? You know me. I made a lot and spent a lot. I'm not the saving type."

"Tell us about some important moment in life in Chicago," Akis prodded him.

"The fact that I was coaching the Olympic Chicago goalkeepers, I wrote that to you. That I sent a guy to the hospital for ten days, I didn't write you. Listen and let me tell you what happened. The first shop I opened was a barbecue place. There were a few tables inside for anyone who wanted to sit and eat, and whoever chose could get shish kebabs or soutzoukakia in take-away packages. I had two employees—a guy who grilled and a waiter to serve. Across the street, just a few yards down, there was a big restaurant owned by a guy who behaved like a cool dude but was also very sneaky. So…one day, he came to my shop and sat down to eat. It seemed strange to me, so I watched him discreetly. So he calls Niko over—my waiter I mean— and while he's talking to him—he supposedly wants something to eat—so Nikos shows him the grilled meat. Nikos turns to look towards the place he was pointing to and then the dude suddenly and sneakily throws a sucker punch to his head. The kid was dazed, and I ran over and told the guy in English: 'What are you doing…asking for trouble? Just leave my store.'

He played it all laid-back, and another guy who accompanied him told me that the waiter insulted him. As we're talking, I say:

'Whadaya want? Why don't you leave my shop? Do you want me to send you to the hospital, or do you prefer the cemetery?'

Then he tried doing me the same trick he used on Nikos and says: 'Look over there where you grill…I see a mouse.'

Having figured out his next move and expecting his sneaky sucker punch, I pretended to look where he was looking, but out of the corner of my eye, I was waiting for him, and when his hand went up to hit me, I stopped him with my left and then with my right I threw him a punch right in the face with all my might. With the blow, the dude falls to the ground, dragging along two glasses of beer served to them, so blood has mixed with the foam…first time, I saw blood foaming. His buddy was scared…he probably thought *now it's my turn* and apologized to me for the inconvenience. I called an ambulance to come, so in a while, they came and picked him up to take him to the hospital."

"What happened next?" young Kostas asked.

"To make a long story short, he stayed in the hospital for ten days because he had a broken bone in his nose, but his eye was also injured to the point that he needed treatment by an ophthalmologist. In addition, he suffered a concussion and did not remember anything about the incident for three days. It wasn't my fault. I had warned him. *What do you like most, the hospital, or the cemetery?*

He was lucky he stayed in the hospital for only ten days, but I almost got into more trouble. He filed a complaint with the police, and they called me to the police station, where they informed me of the injury I had caused him. They didn't believe that his injury was caused by just one of my punches. But the guy had an arrest record this long from allegations against him of sneaky attacks, witnessed by both my employees and another black guy to whom I often gave a bunch of souvlaki sandwiches because he lived in wretched conditions. So, the judge decided to acquit me and dismissed the complaint as unfounded. I didn't have to pay anything for the incident. Remember back then with the butcher? I broke his ear and had to give him four gold coins. Remember that Eftychia?"

"I do remember what you're asking. That beast who slaughtered Koko that we'd tamed and was like a human person! But I want you to tell me. Was there a sequel to this case? Did any gangsters set a trap for you?" Eftychia asked, full of concern about the aftermath.

"Absolutely nothing happened. When he came out of the hospital, he came by in front of my store one day while I was at the door, and I saw him. I told him then: *'You should walk on the sidewalk on the other side of the street because it's not secure on this side.'* Since then, I haven't seen him on my sidewalk again."

Then Akis asked.

"We learned about your fishing, Thanasis. As you wrote us a while back, is it true that there are still lots of fish?"

"Ah yeah, a lotta good spots for fishing, but very strict laws. Where you'd go fishing, there were signs informing you what size fish you were allowed to catch from each species. If you caught a smaller one, you had to throw it back. Otherwise, if you were checked, you were fined. For a repeat offense, they cancel your fishing license for one year. So, one day I went fishing when I was in Florida. There was a nice small harbor with a breakwater to protect the boats. On the inside of the breakwater, there were anchored boats, both small and large, most of them large because the Americans all prefer them to be large, and outside the breakwater, many people were fishing. So, I went there too, feeling like a poor relation. Everyone was holding some huge poles with mechanisms, while I had just a simple line wrapped in cork, rigged with two medium-sized lightweight hooks, so that it would sink slowly, and I could catch the fish circulating higher than the seabed. To my right was a stocky guy wearing a straw jockey hat, and to my left, a woman was fishing. I started taking out one fish after another. Some little ones I threw back. Soon the man fishing at a few yards on my left and not getting anything out got upset that with my simple line, I could fill a basket. He almost broke his fishing rod in frustration and left all upset.

"The woman who was fishing on my right came up to me and asked me what I was doing that I could catch a lot of fish so easily. Then I told her a joke. You know, some Americans are very naïve. I tell her I talk to the fish before throwing them back. I ask them to bring me other larger ones because I don't like small ones. 'I don't believe it', the woman said. So, I picked up a fish I had just caught, squeezed it a little in the throat, and it made a sound. Then I pretended to talk to it and threw it back, saying 'Send me back another fish that would be bigger than you are.' It was hilarious. Very naïve, the Americana. She almost went crazy when she saw me pulling out a large fish in just two minutes."

"Now that you've come here, what happened to the pizzeria," Aristides asked.

"I sold it."

"And what'll you do when you get back?"

"I've bought the rights for one year to operate a machine next to a main road where they buy newspapers by putting coins in, which gives change up to twenty dollars. I'll be taking care of it starting the first of January. So, I'll have more free time to fish."

"Not only to catch fish but also for women," Akis added, who always liked to tease him.

The conversation then turned to another episode that had taken place in a café. He described how he took part in organized arm-wrestling games, becoming the first unbeaten player in the neighborhood up to that point. To everyone, this feat seemed like a lie, but then Thanasis took out of his back pocket a folded paper—quite worn—which everyone saw was a certificate with his name on it for winning the arm-wrestling competition.

"By the way, tell us, Thanasis. You were married to an American woman for so many years and didn't get American citizenship?" Akis asked.

"Oh yeah… I was about to get it—just a formality—but I was annoyed with the oath I had to take."

"What oath?"

"To say that I accept, if necessary, to fight against my first homeland, where I was born, namely Greece."

"What are you saying, Thanasis? We're allies with the United States of America!"

"Yes, but I couldn't swear to something I didn't believe in. Listen. To fight against Greece? I shudder to even think about it."

"Hey, Thanasis…Are you saying that whoever gets American citizenship must take such an oath?"

"Yes, because many ethnicities gather there, and America wants them all to become one nation."

"Well done, Thanasis," Eftychia then said. "You did well not to take the oath. Your grandparents would turn over in their graves."

A lot of time had gone by, and Aristides was the first to get up to leave, anxious about Koralia's nagging. Soon they all left, and in turn, Thanasis left to go and play some backgammon, as he informed his mother.

The following month went by relatively smoothly, but Eftychia, who had learned to live in complete freedom for years, began to get irritated now that Thanasis was around and even worse now that she saw him meddling in her kitchen. She could not tolerate this any longer, and to her friend Katina, she confided that she was tired of her son and couldn't wait to see him go.

"My man can't even visit me, and I hardly go out with my arthritis," she told Katina. "I can't wait for when it's time for him to leave. I was fine while he was away. To think, just the other day, he asked me for a loan. Is it possible? From me? A loan!"

"Yes, but you've been taking his pension for so many years," Katina took her dig.

"Big deal, his pension. Nickels and dimes," Eftychia replied.

"But you've got another pension as Barlabas' widow," Katina countered, who was always somewhat jealous of Eftychia because she had resolved her financial affairs to her benefit.

"What can I do with it? With Kotsos for so many years, I suffered from his filth and his stinginess. The only good thing he did was write poems. Some I still remember. One of them even became a popular song. Oh, what was it called? I forgot it now. It was sung to the rhythm of "Yupi Yaya" right after the Germans left and the English were here with the Hindus...[14] Anyway, what was I saying? Oh yes, with the divorce, everything was arranged. Barlabas had signed it…but at the last minute, I hesitated and didn't sign. So lucky for me, I now have his pension. Of course, I took care of him. He was underfoot in my way for so many years. He'd also had a stroke…constantly lying around for months."

"Not that you had him underfoot. You probably want to say you had him sleeping in the kitchen. Well, now you can't complain, can you? Most years, you enjoyed your life, you had your friends, and even now, you have your man," Katina said, getting in her dig and

---

[14] The lyrics written by Kotsos Barlabas referred to a Greek woman who gave birth to a …dark skinned baby!

knocking her down to size. She was always jealous of Eftychia's success with men.

As the two girlfriends were chatting, a bunny rabbit who at that time was living as a pet in Eftychia's house was chewing on the leather of a shoe. When Katina decided to leave, she bent over to put on her shoes which she had taken off because they were too tight for her. Then she realized that the rabbit had dealt with one of the two shoes to quite an extent.

"Oh! It was my shoe it was eating, and I thought it was yours," Katina exclaimed, who had long since seen the rabbit chewing on the shoe but had been happily indifferent, thinking it was Eftychia's. "The naughty rabbit vandalized me! God help us, Eftychia, with your animals! They're sheer destruction! I wonder how you tolerate them."

"I know it well, but the worst part is that I put up with my stubborn, good-for-nothing older son. Listen to this. After twenty years in America, he returned with a shirt and one change of clothes. I see it and can't believe it."

"Well, things could be worse," Katina said cheerfully and tried to button her shoe, but in vain, for half the strap had been eaten by the rabbit!

"Hey, Eftychia, I'm leaving now," Katina said, slightly confused, and proceeded to leave, dragging one of her feet on the ground so that her shoe wouldn't fall off!

"Be well," Eftychia said. "And I'll wait for you to come tomorrow when I'm making a nettle pita!"

37

The Last Page

Thanasis left for Chicago again, where he set up his new business. Just as he had planned, he bought the rights to a simple newspaper vending machine, but he immediately faced a snag with this job that the poor guy had not imagined. Somebody would have to fill the machine with newspapers every day. This obliged him to be there at least once every twenty-four hours, depriving him of the joy of fishing trips. He would also be obliged to collect the money and place small coins in the machine so it could give change. But to this problem, Thanasis also found the solution by granting the right to use the device for two days of the week to a Greek friend of his, one of his old employees, Dimitris, who oversaw the machine on Tuesdays and Wednesdays. So, Thanasis went fishing on these days and kept on his behalf three weekdays plus the weekends when the newspapers were somewhat more expensive, and the profit was greater.

He lived in a spacious one-room studio except for the bathroom in a separate room, but this studio served all his needs. So, as was his habit, Thanasis spent as much money as he made, but he limited his basic expenses quite a bit.

During that same time, his mother lived alone in her apartment in Greece but did not cease being sociable or receiving visits from her relatives and friends. She now also "read the cup"—pro bono—for companionship, but in a kindly way she would tell her friends to bring her some coffee occasionally, thinking about not damaging her finances. At the same time, every night, she received the visit of her last admirer and friend, the ever-youthful lover, Epaminondas. He was at least five years older than her but dapper and well-preserved. Every night before arriving, he would call her from the corner kiosk next to the apartment building where Eftychia lived to ask if the coast was clear, and if her son or other visitors were not at home. He would go up and stay until late at night chatting with Eftychia.

There was an emotional attachment between them, as it is said, although such a thing is rare at such an age since Epaminondas was close to ninety. Akis, who realized what game was being played, had called the phenomenon "a ridiculous senile love".

One night, however, Eftychia's beau did not appear or even call. The next day Eftychia knocked at the apartment next door and asked them to start bringing her the newspaper *Macedonia* every morning. As soon as she got her hands on it, she hurriedly found the social pages and searched the funeral notices. On the fourth day, she got the newspaper and read about the announcement of Epaminondas' funeral. It was the news that she had both feared and expected with concern.

His funeral was to take place in a village outside Thessaloniki, and the grieving relatives were children, grandchildren, and great-grandchildren. Helpless with her arthritis, Eftychia could not attend funerals, especially those in distant churches. After all, how would she appear to his children? As what? As a mistress? She was forced to stay at home with her grief. At dusk, she even lit a candle. This is where her last love had ended, and she probably didn't have much energy left for another since she was already 86 years old.

The truth is that she had no illusions about her age and the inevitable fate of every human. Still, thanks to her perpetual female vanity, she continued to dye her hair blonde and wear clothes in vivid colors. She rejoiced in receiving more than any other gift, the cologne that Akis gave her occasionally.

Visits to her house continued while cups of coffee—both upright and turned upside down—were still on the agenda, but they were gradually diminishing due to deaths and illnesses. One after another, her friends were passing away. Katina was the last to die. They found her in the bathroom of the house where she lived alone. Her discovery was made because the ceiling of the lower apartment had become very damp from the water that flooded outside the bathtub in Katina's apartment. An autopsy was performed, and the cause of death was diagnosed as a massive myocardial infarction.

With this and that, a few more years went by with fewer and fewer visits to Eftychia's house. She was very distressed by her arthritis and did not leave the house. Recently, after the loss in a car accident fatally injuring careless Bibo, she also stopped having a pet dog. Besides, she couldn't go up and down the stairs to care for the dog's needs. She complained that almost everyone had forgotten about her, even God. One day some distant relatives picked her up to take her to the traditional barefoot fire-walking rituals in the town of Lagadas. There she enjoyed herself but at the same time got quite tired. So, when she returned home that night, she lay down, and as she was feeling tired, she again had the same thought which often came to her mind and even evolved into a repeated monologue: *Oh my God, You forgot me, so why not take me... don't You see I'm too old.* She called her sister in Chicago and talked to her for some time without worrying about the phone bill. She said she had a lovely time at the barefoot fire-walking rituals but was very tired and not feeling well. She did the same with Thanasis, who was cooking moussaka when she called.

"Hey, Mom…How are you doing? Are you all right? I just baked a moussaka, and it will be first-class like yours."

"Come on, you fool. I don't feel well. I think this is the last time I'm making a phone call to you. Good luck with your moussaka. I'm going to sleep now. So, be well and farewell and be careful not to get into trouble and get killed by a gangster."

She hung up the phone, scooped a quantity of face cream of her own making, and spread it on her face—a night cream of course—and fell asleep.

In the morning, she was not awakened by the sound of pigeons on her balcony, as had been the case in recent years. She had passed away calmly and simply in her sleep. No one answered Aristides' daily morning phone call, and her son, who came over to check on her with the idea of death in his thoughts, found her motionless in bed. And a detail that should not be forgotten. She was wearing her dress, not her nightgown, and was uncovered. Ready for her funeral. Next to her was a bottle of cologne. It was all she needed to be anointed by the priest.

Her funeral took place the next day. They tried calling Thanasis to inform him, but he was only located after the funeral, so he did not come.

A year after the death of his mother, Thanasis returned to Greece. Once again, he didn't have much luggage, although he was coming back for good. When he arrived in Thessaloniki, his brother was waiting for him at the airport and drove him to the apartment that had been left unused after Eftychia's death. Once there, Thanasis organized himself as he wished. He lived with the essentials, having greatly limited his needs, his biggest expense being cigarettes. His social life followed the hereditary pattern of Eftychia's. Friends visited him almost daily for conversation, ouzo, and backgammon. Every day he went to the neighborhood café for backgammon, and in the evening, he watched TV. He also went to the bank, where he found enough money from the pensions accumulated in recent years since his mother had minimal expenses.

Everything was going well except for his eyesight. The ophthalmologist who examined him diagnosed "macular degeneration," an incurable condition. He was gradually losing sight, and a year after the diagnosis, he could only see the location of the furniture. He stopped turning on the TV and started listening to the radio. He found a station specializing in sports and began to call a specific midnight show at night. He expressed his opinion on every issue— sports or not—and with time became very popular. A reporter nicknamed him "the President," and everyone would wait for the president to call in to give his opinion. In fact, he had become a key contributor to this show even though he could no longer leave his house.

Various employees of the radio station paid him visits to his hermitage. Once, a special festive evening was organized in his honor. When he got out of the car that brought him, the people's cheering was reminiscent of a political leader's reception. Thanasis Barlabas was pleased by the people's displays of admiration, and it was precisely at that point in his life (although almost blind) he had nothing to complain about. He was happy with himself and the life he had led until then, and above all, he liked that he was popular with many people and that he could finally express his opinions about events, politics, and sports every night.

"Why did America want to attack Serbia? To test new weapons or to spend the stocks of missiles that had filled its warehouses?"

"America has no business going to Afghanistan. They will be defeated just as the Russians were in the past."

"No economizing is attempted by the government and its officials. Why should they change furnishings for every new minister? Why should the Prime Minister change all the furniture in the Presidential palace? Will a disease from the previous administration get transmitted? The only thing that should be changed is the phones, so there would be no bugging!"

"Why does the Ministry of Environment, Physical Planning, and Public Works advertise the metro rail system with full-page advertisements in the Sunday newspapers? 'The Subway Is Being Built,' the ad reads. When it's finished, we'll see it and know about it.

So now, Mr. Minister, why are you paying money for advertising? Is it to stifle the mouths of journalists and not criticize the government?"

"Why are we sending financial aid to Skopje and Albania? To gain their 'gratitude' or to make them think that we're afraid of them, and that's why we're enticing them?"

"Is there that much money falling out of our pants? By some chance, did we get out of that tunnel that P.M. Papandreou was talking about, and we had no idea?"

"Why do a whole bunch of journalists travel for free on every minister's or prime minister's trip? So that they don't write unpleasant things about the government?"

"Why do some ministers suddenly become rich? On their salary?"

"Was it necessary to organize Olympic Games to bankrupt the economy?"

"Why is the Iraklis soccer team changing its coach? It's not his fault. It's the players who are indifferent. Besides, he doesn't have good defensive players and allows a lot of goals."

"Why do Greek teams get older players in transfers? To allow goals in the second half when they run out of oxygen."

"The newspapers wrote about the impending transfer of an American basketball player to the ARES team for 50,000,000 drachmas. How is it explained that ten days later, it was announced that this same player was transferred for 30,000,000 drachmas to an Italian team? I ask now: We have the same climate; we are Una Faccia, Una Razza. So why did the black guy prefer to go to Italy for

less money? Apparently, they announced other things here while they would have given him less! Many team presidents and managers swindle deals and make dirty money. They would probably feel pain for their team and pay them out of pocket. Sure Impossible!"

"Not as many foreign players should be playing on our teams, because new Greek players don't try out, so they can become a strong National Team."

These comments of his were followed by exclamations from the journalists of the radio station: Say it again, Mr. President! May the Lord bless your words! And the more applause Thanasis heard, the more he was aroused and spoke out even more.

One day the doorbell rang, and when Thanasis asked who it was, he heard someone speaking English. He opened the door without having figured out what was going on. In front of him, he stood a forty-something attractive-looking man. He had curly black hair, attractive dark brown-black eyes, a straight nose, and slim facial features. His expression was serious, and it betrayed a shock or concern, but he soon said to him resolutely in an Australian accent:

"Are you Thanasis Barlabas?"

"Yes, of course. What do you want?"

"My name's John, and I'm your son."

Thanasis nearly passed out. After drinking some water from a glass that had been forgotten at the table, he sat down in a chair and began asking questions. But he didn't have much to ask. His son began to narrate.

"My mother had gotten pregnant, but you left for Chicago and probably didn't know about the pregnancy. She didn't have time to tell you. My mother soon married an Australian she met in Germany, where her father worked. When I was seven years old, my mother, who had two other girls by then, wasn't getting along with her husband, and they broke up. My sisters and I entered an institution, and our mother came to see us every fortnight because she worked in another city. So, I never had a close bond with my mother or sisters. They were like little blonde English girls with fair skin. I was dark-haired and didn't look like the Australian I thought of as my father. A few years ago, my mother decided to return to Greece, so she came to Thessaloniki and lived alone in a small apartment she had inherited from her parents. Two years later, I came to Greece to see her because she had heart problems. I stayed with her for a month, and we talked much more than in all previous years. Then, perhaps because she was afraid she might die suddenly, she finally confided her huge secret to me. The Australian officer was not my father. My birth father was a Greek she met when she lived in Thessaloniki but had emigrated to America. I learned then that my father's relatives still lived in Thessaloniki. I asked their last name, and she told me it was that weird name, Barlabas. I asked my mother to search the phone book for a phone number, and she quickly found a number in the name of Aristides Barlabas. The sequel was simple. I took the number and spoke English with a young man who, as it turned out, was Aristides' younger son. I learned your address from him, and that's how I found you."

As he spoke the final words, John's eyes became tear-filled, but his father's eyes weren't any less brimming with tears too. As he listened to his son narrate the above, the shock he received was enormous.

He was about to speak, but he had the impression that he had lost his ability to speak. He went ahead and hugged his son. He didn't know what feelings his visitor had for his father—that is, for himself—and that filled him with anxiety. But soon, this question was resolved, and the agony was gone. John, who grew up in an orphanage without ever seeing his father and with only rare meetings with his mother, had lived with the dream of meeting his true father. Now the great moment had arrived. That blessed moment when he found and loved him deeply, regardless of whether or not he was to blame for the bad outcome of this affair many years ago. His mother had told him that her family excluded the possibility of accepting the common unsophisticated Thanasis as a son-in-law who had no degree or property and was not suited to their upper-class level. These diplomatic officers, consuls, ambassadors, and persons of the diplomatic corps generally have a relative conceit and move through gold-plated halls eating with gold cutlery. Thanasis had no chance of accepting himself among them.

However, there was the matter of pregnancy. The circumstances might have taken a different path if he had known about this development. But he left for Chicago, as had long been planned, and at the same time, the Australian was the lifeline in the situation. He had met his mother (apparently, he had a relationship with her) two weeks before she came to Greece from Germany and got tangled up with Thanasis, which also caused the pregnancy.

Thanasis and John spent many hours in conversation that day, and both said a lot. They had to learn about each other. The son recounted his life in the orphanage to the father and mentioned touching details, including that he'd waited for his mother to visit. She did not come on the visiting day, and tears filled his eyes, but he would restrain the tears so that the other children would not see his suffering. When he grew up, he learned the skill of plumbing and worked in construction at the head of a workshop but could not save money. He spent money easily. He had inherited the waste gene from his father.

Thanasis again told him his own stories. Stories of the Occupation, stories about the English aviators he had rescued, about Germans he worked for (but also stole from), about his business with the English, about soccer, about his loves, about his life and business in Chicago, about his marriage with Kay, the decision to return in Thessaloniki, but also about his last hobby talking live over the phone on the radio. In the end, the two hugged each other tightly when the initial reticence had disappeared entirely.

John continued visiting his father and having long conversations with him for a month. He told his mother, Maro, that he had found Thanasis and would like to see them living together. But she didn't want that and refused. Now elderly with time, having changed her appearance and suffering from severe heart disease, she did not want to meet her great-old love. Maybe she held some grudge against him for leaving; perhaps she didn't want him to see her as an older woman.

Who knows? The soul of a human is an abyss! When one day, at the urging of his son, Thanasis called her on the phone, she did not answer when she figured out who it was but just kept the line open until he was disheartened and hung up. Their old love had been completely extinguished, but John's bond with his father began to form and strengthen.

Maro asked her son to stop seeing Thanasis. She seemed jealous that he was also taking a share of love, but he did not listen to her and continued to see him often but did not tell her. After a month's stay in Greece, John returned to Australia, but he often called his father, and they talked for hours. The following year he came back and stayed for another month. He also came a third time when his mother became seriously ill and basically barely caught up with her still alive two days before she died.

A few months before Thanasis discovered he had a son, it became known that his brother Aristides had lung cancer. Unfortunately, despite the surgery he underwent, he could not escape the call of death and died relatively soon after suffering quite enough. At his brother's funeral, Thanasis could not hold back his tears. He returned home in Akis' car, crushed mentally and physically. This was the last time he went out of his house.

A few days later he began to recover somewhat and with the fighting spirit that characterized him and he had inherited from his mother, he did not give up. He started calling the radio station again, but always with less enthusiasm. He smoked almost constantly despite the urgings of Akis to the contrary, who visited him from time to time and brought a doctor friend to examine him.

"Thanasis, I came last night and knocked on the door for quite a while, but you didn't open it for me."

"Oh, I understand. It was probably when I was taking a bath. I take a bath twice a day. (This habit of his had become second nature since the old days when he had to be ready at any moment for a sexual encounter!). Akis, before you come, call me on the phone so I know you're coming, and I'll be waiting for you and on the watch to open the door to you."

"Fine. I'll call you because sometimes you might not hear the doorbell," Akis said, who was no longer in the mood to argue about smoking.

The reason Thanasis preferred his cousin to call him ahead of time was so he could open the windows to let fresh air come into the house as much as possible, of course, because he could not stand the nagging of anti-smoker Akis about smoking, as he was not about to quit even though it had damaged his lungs seriously. The physician who saw him told Akis verbatim: "Your cousin has severe pulmonary emphysema. He will not last long and will likely die with a cigarette in his mouth!"

Thus, from too much smoking and the many colds he caught caused by frequent bathing, Thanasis' respiratory function was significantly affected. Eventually, after a cold with a fever, his condition deteriorated significantly. He was urgently transferred to a hospital and was admitted to the intensive care unit for the gravely ill.

After Akis notified John by phone, John took steps to get a plane ticket immediately and was on the flight from Sydney to Thessaloniki as soon as possible to see his father still alive. As soon as he arrived, he met with Akis, and they went to the hospital together. Once there, full of anxiety and tear-filled eyes, he saw his sick father, who was in critical condition and still alive under sedation on the ventilator. But how long would he last like this?

John continued to visit him every day. He would sit as long as the doctors allowed him and watch him.

Thanasis lasted in the respirator for fewer than eight days. Very few people attended his funeral. His son, his nieces and nephews, his cousin Akis with his wife, and a journalist from the radio station were in attendance.

Thanasis was the last member of the Barlabas family to leave this earthly world. His mother, Eftychia, and he had lived as they wished, drinking the nectar of life as bees suck it from blossom to blossom. Thanasis Barlabas was undoubtedly a little frivolous and shallow, but he was very good-hearted. He prided himself on his exploits and somewhat exaggerated them as the genuine amateur fisherman that he was. He lived like another "Zorba," like that hero of Nikos Kazantzakis, the author. He was also one of the many little Zorbas who were born Greeks, and with their wit and intelligence as their primary weapons along with their negative traits, struggled in life but had as a priority their contentment with the women they were in love with. No one can accuse him of not being hardworking, competitive, and inventive. Despite being incorrigibly wasteful, he overcame difficult situations with these resources. He had a heart of gold, and as he was very compassionate, he helped many people.

He was a genuine male version son of Eftychia's except that his mother had evolved from life's difficulties, not into a wasteful person but a saver. As she often said in her old age, *If I, the uneducated Eftychia Barlabas, were minister of finance, Greece would have financial surpluses, while now that it is ruled by educated wasteful politicians, some of whom have never worked a day in their lives to appreciate the value of money, Greece is in constant danger of being bankrupt!*

After the funeral, Akis invited John, Aristides' children, and the journalist for lunch at a beachside restaurant. When the meal was over, they talked about Thanasis for many hours. It was pretty late when they sat down to eat, and with the conversation, the time had gone by without them realizing it. The sun began to make its way to the west, filling the horizon with the clouds glowing in lovely shades of orange and the blue sky that was inevitably darkening towards purple.

"John, look what a beautiful sunset Thessaloniki has," Akis told his Australian nephew. "John, please, look at the beautiful sunset because tomorrow you leave, and you'll never see it again. To see these images, it is worth living in Thessaloniki."

After some interruption in the conversation for about a minute, while everyone was gazing with admiration at the departure of the sun which was taking place in a unique feast of colors, Akis added:

"John, think about it. If you can come to Greece, your roots are here. You're a good plumber, and if you learn a little Greek, you'll be able to acquire a good clientele. Think about it. Sunsets will be waiting for you, as well as a Greek woman, to start a family, a family like Thanasis did not manage to have with your mother."

"I'll think about it," John replied, preoccupied, not letting go of his gaze towards the west, which was now getting darker while at the same time mixing more orange with purple, an image that could be a real challenge for those artists who might have perceived it. The beautiful view of the west, with the sun sinking into the sea next to Mount Olympus—the mountain of our ancient gods—passed through John's tear-filled eyes that blurred the view creating the aura of an impressionistic painting.

Before John left for Australia, Akis also gave him some of Thanasis's old photos and one of the soccer team in which he played goalkeeper. His father was even holding the ball, as goalkeepers are used to doing in pictures. In this photo, he was balding quite a bit, and at the time it was taken, he must have been at least 40 years old.

Thanasis liked to play soccer and considered life a game he wanted to win. Often, however, he took risks by playing too much attack and neglecting his defense. So whatever money he earned, he soon spent unwisely.

That same night Akis saw a dream in his sleep. He saw a ship battered by the waves and a woman giving birth in the captain's bunk. He saw three little girls growing up with their mother facing many difficulties. He saw the oldest one, Eftychia, marrying first and having two children, but she was too young to marry. He saw her getting beaten by her husband, much older than her—Kotsos Barlabas—but a little later living her life very freely since she was able to escape the oppression of Kotsos, who, as he got older, lost his place of primacy and was relegated into the background. He saw Eftychia's sister, Electra, getting married for a second time and giving birth to a boy, but dying very young before she was forty. He saw his Aunt Eftychia having in her house her own two boys, a goddaughter, a nephew, a man in her bed and another in the kitchen, but also dogs, cats, hens, a hedgehog, a rabbit, a goldfinch. Among all these people, he saw Aunt Antigone coming from Chicago loaded with gifts. She had brought him a wristwatch, but something happened, and the wristwatch was lost after Thanasis grabbed it in his hands. It was something of a juggling act. He was looking for the watch everywhere and couldn't find it. It was gone. He carelessly bumped into Kotsos Barlabas in the narrow hallway of the house and heard him saying his well-known refrain: *Crowds, crowds, from here, somebody needs to go.*

Then suddenly, he saw an older man appear in front of him who seemed to be blind. Someone, who did not understand who he was or how he was there, told him that the old blind man was the ancient poet. Yes, Homer, it must have been. That is why he was blind, but Akis saw that he also looked like Thanasis, and a dog was jumping joyfully around him. He was reciting some verses with an enviable delivery style but in modern Greek. Was it Homer or Thanasis? The persistent question tired his mind so much that he felt it aching. And the poet said...

Even as are the generations of leaves,

such are those also of men.

As for the leaves,

the wind scattereth some upon the earth,

but the forest, as it bourgeons,

putteth forth others

when the season of spring comes

even so of men,

one generation springeth up

and another passeth away.

(Homer Il. 6. 147-150)

The fallen "generations of leaves" were Grandmother Georgia and Dimitris Mavrothalassitis, their three daughters, also dead now, as well as Thanasis and Aristides. The "others" were children replacing the old generations for the time being until they too would depart like those autumn leaves. He was Akis, the child of Electra, a man now with children of his own and the two children of Aristides, but also John, the Greek-Australian son of Thanasis. In Chicago were the children of Antigone with their children and grandchildren, who numbered more than eighty people together.

Life went on in Thessaloniki, Chicago, and Sydney with its ups and downs, joys and sorrows, successes, and failures. The descendants of the refugee family had survived and multiplied thanks to their constant battle to survive, following the example of their parents. And, perhaps from many of their ancestors, there were molecules in their DNA—yes, DNA from their toughened, die-hard roots—this great race of humans that did not give up easily and always engineered solutions to difficult problems, like Odysseus (Ulysses) in Troy. Since those ancient times, their race held fast, and they spoke nearly the same language and possessed the same character traits. In Odysseus' time, they spread out only in the Mediterranean and Europe, and later with King Alexander they expanded to distant Asia—while now they were scattered both in the new continents—the Americas, as well as Australia. That is, they had spread throughout the earth.

THE END